HORNBLOWER AND THE JOURNEY HOME

HORNBLOWER AND THE JOURNEY HOME

BY

JAMES KEFFER

www.penmorepress.com

Hornblower and the Journey Home by James Keffer

ISBN-13: 978-1-950586-83-7(Paperback)
ISBN—978-1-950586-84-4(E-book)

BISAC Subject Headings:
FIC014000FICTION / Historical
FIC032000FICTION / War & Military
FIC047000FICTION / Sea Stories

Cover Illustration by Christine Horner

Address all correspondence to:
Michael James
Penmore Press LLC
920 N Javelina Pl
Tucson, AZ 85748

Dedication

To Christine—Thanks for everything. I love you.

PROLOGUE

Napoleon Bonaparte fell back on his camp bed in pain, the effort of dictating a new will was more exhausting than he'd imagined. He squeezed his eyes shut and held his breath, trying once again to conquer it by sheer will. The trouble was, the will he had once used to dominate the continent of Europe was no longer able to dominate even his own body. He shuddered as the agony finally subsided and he let the breath out in a long, slow, sad exhale. He asked the date and was told the day was April 15, 1821.

He was dying. He was sure of that now, no matter what his loyal followers told him. The pain in his stomach, which had long since settled itself into a steady ache that was growing in intensity, punctuated with a stabbing sensation that left him totally incapacitated, could mean nothing else. He was resigned to his destiny now, and he found comfort in the fact that he would soon be with Josephine again. The thought of her pleased him and he smiled, at least on the inside. He remembered her smiling face and wished, not for the first time, that he had known her when she was younger. The great irony of his life was that the woman he loved above all others had been unable to give him an heir simply because she was past the age of childbearing. He regretted that he had had to divorce her for the sake of his Empire. With a son of their own, he would have been content to have her by his side for the rest of their lives.

He opened his eyes and stared into the space above him. He had no time for such dreams; he knew that every minute was precious if he was to complete this last task before death succeeded in wearing him down and winning the final victory. He turned his head and tried to focus his eyes on the shape sitting beside his bed, but even that small effort was almost beyond his capacity now. Slowly, the image of the faithful Marchand came into focus.

"Marchand?" Napoleon whispered. "Has all been written? Exactly what I have said?"

"Yes, Sire," Marchand replied.

"It is well," Napoleon said, furrowing his brows in an effort to concentrate. "Now, there is just one matter more to settle, and that is my final resting place."

Marchand turned to the secretary who was charged with taking the Emperor's dictation and saw that the man was ready, quill in hand. He turned back to the Emperor. "We are ready, Sire."

Napoleon closed his eyes and rolled back onto his pillow, resting for a moment and marshaling his strength for this final effort. He drew as deep a breath as he could, then he began.

"It is my wish that my ashes repose on the banks of the Seine, in the midst of the French people, whom I have loved so well." Napoleon closed his eyes again. Marchand and Montholon would see to everything else.

Nine days later, he felt strong enough to write out an additional codicil in his own hand, completing his last will and testament. Marchand took the document from his

Emperor's hand and made sure the codicil was properly witnessed before taking it out of the room. A copy would be made and forwarded to the Emperor's family in France.

Marchand left the Emperor's bedchamber, softly closing the door behind him. In the antechamber, he paused and looked at the document he held in his hands. The last will and testament of Napoleon I, Emperor of France. Marchand looked back at the Emperor's door and wondered if the document he held would make any difference at all. Normally, a will would be submitted to a judge and go through probate to be executed according to the desires of the deceased. But in this case, the judge was England, and Marchand doubted very much whether there was anyone in England who cared what Napoleon wanted done with his remains.

CHAPTER 1

Adolphe Thiers sat back in the overstuffed, high-backed leather chair behind his ornate, solid oak desk in his office and pondered the future of France. He glanced at the calendar and took note of the date, March 2, 1840. Just the previous day, Thiers had been summoned to appear before King Louis-Philippe and asked to form a government. This was the second time in the he had been called upon to render such a service to his country, and now, after only twenty-four hours in office as Prime Minister of France, Thiers was beginning to wonder how he was going to succeed.

The problem was the king. Thiers shook his head. In his opinion, Louis's only mission in life was to avoid Louis XVI's fate. Thiers thought this made the king too susceptible to any stray wind of political thought of the mob that was the population of Paris. Louis Philippe's stated goal, on being swept to the throne of the July Monarchy nearly ten years ago, was to take the best parts of all past governments of France and combine them into one, but the overwhelming majority of cabinets formed for the governing of the nation had been conservative in nature. Louis accepted the idea of popular sovereignty when he was crowned "King of the

French" instead of the traditional "King of France" used by his ancestors, but for some reason, the king had never captured the hearts of the people. The people wanted to be led, not carried along by every whim of the mob, and Thiers was fast coming to the conclusion that Louis-Philippe simply could not lead.

He sighed in disgust and allowed his eyes to roam around his office. It was only his second day, and he had not had a chance to have the room decorated to his taste. As he looked around, his gaze fell on a portrait of the Emperor Napoleon, probably hung in this place of prominence over the mantel by Soult, his predecessor. *Now there,* thought Thiers, *was a man who could lead.* Thiers arose and walked over to the portrait. He wondered idly who the artist was. Probably David, a favorite of the Emperor's. The portrait showed the Emperor on horseback, riding through a crowd of cheering soldiers. That was what France needed today, he decided. France needed the Emperor to capture the people's hearts and unite them for the sake of the nation. Thiers turned away from the portrait and began to pace the room. Sadly, Louis was not Bonaparte; he could never garner the imagination and adoration of the people that way. Thiers approached the portrait again and stopped to study it. The Grande Armée had literally marched to their deaths, all for their love of Bonaparte. He shook his head as he thought of Bonaparte's fate. He had no love for the man, but nobody deserved to be exiled and forsaken, left to die on a godforsaken English rock, as the Emperor had.

Thiers looked again at the portrait and considered. What if Louis could align himself somehow with all that was good in the people's memories of the Empire? Not the constant warfare, of course, but Thiers had to admit that the Emperor did a great deal of good for France, from the Code Napoleon to creating a working tax-collection system and a solid industrial base that were the envy of every court on the continent. He studied the eyes of the portrait and suddenly wished he could ask the Emperor his advice. Thiers's head tilted to one side and his eyes narrowed as a thought struck him. What was that English saying he had heard once? *If the mountain will not come to Mohammed...?*

Thiers resumed his pacing with renewed vigor. What if there was a way for the king to tap into the resurgent popularity of the Empire? Could Louis be persuaded to make a pilgrimage to the Emperor's grave on St. Helena? Would the English permit such a pilgrimage? Thiers paused by a window that had a full view of the Arc De Triomphe, commissioned by the Emperor in 1805 to celebrate the victories of the Grande Armée but only completed four years ago. *Yes,* Thiers thought, *there is an opportunity here, if the king could be convinced to cooperate.* Thiers resumed his pacing, his chin on his breast and hands clasped behind his back as he tried to conceive of a plan to allow Louis-Philippe to ride the coming wave of the Bonapartist revival. Soon his pace slowed and his brow wrinkled as he came up with scheme after scheme, only to discard each, as the reasons became apparent why the king would not participate. Finally, the Prime Minister of France came to a halt in front of the Emperor's portrait and admitted defeat, at least to himself.

"Why couldn't you be buried in France?" he asked the portrait. "At least then the king might make his pilgrimage..." He stopped in mid-sentence as another thought struck him. He returned to his desk and began drawing up a memorandum. After all, he thought as he wrote, why *couldn't* the mountain come to Mohammed?

He wrote for the better part of an hour, carefully outlining for his own information points for and against his idea, ensuring that every objection was provided for and countered. He had to be able not only to convince the king of the political merits of his idea, but also to show how his whole-hearted participation would endear him to the hearts of the French people, and especially the population of Paris. He frowned at a fresh objection, one that sprang fully formed in his mind, and he needed another twenty minutes of writing to finally overcome it.

Finally, he was able to set his pen down, confident he would be able to convince the king. He stepped into the outer office and ordered a carriage. Within a half-hour he was riding through the streets of Paris on his way to the palace. One of the perks of being Prime Minister, which had been brought on by the wave of popular sovereignty that swept Louis Philippe to the throne, was the access he enjoyed. Thiers was able to see the king on state business at almost any hour of the day. He sat back as his carriage sped through the Paris streets toward the Palais-Royal and hoped that the king would see the wisdom of his proposal. In the past, Louis had proved himself cooperative if the proposal would increase his appeal to the masses—which was why he'd agreed to the condition of popular sovereignty in the first place—but occasionally the king's words or actions reminded his ministers that he had just enough Bourbon blood running through his veins to recoil from anything even remotely connected to the Bonapartes. Thiers shrugged and decided he couldn't blame the king; Louis had once told him that he had seen his name on a list, supposedly created by the Emperor during the Hundred Days, of royalists who were to be executed immediately upon capture.

The carriage arrived at its destination, and a footman hurriedly opened the door for the Minister. Thiers descended and marched directly into the palace, ignoring the various attendants he passed along the way. He was announced and admitted to the king's private study.

Louis-Philippe was sitting behind his desk in the corner

of the room, writing a letter. Thiers waited patiently. The king finally put down his pen, but the look on his face told Thiers he was far from satisfied with his efforts.

"Good morning, Minister," Louis said as he rose and came around the desk. Thiers had bowed as soon as the king noticed his presence. Louis shook his hand (a gesture he'd acquired due to popular sovereignty) and motioned him toward a leather settee. "How may I be of service to you today?"

Thiers waited until they were both seated before speaking. "I thank you for seeing me on such short notice, Sire. Has Your Majesty noticed that there seems to be a resurgence of nostalgic feeling regarding the Empire?"

Thiers immediately saw his sovereign tense at the mention of the Empire and reminded himself to tread with care. The king looked sideways at him, suspicion written all over his face. "I believe I have heard something of the sort, Minister; why do you ask?"

"I mean no offense, Sire," Thiers said, "but I believe we may have an opportunity here to endear Your Majesty in the hearts of the people."

Louis looked intrigued. "What are you saying, Minister? How?"

Thiers chose his words carefully. "Sire, I cannot explain this nostalgia of which I spoke, but I do recognize it and see in it an opportunity upon which we must act before the opportunity is lost. If we can align ourselves with popular sentiment, the people will embrace the monarchy and take you into their hearts like never before."

The king looked incredulous. "And just how do you propose we do that, Minister?"

Thiers smiled. "Sire, I believe you need to bring the Emperor home."

Francois Guizot sat in his office in the French Embassy in London, waiting for the arrival of the day's diplomatic bag from Paris. The rain was falling outside, as seemed to be the case nearly every spring afternoon in this benighted country, and Guizot was glad to stay inside. He arose and walked over to the second-story window overlooking the street, and watched the Londoners below dashing through the rain, some trying desperately to hang on to their umbrellas against the wind, others just turning up their collars and trudging on toward their destinations. Guizot shivered in sympathy.

A knock at the door heralded the arrival of the bag. The aide deposited the pouch on his desk, and Guizot sighed as he went to the desk to examine the day's deliveries. He expected another routine, boring day of the usual correspondence from his Foreign Ministry. Those expectations vanished when he saw the envelope bearing the seal of the Prime Minister's office. What could Thiers want of him, and why did the request not bear the seal of the Foreign Ministry? Guizot deliberated; perhaps this was one of the niceties of the Prime Minister also being the Foreign Minister, or perhaps Thiers wanted to get his attention.

He turned the envelope over and wondered idly what was inside. He broke the seal carefully and withdrew the pages. He unfolded them and read slowly. His brows knit together as he reread the letter to make sure he had not misunderstood its contents. He set the pages on his desk and leaned back in his chair, steepling his forefingers together as he thought over his instructions. He shook his head; his orders were signed by the king, but Guizot could sense the hand of Thiers behind this. Who else would try to use the resurgence of the Empire to benefit the king, who, after all, was still a Bourbon, even if he was from a different branch of the family?

Guizot leaned forward and picked up the pages again. His instructions were quite clear, so he walked over to the bell cord and gave it two good tugs. Within seconds, a servant entered the room.

"Yes, Ambassador?" he asked.

"Henri, I need to go to the Foreign Office at once."

"*Oui*, Ambassador." The servant bowed and left. Guizot knew that arrangements would proceed as quickly as possible, and he would be notified when all was in readiness. He wondered how the British Minister would react to the request he was to make. He could always fall back on his good relations with the new queen, if Palmerston proved to be difficult. Overcoming an obstacle as obdurate as a reluctant Foreign Secretary would certainly ingratiate him with the king, possibly even putting him in line to succeed Thiers when his government fell. For a moment, Guizot got caught up in the possibilities for his future, but he was rescued from his fantasies by the arrival of the faithful Henri, to announce that his carriage was ready.

The ride to the Foreign Office was short but agreeably dry, the rain having paused long enough for his journey through London. When he arrived, the attendant took his coat and hat and showed him into a waiting room.

"The Foreign Minister will be with you in a few minutes, Mr. Ambassador," he said.

"Thank you, John," Guizot said. The attendant bowed and left the room, closing the door behind him.

Guizot sat and waited, trying to foresee how the conversation would go in his mind. He finally gave up and instead studied the new portrait of Queen Victoria that had been added since he was last here. It was a good likeness, and he thought the Queen benefited from her recent marriage to the Saxon Albert. Now the entire nation was celebrating the Queen's pregnancy, hoping that the fall would see an heir to the throne.

Guizot turned when he heard an attendant enter the room.

"Pardon me, Ambassador," he said, "but the Foreign Minister will see you now. Will you please follow me?"

Guizot bowed and was led into the presence of John Henry Temple, 3rd Viscount Palmerston, Foreign Secretary of the British Empire. Guizot envied the man his rugged good looks, complemented as they were by eyes that were said to melt a woman's heart on command. He bowed as the Foreign Secretary stood and came around his desk.

"Mr. Ambassador," Palmerston said, "how good to see you again."

"Thank you for seeing me, my lord," Guizot replied. "May I offer my belated congratulations on the occasion of your marriage?"

Palmerston shook the Frenchman's hand. "Thank you, Mr. Ambassador. Will you have something to drink? Some port to fight off the chill from the rain, perhaps?"

"Yes, thank you, my lord."

Palmerston poured their drinks and led the way to a comfortable settee, set off in the corner of the room. He handed his guest a glass of port, and the two men saluted each other and sat. Guizot was glad for the warmth of the liquid going down his throat.

The Viscount set his glass on the table before the settee and sat back. "It is good to see you, Francois," he said. "How may I be of service to you?"

Guizot set his drink on the table and reached into his coat pocket for the letter from Thiers. "I have just this morning received an urgent request from my government. Minister

Thiers has instructed me to communicate to you the request of King Louis-Philippe to the British Government for permission to exhume the mortal remains of the Emperor Napoleon and return them to France."

Palmerston was surprised by the request, as he had heard nothing from any of his intelligence sources on the Continent regarding this. He reached for his glass and took a slow sip of the excellent port to give himself a moment to think. Guizot was known to be on the conservative end of the liberal forces in French politics, while the new Prime Minister was quite the opposite. The Viscount pursed his lips in concentration; the request itself was a simple one, from the British point of view, but it would be interesting to hear his guest's opinion. "I will be glad to bring that to Lord Melbourne and the Queen on your behalf, my friend," he said. "But tell me, Francois, what do you think of the idea?"

Now the Ambassador took a long, slow sip of his drink. What should he say? How honest should he be? Palmerston was a social friend, but they were hardly in a 'friendly' setting. Guizot took a deep breath and exhaled slowly. He sat back and folded his hands in his lap. "I ask you to remember, my lord, that I have only seen this request today," he said, "and I confess, I did not expect anything of this sort from my government." He looked at the ceiling and sighed, then he lowered his gaze to his hands. "I am concerned. Personally, I will tell you I am not in favor of the project. The Emperor made order out of chaos, and for a time made France the master of all Europe." He quickly held up his hand to forestall any comment from the Viscount. "I am not saying I am in favor of the constant warfare and the appalling loss of life. The Emperor murdered and lead to their deaths hundreds of thousands of Frenchmen. He did, however, initiate many good policies for France, policies that are still benefitting the nation today. My personal opinion is that he deserved to be exiled from France forever for his excesses. Personal feelings aside, however, I am concerned that certain... extreme elements may try to use the occasion to overthrow the king and install the Bonapartist Pretender you are currently harboring in your country."

The Foreign Secretary picked up his port and drained the glass in a single draught. He set the glass on the table, sat back in the settee, and looked at his guest. "Ambassador, I believe we are quite in agreement."

Guizot did not expect to hear his counterpart agree so readily. "And the request from my government?"

The Viscount smiled. "You may consider it granted."

Guizot actually blinked at that. "Pardon?"

Palmerston picked up his glass and rose to refill it. Guizot refused his host's offer of more refreshment; Palmerston went about his business and returned to his seat. "There will be no problem with your king's request. You may remember that my government already promised, back in 1822, that the Emperor's remains would be returned to France upon request. Besides, the queen has let it be known in council that she wishes to improve relations with France."

Guizot nodded in thanks. "I am grateful, my lord. I shall get word off to my government at once. I understand the king is most anxious to have the project completed."

Palmerston rose, and Guizot followed suit. The two shook hands and the Foreign Secretary escorted his guest to the door. "Please keep me informed, Mr. Ambassador," Palmerston said. "I am sure Her Majesty will want to send a special delegation to honor the event."

"I will, my lord. Good day."

Palmerston closed the door and went back to his desk. He needed to consider what had just transpired before he wrote his report for the Prime Minister. He sat down behind the desk, opened the humidor, and carefully went through his ritual of selecting a cigar. He clipped the end and lit the cigar, taking great pleasure in puffing life into it and blowing a large cloud of blue smoke toward the ceiling.

So, the French were going to bring the Emperor home. The Viscount's initial reaction to the news was one of foreboding. The occasion was simply too good an opportunity for the Bonapartists to pass up; who knows, with a little luck, they may just be able to manipulate the mob into allowing them to seize the throne. Palmerston's eyes narrowed at the thought. Who would the Bonapartists put forth to wear the crown? He couldn't see any of Napoleon's brothers being fit candidates, which left Louis-Napoleon, who just might be able to carry the thing through. Palmerston wished, not for the first time since the Pretender had arrived on English soil, that he could lock him up for a year to remove him as a player in the already unsettled world that was French politics. Better still, he mused as he puffed, why not let this new Napoleon follow the original straight to St. Helena? Palmerston nodded to himself as he sent another cloud of smoke heavenward; that would be a fitting end.

The Foreign Secretary also knew there wasn't a single thing he could do. The new queen was infatuated with the Pretender, and Palmerston wondered whether any coup attempt by the Bonapartists to put Louis-Napoleon on the throne would have at least her tacit approval. He closed his eyes and rubbed his temples in an attempt to ward off the headache he feared was coming on. Finally, he sighed, put his cigar in the ashtray, and picked up his pen. Lord Melbourne was going to have a busy night of reading.

King Louis-Philippe of France stared out the window of his study and wondered once again if he was doing the right thing. The note in his hand, delivered by special messenger just minutes ago, told him that Minister Thiers would be calling on him at 2:00 pm, almost certainly to discuss his latest scheme, the return of Emperor Napoleon's remains to France. The idea frightened Louis, not only because of Bonaparte's renewed popularity with the masses, but also due to the execution of Louis XVI. That fateful day would always be in the back of the mind of every King of France from Louis XVIII onward, a warning not to disregard the rumbling of the mob or rumors that drifted in from the streets of Paris. Louis knew he had to tread carefully when he placed himself at the head of this business; one false accusation that got the ear of the mob could cost him his life.

He turned and walked over to the large, empty fireplace on the opposite wall. The fireplace was over two hundred years old and dated from the reign of Louis XIV. Over the mantel hung the famous portrait of the Sun King at the siege of Namur in 1692. Louis took comfort in this particular portrait, showing as it did Louis XIV victorious and firmly in charge of the nation. Louis-Philippe envied his famous ancestor the control and authority he exhibited throughout his reign, envied the successes that made him the greatest ruler in the history of France—until Bonaparte.

The king sighed and turned away from the portrait. The Sun King would never have allowed an upstart like the Emperor back into the country, Louis was sure of that; he would leave that blasted usurper to rot on that godforsaken English island, and Louis would love nothing better than to follow his illustrious ancestor's imagined example. Unfortunately, there were forces at work in the nation that were beyond even the king's powers to suppress. He had to accommodate them, and one of the biggest was this resurgence in popularity of the Empire and its ruler. When Thiers had come to him with the suggestion that they ride this wave of enthusiasm rather than be swamped and possibly overthrown by it, he could hardly bring himself to agree. Like all Bourbons, Louis considered the Empire to be an outgrowth of the Revolution, and the Revolution had murdered his kinsmen. Despite his misgivings, he had allowed Thiers to explore the possibilities.

The clock on the wall chimed the hour of two o'clock, and a page announced the arrival of Minister Thiers. The Prime Minister strode into the room and bowed before his king.

"Sire," he said. "Thank you for seeing me."

The king nodded. "Minister, what can we do for you?"

"I have just received the report from our ambassador in London, Sire," Thiers said. "The English have agreed to our request."

Louis turned and looked again at the portrait over the fireplace before addressing his minister. "Minister, I am having doubts about the wisdom of this venture."

Thiers had expected something of this sort. "Sire, this is a grand opportunity for us to connect you to the people. Remember, Sire, it was disconnect that ruined both Louis XVIII and Charles X—the people saw the monarchy as oppressors and not leaders. We need to take every opportunity to make sure this does not happen to you."

Louis frowned and turned away. Thiers watched his king wander over toward the portrait of Louis XIV and stare at it. When he turned back, the minister could read on his king's face the battle that was raging inside, and he decided to wait to see which side won. He saw the king pace back and forth, pause to look at the portrait, pace again and then pause again. Thiers was used to this with Louis-Philippe; the king wanted to be a liberal monarch, but always in the back of his mind a small voice reminded him that he was a Bourbon, with 300 years of absolute rule behind him. The Bourbon part rebelled when the king wanted to indulge his liberal side, almost as if he was haunted by the ghosts of his ancestors, accusing him of betraying his heritage.

Finally, the king settled the issue within himself and returned to his minister. "Very well, Minister," the king said. "We shall proceed with the project."

"Excellent, Sire," Thiers said. "May I suggest you place the Prince de Joinville in command of a naval force to retrieve the remains?"

The king turned away from the window where he was watching some birds. "Do you really think that is necessary, Minister?"

"Absolutely, Sire. We must treat the Emperor with the pageantry and honor that are his due. Besides, we must guard against those who may not want to see this enterprise succeed."

Louis walked over to a settee and sat down, indicating Thiers to join him. The king looked thoughtful. "The Ultra-Royalists would certainly applaud anything that prevents Bonaparte's return, while the Bonapartists may try to whip the mob into a frenzy and use the occasion to stage a coup." Louis said, nodding as he spoke each point in turn. "I see what you mean, Minister. We shall command the Prince de Joinville to take command of a naval force and sail to St. Helena to bring back the mortal remains of the late Emperor. One ship should suffice, perhaps our newest frigate. Sleek and powerful, as the Emperor himself once was. Work out the details, Minister; we should like to see an outline within the week."

Thiers rose and bowed. "As you command, Sire."

Adolphe Thiers sat in his office and quietly awaited his next appointment. The news from Guizot in London had been better than he could have hoped for. Thiers was now confident that he could safely send Admiral Roussin, his Minister of Marine, to England on a private mission. Thiers rose from his desk and began to pace. He knew he was walking an incredibly fine line, guarding against either the Bonapartists or the Ultra-Royalists taking advantage of the proceedings to further their own aims, while ensuring that the people took the king into their hearts. Thank heavens he had been able to convince the king to take the security precautions seriously! But still, he could not quell the growing uneasiness in the pit of his stomach. Something was going to happen—someone was going to interfere with the return, but who, and how? He thought that the trouble, whatever it would be, was most likely to take place somewhere between the time the Emperor's remains landed in France and their arrival in Paris. But who the troublemakers would be was anybody's guess. The list of possibilities was nearly endless.

His thoughts were interrupted by a knock at his door. His secretary opened the door and announced a man Thiers firmly believed was not on that list. Charles Francois Marie, Comte de Remusat, sat in his cabinet as Minister of the Interior and was a political ally against the Ultra-Royalists and the Bonapartists.

"Monsieur le Comte," Thiers said, "thank you for coming. Allow me to get straight to business. His Majesty has commanded that we bring back the mortal remains of the Emperor Napoleon from St. Helena so that he may be given a proper funeral here in Paris."

De Remusat smiled. "Excellent. Who gets the honor of going to St. Helena?"

"The Prince de Joinville."

The Comte nodded. "So how may I be of service to you, Minister?"

Thiers poured them each a drink, and the two men sat on

a leather divan across the room from his desk. "The *Chambre des Deputes* is in session tomorrow. I want you to go and announce to them that the king has commissioned the Prince de Joinville to take a frigate to St. Helena to bring the Emperor home."

De Remusat stared, and then he grinned. Clearly, he enjoyed the idea of being the one to make the announcement to the deputies and the nation. Thiers imagined his friend was grinning in anticipation of the reaction of the Ultra-Royalists. He watched the Comte shake his head, as though he could not believe his good fortune.

"It will be my pleasure, Minister."

At 11:00 am, de Remusat walked into the Hall of Deputies and asked the President for permission to address the assembly. The President agreed and gaveled the deputies to order. The Comte mounted the rostrum and said:

"Gentlemen, the king has commanded His Royal Highness, the Prince de Joinville, to take a frigate to the island of Saint Helena to retrieve the mortal remains of the Emperor Napoleon. We come to ask you for the means to receive them onto French soil in a dignified fashion and to raise a fitting, final resting place for Napoleon. The frigate charged with this historic responsibility will return to the mouth of the Seine, where the Emperor's remains will be transferred to another ship for the journey upriver to Paris. They will be deposited at Les Invalides. A solemn ceremony, a major religious and military procession, will inaugurate the tomb which must hold him forever. He was Emperor and King; he was our country's legitimate sovereign. Thus, he could be buried at Saint-Denis, but Napoleon must not receive the ordinary burial of Kings. He shall reign and command in the fortress where soldiers of the fatherland will always rest, and where they will always inspire those who are called to defend her. Art shall elevate a worthy tomb under the dome, in the middle of the temple consecrated to the God of armies, if any tomb can be worthy of the name that will be engraved thereon. We do not doubt, gentlemen, that the Chambre shares with patriotic emotion the royal idea that we have now expressed before it. Henceforth France, and France alone, shall possess all that remains of Napoleon. His tomb, like his memory, shall belong to no one but his country. The monarchy of 1830 is, indeed, the sole and legitimate heir of all the sovereigns of which France can be proud. Without doubt, it belonged to this monarchy to first rally all the powers and reconcile all the vows of the French Revolution, to fearlessly elevate and honor the statue and the tomb of a hero of the people, for there is one thing, and one only, which does not fear comparison with glory—and that is liberty!"

And the room went wild.

Louis-Napoleon Bonaparte, nephew of the Emperor and currently the leading (and, in his mind, the only) Bonapartist candidate for the French throne, sat at the desk of his study at Nash House, his current residence in London. He was working on an article for a Paris newspaper which he hoped would bring to light the current French government's neglect in certain matters, while at the same time reminding the populace of improvements made under Bonapartist rule. It was tedious work, but he wanted to turn the people's minds as well as their hearts.

The door burst open, startling Louis and causing his pen to go awry, ruining an entire page of manuscript. A curse escaped his lips as he turned to find his secretary, François Courbet, rushing into the room, waving some papers in his hand. Louis buried his annoyance and calmed himself. Alone among his household, François could interrupt him at any time and for any reason.

François Courbet had been an orphan on the streets of Bern, Switzerland, when Louis and his family arrived to live in exile in 1815. Louis's mother allowed young François to stay with them as a companion and playmate for her son, and the two were soon inseparable. François became his prince's first and most important lieutenant.

"What is it, François?" Louis asked.

"A message, my Prince," he said excitedly, "from our man in Ambassador Guizot's office. The French government is petitioning for the return of the body of the Emperor for reburial in Paris!"

Louis stared at the man, stupefied by what he heard and disbelieving. What foolishness was this? He took the pages from his secretary and hurriedly read them. He frowned and read them through again. *This must be a trick,* he thought, *to get me to return to France so my enemies can imprison me again. Well, it will not work!*

He looked up. "You believe this nonsense?" he asked.

"I do. Our man swears the seal of the foreign ministry was intact when the message was received. It was signed by Thiers himself."

Louis grunted. Thiers was weak, but he was also an opportunist. *He knows that the star of my great uncle rises again, and he hopes to use this to the advantage of his ridiculous Bourbon master!* He shook his head. *Ah, no, little man; it is I who shall rise with my family's star. I am the one France will call to sit on my uncle's throne!*

Louis dropped the pages on his desk and leaned back in his chair. "You have seen these?" he asked. Courbet nodded. "And?"

François inhaled deeply and stared out the window. Louis

crossed his arms on his chest and waited; he knew this habit of his secretary. The man's mind was calculating and planning at a furious rate. Soon his eyes blinked and he exhaled loudly. He turned to his prince.

"There are two questions," he said. "The second depends upon the first. What will be our position on the return?"

Louis narrowed his eyes. "What do you mean?"

"Do we welcome the return or use it as an opportunity to hurt the Ultra-Royalists?"

"Hurt them? How?"

"By sabotaging the return in such a way that blame falls on Angoulême and his followers."

Louis pursed his lips and drummed his fingers on the desk. He saw at once that François had raised the crucial question. The body of the Emperor was the holy icon of the Bonapartist movement, and the chance to have it entombed in Paris as a permanent reminder of the glories of the Empire was too good to ignore. He shook his head.

"No," he announced, "we cannot risk any interference. We stand to gain too much. The Emperor's remains must be returned to France."

"I agree," François said. "This leads to the second question: What shall we do to ensure this comes to pass?"

Louis frowned and closed his eyes to think. *What can we do? I must not give the Ultra-Royalists occasion to use the return against us. Our actions must be covert. But what to do? I need more information.*

"Send a coded message to our agent in the foreign ministry in Paris," he said. "Use the courier. Tell our agent I need all information regarding the return of the Emperor's remains as quickly as he can get it to me."

"Yes, my Prince." François bowed and left the room.

CHAPTER 2

Admiral Lord Horatio Hornblower nodded in greeting to the townsfolk as he strolled through Smallbridge with his wife, Lady Barbara, enjoying the pleasantly cool May evening. In some ways, he likened their promenades to the walks he used to take on the quarterdeck of a ship, the master surveying his domain. Yet as soon as the idea came to him he knew the comparison to be flawed; those walks were for exercise or the contemplation of some problem regarding ship's business, whereas his strolls about Smallbridge were strictly for relaxation and socializing with the villagers. A squeeze on his arm reminded him of an added benefit—the company of his wife. Hornblower looked down to her when a tug followed the squeeze.

"Let's stop for a moment, Horatio," his wife said, pointing to a red brick house with a green door. "Mrs. Jenkins' little girl had a fever, and I want to see how she is doing."

"Of course, my dear," Hornblower said. He let her hand fall away from his arm and looked around, his eyes finally falling on a group of men in front of a pub, listening as one of their number read aloud from a newspaper. He motioned toward the group and said to his wife, "You go ahead, dear; I shall walk down to the pub and find out what's happening in the world."

Hornblower studied the group as he crossed the lane. The one who was reading had his back to him, and whatever he was reading so captivated his audience that none of them noticed his approach. "Good evening," Hornblower said.

"Evening, yer lordship," several of the men replied. Some tipped their hats while others bowed.

Hornblower nodded his acknowledgement before turning to the one holding the newspaper. "Well, Matthews, what were you reading?"

"I was just reading to the boys about the Frenchies forming a new government, milord," Matthews answered.

"Didn't they just do that a year or two ago?" someone asked.

"Why don't their king just run things?" someone else threw in. "Ain't that the way it's been since they got rid of Boney back in '15, milord?"

"Not exactly," Hornblower said. "This king came to the throne ten years ago, but he did so under a constitution, much like our own Queen Victoria. He has a prime minister who runs the government for him, and that's who Matthews was reading about. It's not like it was before the revolution."

"Did you hear, milord?" a big man in the back asked. Hornblower recognized him as Palmer, the village blacksmith. "Another Bonaparte is trying for the French throne."

"What?" Hornblower said. He turned to Matthews. "When? Which Bonaparte?"

Matthews was already searching through the paper to find the story. After a moment, he said, "Here it is, my lord. Let me see, now; it says here just that Louis-Napoleon Bonaparte is the heir-presumptive of the Bonapartist faction.

It says he tried to stage a coup a few years ago at Strasbourg, but the police foiled the plot and arrested him." He looked up at Hornblower. "Milord, ain't he the one who lives outside London?"

"I believe so," Hornblower said.

Matthews grunted, and several of the men in the crowd made faces of disgust, allowing Hornblower to see what they thought of the Whigs for allowing this Bonaparte to stay in the country. Privately, Hornblower agreed with them, although he would never say as much to Barbara.

At that moment, the Lady Barbara walked up to the group. All the men removed their hats and bowed, and Barbara beamed. Hornblower never ceased to marvel at the way his wife was adored by the villagers. He smiled at the thought, for he knew that Barbara returned the affection in full. Prepared for her role both by birth and by training, she was completely at home with the peasantry. Hornblower wondered once again if that was what had made her marry him, but he was determined not to ask.

He offered his wife his arm, and they bid the men farewell. They had gone barely twenty paces down the lane when a familiar voice stopped them.

"My Lord! My Lord!"

They turned to find Captain Bush coming up the street. He was moving fairly swiftly, considering his peg leg. They waited for him to catch up to them, and Hornblower could see in his eyes that something was up. He wondered what had his old friend so excited.

"Good evening, Captain Bush," Barbara said with a smile. Truth be told, Barbara had been even more pleased than Hornblower when Bush retired from the navy and bought a small estate outside Smallbridge for himself and his sister. Barbara had told her husband that she felt better whenever he sailed with Bush; for some reason, she thought Bush would always make sure Hornblower came home alive. Hornblower had mentioned this to Bush on the voyage to St. Helena, and even now, twenty years later, Hornblower still smiled at the memory of how embarrassed Bush had been by the compliment.

"My lady," Bush said, bowing over her hand.

"Captain?" Hornblower said. "What has you chasing us down in the street?"

Bush grinned at his former captain with a cryptic smile. "Well, my lord, it seems you have a visitor."

Hornblower's eyebrows rose. "Really? Who?"

"I'm not sure, my lord," Bush said. "I was walking past your house when Brown emerged from the front door. He hailed me and asked that I find you right away. He said you had a visitor." The look on Bush's face made it clear he knew nothing more of the matter.

Hornblower looked at his wife. "My dear, I believe we'd best head for home."

"So it seems, my husband."

Hornblower smiled at her and turned to Bush. "Captain, will you accompany us?"

"Gladly, my lord," Bush said, and the three of them set off back the way they came. Hornblower forced himself to walk at a moderate pace, so as not to tax Bush. Brown met them as soon as they entered the house.

"A gentleman arrived not long after you left, my lord," Brown explained. "I told him you were out, but he insisted he must wait for you, that the matter could not wait. He handed me his card, but it's not in English, my lord. I put him in the library and was about to head out to find you when I saw Captain Bush and asked him to deliver the message." Brown held up a silver salver with the card on it. Hornblower picked it up and studied it, then he showed it to Barbara.

"Well, Bush," Hornblower said, "This announces Admiral Albin Roussin, French Minister of Marine and the Colonies."

Bush pursed his lips and let out a low whistle. Hornblower could only nod his agreement. He looked at his wife and sighed. "Well," he said, "let's not keep the good admiral waiting."

The three of them paused at the library door, and Lady Barbara reached up to kiss her husband on the cheek. "I shall wait for you in the conservatory, Horatio."

"Very well, my dear." Both he and Bush bowed as Barbara left them.

Hornblower opened the door and led Bush into the library. He saw his guest examining some books on the shelf. He was interested to see that the Frenchman was wearing his naval uniform rather than civilian clothes. Roussin was tall, nearly as tall as Hornblower himself, clean shaven and graying at the temples. The French admiral carried himself with the air of someone who had earned his position by deeds and not by birth. Hornblower noted the *Légion d'honneur* pinned to his chest, the white enamel cross with a gold medallion in the center surmounted by a gold crown—unmistakable to anyone who had ever seen it.

"Monsieur," Hornblower said, "I am Lord Horatio Hornblower. How may I be of service to you?"

The Frenchman bowed. "Thank you for seeing me, my lord. I am Admiral Albin Roussin, and I currently serve as Minister of Marine and the Colonies for his majesty, King Louis-Philippe of France. I have come at the direction of the king's Prime Minister to make a request of you."

"Yes?" Hornblower said. "And what request is that? Pardon me, Minister, but won't you sit down? Will you have something to drink? This is my friend, Captain William Bush."

Roussin sat. "An honor, Captain. I have heard your name, of course. Thank you, no drink, my lord. As I said, I am here at the direction of my government on the king's business. I shall try to explain." Roussin took a moment to gather his thoughts before continuing. "Recently in France, there has been a change in the attitudes of the French people. The memory of the excesses of the Bourbon kings Louis XVIII and Charles X, along with the enlightened leadership of our sovereign King Louis-Philippe, have together created a climate of nostalgia for the days of the Empire. My king has instructed our ambassador in London to make a formal request for the return to the French people of the mortal remains of the Emperor Napoleon, currently interred on the island of St. Helena. Your government has kindly granted that request."

Hornblower and Bush looked at each other for a moment before Hornblower looked back to his guest. "I am gratified to hear this, Minister. I am sure you know I was governor of St. Helena for nearly a year and so knew the Emperor well. I can imagine nothing that would please him more than to have his remains returned to France. But what is this request you have of me?"

"My lord," Roussin said formally, "my government would like to request your presence as the official British representative at the exhumation of the Emperor's remains."

Hornblower stared at the Frenchman as he fought to bring his racing mind and emotions under control. If there was anything that was anathema to Horatio Hornblower, it was being caught off guard. The official British representative? Returning to St. Helena was literally the last thing on his mind when he'd entered the library.

"Monsieur," he said to his guest, "you do me great honor.

I will admit to you privately that I counted the Emperor Napoleon as a friend, and nothing would please me more than to be present at such an event. Unfortunately, what you ask is not in my power. Only the Queen may appoint official representatives of the British Crown."

Roussin smiled. "Of course, my lord. I merely wished to gauge your interest in the prospect." He reached inside his coat and withdrew a letter. Hornblower immediately noted the official seal of the British government. "I hope it does not offend you, my lord, but on instructions from my government, I first visited your Foreign Office and discussed the possibility with Lord Palmerston. He gave me permission to seek you out and see what you would say to the proposition. If you agreed, I was instructed by Lord Palmerston to give you this letter." Roussin lifted his eyes from the letter to Hornblower. "So, my lord, do you accept?"

Hornblower held his visitor's gaze while his mind turned over options at lightning speed. He could feel Bush's eyes on him, and he knew his friend was curious as to the answer. Truth be told, Hornblower himself was curious. In the end, he knew there could only be one answer. He held out his hand for the letter.

The Frenchman smiled as he handed it over. "Thank you, my lord. It might interest you to know that I have spoken to General Gourgaud, whom you may remember was a member of the Emperor's household on St. Helena. Gourgaud remembers you distinctly, and he claims to recall several conversations with the Emperor regarding you. While I do not know the substance of those conversations—perhaps you can ask him yourself when you see him—I do know that the Emperor considered you a brother-in-arms as well as a personal friend, and I believe he would be pleased and gratified that you have agreed to attend."

Hornblower sat back in his seat, setting the envelope

unopened in his lap. "Tell me, Minister, what is your personal feeling on bringing the Emperor's remains back to Paris?"

Roussin pursed his lips and studied his hands for a few moments while he gathered his thoughts. "My lord, I will tell you that I personally favor the return. The Emperor, for all his faults, was in truth the greatest ruler in the history of France and possibly amongst the greatest in the history of the world. He deserves an honored burial in the country he made his own."

Bush nodded, and Hornblower said, "Well said, Minister. What fears do you, or your government, have?"

The Frenchman's eyes went from Hornblower to Bush and back again before he answered. "You must understand, the political situation in France is very precarious at the moment, my lord. Despite his attempts at reform, the king is coming to be seen by the populace as governing more and more conservatively, and there are those who fear that he will end up behaving like his predecessors. He hopes that by bringing Bonaparte home, so to speak, he will be able to tap into the rising swell of nostalgia regarding the Empire that is currently sweeping through France. I personally have my doubts as to his ability to succeed in the matter, but as I say, this is just my personal belief.

"There are two major forces to consider regarding the return of the Emperor's remains. The first are, of course, the Bonapartists. They will no doubt see the return as a great victory and perhaps even as a vindication of the Emperor in the eyes of history and the French people. It is possible that they will try to use the occasion to call for a restoration of their dynasty or even to stage a coup to try to take over the government. The problem for them is that they have no-one who is capable of capturing the hearts of the people as the Emperor did. Three of the Emperor's brothers are still living, but none of them are considered fit for the throne. They would put forth Louis-Napoleon Bonaparte as their candidate; he is the son of Napoleon's brother Louis, formerly King of Holland until Napoleon annexed it in 1810. Louis-Napoleon has a certain charm, but he is considered unstable and therefore unpredictable. I believe your Queen Victoria is said to favor Louis-Napoleon for the throne, a rumor which has several people in France fearing British aid for the Bonapartists. Have you met the man, my lord? No? I have met him on several occasions, and personally I believe that Louis-Napoleon on the throne would be a disaster for France. He believes himself the natural successor to his uncle, and therefore his equal. Gentlemen, I will tell you privately, he is nowhere near the Emperor in either talent or ability. He will have France at war with Europe. And yet, he is the Bonapartist candidate for the throne.

"The other force to be reckoned with are the Ultra-Royalists. These are those who long for a return to the divine right of kings, as it was before the Revolution. Where the Bonapartists would take advantage of the Emperor's return to France, the Ultra-Royalists would try to prevent it at all costs. They consider the Emperor to be the culmination of the Revolution, and therefore they blame him for all the Revolution's crimes and excesses, including the execution of Louis XVI and Marie Antoinette. They tried to kill the Emperor many times when he was alive, and they were quite content to leave him buried and forgotten on St. Helena. They have connections in every court in Europe and with every absolute monarch, all of whom fear a resurgence of the principles of freedom and brotherhood espoused by the Revolution and would do almost anything to prevent another Bonaparte on the throne of France."

Roussin paused to allow Hornblower and Bush to digest what he had said.

Hornblower, for his part, still had one question. "Why me?" he asked.

"A fair question," Roussin answered, "but one to which I am not privy to the answer. I can, however, make an educated guess. There are those in my government who are not ill-disposed to the Emperor's memory. These forces got the ear of either the king or Minister Thiers and suggested that someone should be in attendance who is outside the control or even the influence of any of the political factions that have a stake in the Emperor's return. You are known to have been on friendly terms with the Emperor during your tenure as governor of St. Helena, and you have proved yourself a man of character and honor. In short, the government wants someone to look after the Emperor's interests, so to speak, and as the official British representative, you would have the full weight of the British government and also the Royal Navy behind you."

Hornblower stood, motioning for his guest to remain seated. He walked over to a credenza and returned with a humidor. He opened its lid and proffered it to his guest.

"Would you care for a cigar, Minister?"

"Yes, thank you, my lord." The Minister selected one, and Bush followed suit when Hornblower offered. Hornblower selected one as well before returning the humidor to its place and resuming his seat. Soon all three men were exhaling clouds of smoke toward the ceiling.

"When did you meet the Emperor, Minister?" Hornblower asked.

Roussin stared at his host. "How did you know?"

Hornblower pointed to Roussin's chest. "I have learned that the Emperor alone gave out the stars of the *Légion d'honneur*."

The French admiral smiled and nodded. "I was awarded

this from the Emperor's hand in 1813. I had just been repatriated after being captured when the British took Mauritius and Reunion Islands and was appointed to command of the frigate *Gloire*. Between December, 1812, and April, 1813, we took fifteen prizes, including two sloops."

Suddenly, the light dawned, and Hornblower remembered reports he had read while convalescing following his return from Russia. A glance at Bush told him that he, too, had placed the name. The Frenchman smiled when he saw the recognition on the Englishmen's faces.

"Roussin!" Hornblower exclaimed. "Of course! You drove the Admiralty mad, my dear admiral! I'm afraid I was ashore at the time, recuperating from the typhus, and so was unable to join the hunt for you. Captain Bush was only just returning from the Baltic, I believe."

"That is so, my lord," Bush said.

The Frenchman smiled again and bowed. "I am gratified that you remember me, my lord. I wish we could have met at sea; what a glorious battle we would have had!" Roussin rose, and Hornblower and Bush followed suit. "I must also say, my lord, that it is an honor to meet you personally, and you as well, Captain Bush. I hope we shall meet again."

Hornblower shook his visitor's hand. "You will not be going to St. Helena?"

Roussin shook his host's hand, and then Captain Bush's, with a warmth found only among comrades-in-arms. "Sadly, no. I shall have to wait for the Emperor's return to Paris to honor him. Goodbye, my lord; Lord Palmerston's letter will give you your instructions. Captain Bush, adieu." Roussin bowed. Hornblower rang the bell, and the faithful Brown appeared in the doorway. "Please show our guest out, Brown," Hornblower said. He turned to Roussin. "Farewell, monsieur. Perhaps we shall meet in Paris."

The Frenchman followed Brown out of the library. Hornblower waited until the door was closed behind them before turning to Bush. "Well, Bush, now we know. I remember reading reports in early 1813 about a French frigate that was plundering our convoys, but we never caught it. I wanted to go to London and offer to go after it, but neither Barbara nor the doctors would allow it."

"I can well imagine, my lord; as I recall, you very nearly died of the typhus. I had received orders to bring *Nonsuch* and the bomb ketches to the Nore. When we arrived, I found Admiralty orders for *Nonsuch* to report to the blockade squadron at Brest, to help compensate for frigates that had been released to search for our friend." Bush's eyes went to the library door and back again. "But they never caught him."

Hornblower nodded. Those days were long gone, although he had to admit, at least to himself, that he missed them sometimes. He pondered the letter in his hands and thought about St. Helena and his time there with Bonaparte. The island had very nearly been a death trap for him, and almost taking the life of his son through an attack of dysentery. The near-tragedy had had an unexpected outcome in that the boy's illness had softened the Emperor's heart towards him. The Corsican became a source of solace and strength as Hornblower anxiously awaited word on his son's condition, and Hornblower always considered himself to be in the Corsican's debt. He turned the letter over and studied it. He wondered if he would finally have the chance to repay his friend.

CHAPTER 3

Hornblower broke the seal on the letter. It turned out to be a single page in length, with but a short, intimate paragraph handwritten over the powerful signature.

My Lord,

Since you are reading this letter, you have agreed to the request of the French Government, made through their Minister of Marine, to travel to St. Helena as the official representative of the British Government at the exhumation of the mortal remains of Napoleon Bonaparte. You are therefore requested and required to present yourself at the Foreign Office within the coming week for consultations on the particulars pertaining to your mission.

Palmerston

Hornblower handed the letter to Bush before walking over to the bust of the Emperor that stood unobtrusively in a corner of the room. He stood and stared at it for several minutes, remembering his friend and wondering what Bonaparte would think of the plans to return him to France. Hornblower became aware that Bush had joined him, standing silently behind his shoulder out of respect for his friend's need to think. It was one of the qualities he loved in Bush. He had not always possess it; the ability had developed over the course of many years and even more painful encounters. That was another thing he loved about Bush, the way his friend had changed to allow their friendship to deepen through the years. Hornblower was not by nature a praying man, but over the years he found himself thanking whatever Powers there be for bringing him together with William Bush.

"What do you think, Bush?" Hornblower asked.

"It seems fairly straightforward to me, my lord," Bush said as he handed the letter back to Hornblower. "I don't understand why the French *government* would ask you to attend. As I recall, they were among the ones who did not like that you and Bonaparte were becoming friendly."

Hornblower nodded and looked at the bust again. "That thought had occurred to me as well. Perhaps Lord Palmerston will be able to shed some light on that little mystery." He nodded to the bust before walking out of the room. Bush hesitated for a moment, his eyes going back and forth between his friend's retreating form and the bust, then followed Hornblower out of the room.

Hornblower found his wife in the conservatory, sipping tea and reading a letter. She looked up and smiled when her husband entered. She held up the letter for his inspection.

"A letter from Richard, my dear?" Hornblower asked as he sat down.

"Yes," Barbara said. "He still wants us to come to

Edinburgh this summer. Oh, hello again, Captain Bush. I didn't know you were still here. Really, Horatio, we simply must make it up to see Richard and Elizabeth. Little Barbara will turn a year old in a few months, and it would be wonderful to celebrate with my granddaughter."

"Yes, well," Hornblower said, as he handed her the Palmerston letter, "you may have to go alone. Trade letters with me."

He sat back on the window seat to read the letter from his only surviving son. In the years since his return from St. Helena, Richard had grown into young manhood at Smallbridge. To his father's surprise—and carefully concealed disappointment—Richard chose not to enter the Royal Navy. Instead, he'd decided to follow in the footsteps of Hornblower's father and study medicine, enrolling at the University of Edinburgh Medical School in Scotland. In his third year, Richard had met and fallen in love with Elizabeth Cosgrove, daughter of the school's headmaster. After graduation, Richard completed his internship at Edinburgh's St. James' Hospital. Professor Cosgrove arranged for Richard to purchase a practice in the wealthy village of Leith, two miles outside of Edinburgh. The practice was a success, and Richard and Elizabeth were married in 1837. A year later, a daughter was born, whom Richard name Maria, after his mother. The name proved unlucky, however, for the little girl died suddenly, after only four months. Hornblower and Barbara were devastated—Hornblower particularly so, mourning again the loss of his first wife and a daughter of the same name. Another daughter was born in 1839 whom Richard named Barbara, after the stepmother who had taken him in and raised him when his mother died in childbirth and his father was still out to sea. The child thrived, and Lady Barbara loved nothing better than to dote on her namesake at every opportunity.

Hornblower looked up from Richard's letter to find his wife staring at him in wide-eyed disbelief. He and Bush shared a laugh at her expense, and Hornblower spent the next hour recounting the Frenchman's visit as his wife listened closely. When he finished, his wife looked off into the distance, considering his tale. Hornblower saw her eyebrows rise, and she smiled and shook her head. He waited for her to explain.

"It seems, my dear husband," she said, "that we have one more service to give to our friend on St. Helena. You will go, then?"

Hornblower took the Foreign Secretary's letter back from her. "I feel a debt to him. Had he not been there for me, after you had to return with Richard to England, I don't know what would have happened." He looked up at his wife. "Those were dark days for me. He was my anchor when you could not be."

"I know," she said. "I have always regretted that I was not able to return to the island while he was alive and thank him for what he did for you." She looked away. "He deserved better, at least at that point in his life."

The three of them sat there for a while, each remembering the Corsican in his or her own way, each hoping he would finally be at peace once his remains were entombed back in France.

It was Barbara who stirred first. "Oh, Horatio, I just remembered. I received a note this morning; we are to have a guest for dinner."

"And who would that be?" Hornblower asked, but before his wife could reply, Brown appeared in the doorway.

"Your pardon, my lord," he said, "but the duke has arrived."

The three rose as Brown stepped aside and the duke of

Wellington marched into the room. Barbara stepped forward to greet him, hugging her brother warmly and giving him a kiss on the cheek. She held the duke's arm as they walked back to Hornblower and Bush.

"As I was about to say, Horatio," Barbara said, as her brother nodded greetings to the two men, "I had just received a note from Arthur shortly before you came in, saying he was passing through the area and would join us for dinner if it was convenient."

Hornblower was genuinely pleased to see his brother-in-law, especially today, and he shook the duke's hand warmly. "I'm sure Arthur knows he is always welcome at Smallbridge. In fact, his timing is exquisite. Events are conspiring to return me to St. Helena, Your Grace, and I should very much like your opinion on the matter."

"Delighted to be of service, Hornblower," the duke said. He shook Bush's hand. "How have you been, Captain?"

"Very well indeed, Your Grace," Bush said. "Thank you."

Barbara steered her brother to the settee against the wall while Bush resumed his seat and her husband went to pour each of them a drink. Hornblower delivered the drinks and then sat next to Bush on the divan, across from the duke. Wellington, for his part, simply sipped his drink and waited patiently for his host to fill him in on events and their connection to St. Helena.

Hornblower, too, sipped his drink before beginning his tale. "I had a most interesting visitor today, Arthur—Admiral Albin Roussin, French Minister of Marine. He told me the French were going to bring the remains of the Emperor Napoleon home from St. Helena and bury them on the banks of the Seine in Paris."

Hornblower watched the duke's left eyebrow rise a fraction at the news—he wondered if it was a family trait—

before he looked at his drink as he swirled it in his hand. "Yes," he said, "I heard something of the sort only yesterday in London. It seems King Louis, or at least his new prime minister, Thiers, is trying to ingratiate himself with the Paris mob. Apparently, Boney has been gone long enough to be back in favor with the masses. Perhaps they have forgotten the millions dead across Europe, all because their sainted Emperor could not bring himself to stay within his own borders."

"Do you see this move enabling the Bonapartists to seize the throne again?" Hornblower asked.

Wellington thought for a moment before shaking his head. "I can't see how. Napoleon has—what?—three brothers still alive, isn't it? None of them can capture the people as the Emperor could. Who else could they put up?"

"What about that Pretender who is living outside London?" Bush asked.

The duke shook his head. "I don't think so. Louis-Napoleon is the most charismatic of the lot, but from what I am told he is also very nearly insane. Should he ascend to the throne of France, I don't think it will be too long before he tries to emulate his famous namesake and has France at war with one or more of the European Powers. It will be 1815 all over again."

"As bad as all that, Arthur?" Barbara asked.

The duke shrugged. "He's already tried to seize the throne, so who knows what he would do if he were actually crowned Emperor?"

"Not king?" Hornblower asked.

Wellington laughed, a short, derisive bark. "Have you ever met him? No? Well, let me tell you, his ego is enormous. He will make every effort to eclipse the Napoleon we fought and make a Second Empire that will overshadow the First.

His problem is, he is not his uncle."

Hornblower and Bush sat back and caught each other's eyes. Bush stirred.

"But, Your Grace, if this Pretender is so dangerous, why is he allowed to stay in England? Why isn't he already on St. Helena, or at least in the United States or Canada?"

The duke shrugged. "A very good question, Captain, for which there is a very simple answer. Our beloved queen has been charmed by him. One of Victoria's policies—encouraged by Melbourne, I might add—is to improve our relations with France. She feels that having Louis-Napoleon on the throne will turn France into Britain's best friend on the continent." He grunted. "What she doesn't realize is that once that maniac ascends to the throne, France won't want any friends in Europe, only vassals."

"Well," Barbara said, "let's hope it doesn't come to that."

"Tell me, Hornblower," the duke said, "what was Roussin's opinion of the Emperor's return?"

"Personally, the admiral is in favor," Hornblower said. "Privately, however, he is concerned. I believe he holds the same fears for the future of France as you do yourself, Your Grace. He also fears that the Ultra-Royalists will make some attempt to prevent the return, although he has no idea what the consequences of such an occurrence might be."

"And what does all this have to do with your returning to St. Helena, Hornblower?" the duke asked.

"Roussin was sent on behalf of the French government to ask that I attend the exhumation as the representative of the British government."

That made the duke blink. Hornblower was quietly pleased; it wasn't often that the duke of Wellington was left speechless. Even Lady Barbara hid a small smile at her brother's discomfort.

"Extraordinary," Wellington said. He stared at his drink for a moment before draining the glass. He looked at the empty glass again before setting it on the table. "Don't take this amiss, Hornblower, but what you say worries me."

"Why is that, Your Grace?" Bush asked.

The duke drummed his fingers on his thigh. "Because, my dear Captain, we may now presume that someone in the French government is very concerned about Boney coming home. Probably one of his friends or family, since they wanted someone in the British delegation who was friendly with Bonaparte on St. Helena to be there. Hornblower is the natural choice from the Bonapartist point of view."

"Do you think Roussin might be right about the Ultra-Royalists, Arthur?" Hornblower asked.

"I don't know," the duke replied. "It's certainly possible. They hate Boney as the result of the Revolution, and their connections to the other courts on the continent would give them plenty of allies and support, should they choose to act. I must admit that I can no more predict what the result would be than can Roussin. Any attempt on their part would almost certainly provoke a response of some kind from the Bonapartists, and should they succeed—say they sink the ship carrying his remains, for example—it may send France into a civil war and condemn Louis-Philippe to follow in the footsteps of Louis XVI. If that happens, I believe even Queen Victoria will go to war."

They sat quietly, contemplating what the duke had prophesied, while Hornblower rose and refilled their glasses. The duke thanked him and said, "So, what will you do?"

Hornblower handed him the Palmerston letter, which the duke read; he grunted as he returned it. "Well," he said, "at least the Foreign Office is taking this seriously. I would advise you to seek out Richard while you are in London, Hornblower. He may have some good advice for you."

Brown stepped into the conservatory at that moment to announce that dinner was served. Bush joined the Hornblowers and the duke for the meal. Afterward, both Bush and the duke made their farewells, leaving their hosts to ponder the future.

"Shall I have Brown pack for you, Horatio?" Barbara asked.

"Please," her husband answered as they walked out to sit on the terrace.

"How long will you be gone?"

"I have no idea. Palmerston gave no hint as to the number of 'particulars' he wished to discuss, plus Arthur thought it would be a good idea to hear Sir Richard's thoughts – I suppose three days, as a worst-case scenario. If it is any longer, I will send you word."

Brown proved to be as efficient as ever, and the bags were packed and loaded onto the coach shortly after dawn. Hornblower breakfasted early with his wife, as was their custom. She walked him out the front door to where the coach was waiting for him. He bent down and kissed her as they said their goodbyes.

"Greet Richard for me," she said as he boarded. "Try to get him to come visit."

"I will," Hornblower said as he reached out the window and squeezed her hand for a moment. He waved as the coachman whipped up the horses and the coach pulled away from the door, holding her eyes until the coach rounded the corner and she disappeared from view.

He pulled his head back inside the coach and made himself comfortable. He was once again reminded how fortunate he was to be married to Barbara, who was so strong and calm, never questioning his orders or making a fuss about his being needed. Maria would have been beside herself with worry, asking questions Hornblower could not answer and begging him at the same time not to go. He felt the pang of guilt that plagued him whenever he compared Maria to Barbara, and he dismissed it from his mind only with great effort.

He determined to put all thoughts of women out of his mind by concentrating on his mission. Returning to St. Helena held no appeal to him whatsoever; only the debt he felt he owed the Corsican made him accept Roussin's request. In a strange way, Hornblower was glad he had met Bonaparte so late in his life, after his ego had been moderated somewhat by defeat and exile. Hornblower now realized that much of their relationship was founded upon a mutual pain—the loss of a son, feared on Hornblower's part, but all too real for Bonaparte. As grateful as he was for the Corsican's help during those dark days, Hornblower often wondered what had caused him offer a hand of friendship and support to the hurting governor, when he could just as easily have used Richard's illness as a dagger, or simply withheld his support and allowed Hornblower to wallow in his suffering and misery.

Hornblower had been amazed that Bonaparte had chosen consolation over confrontation. He'd always had a word of comfort or encouragement, and Hornblower was thankful that he had been discreet as well. The only one who had full knowledge of the relationship the two men enjoyed was Mr. Brewer, and Hornblower knew his aide had kept, and would continue to keep, his confidence.

He smiled at the thought of his one-time protégé. It had been more than twenty years since he had become Brewer's patron, and in all those years he never had cause to regret his decision. No matter where Brewer had served, whether it was as his secretary on St Helena or as a lieutenant to Captain Bush in the Mediterranean, whether in command of a frigate or a sloop of war in the Caribbean or of a frigate off the West African station, Hornblower had never received a poor report of Brewer's conduct or performance. Brewer had also been faithful to his promise to write Hornblower regularly, and had stayed with them at Smallbridge when he had occasion to pass through the area. Hornblower had no reason to regret reviving the old custom of allowing a retiring station commander to grant one promotion from midshipman to lieutenant and one to post captain, which he used to promote Brewer to post captain in the frigate HMS *Phoebe*. Brewer's latest letter said he was in Plymouth, overseeing the fitting out of his newest command, HMS *Iris*, a brand new 26-gun frigate.

Hornblower looked out the window with a frown as he thought about his return to St. Helena. The more he considered his meetings with Roussin and then with Wellington, the more he realized the possibility of an international incident arising, especially if the Ultra-Royalists received aid from a European power and succeeded in disrupting the Emperor's return. He recalled Roussin's speculation that his government wanted someone who would "look after the Emperor's interests" and the full weight of those words now dawned on him. Hornblower shook his head in wonder. How ironic, he thought, that after more than twenty years of fighting Bonaparte as a young man, here he was in his old age as the one being sent by the French government to protect his interests.

Hornblower pulled a pencil and a sheet of paper from his bag and began to make notes, but he had to give up in frustration after only a few minutes. There were just too many unanswered questions coming to his mind; he would just have to wait for his meeting with Palmerston and maybe his brother-in-law, Richard, before he would have a clearer picture of what was ahead of him. He sat back and watched the countryside roll by. He hated this sort of forced inactivity. He needed something to engage his mind; he hoped to consider this St. Helena business in detail during the trip, but he simply did not have enough data. No, he had to wait for his meeting with Palmerston.

Hornblower leaned his head back and closed his eyes, and when he did, an image appeared. The image was that of a plate he had mounted on the wall of his library in Smallbridge, which bore a picture of the French army camp at Boulogne in 1805. It was the plate that the Emperor had given him as a going away present when he left St. Helena. He smiled at the memory and allowed his mind to wander back to his time spent with the man who was the greatest threat to England's safety and security since the Spanish Armada.

The two men had spent countless hours together, sometimes discussing their careers, but sometimes speculating about what might have been. Hornblower recollected a particularly vigorous discussion on what might have happened had Villeneuve been able to lose Nelson in the West Indies. Trafalgar would never have happened, the Emperor theorized, and the French fleet would have swept into the English Channel, gaining control of it long enough for the *Armée d'Angleterre*, or Army of England, to cross the Channel and end the war in his favor.

Hornblower had protested. "But aren't you forgetting, sir, the English squadron blockading Brest under Admiral Cornwallis? He had fifteen ships of the line outside of Brest, along with additional forces blockading Rochefort and Ferrol? How would you get past those?"

Bonaparte waved the governor's objections aside. "I should have ordered all French forces along the Atlantic coast to sea at once. If I recall correctly, Admiral Ganteaume had something like twenty sail of the line at Brest, with additional forces close at hand, say perhaps thirty or thirty-five of the line altogether. Combine that with the force Villeneuve was bringing up the Channel, and England was doomed."

Hornblower had retorted, "You would have had to sink every ship in the Channel Fleet. No fleet was capable of that kind of domination over the Royal Navy. The Spanish certainly wouldn't have been any help."

The Emperor had shrugged. "You may be right, Governor, but they were not a major part of my plans, in any case. Everything depended upon Villeneuve shaking off Nelson in the West Indies and arriving back off the coast of France with two or three weeks' lead. That would have been enough."

"What would you have done then?" Hornblower asked.

Bonaparte had considered answering. "I would have advanced on Canterbury or London, in order to draw the English forces into a battle. One or two good battles and the English would have surrendered as quickly as the Austrians. My peace terms would have beggared your country: reparations that would have left England unable to finance the coalitions of 1806-1811, plus the virtual dismantling of the Royal Navy to include the burning of all of its ships of 90 guns or more, along with the surrender of one half of your frigates." Bonaparte smiled. "I would also station an occupation army on your island—a combined French-Irish force." The smile was topped by a glint of steel in the Emperor's eyes. "Your country would be helpless."

Riding in his carriage, more than twenty years later, Hornblower remembered the cold chill that had gripped his heart at the Emperor's words, for he knew that, had Villeneuve managed to lose Nelson in the West Indies, history might well have unfolded exactly as the Corsican described. The shiver that ran down his spine now had very little to do with the weather.

He looked out the window again, and he wondered at how fortunate England was to always seem to have the right man in the right place at the right time to thwart Bonaparte. There was Pitt, who organized the finances that paid for the coalitions that never let the Corsican rest; Nelson, who clung to Villeneuve tenaciously until he could destroy him at Trafalgar; Wellington, who met Bonaparte himself at Waterloo and ended his dreams for good. Hornblower smiled. Providence had definitely been on their side.

He passed the remainder of his trip to London in quiet reflection. He took a room at the Trafalgar Inn, which was a short walk from the Foreign Office. He sent a short note to his brother-in-law, Richard, saying he was in London and asking to meet him for supper the day after next. He dined alone before retiring to his room to spend the evening reading.

He breakfasted early and walked to the Foreign Office for his appointment with Lord Palmerston. The morning was damp, and Hornblower noticed how different Londoners were from the folk he met whenever he walked through Smallbridge. The people he passed this morning walked with their heads down, cramming into the coffee shops for breakfast and going through their daily routines without a glance or a word for passersby. Hornblower realized that not a single person of the thousands who were all around him this morning had the slightest idea who he was. In the much smaller fishbowl that was Smallbridge, everyone who passed him greeted him by name, but here, if it weren't for his dress, he would be considered little more than a common laborer.

Hornblower chided himself for his vanity and quickened his pace. Upon arriving at his destination, he was shown almost immediately into the presence of the Foreign

Minister, John Henry Temple, 3rd Viscount Palmerston.

"Hornblower!" the Viscount said, as he came around his desk with his hand extended. "A pleasure to meet you at last." Hornblower shook the Secretary's hand and bowed. Palmerston nodded his acknowledgement and led Hornblower to two chairs set off in a secluded corner of the office. A servant placed two glasses of Madeira on the table in between. Hornblower could see that all he had heard about the Foreign Secretary and his fabled good looks and easygoing manner were true.

"Thank you, John," Palmerston said, dismissing the servant as he picked up his glass and raised it in salute to his visitor. Hornblower did the same, and the two men drank.

"The Secretary set his glass on the table and sat back in his chair. "I'm glad you are here, Hornblower. Tell me, what do you think of all this?"

"I confess to being a bit bewildered, my lord," Hornblower said. "I can understand the king trying to tap into the swelling nostalgia for the Empire instead of trying to quash it and risk an uprising. I still don't understand why the French government would ask me to be an official British observer."

"Did you ask Roussin why?" Palmerston asked as he began to stroke his chin between his thumb and forefinger.

"Yes, my lord; he said that he did not know any official reason for the request. I will tell you, my lord, that my brother-in-law, the duke of Wellington, happened to stop by my house in Smallbridge on the same day that I was visited by Minister Roussin, and I told him of the visit and asked his opinion. He said he was very troubled by what I told him. He is of the opinion that someone in the French government is also concerned. Probably one of his friends or family, since they want someone in the British delegation who was friendly with Bonaparte on St. Helena. He thought I would be the natural choice from the Bonapartist point of view." He paused when he saw the look on the Viscount's face. "Pardon me, my lord, but may I ask what is so amusing?"

Palmerston held up his hand as he shook his head. "Pray forgive me, sir, but I confess to finding myself astonished. I believe this may be the first time in memory that your Duke and I have been in perfect agreement!"

Hornblower, in his turn, allowed a smile to creep onto his face. He could well imagine what Wellington himself would say when Hornblower eventually relayed this conversation to him.

Palmerston picked up his glass, swirling it gently and studying the contents for a moment. "I, too, am concerned, Hornblower, very concerned by Roussin's request. Were I to make a guess, I would say it was a ploy by Thiers to throw at least part of the security of the operation on to the Royal Navy, but I will confess I have no hard evidence to support that suspicion. I am afraid that I find Minister Roussin's version entirely believable, but I also find the duke's to be so as well. I believe we need to take a deeper look into the political factions in France and what they might be planning."

The Viscount drained his glass. He set the empty glass on the table and rose. Hornblower followed his example. He watched as Palmerston went to the door and called for a carriage. He closed the door and walked back to where Hornblower was still standing. He smiled when he saw the bewildered look on his visitor's face.

"Sorry, old boy," he said, "I forgot to tell you. Her Majesty is aware of the request for your participation at St. Helena. I'm afraid she wants to speak to you. You see, dying alone in exile transformed Napoleon from a tyrant into a mere human being and resulted in much soul-searching in England about the morality of his captivity. I suspect the

Queen, in her own way, is looking to make amends."

Hornblower followed his host out to the carriage and climbed in behind him. The footman shut the door behind them, and Palmerston leaned forward.

"Windsor Castle, driver!"

CHAPTER 4

Hornblower rode in silence beside the Viscount as the carriage weaved its way through the streets of London. He had never been to Windsor, and he was greatly impressed riding up the drive approaching the castle. Originally built in the 11th century by William the Conqueror, the castle had been used by every reigning monarch since Henry I. Most recently, Windsor underwent an extensive restoration by George IV, who persuaded Parliament to vote £300,000 for the project in 1824. Sir Walter Scott described the restoration as "a great deal of taste and feeling for the Gothic architecture." Queen Victoria and Prince Albert made Windsor their primary residence. The carriage drove straight through the gates and pulled up to a doorway.

Palmerston turned and said, "I will not be staying with you during your audience. The message I received asked me only to deliver you to the Queen. Be sure to come and see me tomorrow morning, and we shall finish your briefing."

"Yes, my lord," Hornblower said.

A page opened the door on Palmerston's side, and the Foreign Secretary exited without a word, leaving Hornblower to catch up to him. The stone edifice towered above them, grey against an overcast sky. The passed beneath the great archway.

At the castle entrance, Palmerston was greeted by a footman. “I have an appointment with the Queen,” he said.

The footman checked his appointment calendar. “Very good, my lord,” he said. “The Queen is in the Waterloo Chamber with Prince Albert. If you will follow me?” Without waiting for a reply, the man lead the way though the grand entrance hall of ribbed columns and down a hall. He stopped and put his ear to a door, then knocked, opened the door and stepped inside.

“Viscount Palmerston and Admiral Lord Hornblower!” he announced. The footman stepped aside to allow the two men to enter, and then he left, closing the door softly behind him.

Hornblower was in a long room, the walls of which were covered with portraits of those who had played a part in the Waterloo campaign. The largest was of his brother-in-law, the duke of Wellington. The center of the room was dominated by a very long and narrow banqueting table, and two people were at the far end. Palmerston bowed deeply in their direction, and Hornblower followed suit. The two men walked along the near side of the table.

Hornblower thought for a minute that the faces at the other end were Prince Albert, the Queen’s husband, and a child. To his immense embarrassment, he realized that it was the Queen herself who was sitting there. As the two men approached, Victoria rose and stepped to the side of the table. Hornblower could see now how very petite she was, barely five feet tall and almost frail looking. Palmerston stopped in front of her and went down on one knee. Hornblower did likewise and lowered his gaze.

“Thank you for coming, my lords,” the Queen said, in a sweet yet firm voice. “You may rise.”

Both men stood. They seemed to tower over the young Queen, Hornblower especially, but Victoria seemed completely at ease as she resumed her seat.

"If Your Majesty will excuse me," Palmerston said, "I have urgent business at the Ministry."

"Of course, my lord," Victoria said. Palmerston bowed to the royal couple and retreated from the room.

"Sit here, next to me, Admiral," Victoria said.

"I thank you, Your Majesty," Hornblower answered. He sat in the seat on Victoria's right, with Albert across from him.

"My lord," the Queen said, "we wished to speak to you regarding your mission to St. Helena. It is our understanding that Admiral Roussin, the French Minister of Marine, came to see you with a request?"

"Yes, Your Majesty," Hornblower said.

"And that request was that you attend the exhumation of the remains of the Emperor Napoleon for their removal to France."

"Yes, Your Majesty."

Victoria glanced over to Albert and gave him the merest fraction of a nod. Albert took over the questioning.

"What are your personal feelings about the return, my lord?" he asked.

Hornblower paused to gather his thoughts, choosing his words with care. "I am in favor of it, my Prince, mainly because I know it to be a wish of Bonaparte's."

"You knew him, then?" Albert asked.

Hornblower replied, "Yes, my Prince, from my time as governor on St. Helena."

Victoria looked up at him. "Tell us, my lord, what sort of man was he?"

Hornblower sighed. "You must understand, Majesty, that

the Bonaparte I knew was not the Bonaparte of 1805 or even that of 1812. The defeat at Waterloo and exile to St. Helena had done much to change him from what he was." Victoria and Albert both nodded, so Hornblower continued. "He was a man in great need of intellectual stimulation. Before I arrived, he found it in twisting the then-governor's nose and embarrassing him at will. I was sent mainly because of the similarity of our backgrounds. The hope was that I could deal with him man-to-man."

"And what is the similarity in your backgrounds?" Victoria asked.

"We are both men born not to a noble family, who have achieved noble rank based on our achievements, our military victories, alone. We rose through the ranks of our respective services."

"We see," Victoria said. "Please continue."

"What softened him most was nothing I said, but the presence of my son, Richard, who was the same age as Bonaparte's son, the king of Rome. Remember that, after Waterloo, the Empress Marie-Louise and her son were taken into 'protective custody' by her father, the Emperor Francis of Austria. Together with his minister, Metternich, they determined never to allow Bonaparte to see his wife or son again." He saw the Queen's hand go to her stomach, and he recalled the recent announcement of her pregnancy. He looked at the prince. "Imagine yourself in Bonaparte's place, my Prince. They were all he had left at that point, and he missed them terribly. Bonaparte took a liking to Richard, and he asked if he could spend time with him—always in our company, of course—since he could not with his own son." His face softened at a memory. "He gave Richard a present of two sets of wooden army men, a blue set that was the French army and a red set that was either the Russian or Austrian army. Do you know, he actually got down on the floor and played with the toy soldiers with my son. They refought all the major battles of his reign, and he explained to Richard all about strategy and moving men around a battlefield. It was really something to watch." Hornblower suddenly remembered to whom he was speaking. "I beg your pardon, Majesty."

Victoria smiled and nodded. "We understand, my lord, and we thank you for your insight. We pray your dear wife does not mind our calling upon your services once more."

"We are both humbled that I can be of service, my Queen."

Prince Albert spoke up. "Admiral, if you were the Ultra-Royalists, how would you achieve their ends?"

Hornblower thought for a moment. "My Prince, I would attack and sink the French ship carrying the remains on its way back to France."

Albert shared an apprehensive look with his bride. "That would cause war."

Hornblower nodded. "Perhaps the very thing the Royalists want: to topple Louis-Philippe and bury the Bonapartists at a stroke."

"We have made it a cornerstone of our policy," the Queen said, "to improve our relations with France. Tell me, Admiral, what is your opinion of Louis-Napoleon Bonaparte?"

"I have never met him, Your Majesty," Hornblower said.

"We believe he is the best hope for France," the Queen said, "but we are aware that he has many enemies."

Albert leaned in and said, "Tell us, Admiral, what do you think Britain should do regarding the return?"

Hornblower thought for a moment. "Assign one or two frigates to escort the French ship carrying the remains back to France."

"A fine idea, my lord," Victoria said. "We shall speak to our First Sea Lord regarding this." The Queen paused for a moment, then said formally, "My lord, we desire you to go to St. Helena as our official representative. You have our instructions to see that the remains of the Emperor Napoleon reach France safely. We shall send a letter to Lord Palmerston, giving you our royal backing." Victoria rose, signaling the end of the audience. Hornblower and Albert followed suit.

"Thank you for coming to see us today, Admiral," the Queen said. "May God bless you on your journey."

"Thank you, Majesty," Hornblower said. "May I offer my congratulations on the coming child? Lady Barbara and I shall pray for a safe delivery and health for you both."

The Queen smiled, and Albert said, "Thank you, my lord. We are honored by and cherish your prayers."

Hornblower bowed and left the room.

A carriage was waiting outside to take him back to the inn. Hornblower sat back in the plush seats and resisted the urge to look over his shoulder to watch Windsor Castle recede into distance. He folded his hands in his lap and thought about his audience with the Queen. She obviously expected him to ensure safe passage for Bonaparte's remains to France. Just what kind of authority he would possess to make that happen could well depend on what the Queen's letter would say, and he hoped to discover that tomorrow morning when he met again with Palmerston.

He took in the exquisite scenery that flowed past him. He had to admit, he was impressed with the young Queen. He had heard his brother-in-law, Arthur, say that the Queen was very young and inexperienced, and so might be subject to manipulation by Melbourne or others, but after speaking with her, Hornblower had his doubts about that. She seemed to possess a commanding personality; if she could manage to surround herself with the proper counselors, Hornblower thought she stood a good chance to develop into a great monarch. He thought Albert would do well for her; they seemed to work well together.

Dinner at the inn was a delicious steak-and-kidney pie. He washed it down with a pint of the local ale, for which the inn was famous, and then he wrote a note to his brother-in-law, Sir Richard Wellesley, asking if it were convenient for him to stop by that evening to discuss some pressing matters. This he sent off by special messenger before retiring to his room to relax and do some reading.

A knock on his door made him look at the clock on the wall, and he discovered that nearly three hours had flown by. He opened the door to find a messenger bearing a note from Sir Richard that said he was expected for supper at eight o'clock. That suited Hornblower admirably, so he picked up his book again and lost himself in Gibbon, still his favorite author after more than thirty years. He had time to finish the chapter before readying himself for the evening.

Hornblower heard a clock striking the hour as he stepped from his carriage and mounted the steps to Richard's front door. Montrose, Richard's butler, opened the door just as he approached. "Good evening, my lord," Montrose said, as he took Hornblower's coat, hat and stick. "The master is in the library. If you would be so good as to follow me?"

Hornblower allowed the servant to lead the way, though he knew it well enough. He paused when they arrived and allowed Montrose to announce him. When the butler stepped aside, he entered the room to find his host sitting in a chair in front of an empty fireplace, reading a letter. Richard rose and came over to shake Hornblower's hand.

"Hornblower! Good to see you." Richard wrung his hand

heartily. "Montrose, the port, if you please. Come, Horatio, sit here." He indicated a chair opposite his own. Montrose appeared a moment later, bearing a silver tray with two glasses of port. He held it low, and each man helped himself. Richard raised his glass in a toast.

"To Bonaparte," he said, and both men drank.

"You look surprised," Richard said.

Hornblower shrugged. "You seem especially well informed."

Richard smiled. "Rumors fly around this town, old boy, especially when the Foreign Secretary is visited first by the French ambassador and then by their Minister of Marine. It wasn't hard to ask a question or two in the proper quarter." He took another sip of wine, then set the glass on the small antique table between the chairs before sitting back and making himself comfortable. "Tell me about Roussin's visit."

Hornblower spent the next half-hour recounting his visit with the French admiral, ending with the request that he attend the exhumation and the letter from the Foreign Secretary. Richard listened intently, interrupting only twice for clarification. When Hornblower finished, he leaned his head back and closed his eyes for several minutes, digesting this new information. When he finally opened his eyes, it was to ask a question.

"Why did you agree to go?"

Hornblower smiled and shook his head. "Really, Richard, do you have to ask? You read my reports, not to mention the personal letters I sent you from St. Helena." When his host remained silent, Hornblower sighed. "You sent me to St. Helena to make Boney behave. While I was there, we formed a friendship of a sort, stronger than either of us would have cared to admit, even privately, to anyone. Barbara knew about it, of course. He was the one who helped me through the torment of Richard's illness. I never got the chance to repay him for his kindness or his discretion." Hornblower shrugged. "Now I can."

"That's one of the things I like about you, Hornblower; you are what you are. There is no pretense with you whatsoever." A small smile crept across his brother-in-law's face. "I imagine that is one reason my sister fell in love with you."

"The Queen has promised a naval escort for the return," Hornblower continued, "and she is supposed to write me a letter that would allow me to call in any resources necessary in the event of an emergency."

"Well," Richard said, "that's a start. What does your schedule look like?"

"I'm to meet with the Foreign Minister tomorrow. I do not have a departure date yet."

Richard nodded. "Good. I am by no means considered a friend of the current Foreign Minister, but even I will admit to you privately that Palmerston is good at his job. I would advise you to listen closely to what he tells you to do."

"Who is the governor now?" Hornblower asked. "Not Lowe, surely?"

Richard thought for a moment. "No, his name is Middleton. No, wait, that's not right. What is his name? Middlemore? Yes, that's right. One of Arthur's last appointments before he left the Ministry. Good man."

"Do you know him?" Hornblower asked. "Will he give me any trouble when I get there?"

"I met him once or twice," his host replied. "Couldn't really tell you anything about him, though. Middlemore's still in the Army—a major general, I believe. I have no doubt that the letter you carry from the queen will bring him around."

Hornblower sat back, reassured that he would not have to deal with Lowe or any of his ilk. He took a slow drink of wine to hide his uneasiness at his host's remarks. Thankfully, Richard did not dwell on the subject.

"Tell me, Hornblower," he said, "do you think there will be a fight before this whole thing is over?"

Hornblower thought for a moment before answering. "Possibly. The best place for such a move, presumably by the Ultra-Royalists, would be at sea. If they can sink the transport, all their problems would be over. In order to do that, they would need a fast warship. If they believe the transport lacks an escort they will think that a frigate would do the job, or perhaps two sloops, but where would they get them?"

"Russia," Richard said as he rose to refill his glass. "It is well known that Nicholas has no taste for anything that smacks of revolution or enlightenment for the peasantry."

Hornblower considered this. "Enough to risk a war with France and possibly Great Britain?"

"I'm afraid so. If Nicholas plays this right, he may just be able to rouse the courts of Austria and Prussia against the specter of a new Bonapartist France rising to spread the principles of the Revolution again."

Hornblower was alarmed by this, yet incredulous at the prospect his brother-in-law proposed. Richard read all this in his face and leaned forward to speak quietly and in earnest. "I will let you know something, Hornblower. When the Allied Powers restored Louis XVIII the second time, after the Emperor was beaten by Arthur at Waterloo, a secret protocol was signed among the Powers of Europe, committing them to armed intervention in the event of any sort of revolutionary activity in France. I can well imagine Nicholas calling the courts of Europe to act upon it, especially if it looks like that loud-mouthed pretender, Louis-

Napoleon, might ascend to the throne. Should such circumstances come to pass, Britain would act immediately to seize the channel ports, if only to keep the French navy out of the hands of the Russians."

Hornblower sat back and began to realize just how real the possibility of war was, should the Emperor not make it to his new resting place safely. He was about to speak when Montrose entered the room and announced that dinner was served. Both men followed him to the dining room to enjoy the feast of stuffed duck, ragout of pork, French beans, and fresh young carrots, all of which were among Hornblower's favorites. The dinner conversation was strictly about family, with Richard telling Hornblower about his children's adventures and Hornblower relating his son's latest letter. Coffee was brought after the meal, and the men retreated with their cups to the library to smoke cigars.

The Marquess blew a blue cloud ceilingward and said, "I would advise extreme caution on this trip, Hornblower. You may prevent a war if you act appropriately, or you may start one if you don't. I must say, I don't envy you."

Richard rose, and Hornblower followed his host to the front door, where the faithful Montrose was waiting with his things. The two men shook hands.

"Give Barbara my love," Richard said, "and say hello to Boney for me."

The morning found Hornblower standing across the desk from the Foreign Secretary. Palmerston handed him an envelope containing the Queen's letter.

"You may open it and read the letter," he said.

Hornblower carefully opened the handmade envelope and took out the letter. He unfolded the page and read exactly what the Queen had told him would be there, that

Lord Hornblower was operating as her special representative and should be extended every courtesy in any request he should make upon the resources of the British Empire. He refolded the letter and carefully replaced it inside the envelope.

"You should keep that letter on your person at all times," Palmerston said. He handed Hornblower a set of papers. "These are your sailing orders. You are to report to HMS *Iris*, currently fitting out at Plymouth. The captain is being sent a copy of your sailing orders, along with an additional note signed by Admiral Dunston, informing the captain that he is to defer to your wishes."

"Who is the captain?" Hornblower asked.

Palmerston looked at his papers. "The captain is one William Brewer."

Hornblower smiled but said nothing.

Palmerston raised an eyebrow but did not make any inquiry. "Please be seated, my lord," he said. "It has become necessary to inform you of something that may affect your mission, and that is the French support for Muhammad Pasha in Egypt. Thiers's policy of support of the renegade, in the face of opposition from nearly every other European Power, may lead to war. My instructions to you, my lord, are not to worry about Egypt until you hear officially from the government. Until then, you have broad powers, which you will be expected to exercise at your discretion. Just remember, Hornblower, you may have to answer for your actions, so be careful."

"Yes, my lord."

"HMS *Iris* is scheduled to be ready for sea within the next fortnight. Please send a note to the captain and inform him when you want to be ready to sail. I'm sure a clerk at the Admiralty can take care of that for you. I would think you'd need to sail within the month at the outside."

Palmerston dropped his pen on his desk and sat back in his chair. "I wish you a pleasant voyage, Hornblower, with no troubles, although I doubt you shall get it. Just make sure you don't start a war, although this Egyptian business may take things wholly out of your hands. Still, I know you've been in tight spots before, and I have confidence in your judgment."

"Thank you, my lord."

The Viscount rose and put forth his hand. "Good luck to you, Hornblower. Report to me after you return."

Hornblower shook the Foreign Secretary's hand, bowed slightly, and left the room.

Inside the French Chamber of Deputies, the fight was on. The Chamber was in full debate over the bill to fund the retrieval of the Emperor's remains from St. Helena, and Alphonse de Lamartine did not like the way the debate was going. The overwhelming majority of deputies seemed to be carried along with the wave of Bonapartist sentiment created when the king, no doubt put up to it by his toady Thiers, announced the plan. Lamartine turned on his bench to look at Thiers, who was sitting on the other side of the chamber and looking as if he had very few friends left in the world and was in danger of losing those. Alexandre Glais-Bizoin had seized the floor of the chamber, a fact which made Thiers look even more miserable.

"Bonapartist ideas are one of the open wounds of our time," Bizoin cried. "They represent that which is most fatal to the emancipation of peoples, most contrary to the independence of the human spirit!"

Several deputies seated around Lamartine jumped to their feet and cheered, while others around Thiers let their disapproval be known as well. Bizoin made his way back to his seat, and Lamartine was troubled to see Odilon Barrot step up to the podium. Not only was Barrot a fine speaker, he was also a defender of the Empire. Much worse, in the eyes of Lamartine, was the fact that Barrot was a friend of Louis-Napoleon Bonaparte.

Barrot stood at the rostrum and faced his colleagues. His speech was basically what Lamartine expected, a praising of the Emperor's accomplishments while asking forgiveness for his wars. Unfortunately, given the rising tide of Bonapartist sentiment in the chamber as well as in the nation, his words would be more than enough to sway the votes. It was beginning to look more and more as though this situation would demand Lamartine's direct intervention. This measure was dangerous and had to be stopped.

Lamartine scowled as he recollected an encounter with Thiers outside of the chamber before the start of the current session. The minister had intercepted him on his way into the chamber and urged him not to interfere with the vote on the measure.

"No, I will not sit silently," he had replied. "Napoleon's imitators must be discouraged."

"Oh! Such fears are groundless!" Thiers had exclaimed. "Who could think to imitate him today?"

Lamartine had paused and looked down at the smaller man. "I do beg your pardon, I meant to say Napoleon's parodists."

The look on the minister's face had been richly rewarding.

Now, in the chamber, Lamartine decided the time was right. He cast one more look across the chamber. Thiers sat on his bench, looking miserable, and the hopelessness on his enemy's face brought a smile to his own. He rose, walked to the podium, and faced the assembled deputies.

"Gentlemen," he said loudly, raising his hand to call for silence and their attention, "I rise before you today to state my belief in no uncertain terms that this measure before us today, this return of the remains of Napoleon Bonaparte to these shores, is not a good idea, and I stand firmly against it. Although I am an admirer of this great man, I am not enthusiastic about him. I do not prostrate myself before this memory; I am not a follower of this Napoleonic religion, of the cult of force that for a time some have wished to substitute in the Nation's spirit for the serious religion of liberty. I also do not think it good to deify war, to encourage these over-impetuous bubblings in the French blood, that make us appear impatient to wreck ourselves after a truce of 25 years —as if peace, which is the good fortune and glory of the world, could be the shame of nations. Let us, who take liberty seriously, make our views known in a measured way. Let us not appeal to the opinion of a people who better understand what dazzles them than what serves them. Let us not efface our monarchy of reason, our new, representative and peace-loving monarchy. It would end up disappearing from the people's eyes. It is good, Gentlemen; I do not oppose this, I applaud it: but pay attention to these encouragements to genius at any price. I am doubtful for the future. I do not like these men who have liberty, legality and progress as their official doctrine, and as their symbol a sabre and despotism. I invite France to show that she does not wish to create out of these ashes war, tyranny, legitimate monarchs, pretenders, or even imitators."

Thiers, knowing this last was aimed squarely at him, looked devastated. Lamartine stepped down, not knowing whether or not his intervention would be enough to send the bill down to defeat. In the end, it was not, as the deputies voted overwhelmingly to fund the return. He did have a small measure of revenge, however, when, by a vote of 280 to 65 the deputies refused to increase the funding for the venture from one to two millions.

Lamartine walked out with his friend Glais-Bizoin. "The Napoleonic myth is fully developed."

Bizoin nodded. "So it would seem. The return will serve to restore the crown to his head. I fear for our country."

"As do I, my friend," Lamartine said, his voice heavy with resignation. "As do I."

François searched the house for his prince. He found Louis-Napoleon in the museum, the name the prince gave the room used to display his collection of Napoleonic memorabilia.

"My Prince," he said.

Louis turned. "Yes, François?"

The secretary held out an envelope. "The courier just arrived from Paris."

Louis took it from his hand and smiled. "Excellent. Let us go to the library."

François followed his master to the library. He closed the door behind him before taking his usual stance inside the door while Louis went to his desk. He opened the envelope and carefully read the pages inside. He turned back to his secretary.

"So," he said, scanning the pages to verify details, "the king is sending his son, the Prince de Joinville, to St. Helena in the frigate *la Belle Poule* to retrieve my uncle's remains and bring them to Le Havre. From there, they shall travel by river to Paris." He set the pages on the desk and considered the information. "It says that the prince will sail from Toulon. François, do we have a man in Toulon we can get onto *la Belle Poule*?"

"*Oui*, my Prince," came the answer. "Henri Girot. His father served with distinction during the Empire and was personally decorated by the Emperor at Wagram. Girot is currently a lieutenant in the shore facilities at Toulon, but a word in the right ear in Paris should get him transferred."

"Arrange it at once. I shall write a letter to Girot, so he understands exactly what we want him to do." Louis rose and began to pace as he spoke. "He will act as the last member of the Emperor's Old Guard, a secret bodyguard, if you will."

"Indeed, my Prince."

Louis ceased his pacing. "Good. I shall write the letter immediately, and the courier can take it when he takes your note to Paris. Is there anything else?"

"One thing, my Prince. We have received another message from our man in the French ambassador's office in London. He says Minister Thiers has asked the British to send a representative to the exhumation."

"Really? Who were they asked to send?"

"Horatio Lord Hornblower," François said. "He was briefly the governor of St. Helena during the Emperor's exile."

Louis looked nonplussed. "And *Thiers* asked them to send this person? Why?"

"I do not know, my Prince," François replied. Louis admired his secretary's ability to remain unflappable. "But our man reports that Admiral Roussin was sent to visit him and make the request."

"The Minister of Marine?"

"*Oui*, my Prince."

Louis dismissed his secretary to his task and resumed his pacing. Why would the French ask for a special British representative, and why this Hornblower? Granted, there were rumors that he had been friendly with the Emperor while he was governor, but that was more than twenty years ago. Louis frowned. *Could it be that I am overthinking this? A British representative certainly would not be an impediment to the return; if the British government didn't want the return to happen, they would simply have refused the French request.* He grunted. *Especially with the new queen, who has stated her desire that relations improve between the two nations.* A dismissive shake of the head. *No, I think we can eliminate Hornblower from our calculations and concentrate on stopping any interference by the Ultra-Royalists.*

Satisfied with his thinking, at least for the moment, Louis sat at his desk and began to compose his letter to Lieutenant Girot.

In his chateau outside of Paris, Louis-Antoine d'Artois, Duke of Angoulême and Legitimist Pretender to the French throne, read with interest a report he had just received from his agents in the French Chamber of Deputies.

"So," he said to no-one in particular, "the deputies have agreed to finance the return of the Upstart's remains from St. Helena? That is surprising."

"Hardly so, my lord," Porthos said, "considering the nostalgia for all things relating to the Empire that is all the rage in Paris at the moment."

The duke looked at his friend with hooded eyes. Porthos was the one man responsible for secreting him from France after the fall of his father Charles X in 1830 when Angoulême himself hesitated, almost to the cost of his life. This act of selfless devotion had earned Porthos the right to speak his mind at all times in the duke's presence, often (as now) to the duke's consternation.

"Indeed, Porthos?"

"Yes, my lord. The Chamber of Deputies voted to fund the return overwhelmingly."

"Interesting," Angoulême said. He walked back to his desk and sat down, lost in thought. *If Paris goes over for the Bonapartes, France will surely follow, effectively ending my chances of ever reclaiming our family's throne.* He scowled at the thought of the Paris mob. He knew it was perfectly possible that if the Emperor's remains were welcomed into the city, Louis-Napoleon could be right behind.

Angoulême cursed under his breath and wished again that his uncle, Louis XVIII, had allowed his father, when he was the Comte de Artois, to kill Louis-Napoleon during the Second White Terror. But the boy had been not yet ten years old at the time, and the king had recoiled at the idea of murdering a child, even a Bonaparte. Angoulême shook his head in disgust. *Too bad,* he thought. *It would have cut the Bonapartists off at the knees and made things easier today.*

Porthos turned to him. "So, my lord, what are you going to do?"

The duke blinked, roused from his train of thought. "Do? About what?"

Porthos looked at him in something close to disbelief. "About what? About the Emperor's remains coming back to France!"

Angoulême's eyes narrowed as he considered his friend's words. He sat back in his chair, and his gaze fell on the portrait of his uncle, Louis XVI, painted shortly after he assumed the throne in 1774. It was his favorite portrait of his uncle; he felt it captured his spirit, his joy for living, his inherent goodness for all to see. It also reminded him of the way the Paris mob turned on his uncle and callously snuffed out that goodness on the guillotine. His brows furrowed, and he felt the knot of rage in his stomach. The Revolution had killed his uncle, and the Revolution had given prominence to

Bonaparte. Porthos was right; he had to act. But how? He sat back in his chair and began to think out loud. Porthos sat on the other side of the desk and listened; it was their usual way of brainstorming an important decision.

"The problem is to prevent the Emperor's body being brought back to France," Angoulême mused aloud, "and the question is how." Porthos was silent. He never spoke while the duke was musing thus, unless he was spoken to directly or if the duke wandered into gross error. "So, how do we stop the entourage from reaching France? No! That's not the question! Not France, but Paris! How do we stop them from reaching Paris?" He held his chin between a thumb and forefinger for a minute, then, resting his elbows on the arms of the chair, steepled his fingers in front of him. "We have two options, and those are to prevent the ship from ever reaching France, or if it does, to destroy body before they reach Paris."

Porthos inclined his head. Good so far.

"In order to prevent the remains from reaching France, we would have to blow them up, either on St. Helena or on the transport, or else sink the transport ship while at sea. The latter would obviously be the more difficult option, as it would require a warship with a moderately-trained crew. The king will surely send a frigate, at the very least, and the British will have warships in the area in any case." He leaned his head back and closed his eyes.

"Pirates?" prompted Porthos.

The eyes opened again and stared out into space for a moment. "Pirates? No, I don't think so. Pirates would have neither the incentive nor the skill to take on a navy ship in open waters and destroy it." Angoulême rose quickly and began to pace. "No, we need something better."

"The Swedes?" Porthos mused aloud. "Charles XIV John —the former Marshall Bernadotte—has no love for his former Emperor."

The duke paused and looked at Porthos, as though noticing for the first time that he was in the room. Porthos fell silent; he had said too much and he knew it. Now he had to wait to see which way his master would turn.

Angoulême's eyes narrowed, and after a moment he looked away. "The Swedes?" he said, and Porthos relaxed a little. "The Swedes?" he said again as he resumed his pacing, head down and eyes narrowed in concentration. "The Swedes... no, I don't think so. Charles has no interest riding on stopping a Bonapartist ascension in France." The pacing continued for about a minute before the duke stopped in mid-stride and his head came up, his eyes wide open as an idea erupted in his mind.

"Perhaps not the Swedes, my dear Porthos," he said as he went to his desk and sat down, "but who *would* be interested?" The duke reached into a drawer and pulled out some paper.

Porthos frowned. "Who, Your Grace?" He began counting off the various courts on his fingers. "The Austrians and the Prussians suffered much at the Corsican's hands, but they have no navy.... The minor German states as well, but they, too, have no warships. The Spanish navy is still the joke it was in 1805, and Venice and Naples do not even enter into this discussion. That leaves..." Porthos's eyes grew wide at the thought.

Angoulême looked up from the list he was making. "Exactly. The Russians." His pen began flying across the paper again.

Porthos squirmed a bit in his seat and looked decidedly uneasy. "Your Grace, if I may; take care, my lord, rumors abound regarding the tsar's sanity. Even if he could be convinced to lend you one or two warships for your scheme, the chance of keeping the transaction secret and avoiding war is... remote, at best."

Angoulême looked up from his list and considered his friend's words. Finally, he shrugged in resignation. My dear Porthos," he said, "if the tsar cannot be trusted, he will have to be dealt with. After he serves his purpose."

Porthos could only stare wide-eyed at such a statement, for he knew his master to be deadly serious.

The duke smiled. "Arrange for my transport, Porthos. I must see the tsar about a ship."

CHAPTER 5

Lady Barbara Hornblower's eyes went back and forth between the empty trunk and the piles of her husband's clothes that were neatly folded on their bed. She was fast coming to the conclusion that she had either too many clothes or not enough trunk. It would be easier, she was sure, if she knew whether her husband would need both his society clothes and his uniforms or if one or the other would do. Unfortunately, Horatio had not decided yet, so she turned to ask him yet again. She found him as she had left him, leaning against the far wall of their bedroom, arms folded across his chest, staring in the direction of the trunk but not seeing it.

"Horatio," she said as calmly as her rising frustration would allow, "you must make a decision."

Her husband's only reaction to her plea was a blink that brought his eyes back into focus. He looked at her, pursed his lips, and sighed, but he said not a word to ease her dilemma. She folded her arms in a failing attempt to contain her impatience, and her eyebrow rose noticeably. Her husband took note of this, and the result was that his eyes closed and his chin descended to his chest.

Finally, she could bear no more. "Really, Horatio..."

This final demand stirred him to life. He pushed off the wall, walked over to the clothes on the bed and looked down at them.

"I think it would be best for me to wear the uniforms, my dear," he said. "I may need their authority behind me. In any case, I would prefer to say my last goodbyes to Bonaparte as a soldier."

Lady Barbara smiled, for this was the very conclusion she had come to herself during the previous night while her husband slept. His uniforms, with the exception of the two sets on the bed, had been packed in a trunk before he awoke this morning and were even now being loaded on the coach for his departure after their noonday meal.

Hornblower noticed the cryptic smile on his wife's face and realized that she had not moved to pack his clothes. Puzzlement gave way to a smile as reality dawned on him.

"You already packed the uniforms," he said. A statement, not a question.

"Yes, my husband," she said with a nod.

"And they are already being loaded?"

"Yes, my husband."

"And these that I see here are one dress uniform and one service uniform for me to wear on my trip to Plymouth?"

"Yes, my husband."

Hornblower shook his head in silence and smiled broadly. What a woman he had married! He watched Barbara as she directed Marie in putting away the clothes he would not be needing, and once again he felt himself drawn into comparing Barbara with his first wife, Maria. He hated himself whenever he partook in the exercise, and this time he was determined not to descend to comparisons. Hornblower banished the whole line of thinking from his mind with a sigh of disgust.

He pulled out his pocket watch and saw that dinner should be almost ready. He pushed himself off the wall and walked over to his wife.

"Almost time for dinner, my dear," he said.

"Already?" she said with a smile. "My, how the time has flown. Very well, my husband, let us have one more meal together before the country takes you from me once again."

He smiled at her as he offered her his arm, and she nodded her thanks as she accepted it. They walked out together and entered the dining room. Hornblower held his wife's chair before sitting down himself.

The meal was a simple one, yet filling. Lady Barbara paused after taking a sip of wine, then all at once she set the goblet down and looked at her husband.

"Horatio," she said, "what do you think Bonaparte would say if he knew you were coming back to St. Helena to make sure he gets home?"

"I have been wondering about that," he said as he stabbed another carrot and put it in his mouth, thinking as he chewed. "I'm sure he would be pleased, especially if I were able to foil any mischief his enemies have planned."

"Do you really think anyone would cause any trouble? After all, the man has been dead for nearly twenty years."

"He's still the acknowledged symbol of the Revolution, and the Bonapartists are still a viable political party in France. One of the Emperor's nephews tried to overthrow the government only a few years ago, remember?"

Barbara smiled, her eyes unfocused as her thoughts dwelt on the past. "Horatio, do you remember how he used to come to our house on St. Helena, just to play on the floor with Richard? I still laugh when I think of the Emperor of the French, the terror of Europe, on his knees in our house, playing with toy soldiers!"

"I remember," her husband said. He sat back and allowed his mind to drift back through time. "Did you notice? In all the battles he refought with Richard, he never got around to Waterloo."

Her eyebrows shot up. "Really? Now that you mention it, I don't recall that he ever did. Did he ever talk about that last battle with you?"

Hornblower set his fork down and sat back in his chair. His head tilted to the side, as most people's do when they are trying to snatch one particular memory. "I seem to recall that we did. Let me see... yes, I am sure we did." He paused while his glass was refilled. "As I recall, it was after you had left to bring Richard back to England. We were discussing the Peninsula Campaign, and he was very disparaging in his remarks about the British army and its leadership in particular. So, I asked him, if that was the case, how did he account for Waterloo?"

"Really? What did he say?"

Hornblower thought for a moment. "Let me see... he said the weather doomed him; that, and the failure of his marshal to keep the Prussians from joining the battle. I do remember him saying something interesting, though; he said that, even if he had won at Waterloo and scattered the English and Prussian forces, he doubted that his return would have lasted more than a few years at best."

"That doesn't sound like him, even at that late stage in his life. Did he tell you why?"

"He said that France could no longer withstand the combined might of Europe, and sooner or later, it would simply have overwhelmed him. He seemed to think it was inevitable that the Russians, Prussians, and Austrians would eventually copy his methods as much as they could. They learned a great deal from studying his campaigns, he said, and were becoming quite adept at using what they learned against him."

Barbara shook her head in wonder. "Do you believe him?"

Hornblower looked at his wife and shrugged. "I think the truth is that he was becoming tired. Tired of war, tired of being in control, tired of shouldering the burdens of an empire. I can understand, in a small way, as I had similar responsibilities as the captain of a king's ship, albeit on a much smaller scale. He admitted to me that by 1815 he was slowing down. His mind was not as sharp as it once was and he missed things that he would never have missed in 1805. Did you know that imprecise orders from him allowed an entire corps to wander back and forth between the battlefields of Quatre Bras and Ligny, before the fight at Waterloo? Had that corps been present at either battle, it would have tipped the scales decisively for the French, and the battle at Waterloo might never have taken place. Bonaparte was very bitter that he allowed that to happen, and he said he never would have done so in 1805, and it wouldn't have happened at Waterloo, had Berthier been present."

Barbara was confused. "Berthier?"

"His indispensable chief of staff. A genius at moving army corps and divisions around the map of Europe. He refused to join Bonaparte upon his return from exile and died shortly before the battle."

"Ah," she said. "How fortunate for Arthur."

Hornblower raised an eyebrow, but only for a moment. "In any case, he knew that he simply was not the same man in 1815 as he had been in 1805. It seems the enormous energy he displayed in the Consulate and the early years of his reign worked against him in the end, causing him to burn out like a candle."

"Well," Barbara said, "I'm glad we were able to bring even a little joy into his life on that wretched island. I almost wish the government would have allowed him to escape to America and live out the rest of his life in peace."

"Hmm," Hornblower said absently. "Tell me, did Richard ever mention him to you? During his recovery, perhaps, or during the voyage?"

Now it was his wife's turn to stare into space for a moment as she searched her memory. "He didn't say much of anything during the voyage," she said. "I think the first time he said something about the Emperor was a couple months after we arrived back in Smallbridge. He had taken out the box of toy soldiers, and in the bottom of the box we found a note written in French. Unfortunately, the handwriting was so bad that I could not read it! Fortunately, Marie was able to translate it for us. It said that these soldiers were a gift to Master Richard Hornblower from Napoleon I, Emperor of the French. It also said that the Emperor hoped Richard would be inspired to use his life to benefit mankind. I wrote the translation on the back of the note for him. In fact, I think he still has it with him to this day."

She smiled at the memory. "When he brought out the box, Richard said he wished his 'oncle' could be there with him to play with the soldiers, and he asked me why the English had to keep him locked up on St. Helena."

"What did you tell him?"

Barbara sighed. "I told him that this is what happened sometimes when you lost a war."

"True enough," Hornblower said as he rose. "I must change before I leave, my dear. Thank you for a wonderful meal."

She rose and walked with him. "I wish he was still alive,

Horatio, and we could go visit him, rather than escort his remains back to France."

A sad look came over his face for just a moment. "I wish it as well, but this is the best I can do to repay the debt I owe him."

A half-hour later they were walking out to the carriage. Brown was supervising the loading of the last of Hornblower's luggage.

"Well, Brown," Hornblower said, "take care of things while I'm gone."

"You know I shall, my lord."

Hornblower stepped into the carriage. "Don't forget to look in on Captain Bush from time to time."

Brown bowed. "Aye, my lord."

Hornblower reached out and held his wife's hand for a moment before the coachman got the horses moving. He blew her a kiss and leaned out the window, watching her until the carriage rounded the bend in the road.

His Royal Highness, the Prince de Joinville, third son of King Louis-Philippe of France and a captain in the French Navy, paced the anteroom to his father's study in the Palais-Royal, awaiting his summons into the royal presence. Although no reason was given for his summons from the naval base at Toulon, he had little doubt about why his father wanted to see him. The news of the plan to retrieve the Emperor's body from St. Helena had electrified the nation, and who better to appoint to the task than a prince of the realm? Not that the prince was flattered; he had better things to do than to gather the bones of the Usurper and pretend it was a glorious moment for France. Unlike his father, Joinville was not so willing to overlook the murder of Louis XVI and his Queen, but he was also smart enough to understand that, to make his position known would do him no good whatsoever.

The door opened, and the page appeared. "Your Royal Highness," he said, "His Majesty will see you now."

Joinville marched into the study to find his father writing something at his desk. He waited until the pen was set down before speaking. "You sent for me, Sire?"

"Yes, my son," the king said. He placed his hand on a packet of papers on the corner of his desk. "I have orders here for you to report back to Toulon and take *la Belle Poule* to St. Helena. Your mission is to bring back the mortal remains of the Emperor Napoleon I to France for reburial here in Paris."

It was just what the prince had feared, but he could do naught but bow. "Yes, my King."

"You will receive further orders when you return to your ship." The king turned and noticed the look on his son's face. He softened his tone and spoke as a father to a son. "You do not understand why I am doing this, or at the least you do not approve. Trust me; I do this to ensure that you may one day sit on this throne."

Joinville looked up at his father. "You do this because of the people."

"Yes."

"May I remind the king that these are the same people who murdered your cousin and his queen?" Joinville said with disgust in his voice. "They are also the same ones who put this usurper on his throne. On *our* throne."

The king stared hard at his son, obviously trying to control himself. "This is politics, Joinville. We will do what we must." The king returned to his desk and picked up his pen. "Keep me informed as to your progress."

The king began writing again, completely ignoring his

son. Joinville bowed correctly and left the room. He did not stop walking until he entered his carriage and flopped angrily in his seat.

"I take it the meeting did not go well?"

The voice belonged to Colonel Hernoux, Joinville's aide-de-camp. Several years older than his twenty-two-year-old Prince, the colonel was an old hand at handling his superiors. He had served Joinville for the past three years, and the two men got along very well.

The prince shrugged. "Just as I feared. We are to go to St. Helena and return with the coffin of the Corsican." Joinville made a face as though he had swallowed something sour and looked out the window. "I almost wish I could find a way to fail on this mission, Hernoux."

"But you have never failed, my Prince," Hernoux said lightly, "so to fail now would almost certainly incite the mob."

Joinville looked over at his friend, who was now also staring out the window at the passing Paris scenery, and shook his head, amused to remember that his friend tended to forget that he himself had arisen out of the peasantry.

"It matters little, Hernoux," the prince said. "I must do as my King commands, even though I believe he is paving the way for us to be living in England again."

Hernoux turned to look at his friend, the smile on his face fading quickly once he saw that his captain was not joking. "My Prince?"

Joinville sighed and looked out the window. "What can this achieve, but to make us look weak compared to the Bonapartists? Surely the Ultra-Royalists will move to put that fool Angoulême on the throne." He shook his head. "That would make the Austrians, Prussians, *and* the Russians very happy."

Hernoux shrugged. "It would make us weaker yet to fail, my Prince. We must carry out our orders, I'm afraid, and trust that your father knows what he is doing."

Joinville grunted. "Thiers, you mean. I do not for one moment believe this project was my father's idea."

"Be that as it may, we must succeed. I fear worse consequences for France if we do not."

"Humph." The carriage was passing through the outskirts of Paris now, and the beauty of the countryside revived Joinville's mood somewhat. A pretty farmer's daughter waved at the carriage as they rode past, and the gesture gave him an idea.

"You know, Hernoux," he said, a sly smile creeping into the corner of his mouth, "there's no reason we can't have a little fun on the way, is there?"

Hernoux grinned. "What did you have in mind, my Prince?"

Joinville sat back and turned towards his friend. "What say we take *la Belle Poule* and stop at a few places en route, for a ball, shall we say, or at least a visit to a governor or two? We can also use these stops to allow the world to keep track of our progress as we journey to bring home the greatest military mind of all time."

Hernoux's mouth quirked at the sarcasm written all over his captain's face. "And where would you like to put in to port, my Captain?"

Joinville smiled and leaned back. He closed his eyes and imagined their probable route. "I will not receive my final orders until we reach Toulon, but when I think of the probable route, Cadiz and Madeira come to mind. There's also Tenerife and Bahia." The prince sighed and smiled. "At least we can have a little pleasure cruise, eh, Hernoux?"

"I hear and obey, my Prince and my Captain," Hernoux

intoned with a matching smile.

In his office in the heart of Paris, Adolphe Thiers paced back and forth. The king was to have met with his son, the Prince de Joinville, today to give him his instructions for the trip to St. Helena. Louis-Philippe had denied Thiers's request to be present, and the minister worried that the king might change his mind from the mission details they had discussed the day before yesterday. Added to that was the fact that the prince, despite being a successful naval officer, was much more drawn to the Ultra-Royalist camp than his father and might object to the assignment. Were that the case, Thiers did not trust his King to stand his ground. Unfortunately, there were some things one simply could not say to a king, and "Please don't mess this up; just say what I told you to say" happened to be one of them.

Thiers paused his pacing when his secretary opened the door to announce the arrival of his Minister of War, General Amédée Despans-Cubières. Despans-Cubières was a veteran of the battles of the Empire, and he was devoted to the memory and person of the Emperor.

"Ah, General," Thiers said as he walked over to shake his visitor's hand, "come in, come in. We must discuss security arrangements."

The two men sat in overstuffed leather chairs before an empty fireplace and allowed servants to set drinks and pastries on the table in between. Thiers waited for them to withdraw before speaking.

"General, I am very concerned that the entourage will be attacked on the journey from the coast to Paris."

Cubières shifted in his chair as he helped himself to a pastry. "I have troops ready to escort the Emperor to Paris."

Thiers sipped his drink and set the glass down. "That

won't do, General. The last thing we want is for French troops to have to open fire on the populace. That's what it will look like, you see—either the Bonapartists or the Ultra-Royalists will cry out to the press, who will repeat it to the people without bothering to question whether it is true or not. 'The Government fired upon innocent civilians!' No, General, we must find another way."

"What do you suggest?" the general asked.

Thiers smiled. "What would the Emperor have done?"

"He would have had Fouché and his secret police arrest all suspects before the remains ever got here."

Thiers waved his hand. "Not a bad idea, but nothing we want to do ourselves. What other options are there?"

"We can clear the route with a whiff of grapeshot," the general mused. "I seem to recall the Emperor doing that once."

Thiers shifted uncomfortably. "Seriously, General...."

Cubières thought for a moment. "We can avoid some of the towns and villages we were going to pass through, but that leaves us in the countryside for a very long period of time, and the attackers—whoever they may be—would have plenty of time to set up an ambush or simply attack at night, when the procession makes camp for the evening. Either way, there will be casualties, Minister. On both sides."

Thiers took a swallow of his wine. He swirled the dark liquid in the glass and lost himself for a moment in the currents. How could they eliminate the chances for partisans to set a trap? Of course! He set the glass down and looked over at his guest.

"I have it, General!" he cried. "We eliminate the problem by taking away the opportunity. We change the route! Let the Emperor arrive in Paris by fast steamer up the Seine!"

"Marvelous!" the general said. "It should be no problem

to have the steamer escorted by several gunships. That way, we would only have to guard the route from the riverbank to the burial site."

Thiers raised his glass in salute. "See to it, General. We will see this thing through yet!"

CHAPTER 6

Hornblower was shown into the office of the port admiral. The office itself he thought overly ornate, with paintings crowding the walls and artifacts, obviously looted from the Caribbean, on display. Admiral Richard Wright was a small, mousy man, quick of temper with a sharp, pointed nose and close-set, beady eyes that made him look almost paranoid. He was a distant relative of Cornwallis and was rumored to have made full use of his family connections to advance his career. He was sitting at his desk writing, but he put down his pen when Hornblower entered. He rose but stayed in place, so that Hornblower had to cross the room.

"Good to see you, Hornblower," he said as the two shook hands. "It's been—what?—more than thirty years since we were fighting together against Boney? And now here you are, helping him to return to France."

"Kind of you to remember me, Admiral," Hornblower said.

Wright motioned his guest into a chair in front of his desk while he walked over to a table in the corner of the room and poured them each a glass of wine. He handed one to

Hornblower and sat behind his desk with the other, raising it in salute.

"To England."

Both men drank, and Wright set his glass down and sat back in his chair. The look on his face was one of obvious disapproval, and Hornblower braced himself for what was coming.

"I cannot say I approve of your mission, Hornblower," the admiral said.

Hornblower looked at the dark liquid in his glass and guarded his voice. "It would seem the Queen and Foreign Secretary disagree with you."

The port admiral leaned forward on his desk, his fury visible on his face. "This country did not grow strong by aiding the French! Why, it's entirely possible we will be at war with them again in a few months over this Egyptian business." He looked out the window. "No good has ever come from helping the French."

Hornblower's eyes narrowed slightly. "When I saw the Queen regarding my current mission, she made it very clear to me that she intends to improve our relations with France."

The admiral's eyes snapped to Hornblower at that, and Hornblower thought he saw rage and hatred there, but Wright recovered quickly. He grunted and said in a low voice, "And that would be just fine with you, I suppose."

Hornblower's chin rose slightly. "Just what do you mean by that, sir?"

Wright sneered. "You're practically a frog now, aren't you? Ever since Boney turned your head! That's why the frogs asked for you to go now, isn't it?"

Hornblower jumped to his feet, his left hand automatically going to the hilt of his sword. Wright's eyes grew wide, and he seemed to shrink back into his chair.

Hornblower's eyes threw daggers at the admiral, and his lips were pressed into an angry thin line, mainly because he did not trust himself to speak. After a moment or two, the admiral blinked and picked up his glass, draining it in a single draught. He set the glass on the desk and looked out the window, ignoring Hornblower completely.

Hornblower allowed a small smile to curl the corner of his mouth.

"That's what I thought," he said softly. He turned and left the office without looking back.

Outside, Hornblower boarded a coach and headed for the port. He was fuming. He hated the narrow-minded thinking of officers like Wright, and he was done making allowances for them. He sat back in the coach and closed his eyes, willing himself to calm down and think.

In less than a minute, his eyes were open again. It was no use. He had come very close to challenging Wright to a duel over his slander, something that he had not done since his days as a midshipman on the old *Justinian*. He shuddered. It wasn't often that he came so close to losing control like that. And how many more officers would he meet during the course of this mission with that same thinking? Hornblower shook his head.

A glance out the window told him he was nearing the harbor and his much-anticipated reunion with Captain William Brewer. That thought cheered him considerably. Brewer was the great success story of Hornblower's patronage. Many of Hornblower's contemporaries had offered patronage to those they considered to be worthy young lieutenants struggling for promotion in the peacetime Royal Navy, only to have their favor taken advantage of by young officers of privilege, who would rather drink or charm their way to promotion than to earn it by their deeds. Not so with Mr. Brewer. He had worked his way up by merit. Hornblower had been able to steer him to a couple choice assignments.

The carriage stopped at the wharf, and Hornblower got out. He quickly made arrangements for his transportation out to HMS *Iris*. His dunnage was loaded, and he was soon in the stern sheets as they made their way over the choppy waters of the harbor. Hornblower looked around at the new-fangled steam ships, most having paddlewheels but a couple equipped with screws, and he marveled at the march of progress. He wondered how long it would be before the Royal Navy had a steam-powered warship. *Probably not very long*.

They cleared a three-decker, and the captain of the boat touched his arm. "Begging your pardon, my lord," he said. Hornblower turned, and the captain pointed to a small ship directly ahead. "HMS *Iris*," he said.

Hornblower studied the ship as they approached. He judged her a large sixth-rate and counted gunports for a total of 26 guns. Probably around a thousand tons, with the clean lines of a new ship. As they approached, their boat was challenged, and the boat captain stood and gave the correct response. Hornblower felt a lump rise in his throat as he prepared for the transfer.

He glanced up and saw the bosun's chair being swung over the side for him, but before he could say something, he heard a familiar voice.

"Belay that chair, you lubber! He's an admiral, don't forget, with more time aboard Her Majesty's ships than you have breathing God's good air! Now stow that thing and stand ready!"

Hornblower smiled as he timed the jump, managing to hang on, even if just barely. He wouldn't be the first admiral to fall into the drink, but soaking wet wasn't the way he wanted to begin his journey. He climbed to the deck and stepped on board as the bosun's mates played their pipes and the officers saluted. Hornblower saluted the quarterdeck and then walked over to where Captain Brewer was standing with his officers. The group saluted smartly when he arrived, Brewer with a smile on his face but the others looking as though he were coming aboard to preside over their courts-martial. Hornblower hid his own grin and made a mental note to ask Brewer what he had said to them before he arrived.

He stopped right in front of the captain and returned his salute, slowly and deliberately. The captain's eyes danced with joy; Hornblower could hardly contain his own. He lowered his salute and shook the captain's hand.

"Welcome aboard, my lord," Brewer said formally.

"Thank you, Captain," Hornblower said. "You may present your officers."

"Very good, my lord," Brewer turned to the lieutenant immediately behind him. "May I present my first lieutenant, Mr. Dean?"

The lieutenant saluted.

Hornblower nodded, and Brewer smiled and moved to the next two men.

"My lord, this is Mr. Jason, my second, and Mr. Cooksley, my third."

"My lord," Jason said as they both saluted.

Hornblower nodded again.

Brewer stepped to the next group of three men.

"May I present my warrant officers? This is Mr. Sisk, the surgeon, Mr. Priestley, the master, and Mr. Shannon, the purser."

The three men saluted and mumbled a greeting, and Hornblower nodded his acknowledgement.

"And here we have Lieutenant Blake, in charge of our marines."

"An honor, my lord," Blake said.

"Thank you, Mr. Blake," the admiral replied.

Brewer led his admiral to the next group. "These are our young gentlemen, my lord. May I present Mr. Ford, senior midshipman, and these are Mr. Cabot, Mr. Paddington, and Mr. Youngblood."

The four saluted, the youngest two looking at Hornblower as if he were the archangel Gabriel.

"Gentlemen," Hornblower said with a nod. He turned to address the group. "Gentlemen, I look forward to a successful voyage with you."

"Thank you, my lord," Brewer said on behalf of his crew. "Now, if you will follow me, I shall show you to your cabin."

Hornblower nodded and stepped back, and Brewer led him below deck. They turned aft.

"Mind your head, my lord," Brewer said.

Hornblower ducked and followed his captain aft. Once they entered the cabin, Hornblower broke into a wide smile.

"Brewer, it is good to see you again!" he said. "Tell me, what did you tell them about me? They looked like I was here to see them drawn and quartered."

Brewer laughed and tossed his hat onto his desk. Hornblower sat down on the settee under the stern windows.

"Nothing, really, my lord," Brewer said. "I'm afraid some of the old legends have been circulating below decks ever since they heard you were coming on board."

Hornblower shook his head and laughed.

Brewer gestured around him. "This is yours, my lord. I've had my things moved into the chart room for the duration. I hope you won't mind dining together, although I'm sure we'll get an invitation to the wardroom before long."

"That's fine, Captain," Hornblower said. "It's been a long time, William. I look forward to hearing all about what you've been doing."

"Of course, my lord. And how is Lady Barbara?"

"She is well. She spends much of her time these days looking after Captain Bush."

Brewer sighed. "He wrote me how lonely he has been since his sister passed away. I'm glad Lady Barbara can do him some good. And Master Richard?"

"He's doing well at his practice. We were looking forward to joining them for little Barbara's first birthday, which unfortunately I am going to miss, due to this mission."

"The call of duty," Brewer sighed. "We will hear it as long as we are breathing, I suppose."

Hornblower nodded, and the conversation lagged as two seamen brought in his sea chest and set it against the bulkhead. They saluted and left the room.

"And now, if you'll excuse me, my lord, I'm needed on deck," Brewer said. "We sail on the morning tide. Supper will be at the turn of the first dogwatch, if that is convenient. Of course, I understand if you'd rather dine alone."

Hornblower looked up and realized his mind had wandered. He smiled by way of apology. "Not at all, Captain. Forgive me; I was lost in thought for a moment. I very much look forward to dining with you. We have much to discuss."

Brewer bowed and excused himself. After he was gone, Hornblower inspected his surroundings. The sleeping compartment was small, but more than adequate for his needs on this voyage. He raised his eyebrow at the sight of the cot set up in the corner of the room; apparently the captain was afraid he might not be able to swing up into a hammock anymore. Hornblower was suddenly grateful that he would not have to make the attempt. A small desk and a chair were crowded into the back corner and took up the rest of the available space.

A throat being cleared behind him interrupted his observations. He turned to find a very short man standing in the doorway, and he remembered that this was the captain's famous servant. What was his name? Albert? No, that wasn't it. Edward? No.... What was...? Yes! Hornblower smiled as the name came to him.

"Alfred!" he said. "Good to see you again. How have you been?"

The servant bowed. "Very well, my lord. It is kind of you to remember me. Is there anything you require?"

Hornblower was about to decline, but a tightness in his belly reminded him that his shortened interview with the port admiral had cost him his dinner. "As it happens, I missed my dinner. Would you by chance have something small that can tide me over until supper?"

"Yes, my lord. Would fruit and cheese suffice?"

Hornblower nodded. "Thank you, Alfred; that will do nicely."

The servant bowed and disappeared, returning with a tray laid out with a selection of fresh fruit and cheese together with a decanter of wine. Hornblower eyed the tray hungrily. "Thank you, Alfred," he said. "I have some supplies coming aboard. Please see that they are stowed."

"Yes, my lord."

The servant left the cabin, and Hornblower did justice to the tray. He particularly savored an aged Rochefort cheese; it was better than any he had tasted for a long time. He sat back in his chair, entirely satisfied for the first time since he left Smallbridge. He sensed the gentle swaying of a ship at anchor, and he felt as though he had come home. Almost as soon as the thought entered his mind, he chided himself and dismissed it. He rose, picked up his hat, and went out on deck.

Night was just beginning to fall, and Hornblower enjoyed the evening breeze. He stood off to the side of *Iris's* quarterdeck, watching Brewer and his crew make their final preparations for sea. Several times, he began to give an order regarding the rigging or stowing the last-minute supplies coming on board, then chided himself and did his best not to interfere. Not that they were doing anything wrong; it was just that the habits of command was still so much a part of him.

He looked around at the sailors moving efficiently at the various tasks necessary to get a ship ready for a voyage, and he felt a heaviness in his heart when he realized that many of them were young enough to be his grandchildren. He had worried from time to time back in Smallbridge that age might be affecting him, that "old age" might be sapping his faculties, but he would not allow such worries here, on the deck of a queen's frigate and in front of Captain Brewer and his men.

He was spared from any further musings by the approach of Captain Brewer. Brewer saluted, as Hornblower was in uniform.

"A fine ship, Captain," Hornblower said. "I wager she'd fly over the waves if you let her go."

Brewer agreed. "She made twelve knots easily on her trials, and her turning radius is tighter than any ship I've sailed in since *Lydia*." He paused to look around the ship, and Hornblower could see the familiar look of pride in Brewer's eye that only a captain can possess.

"She's not as big as I would like," Brewer continued, "but she'll pack a wicked sting. We have eighteen 24-pounders below."

Hornblower remembered the pride he'd felt upon taking command of HMS *Lydia* over thirty years ago. He looked around the deck in silence until he heard eight bells toll.

"Well, my lord," Brewer said, "shall we adjourn to the cabin and see what Alfred has set out for us to drink? Supper should be ready before long."

"A fine idea, Captain. Lead the way."

Brewer led Hornblower to the cabin and held the door open for his mentor to enter. Hornblower walked back to the stern cabin and stood in front of the windows to admire the view to the west of the harbor. Behind him, he heard Brewer call to Alfred for some wine. The sun was sinking below the horizon, and its glow silhouetted the landscape. He was so taken by the view that he did not notice Brewer come up beside him until he spoke.

"Beautiful, isn't it?" the captain said, handing his admiral a glass of wine.

"Yes," Hornblower said as he accepted a glass. "So tell me, William, how's Elizabeth? Did you manage to spend much time with her before taking up your new command?"

Brewer grinned sheepishly. "Not nearly as much as either of us would have liked."

Hornblower gave a knowing smile. "Have you given any more thought to moving to Smallbridge? Barbara would dearly love to have Elizabeth close by."

Elizabeth Danforth was the daughter of the governor of the Caribbean island of St. Kitts who had captured the heart of then-Lieutenant Brewer nearly twenty years ago. He'd once told Hornblower that he had sailed his sloop HMS *Revenge* into the harbor and gone to see the Governor. Elizabeth had interrupted the meeting to ask her father a question, and Brewer hadn't heard another word the Governor said. Elizabeth was tall and beautiful, with chestnut hair and eyes that sparkled, and she was tremendously gifted when it came to music. Her father had encouraged her to play the piano, and Elizabeth was a master of the instrument. When Hornblower was first introduced to her, he remembered wishing, for a fleeting moment, that he was twenty years younger and single.

"I'm afraid not, my lord. Elizabeth is quite taken with London. The only time she leaves is to visit her father in Northumberland."

Hornblower nodded. "I quite understand. Still, remind her to stop by and greet Barbara if she is ever in the area."

"I shall, my lord, and thank you. And how is Captain Bush?"

Hornblower smiled. "Still active, Captain. He seems to be slowing down a little, but he still walks around the town nearly every day. Brown goes to see him to help with what work needs to be done around the house. He often eats supper with us, and we play whist every week. Do you know, I believe that he looks after the town folk just as though they were his crew!"

Brewer laughed. "In that case, my lord, you should have the happiest village in all England!"

Alfred appeared in the doorway and announced that supper was ready. The two officers took their seats, and the stewards brought the first course: a fine, hot soup, perfect for the chilly evening, with an aroma that promised ambrosia and a taste that delivered. Alfred followed that with a platter of mutton chops covered in gravy, along with a bowl of potatoes, another of fresh, steamed cauliflower, and plum duff with a gooseberry pie for dessert. Both men did justice to the feast. It wasn't until the last plate was empty that they sat back in their chairs, satisfied and happy.

They rose and retired to the great cabin to smoke their

cigars, leaving Alfred and his mates to clear the table. Brewer held the humidor open while the admiral made his selection, then lit his mentor's choice before picking one out for himself. Soon both men were sitting beneath the stern windows, blowing clouds of blue smoke at the deck above and feeling relaxed.

"Tell me, William," Hornblower said, "how's your crew doing? Have you had much of a chance to work them?"

Brewer looked at the cigar between his fingers. "They are fairly well along, my lord. I have very few who are new to the sea, and about a third claim to have seen battle before." He looked up. "Am I to assume we may expect trouble on this commission?"

Hornblower said quietly, "About the same as the last time we went to this lovely little island."

Brewer smiled grimly. "Once more for queen and country, my lord?"

Hornblower took a slow drag on his cigar before tilting his head back and blowing a long, slow, blue cloud heavenward. He looked at Brewer. "I prefer to think of it as one last chance to repay a debt to an old friend."

Brewer sighed, remembering his own interactions with Bonaparte. There was indeed a debt to be paid, and he was grateful for a chance to settle up.

He knocked some ash from his cigar. "As for gunnery, my lord, we were able to practice twice, for an hour each time, while the ship was out on her trials." He shrugged. "That was all the powder and shot I could lay my hands on. Then suddenly five days ago I began getting powder and shot from shore, obviously due to your coming on board. We are fully stocked now, including small arms for the marines. I intend to have Mr. Dean and Mr. Lynn begin an intensive drill program as soon as we are under way." He paused for a drag.

"Just in case we meet anyone interesting on the way south, you understand."

Hornblower's eyebrows rose a fraction. Somehow, the possibility of prize money on the way south had not entered his mind until Brewer spoke. Pirates still operated off the African coast, and there was a real chance of intercepting a slaver making a run to the West Indies or the markets of the American South.

Hornblower set his cigar in the tray. "I will let you know, Captain, that I carry a letter from Her Majesty granting me the authority to call on any resource of the Empire that is needed to fulfill my mission."

"Ah," Brewer said.

"I will also tell you," Hornblower continued, "that the Admiralty has not put me in command of your ship. I am here as Her Majesty's representative."

"I understand, my lord."

Hornblower frowned, and his eyes fell. After a moment he looked at his protégé. "I'm sorry, William. I have not been myself lately."

"What is it you fear, my lord?" Brewer asked as he refilled his Admiral's glass.

Hornblower sipped his wine as he tried to organize his thoughts. "I'm not sure, William. It's more a feeling, like something is going to go very wrong on this commission, and I have no idea as yet what it might be."

Brewer resumed his seat. He knew that in this intimate setting he could speak freely. "Well, you have no shortage of suspects, my lord. Start with the French, whether Bonapartist or Ultra-Royalist, then throw in the Russians or possibly the Austrians, neither of whom would like to see a Bonapartist revival in France. And just to throw in a little variety, we have this Egyptian situation on the side, which may turn the whole venture on its head."

Hornblower drained his glass and stood, and Brewer followed suit. "It's good to see you again, William," he said. "There's no man I'd rather have standing beside me, except perhaps Bush."

Brewer smiled. "That's high praise, my lord; I pray I may be worthy of it."

"You are, William, you are. Good night."

"Good night, my lord."

Hornblower came out on deck the next morning to a crisp, clear day. HMS *Iris* was going through her final evolutions to be ready to cut all contact with the land upon her master's command. The admiral was pleased to find that every step and order was still familiar to him, even though he had not been to sea for many years. He looked across the quarterdeck and saw Captain Brewer in conference with Lt. Dean and Mr. Priestley. He had just decided to stand off to the side until the captain was finished when Mr. Youngblood, the junior midshipman, came up and saluted.

"Good morning, your lordship," he said cheerfully. "Is there anything I can do for you?"

"Good morning, Mr. Youngblood," the admiral said. "Your first voyage, is it?"

"Yes, sir! How did you know, my lord?"

Hornblower smiled. No midshipman with any experience whatsoever would come up to any admiral—or captain, for that matter—without being bidden. No matter, he decided, the boy would no doubt be corrected very shortly. In the meanwhile, his sense of initiative was refreshing. "Yes, Mr. Youngblood, there is something you can do for me. Can you tell me when *Iris* is scheduled to sail?"

"On the tide, my lord. Should be any minute now!"

Hornblower nodded. "And where is your duty station?"

"The mizzenmast, my lord!"

"Thank you, Mr. Youngblood. You may return to your duties."

The midshipman saluted smartly. "Aye, my lord."

The boy departed just as the captain approached. Brewer looked quizzical.

The admiral shrugged. "Mr. Youngblood was asking if he could do anything for me."

Brewer sighed. "I apologize, my lord. I shall have Mr. Ford instruct him on the proper etiquette for the quarterdeck."

"Quite all right, Captain," Hornblower said. "It was good to hear such unbridled enthusiasm for the Queen's service."

Lt. Dean approached and saluted.

"Ready for sea, sir," he said, addressing his captain. "The anchor's hove short."

"Very well, Mr. Dean," Brewer said. "You may take us out."

"Aye, sir," Dean saluted and turned to carry out his duties.

Dean strode forward. "Stand by the capstan!"

Hornblower glanced toward the wheel. Mr. Priestley was on hand, two of his mates at the wheel, ready to put the ship about when ordered. The marines were at the mizzen braces. Dean's eyes were everywhere, making sure everything was done correctly.

"Loose heads'ls!"

Hornblower felt at home to hear the canvas forward begin to flap in the morning breeze.

"Hands aloft! Loose tops'ls!"

Hands scurried skyward, and soon Hornblower was watching the choreography he'd observed on *Hotspur,*

Lydia, and *Nonsuch.* It still thrilled his soul.

"Man the braces! Stand by!"

"Anchor's aweigh, sir!"

Hornblower felt *Iris* begin to move, her sails thundering under the force of the wind, the men straining at the braces to haul the yard around. Mr. Priestley put the helm hard over, and the ship came around.

Mr. Dean picked up a speaking-trumpet. "Get the fore and main-courses set!"

HMS *Iris* glided across the harbor. Hornblower turned to the captain. "Nicely done, Captain. Have you sailed with Mr. Dean before?"

"No, my lord," Brewer said softly. "You may remember my former first lieutenant, Mr. Greene? He was with me ever since *Defiant*. He was killed in action while we operated with the West Africa squadron some years back. Mr. Rivkins took over for him; he first sailed with me on the old *Lydia,* when Captain Bush took us to the Med to fight the Barbary pirates. He finally had to retire due to his health, and this is my first voyage without him. In fact, the entire crew is new to me, save Alfred and Mac."

"Then you are off to a fine beginning, Captain," Hornblower said. "I am going below to study some material given to me by the Foreign Office regarding our mission. I shall see you at dinner."

Brewer saluted. "Yes, my lord."

He watched as his mentor descended below deck, only his eyes betraying his concern. The admiral was not as young as he used to be.

HMS *Iris* cleared the harbor. Hornblower could tell, because Brewer swung the ship around on the other tack and crowded on more sail so she leapt forward in the water. A look out the stern windows confirmed this. Hornblower was about to call for Alfred to brew him some coffee, which he had laid in store just before the ship sailed, when a thought occurred to him, and he turned to look out the stern windows again. Yes, he saw the wake trailing the ship, indicating its growing speed, and he noted the swells making the *Iris* rise and fall. Hornblower stood in the aft cabin, looking around; something was different. What was wrong? Finally, it hit him —his stomach was perfectly fine! Where was his seasickness? Hornblower stood there is dumb disbelief. Finally, now, at 64 years of age, he was no longer seasick at the start of a voyage! Hornblower threw his head back and laughed.

CHAPTER 7

Louis-Antoine d'Artois, Duke of Angoulême, sat exhausted in an anteroom of the palace in St. Petersburg, awaiting his audience with Nicholas, the tsar of all Russias. He had left Paris with almost no warning and taken a fast coach north out of town, traveling in utmost secrecy and almost without stopping, racing to a small port on the Dutch coast. There he'd caught a small but very fast schooner to take him around the Danish peninsula and through the Baltic to St. Petersburg. He'd come ashore almost immediately upon docking, and ridden directly to the palace. He had been admitted, but he had been kept waiting for nearly four hours.

The duke was convinced that Nicholas was his best chance for help in his quest to prevent the Corsican's remains from reaching France. His only other realistic option was to hire a Venetian ship and equip it, but that would almost certainly mean that he would be betrayed to the world. No, the tsar had to be convinced to order one or two of his frigates to sink Joinville's ship on its way back from St. Helena.

In his exhaustion, the duke raged silently against his

father, King Charles X. When he had been the duke, Charles had tried several times to kill Bonaparte, once on the way to exile on Elba and again after his defeat at Waterloo, but every attempt had met with failure. For years, Bonaparte had carried a vial of poison in case he was ever captured. One of his father's agents had got hold of the vial and switched its contents with something supposedly twice as lethal. In reality, the potion was old and weak, and Bonaparte had survived when he swallowed it in 1814. Then, after Waterloo, the Emperor had escaped Paris before Charles's agents could attack him, and when they set out in pursuit they'd gone down the wrong road, thinking Napoleon was headed for Brest when he was in fact fleeing to Boulogne. After that, he had always been in the custody of the British, either aboard ship or on St. Helena. It had taken years of work for Charles to get Lowe installed on the island, to finish the Corsican once and for all.

And now, even from the grave, Bonaparte still troubled him! Bad enough to have that fool of a cousin on the throne that was rightfully his! But to have the remains of the man who was made Emperor by the Revolution brought back to France was simply too much to endure. The Bonapartists were just smart enough to use the event to whip up the Paris mob in their favor, perhaps even smart enough to convince the mob to accept that idiot Louis-Napoleon as the next Emperor. And if *that* happened, the duke's chances of ever sitting on the throne of his ancestors were over. Louis-Napoleon would surely seek vengeance for the attempts on the Emperor's life. The only way he would ever sit on the throne was to prevent the body of Napoleon I from reaching the shores of France, and the surest way to do that was to sink it in transit. For that, he needed Russian naval support.

The duke stood and made a show of looking at the artwork in the room, but he was actually trying to stay awake. He would dearly love to sneak away for eight solid hours of sleep, but time was of the essence. One of the Tsar's aides had said the tsar was getting ready to leave for Moscow. It was, quite possibly, now or never.

Suddenly the door opened, and a page announced that the tsar would see him now. d'Artois took a deep breath and steeled himself for what was to come. He strode into the room to find Nicolas standing before a huge fireplace, holding an open book. Angoulême thought this a pretense, a theatric—the tsar was not known as a reader—but he wisely ignored this and bowed deeply.

"Majesty," he said.

The tsar looked over at the duke and scowled. "I am not pleased with your king, your grace. He seeks to fan the flames of revolution!" The tsar made a great show of closing the book and replacing it on the shelf. "Is he trying to bury autocracy forever? All that will get him is a date with Madame Guillotine, to share his uncle's fate!"

The sooner, the better, thought the duke, although he knew better than to voice such an opinion in the tsar's presence. He bowed again and said, "It is precisely this topic I wished to discuss with your Majesty."

The tsar sat at his desk. "Tell me, my lord, do you know of the Treaty of Aix-la-Chapelle?" The duke nodded. The tsar referred to a document signed in 1818 by Russia, Prussia, Austria, and Britain. The treaty guaranteed the territory and sovereignty of the signatories, as well as the preservation of their ruling governments.

"I have read the entire document, Majesty," he said, "including the secret protocol." The protocol committed the four powers to military intervention in the event of any revolutionary activity in France.

The tsar nodded. "We have been in contact with our

brothers, the Emperor of Austria and the king of Prussia, and we can tell you that the subject of the Protocol has come up." He leaned forward menacingly. "We will enforce it, my lord, if the Bonapartists stage a coup and re-establish an Empire."

Angoulême held his tongue. He knew the cornerstone of the tsar's foreign policy was to act as the protector of ruling legitimism. Nicholas considered himself the self-appointed guardian against revolution anywhere in Europe. If the Corsican and his times had proven anything, it was that revolution was not confined by national borders.

"Sire, this is the very topic about which I came to see you. I knew that you alone, of all the sovereigns of Europe, would appreciate the potential danger in what the French king is doing."

The tsar seemed to relax a little. "So, there is still at least one man in France with some sense. Do you speak for your family as well?"

Angoulême raised his chin haughtily. "No. I speak for all Frenchmen who wish to see a true Bourbon back on the throne of Louis XIV, not his new prime minister."

Angoulême was pleased; so far, this was going better than he had expected. He knew that Nicholas lacked his late brother Alexander's intellect. He was a paternal monarch who would do anything to maintain his absolute autocratic rule over his people. Immediately after his ascension in 1825, Nicholas had crushed the Decembrist Revolt, led by 3,000 Imperial Army officers and liberal-minded citizens, who had been demanding that the new tsar accept a constitution and a representative government. The duke grimaced inwardly; if his august uncle had acted in the same fashion back in 1789, they wouldn't be in the mess they were today. Angoulême sighed. *The price of weakness.*

The tsar tilted his head. "I think perhaps the Austrians might object to your description, but that no matter. What, then, is your proposal?"

"The answer to that is simple, Sire," the duke said. "Sink the ship."

The tsar's eyes narrowed suspiciously. "That would mean war with France."

The duke's face was expressionless. "Only if someone were to survive and carry the story back to Paris. Ships are lost at sea every year. There are pirates, storms, even the ineptitude of officers."

Nicholas sat back and stared, the disbelief on his face giving way to a sly smile at the corner of his mouth.

"So, my lord," the tsar said, "how may I be of service?"

Angoulême said smoothly, "I was wondering, Sire, if you might have two frigates we might... borrow, I suppose, would be the word."

The tsar stared at him. "I see. And what about the British?"

"What about them, Majesty?"

"Their queen is known to be favorably disposed to both France and the Bonapartist upstart. Will she not wish to honor the Emperor with an escort from the Royal Navy on his way back to your country? If that is the case, sinking the Emperor's remains could very well mean a battle with English frigates and war with England."

"What can England do to the tsar of all the Russias? Can their fleet sail into St. Petersburg or Moscow and dictate terms? Their only option would be a repeat of the French mistakes of 1812, and the outcome would be the same."

Now the tsar smiled openly. "Sit down, my lord, and let us speak of the future security of empires and kingdoms. With you on the throne of France guarding the west while I protect the east from revolution, Europe will enjoy a golden age of autocracy and the divine right of kings."

The two men talked for a short time before a page entered the room and reminded the tsar of his next appointment. The duke hid any signs of annoyance at his subsequent premptory dismissal. Nicolas watched through narrowed eyes as the duke bowed correctly and withdrew from the room. He was still staring at the closed doors when his confidential aide, Prince Kutuzov, entered through a hidden door in the corner.

"You heard?" Nicolas asked.

"As you commanded, Sire," the prince replied.

"And your thoughts?"

Kutuzov shrugged. "He is desperate."

Nicolas frowned. "Go on."

Kutuzov took a deep breath and let it out slowly. When dealing with the tsar, one always had to be careful how one said things. "The duke fears the possible consequences of the return of Bonaparte's remains to France, Sire; that much is obvious. For all his bravado, the duke believes it would lead to a Bonapartist restoration at the hands of the Paris mob. The only man they could put forward to lead the nation is Louis-Napoleon Bonaparte, the Emperor's nephew, son of his brother Louis. Some have speculated that this Louis-Napoleon is insane. He has already attempted to overthrow the French government once. The duke fears that, should he gain power, he would eliminate the house of Bourbon once and for all."

Kutuzov paused and looked at the tsar. Nicolas's eyes were narrow slits and his jaw was set; Kutuzov knew from past experience that the tsar's temper was smoldering. Reluctantly, he continued.

"You heard what he said, Sire. He wants Napoleon's corpse at the bottom of the Atlantic Ocean. To whom can he come to make that possible? There is no one among the courts of Europe but you who possesses a navy capable of aiding him. He thinks nothing of embroiling Russia in a war with England and France to secure a throne that is not even his."

Nicolas stared into space, his eyes focused on some distant point. His countenance was angry.

"The one great failing in my father's reign," Nicolas said in a low, menacing tone, "was his failure to march into Paris in 1790 and end their accursed revolution." He strolled over to the mantle, leaned one arm on the marble and raised his head. "That failure allowed their decadent republic to emerge, which eventually gave way to Bonaparte and the Empire. The French people want to be *led*, Kutuzov, as do the Russian people. Democracies will always fall to corruption. God ordained kings to rule the masses—one strong man to rule and protect the people." The tsar's fist slammed down on the mantle. "I realize that Angoulême wants me to fight his battles for him, to do his dirty work, I believe the saying goes. But we must look beyond this to what may happen, should the Bonapartists succeed in reclaiming the French throne. Europe barely survived the Corsican's attempts to alter the fundamental basis of society. Suppose this Louis-Napoleon manages to reclaim his uncle's throne. He will naturally set out to finish his uncle's work, don't you think? What if he does exactly this, but he avoids his uncle's mistakes? The consequences would be disastrous for kings and autocracy."

Nicolas shook his head decisively and jabbed at the mantle with his forefinger. "I have sworn at the graves of my father and my brother that I would protect the principles of autocracy that safeguard Russia, and the only way to do that is to protect the divine rights of kings everywhere. Everywhere! The Bourbons of France were God's men, chosen to rule that nation. I must do what I can to prevent them from being overthrown again." Nicolas stared at his forefinger tapping the mantle.

Kutuzov stood silently during Nicolas's tirade. Over his years of service, the prince had learned to wait and see what remained once the storm passed. Sometimes, after outbursts like this, the tsar was open to suggestion; at others his mind was immovable. Everything hinged on what Nicolas said next.

"Kutuzov," Nicolas said at last, "we must help him. I do not take lightly the dangers of war with England and France, but the prospective disasters that await every court in Europe in the wake of a Bonapartist restoration are too terrible to ignore. I will not make my father's mistake."

The tsar stared at his aide. "I want you to handle this yourself. Do not go through normal naval channels. Detail two frigates to intercept and sink the French vessel carrying the remains back to France."

"Sire," said the prince, "is there no other way?"

"None," the Tsar replied. "If the remains arrive in France, within a year we shall see a Bonaparte sitting on the throne of France, and this time, it will mean the destruction of Europe." Nicolas stared into the fireplace and nodded. Kutuzov knew the sign; he bowed and left the room as he had entered.

He returned to his office via the secret corridors that allowed him private access to the tsar's study. He sat behind his desk—little more than a large table, actually—and laid a sheet of paper and a pen in front of him. Instead of picking up the pen, he sat back in his chair. The tsar had laid before him an impossible task. The French transport vessel would surely be protected by warships. The duke had made it clear that the only way to avoid war with half of Europe was if there were no witnesses to the sinking. That meant every vessel escorting the transport must be sunk, and every soul aboard every one of those ships must die.

Kutuzov rose and walked over to the large portrait of Peter the Great that dominated the wall to the right of his desk. Before the portrait was a single overstuffed leather chair with a small table to its left. On that table was a silver bell. As he always did when he needed to think, Kutuzov sat in the chair. He picked up the bell and rang it. The unique tone of the bell sent a special message to his servants outside, and within three minutes the door opened and a servant placed a glass of Cognac on the table and left without saying a word.

Kutuzov sipped the nectar from the glass as he stared silently at the greatest ruler in Russia's long history. Kutuzov's family had a long history with the Bonapartes. His own grandfather, the great General Kutuzov, had fought the Emperor at Austerlitz and then saved all Russia when the French invaded in 1812. That campaign had cost him his life; the general's heart gave out as the last Frenchman retreated across the Vistula. The prince drained his glass. Men like Peter and the general seemed conspicuous in Russia these days by their absence. Kutuzov looked to the portrait again. Somehow, he doubted they would be coming back.

He rose with a sigh and paced the room, racking his brain to come up with a way to perform the impossible. He saw no way to accomplish the task given him by the tsar and keep Russia out of the war that would follow against England and France. Kutuzov stopped in the middle of the room and stood tall, his head raised defiantly. A terrible decision had been made. One he did not agree with, to be sure, but it was the only decision that could be made. Bonaparte must die. Again.

He went to his desk and pushed the paper and pen to the side. The bell to his right was a different size and cast from a different metal than the one before the portrait. It was much larger and rang with a deeper tone. He looked down ruefully for a long moment before picking the bell up and giving a vigorous shake. An aide opened the office door and took one step inside the room.

"Yes, my Prince?" he asked.

"Get me Count Alekseyev," Kutuzov said, "at once!"

"Yes, my Prince." The servant bowed and withdrew.

Kutuzov leaned back and closed his eyes. He knew he had about an hour before the count would knock on his door, and he hoped to calm his mind and order his thoughts before then. He discovered almost immediately that this was impossible. Kutuzov opened his eyes in desperation, and looked to the portrait for answers. Kutuzov was not a fool; he was very well aware that thousands of serfs had died during the construction of St. Petersburg, literally worked to death to create a European-style capital for Peter's westernized Russia. But to order the outright murder of hundreds of sailors.... His eyes flew briefly to the small silver bell beside the chair. The prince closed his eyes tightly and cursed bitterly inside his head. Now was not the time to have his senses dulled by drink. That would come later, after the orders were written and signed.

Finally, a knock on the door sounded, and the steward announced the arrival of Count Alekseyev. The Count strode into the room, halting in the middle and bowing.

"My Prince," he said, "you have sent for me?"

"Yes, Mikhail," Kutuzov said. He indicated the chair before his desk. "Be seated. The tsar has given me an assignment, and I need the services of a naval captain to command two frigates we are sending to the South Atlantic. What was the name of that captain you introduced me to at the embassy ball last month?"

"That was Captain Dimitri Eduardovich Baranov, my

Prince," Alekseyev said promptly.

"What do you know of him?"

"He is one of our most experienced commanders, my Prince. As a young lieutenant, he fought the French forces on land and sea during the invasion of 1812. More recently, he has scored several victories over Turkish naval forces in the Black Sea. Within the Navy, he is regarded as a wise and resourceful captain. Sailors fight to serve under his command."

Kutuzov nodded thoughtfully. "Is he still in Odessa?"

Alekseyev's eyes narrowed inquisitively. "I believe so, my Prince. May I inquire what this is all about?"

Kutuzov smiled, but it was a dry, distinctly Russian smile, one that would brook no interference. "No, my dear Count, you may not. Send Baranov to me tomorrow morning. If he has left the city, recall him at once, on my authority."

Alekseyev rose and bowed. "It shall be done at once." He turned and left the room without looking back. Kutuzov watched the door for several minutes after the count departed. Then he reached for the pen and began to write the orders for the operation.

The next morning, Kutuzov rose early, weary and bleary-eyed, and told his servant to bring him a pot of strong, hot tea. The previous evening had been a fight from start to finish; the tsar had to be convinced to sign the orders. Given the specifics of the mission, Kutuzov had said, not to mention the fact that it might cause a war with both England and France, no one but the tsar himself had the authority to commit Russian military forces to this course. This appeal to his position and absolute authority had finally convinced Nicholas to sign the orders.

Kutuzov splashed cold water on his face before sitting down to his usual breakfast of eggs, fried potatoes, sausages, and hot tea. He left the table upon clearing his plate, taking his tea with him to his study. He no sooner sat down behind his desk when a knock rapped on the door. It opened to reveal the excited Count Alekseyev.

"I got him, my Prince!" he announced.

"Whom have you got, Mikhail?"

"Captain Baranov!" Alekseyev paused to catch a breath. "He made it as far as Chornomorsk before my men caught up to him and turned him around. He has been riding all night, my Prince, in response to your summons."

"Thank you, Mikhail," Kutuzov said. "Let's have the captain in."

The count left to retrieve his charge. Kutuzov considered geography. The section of Black Sea coastline mentioned by Alekseyev was fully twenty-five kilometers from Odessa. The count's men had done well indeed.

A second knock announced the return of Alekseyev and Baranov. This time Kutuzov stood to greet his guests. The two men marched up to the desk and stood at attention.

"My Prince," Alekseyev said, "may I introduce Captain Dimitri Eduardovich Baranov? Captain, I present to you your host, Prince Kutuzov, personal aide to the Tsar."

Both men bowed. Kutuzov gestured them to comfortable chairs, the ones for honored guests. As he resumed his own seat, he appraised the man sitting before him.

Baranov was big, even for a Russian. He was around two meters tall, with broad shoulders and a thick, muscular chest. A receding hairline had left him bald on the top of his head; Kutuzov wondered if the captain's marvelous beard had been grown by way of compensation. Baranov sat quietly, seemingly content to let events take their course. This impressed Kutuzov; there were not many men summoned into his presence who remained calm. *Yes,* the prince thought, *this one should do nicely.*

"Will you excuse us, Alekseyev?" he said. "I wish to speak with Captain Baranov privately. Permit me to congratulate you and your men on a fine job of tracking the captain down and bringing him here."

Alekseyev was irritated by the dismissal, but he recovered quickly and stood. He bowed and left the room. A steward closed the door behind him. Kutuzov knew they would not be interrupted.

"A pleasure to meet you, my Prince," Baranov said, in a deep, resonant voice. "May I ask why you have sent for me?"

Kutuzov settled in his chair, his irritation at the captain's speaking first betrayed only by the narrowing of his eyes. *So,* he thought, *our captain is also a man who does not like to waste time. He is not awed by authority, either. This one will bear watching. If he returns, that is.*

"Captain Baranov," Kutuzov began formally, "my information is that you currently command two of His Majesty's frigates. Is this correct? Good. Your ships are at Sevastopol?"

"Yes, my Prince."

"How long before you can have them ready for sea?"

Baranov lowered his brows. "How long a voyage?"

"Your ships will be at sea for six months or more."

"Will I have access to a port to reprovision and get fresh water?"

"Assume that you will not."

Baranov thought for a moment. He placed his wide hands on his knees and stared at his thumbs as he answered.

"Once I return to Sevastopol, provisioning will take approximately a week, assuming the supplies are in the warehouses."

"That will suffice." Kutuzov leaned forward and rested his

elbows on the desk, steepling his fingers before his chin. "I will make available to you the fast packet ship *Minsk*. Leave as soon as the winds allow." He looked at the calendar on his desk. "Today is the 14th. Allowing for a slow passage, let's say you arrive on the 16th. One week to provision means that you should be ready to sail on the 24th. Yes?"

Baranov coughed. *What am I being measured for?* he thought. He blinked and replied, "Yes, my Prince."

Kutuzov rose. "Very good, Captain. Return to your ships and prepare them for sea. Your orders will be delivered to you by the morning of the 24th. Any questions?"

Baranov rose. *Many, but there is only one I dare ask,* he thought. "May I ask why I cannot receive my orders now?"

Kutuzov's eyes flashed at the captain's temerity. "This mission is being conducted in the utmost secrecy, Captain. Orders will only be given to you just before you sail." With a effort, he unclenched his jaw. "I will say that you are being assigned a mission, Captain, that will either ensure the stability of Europe for the next fifty years..." the prince's eyes narrowed, "...or destroy it."

Baranov's jaw worked. "And if I refuse the mission?"

Kutuzov didn't even blink. "You will be shot."

The Captain smiled wryly. "As you command, my Prince."

Kutuzov picked up an envelope from the desk and held it out. "Here is your authorization to take passage on *Minsk*." Baranov took the envelope, and the prince continued. "One more thing: there is a slight chance that this mission will be canceled. If that is the case, your orders will not come. If you have not received them by the morning of the 25th, you may assume you are free to resume your former command."

"I understand, my Prince."

Kutuzov stood with an air of dismissal. "Good luck, Captain. May fortune smile on you."

"Thank you, my Prince." Kutuzov had risen to his feet; now came to attention, then he spun on his heel and marched from the room.

Kutuzov stood there for some time, watching the door and considering the man he had just sent to his death. Then he made his way to the chair before the portrait. He sat and rang the bell.

His Royal Highness, the Prince de Joinville, had to be shaken awake when they finally reached their destination. He stretched inside the coach, extending his arms and legs and shaking his head.

"We are here, my Prince," the aide said. "We have merely to walk down to the dock."

"Dock?" Joinville asked. "Why is *la Belle Poule* in dock?" The prince climbed out of the coach and headed toward the ship.

Hernoux hurried to keep up. He regretted the delay caused by the prince's insistence on a stay of several days at the chateau of one of his many mistresses. "My Prince, orders were sent from Paris after we left. The ship was put into dock and modifications begun for the journey to St. Helena."

"Modifications?" Joinville called over his shoulder. "What modifications?"

"Accommodations for the passengers, my Prince."

Joinville stopped and turned around. "What passengers?"

Hernoux sighed and handed his captain the orders he'd picked up at the dock office before waking Joinville. The prince glanced at the top page before flipping through to find the list of passengers. He could hardly believe his eyes when he read the names. He handed the list back to Hernoux. "Read them to me."

The two men resumed their walk as the colonel read. "Philippe de Rohan-Chabot, attaché to the French ambassador to the United Kingdom and commissioned by Minister Thiers to superintend the exhumation proceedings. Generals Bertrand and Gourgaud, both of whom were with the Emperor on St. Helena. Count Emmanuel de Las Cases, son of Emmanuel de Las Cases, who took dictation for Napoleon's memoirs while on St. Helena. Five men who were personal servants to the Emperor while he was on St. Helena: Saint-Denis, Noverraz, Pierron, Archambault, and Coursot." Hernoux scanned the orders. "We are to be accompanied by the corvette *La Favorite,* under the command of Captain Guyet. *La Favorite* will transport Louis Marchand, the Emperor's chief valet de chambre while on St. Helena."

"What about the modifications?" Joinville asked.

The colonel flipped through the orders until he found the information. "*La Belle Poule*'s steerage is being converted to a candle-lit chapel, draped in black velvet embroidered with silver bees, which were the Emperor's symbol. There will be a catafalque, or raised bed to receive the casket, in the center. It will be guarded by four gilded wooden eagles. The ship will also be painted black for the voyage."

Joinville stopped again. "And just how is all this being accomplished? How is it we are to house a chapel and quarters for all these passengers?"

Hernoux scanned the orders and his face paled. He looked at his Prince and swallowed. "Apparently, this is being done at the expense of our armament."

"What?!?" Joinville exclaimed. He seized the orders and examined the page his lieutenant indicated. Incredibly, it was true. His beloved sixty-gun frigate was losing all thirty-two of its 30-pounders, all four of his 80-pounder Paixhans guns, and eight of his 30-pounder carronades. This would

leave him just sixteen 30-pounder carronades, which were useless at long range, to protect a ship over 170 feet long of 2,500 tons displacement. *Hence,* he thought grimly, *the escort.*

The prince and his aide boarded their ship and were met by Lieutenant Charner, Joinville's second-in-command. The two men had been midshipmen together on the old *Liberte*, and both had advanced more through competence than through Joinville's family connections. Joinville had made sure the two stayed together as their careers advanced.

"Quite a surprise, eh, Charner?" the prince said grimly.

"Yes, Captain," the first lieutenant said with a short bow. "The orders came aboard the day after you left. They were countersigned by the King himself."

Joinville nodded, a dark look crossing his face. He knew better than to take his anger out on Charner. He was too good a lieutenant, too good a friend, to treat that way.

"Did I count right?" Joinville asked. "We are down to sixteen of the 30-pounder carronades to defend ourselves?"

Charner winced. "No, sir, fourteen. It seems that Count Las Cases demanded separate accommodations for his servant."

Joinville stared at him before looking out over the harbor and shaking his head. Finally he sighed and turned back to his lieutenant.

"And the modifications?"

"They should be completed on schedule, Captain. You should see the steerage; it's quite impressive, even if it is for Bonaparte."

The prince grunted. "I'll go below and look it over, then I will be in my cabin. Come to see me later."

Charner bowed. "Yes, my Prince."

Joinville nodded and made his way below. He wandered

more or less by instinct, as his mind was racing. *If Bonaparte were alive to see all this,* he thought, *he'd die from a laughing fit.*

Joinville inspected the work being done in the steerage. He had to admit that the little chapel would be an impressive place when it was completed; too good, in fact, for Bonaparte. He took one more look around and grimaced in disgust. He marched out of the room and did not look back.

He went up to the gundeck and looked over the rooms that were being constructed for the passengers. The walls were of the normal sort that were easily dismantled when the ship beat to quarters. Joinville wondered where the passengers would go for safety during an engagement. He walked aft toward his own quarters, cursing his father—and Thiers—under his breath. Surely, it would have been far better to use an Indiaman for this benighted mission? Merchant ships were equipped for passengers. That would have left *La Belle Poule* intact to act as the official escort.

When he reached his quarters, he found Hernoux working on their itinerary. Fortunately, their orders gave only a broad outline of their mission. This left him latitude for recreation along the way.

His aide looked up. "I believe I have the basics set down, Your Highness. As you suggested, I have scheduled stops in Cadiz, Madeira, Tenerife, and Bahia. If you approve, I shall send out the notifications immediately."

The prince stepped over to the table to study his aide's outline of the proposed itinerary for their journey, and his spirits lifted considerably. *This may end up being quite enjoyable,* he thought.

CHAPTER 8

Philippe de Rohan-Chabot looked around his small cabin aboard *la Belle Poule* and once again considered his situation. Despite his orders from Minister Thiers, he was not quite sure where he stood, so to speak. The Minister had put him in charge of the exhumation of the Emperor's mortal remains, which meant it was technically his responsibility to receive them from the British. He was not at all sure how the Prince de Joinville, whom he had not met yet, would react. His Highness was a Bourbon, and thus had an inbred hatred of the Corsican; did that mean he would be willing to step back and let Rohan take the lead? Or would he opposed the mission, either subtly or directly? Then there was Bertrand and Gourgaud, whom he also had not met; they had soldiered with the Emperor and endured the hardships of the island with him. Would they allow him to fulfill his commission or would they attempt to take over?

Rohan rubbed the bridge of his nose between his thumb and forefinger in an attempt to ease the tension he felt creeping in. Not for the first time, he wondered if he was up to this assignment. More than one of his colleagues (probably motivated by jealousy) had stated both to his face and behind his back, that this was much too big a task to be entrusted to a twenty-five year old. He raised his head and took a deep breath to steady his nerves. *No,* he thought, *I will not allow any of them to hinder me. I must compose myself as if it were the Emperor himself I am going to meet, rather than his corpse.*

He walked out of his cabin to the communal table. It had been set up in the middle of the deck, similar to the gunroom one deck below. He saw an officer sitting there, his back to Rohan, drinking a glass of wine and reading something. The officer turned at the sound of Rohan's door closing. He stood when he saw the newcomer.

Rohan took a step in his direction and bowed. "Philippe de Rohan-Chabot," he said formally. "At your service, monsieur."

The officer bowed as well. "General Henri Bertrand. A pleasure to make your acquaintance. Won't you join me?"

"Thank you." Rohan took a seat one down from the general. The steward appeared, and Rohan requested tea.

Bertrand turned over the papers he was reading. "M. Rohan, am I correct in that you are in command of this expedition?"

"Only the exhumation," Rohan said. His tea arrived, and he thanked the steward. "His Highness, the Prince de Joinville, commands the overall expedition."

"Yes, I am aware of his authority," Bertrand said as he took a drink of his wine. Rohan did not think the general was very impressed with the prince. This would bear watching.

"Tell me, M. Rohan, are you in favor of the Return?" Bertrand asked.

"I serve France," Rohan said. "Minister Thiers has given me a charge, and I shall carry it out."

"Of course," said the general with a fatherly nod. "I was

inquiring after your personal feelings—unless my question offends? If such is the case, please forgive me."

"No, no, General, I am not offended." Rohan considered for a moment. "General, I do not know you, so you will forgive me if anything I say offends you." The older man smiled and nodded once. Rohan continued. "My family is Royalist. My father was, for many years, aide-de-camp to King Louis Philippe when he was duc d'Orleans. I was born in London during the Hundred Days. We have no love for the Emperor. That being said, I personally take no position on the return. Make no mistake, monsieur, I deplore the endless warfare under the Emperor, but I also see many good things he did for our country, from which we benefit even today. My parents had nothing good to say about him, but I have met many in my work at the Ministry who hold different opinions of the man. Some of them think he could do no wrong, but there are some who are more honest in their assessments. Do I think he deserves to be buried in France? Yes, I do. Is it necessarily the best thing for France that it happens now? Of that, I am not sure."

Bertrand studied the younger man through hooded eyes. "Pardon my asking, monsieur, but how old did you say you are?"

Rohan smiled. "Twenty-five, General."

Bertrand shook his head in genial mock-disbelief. "I believe you are well chosen."

Rohan was wondering just what the general meant by that when the door opened and another officer entered. He stopped short when he saw that the room was occupied.

"I beg your pardons," he said.

"Nonsense, Gourgaud," Bertrand said. "Come in! Allow me to present M. Phillipe de Rohan-Chabot." Gourgaud bowed, and Bertrand turned to Rohan. "Monsieur, allow me to present General Gaspard Gourgaud, one-time aide-de-camp to the Emperor Napoleon."

Rohan rose and bowed. "An honor, General."

Gourgaud nodded abruptly, then said, "You've heard who the British are sending, Bertrand?"

"Hornblower? Yes, I heard," the general replied. "A natural choice, surely."

Gourgaud sneered. "Perhaps, but did you know that his presence was requested by *our* government?"

"What!?" Bertrand looked to Rohan for an explanation.

"Don't ask me!" the envoy said. "I know nothing of this."

"It's true, Bertrand!" Gourgaud exclaimed. "The question is, why? Is Hornblower part of a plot to legitimize the Pretender? A sign of the new queen's approval?"

Bertrand shook his head. "I doubt that even a naive, idealist queen would undermine the authority of kings in such a way. I suspect a simpler reason. The Emperor spoke frequently of this Hornblower. He said that the Governor was a man of honor. It is, therefore, natural that his presence would be requested as an expression of mutual respect."

la Belle Poule slipped out to sea the next day, escorted only by the corvette *Favorite*. Joinville stood silent in the middle of the quarterdeck of his frigate while Lieutenant Charner took the ship out of the harbor and set course due south. The prince turned to see two of his passengers, M. Rohan and General Bertrand, standing at the fantail. He walked over to join them.

"Good morning," the young prince greeted them.

"Good morning, your Highness," Rohan said. Joinville noticed that Bertrand had come to attention at his approach and nodded his acknowledgement.

"A fine day to depart, Highness," Rohan said. "A good

omen, I hope."

"As do I, Monsieur," the prince said.

Bertrand observed the prince as he spoke with Rohan. The third son of the king, Joinville was a full captain, and commander of this expedition at the young age of twenty-two. Tall and lean, the prince had a reputation of taking his naval duties seriously and learning as he progressed in rank. Bertrand was privately impressed at this first meeting.

"We shall be making several ports-of-call on our journey south," the prince was saying. "Cadiz, Madeira, Tenerife, and Bahia. Our return journey, however, will be direct. It shall be conducted with all proper ceremony. The Emperor will be brought home with all the honor he is due. Will you gentlemen join me for supper tonight? I shall invite General Gourgaud as well."

"An honor, my Prince," said Bertrand, answering for them both.

"At the turn of the first dog watch then," Joinville said, and he smiled at the looks on his guests' faces. "6 pm."

After the prince had gone forward, Bertrand turned to his companion. "So? What do you think?"

"Of the prince?" Rohan grinned. "Well, it's nice to know I'm not the youngest one out here."

Bertrand chuckled. "Word is that, although family connections got him promoted, the prince has taken the trouble to learn his job. He is considered a competent naval officer, lacking only in experience."

"I hope you're right," Rohan said. "I have a feeling we will not make France again without a fight."

Bertrand looked at him. "You have heard something?"

Rohan shook his head. "Just a feeling."

Henri Girot stood at the fantail and watched as Toulon

sank below the horizon. Ten hours ago, a messenger had showed up at his office at the Naval Armament Office with orders for him to report immediately for sea duty aboard *la Belle Poule*. He was familiar with the frigate, since he had just finished logging receipt of most of her armament. He had been surprised when the messenger told him not to bother returning to his quarters, as his sea chest was being sent on to the frigate. He'd hurried to the wharf and reported aboard less than two hours before the ship set sail.

After Toulon disappeared from sight, Girot made his way to the gun room and entered his cabin, closing the door behind him. He sat on his sea chest and pulled an envelope from the inside pocket of his coat. The same messenger had f handed it to him without explanation just before he'd left the office. In his haste to get aboard the frigate before it sailed, Girot had all but forgotten the envelope.

Now he examined the envelope carefully. His eyes grew wide when he recognized the "N" impressed on the wax seal. He sliced the envelope open with his dagger and withdrew the single sheet it contained. He read it slowly.

> *My Dear Lieutenant Girot,*
>
> *I wish to enlist you in a great undertaking. I have taken the liberty of arranging for you to be reassigned to the frigate* la Belle Poule*. Your mission is to guard my Uncle's remains until they are safely returned to France. I fear the Ultra-Royalists will try to sabotage the enterprise, possibly by desecration during the return trip. Your job is to stop them by any means necessary. May destiny smile on you.*
>
> *Louis-Napoleon Bonaparte*

Girot read the letter two more times before he refolded

the page, put it back in the envelope, and buried it in the bottom of his sea chest. He closed the chest and sat on it again. He rested his head in his hands and closed his eyes. He felt a knot developing in his stomach. *My God! If the prince discovers that letter!* Girot had just come to the conclusion that he must destroy the letter when a knock at his door made him jump.

"Enter," he gasped.

A young midshipman stepped into the cabin and came to attention. "His Highness has sent for you, sir. He is in his cabin and I am to show you the way."

"I shall come at once," Girot replied. He rose and took a deep breath, steeling himself for the worst. He swallowed hard and grabbed his hat on his way out.

He was shown into Joinville's day cabin, where he found the prince talking to his personal aide, Colonel Hernoux, and the first lieutenant. Girot came to attention.

"Lieutenant Girot reports as ordered, my Prince," he stammered.

"Yes, Girot," Joinville took a sheet of paper from his aide, "I see that you are a last-minute addition to our company. Welcome to *la Belle Poule*."

"Thank you, my Prince."

The prince met his eyes. "Are you aware of our mission?"

"No, my Prince," Girot lied. "My orders merely said to report aboard immediately."

Joinville handed the paper back to Col. Hernoux. "We have been commissioned by my father the king to go to the island of St. Helena. There we will take possession of the mortal remains of the Emperor Napoleon and return them for burial in France."

"Mon Dieu!" Girot whispered.

"My sentiments precisely," the prince said sarcastically.

"Your arrival, Lieutenant, is fortuitous, as we are working with a reduced crew due the passengers traveling with us. I have a particular task for you. You will be take charge of the arrangements for transporting the Emperor's body once it is aboard. Lieutenant Charner"—the prince indicated his first lieutenant—"will instruct you on your duties. That is all."

"Report to me at the turn of the next watch," Charner said.

Girot snapped to attention. "Yes, Captain." He turned and marched from the cabin, unable to believe his good fortune.

HMS *Iris* plowed through the gentle waves under all plain sail. The weather had been good so far, and this particular morning found Hornblower on the quarterdeck early, pacing the lee rail, just as he would have thirty years ago. He had been flattered when Captain Brewer had informed him the night before that his old stomping grounds would be ready for him at his usual time; at first he had begged off, claiming he did not wish to interfere with the ship's routine, but Brewer had assured him that his presence would be no disruption, and now Hornblower was glad that he had.

He paced back and forth, his mind turning over and over what he might find when he got to St. Helena and what kind of dangers he might encounter. There were potentials for sabotage even before they left the island. He resolved to prevail upon the governor of the island to have everyone searched before they approached the gravesite. Several people in London had opined that the easiest way for the Ultra-Royalists to put an end to the entire affair would be to simply blow up the body, either before it was exhumed or immediately afterwards. The alternative would be to sink the frigate after they departed the island; Hornblower was reasonably confident that Captain Brewer could assist the

French in preventing that. That left the land option. Hornblower's briefing in London had emphasized that the garrison of St. Helena was only one-tenth what it had been when Bonaparte was alive. Reenforced with some of Brewer's marines, he decided, it should be equal to the task of providing adequate security.

Hornblower finished his pacing at the end of his current leg and was oddly pleased to feel sweat dripping slowly down his back. Another familiarity. He strolled over to where Brewer was standing.

"Good morning, Captain," he said.

"Good morning, my lord. I hope your walk was satisfactory?"

"Yes, thank you. It amazes me how quickly one can fall into old habits."

Brewer grinned. "Do you prefer it to a stroll around Smallbridge?"

Hornblower pursed his lips. "Some things are best kept a secret."

Both men chuckled.

"You know, that's one habit of yours that Captain Bush never picked up," Brewer said. "Oh, I nearly forgot! My lord, while you were pacing, Mr. Dean came to me and extended an invitation for us to dine in the gunroom tonight. He suggested the turn of the first dog watch."

"I hope you accepted immediately on my behalf."

Brewer grinned. "I did indeed, my lord. But I'm afraid there may be the usual questions. Mac has been telling tales below deck."

Hornblower shrugged. "He doesn't forget a thing, does he?"

"Not that I've noticed. Do you know, I asked him if he would consider staying with Elizabeth and running the household—similar to what Brown does in Smallbridge—and do you know what? He turned me down! Said his place was with me at sea. Said he would come ashore when I do."

Hornblower shook his head in admiration. "I've never been anything near the man of prayer you are, William, but I must say that you and I have been blessed as captains with good coxswains."

Brewer could only nod in agreement.

Lieutenant Girot reported to the first officer as ordered. He found Charner on the quarterdeck and saluted.

"Lieutenant Girot reporting as ordered," he said.

"Ah, Girot," Charner said. "Follow me."

Girot fell into step and followed the first lieutenant below. They made their way to the steerage, and Girot paused in wonder as he stepped inside the converted chapel. His eyes settled on the polished black ebony sarcophagus—empty for the time being.

"Impressive, is it not?" Charner commented.

"I believe the Emperor would be... pleased," Girot said slowly.

Intrigued, Charner said, "You don't look old enough to have known the Emperor."

"I meant no disrespect," Girot said, flushing. "My father fought for the Empire in the army. He was decorated by the Emperor after the battle of Wagram. He told us many stories."

"I see," Charner said. "You have a vested interest in our mission, then." He gestured with his arms open wide. "All this is yours. You are responsible for making sure all is ready, and for ensuring decorum during the return journey. Louis!" he called, and an old sailor appeared. "This is Lieutenant Girot. He will be in charge of this area. Girot, this is Louis.

He will assist you in your work. We are traveling under a reduced crew, so he will be your only assistant."

"I understand." Girot said.

"I will leave you two to it, then," Charner said, and he left the chapel.

Girot watched as Louis went about his routine chores in the steerage, surprised that one so old served on this ship. "Louis," he asked presently, "is there still work to be done to make all ready here?"

The old man scratched his nose. "We are ready for the most part, sir." He placed a gnarled hand on the sarcophagus. "This will go ashore when we reach St. Helena, and the coffin containing will be taken from the ground and placed inside for the journey back to France."

"What about security?" Girot asked.

Louis looked surprised. "Security, sir?"

"Yes." Girot was shocked by the sailor's indifference. "What if someone tries to prevent us from arriving in France?"

"That is up to Lieutenant Charner and His Highness, sir," Louis said matter-of-factly.

"Of course," Girot said automatically. He wondered just how much help Louis was going to be.

Hornblower had forgotten how much he enjoyed being invited to the gunroom. It was like being the guest of honor at a banquet. This time he was treated more like royalty. Hornblower was amused by the looks he got when he and the captain entered the room. He was conducted to the seat of honor at the first lieutenant's right hand, and the captain was seated across from him on the lieutenant's left. Standing at the head of the table, Lieutenant Dean welcomed them, bowing to Hornblower. When they were all seated, Dean addressed Brewer.

"I say, sir," he said, loud enough for Hornblower to hear, "when I invited his lordship and yourself to dine, I had thought to request Alfred's services for the evening. But when Carmichael heard of it, he was so deeply wounded that I felt I could not make the offer. So I have left the whole evening in his hands."

"I look forward to the results, Mr. Dean," Brewer replied. "Carmichael has a good reputation around the fleet. Before I brought Alfred aboard, I believe some of your officers were afraid I might steal him for myself!"

"Thank God you didn't, sir! Knowing Carmichael is down here is a great comfort to us!" Dean paused while the stewards filled the glasses with wine, then he rose. "Gentlemen! Your attention, if you please! Mr. Ford, if you would be so kind, sir."

Ford cleared his throat loudly and raised his glass. "Gentlemen, the Queen!"

"The Queen!" echoed around the room, and all drank the sovereign's health.

Hornblower took note that Ford had remained seated while giving his toast. He was about to say something to Brewer when he remembered that King William IV had granted a special dispensation. The king had been a Royal Navy officer before his ascension to the throne, and it was said that he had cracked his head many a time on a deck beam overhead when he had to stand and give a toast. As a favor to his fellow officers, he issued an edict granting permission for toasts to be given while seated. Hornblower smiled; being over six feet tall himself, he, too, remembered having to stand to give a toast only to have the motion of the ship ram his head into a beam.

Conversations broke out in muffled tones all around the

table. Mr. Dean whispered something to the captain, and the captain nodded. Mr. Dean hesitated only slightly, and then turned to Hornblower. "My lord," he said, "a question if I may?" The table grew silent.

Hornblower's brow rose slightly. "Of course, Lieutenant."

Dean looked hesitantly at Brewer before turning back to Hornblower. "Well, my lord, it's just that.... Is it true that when the Tsar of Russia visited you on HMS *Nonsuch*, er... did you actually give him ship's fare, *including ship's bread?*"

Hornblower was somewhat surprised. This was not a question he had anticipated. "But of course, Mr. Dean."

"My lord, how did he react to the weevils?" Dr. Sisk asked.

Hornblower smiled at the memory. "Actually, he took it in good stride. Tapped 'em out like he was born to it."

Brewer grinned. He had heard the story before from Captain Bush.

Mr. Priestley leaned forward. "Beg pardon, my lord, but if it's not too forward to ask, can you tell us what Bonaparte was like?"

Hornblower looked at the sailing master for a moment before looking to the captain.

"Have they asked you yet?"

Brewer shook his head. "Haven't really had the chance as yet, my lord. If you would rather, I can answer the question."

His Lordship considered the captain's offer before shaking his head. "No, thank you, Captain." He turned to Priestley. "To say that Napoleon Bonaparte was the most fascinating person I have ever met, besides my brother-in-law the duke of Wellington, would be an understatement. When your captain and I arrived on the island—he was detailed to me to act as my personal aide and secretary—Bonaparte's greatest problem was boredom. He had nothing to occupy his mind in his exile. And there was nobody there in governance on the island whom he respected."

"My lord," Mr. Shannon said, "I'm afraid I don't understand."

Brewer spoke up. "The Foreign Office hoped that Bonaparte would respect his lordship on the basis of his accomplishments. There was also the similarity in their backgrounds: neither man was of noble birth, yet both achieved titles on the basis of military victories."

"I see," the Doctor said. "So there you were, a man of action who could converse about the things that mattered most to him, not merely a bureaucrat. I see indeed. Tell us, my lord, what was the thing about Bonaparte that surprised you most?"

Hornblower's brows rose. "Surprised me most? Many things about him surprised me, Mr. Sisk, but to narrow it down to what surprised me *most*?" He took a drink of his wine as he searched his memory. Finally, he set the glass down and leaned forward, resting his forearm on the table.

"I suppose what surprised me *most*, Doctor, was the manner of man he had become since being exiled there. You see, all else aside, by the time the captain and I arrived early in 1817, he had been on the island for nearly two years, and it had begun to sink into his mind that this dreary island would be where he would die. That sort of knowledge changes a man. There is no stranger man on the face of the earth, my good Doctor, than an emperor or a king without a throne. Bonaparte was used to administering an entire continent, and now had absolutely nothing to do. It sounds petty, but he used his energies to cause as much mischief as he could. I tell you, my first meeting with Bonaparte was one of the strangest events of my life."

"Strange how, my lord?" the Doctor pressed.

"One of Bonaparte's most potent weapons was his reputation, and he knew how to use it to intimidate. I had to concentrate in order not to fall prey to it." Hornblower nodded, remembering. "Our great 'battles' if you will, were those of the mind. We developed a contest between us regarding who could leave the other speechless. I struck the first blow when, during that first visit, we were discussing how he should be addressed. The previous governors had addressed him as 'General Bonaparte'. When he suggested that he be addressed as 'Emperor', I suggested 'Prisoner Number 1'." Hornblower's eyes crinkled. "I tell you, gentlemen, the look of shock and dismay on his face shall cheer me till my dying day."

It was Lieutenant Blake who laughed first. Before he broke, Brewer saw that the entire table was trying to hold it in, but once the dam was broken, the entire table, with the exceptions of Hornblower and Brewer, erupted in laughter like a volcano spewing lava and ash into the air. Brewer and Hornblower simply sat silent, sharing a smile and a look that no one who had not been there could never understand. The uproar died down.

The Doctor wiped tears from his eyes before turning back to Hornblower.

"My lord, what was Boney's reaction? What did he say to your gracious offer?"

Hornblower sighed in mock-disappointment. "He declined."

Another smaller wave of laughter swept the room. Then Lieutenant Blake leaned in and asked, "My lord, I'm curious. Did he ever discuss Waterloo?"

"He never discussed the battle with me directly, Lieutenant. He was not, however, reluctant to discuss his other battles. I recall translating a conversation between Bonaparte and Captain Bush, who was the commander of the naval detachment patrolling the island, regarding which battle was more important, Austerlitz or Trafalgar. They went back and forth, and I could see that Bonaparte was clearly enjoying himself. After all, this was exactly the sort of intellectual stimulation he thrived upon. Finally, I stepped in and told him I could offer proof that Trafalgar was the superior victory. He looked skeptical and asked me what that would be. I told him it was his presence on this island. His eyes turned to saucers, but he recovered quickly and tried to make some excuse. The truth, gentlemen, in my eyes, is that if Lord Nelson had not succeeded in destroying the French and Spanish fleets at Trafalgar, if Bonaparte had succeeded in getting his army at Boulogne across the Channel and landed in England, I do not believe we would be sitting here today. England owes her current position to two men: Lord Nelson, and my brother-in-law, the duke of Wellington."

Choruses of "Here! Here!" rang around the room, and toasts were drunk to the two heroes of the British Empire. Hornblower waited while Carmichael and his stewards refilled the glasses before leaning forward again.

"It may interest you gentlemen to know," he said, "that your captain has stood before the full fury of Bonaparte's wrath. I take it he has not told you the story, Mr. Dean? No? How typical of him. Please allow me to do so. We had picked up intelligence of a coming escape attempt to get Bonaparte off the island and speed him to America, so I ordered a security crackdown around Longwood, which was Bonaparte's residence. A day or two later, as I approached the door of my office, I could hear Bonaparte screaming at the top of his lungs in his broken English. I burst in to find your captain standing toe-to-toe with Bonaparte and taking everything the ex-Emperor had to throw at him without flinching. Later, Bonaparte told me that Mr. Brewer's courage during the episode had impressed him greatly. I believe that Bonaparte presented the last medal of the French *Légion d'honneur* in his life to your captain."

Dean and the whole table looked astonished. "Sir?" Dean asked. "Is this true?"

Brewer looked embarrassed and shot a later-for-you look at his smiling mentor. He cleared his throat. "Yes, I'm afraid it is."

Cheers erupted. Cries "The Captain!" and "Here's to the Captain!" rang out. As the cries died down, Hornblower turned to Dean.

"Do you mean to tell me that Alfred or Mr. McCleary have not told you any of your captain's deeds?"

Dean shot a mischievous look at his captain. "None, my lord. It is my understanding that they have been threatened with walking the plank if they did."

Hornblower raised his eyebrows and looked to the captain with a sly smile.

"Carmichael!" he called. The servant appeared.

"Pass the word for Alfred and Mr. McCleary."

"Aye, sir."

The officers waited in great anticipation for the arrival of the two men, not daring to speculate what his lordship had up his sleeve. When the two men arrived and stood at attention just inside the doorway, Hornblower addressed them.

"Gentlemen, am I to understand that you have been forbidden to relate tales of your captain's exploits to the crew?"

"That's true, yer lordship," Mac answered for them both.

Hornblower looked to Brewer and made a *tsk-tsk* noise. "Captain, is that really fair?" He turned to the two newcomers. "For the duration of this voyage, you have my permission to tell the tales of your captain's adventures to the crew."

Alfred looked stoical, but Mac broke out into a grin that made his captain's heart sink. Brewer leaned forward.

"Really, my lord?"

Hornblower's face wore a bemused expression, but he nodded his permission.

Brewer pointed a finger right at his coxswain's nose. "Only the true stories, Mac."

Laughter rippled around the table as the big Cornishman's face fell.

"Aw, sir," he moaned, "that leaves all the best ones out!"

"Exactly." Brewer sat back in satisfaction. Only after they departed did he join the others in their laughter.

"You see, my lord?" he said, looking at his mentor in mock-dismay. "Do you see now what I have to put up with?"

Hornblower shook his head decisively. "One more complaint out of you, my dear Captain, and when we return to England I shall take Mr. McCleary back to Smallbridge with me and have Brown teach him all his best tricks."

Hornblower could not help but smile at the speed with which Brewer changed the subject.

The next morning, Hornblower again mounted the deck at the appointed hour and began his exercise. He happened to look up from the deck in time to see Captain Brewer emerge from the stairway.

"Captain," he called out, "would you care to join me?"

"Certainly, my lord," Brewer answered. He fell into step inboard of his friend and mentor, lengthening his stride to keep up. For the first several turns, Hornblower remained silent, and so by custom did Brewer. His lordship must have noticed that his companion longed to say something.

"Captain?" he said. "You may speak, if you feel the need."

Brewer hesitated. "It's nothing really, my lord. I just wished to apologize for the men in the gunroom last night. I hope you did not think them impertinent for asking questions as they did."

Hornblower looked at his companion without breaking stride. "Perfectly all right, Captain. I seem to recall something similar happening on HMS *Lydia* on the way to St. Helena." He stared at the sky as if searching for a memory. "In fact, I seem to recall you yourself asking some of the very same questions."

Brewer smiled. "It was hard not to, my lord, not with Brown and Gerard telling stories, each more incredible than the one before and all of them absolutely true. Add to that the fact that Captain Bush was encouraging them and vouching for every story they told.... We could hardly believe it was so, and yet it was."

The two walked on through several more turns in companionable silence before Brewer spoke again.

"My lord, what do you expect we'll find when we arrive at St. Helena?"

Hornblower sighed. "I presume you mean, will the trouble start there?"

Brewer shrugged.

"Your guess is as good as mine, Captain," Hornblower said. "I am certain there will be trouble somewhere along the line. The first place would be at the grave; they could attempt to destroy the Emperor's remains. An agent of the Ultra-Royalists could be planted among the French dignitaries to throw a bomb into the casket as soon as it is opened." Hornblower hesitated for just a second. He looked up, as if an idea had just struck him. "In fact, Captain, I would not put it past the Pretender to put a Bonapartist agent amongst the French for the same reason."

"What?" Brewer exclaimed. "Why on earth would he do such a thing?"

Hornblower's chin was down again, and he resumed his pacing. "Perhaps in order to use the incident as the basis for a populist coup, to make his own way to the throne."

"I see," Brewer's voice sounded grave. "And the next?"

"There is the obvious risk that someone will attempt to sink the ship on the way back to France. There are two problems with this plan. The difficulty there is, in order to get away with it, they would have to make sure there were no survivors."

That pulled Brewer up short.

"The third chance," Hornblower went on, "will be after the body arrives in France and is en route to Paris. But that will be the responsibility of Minister Thiers and King Louis-Philippe. We must concern ourselves with preventing the first two options."

CHAPTER 9

Minister Roussin was furious. He had begged Thiers to allow him to send a force of frigates and corvettes to escort de Joinville's ship home from St. Helena. He was very much afraid that the duke of Angoulême would attempt to sink *la Belle Poule*, sending the Emperor's remains to the bottom of the Atlantic, along with every living soul on that ship. Roussin had no doubt the duke would find an ally with a frigate or two to spare for just such an adventure.

Thiers had refused his request, saying such a move would make France appear weak and fearful. *Bah!* Roussin thought as he angrily paced his office. *What madness! Better to look weak and have the enterprise succeed!*

He was ashamed and embarrassed that Thiers was using a British frigate and an aging ex-governor to provide the protection. He did, however, realize that this was the best way to avoid either Ultra-Royalist or Bonapartist sympathizers inciting trouble in the crews.

He ceased his pacing, all the angry energy suddenly drained from his body. He stepped to the window and stood, hands behind his back, staring at the Arc de Triomphe below. Commissioned by the Emperor in 1806 following his victory at Austerlitz, construction had been halted by Louis XVIII during the Bourbon restoration. Louis Philippe had restarted the work in 1833, and the monument had been completed in 1836. Roussin found comfort, in a way he could not quite explain, gazing on the arch. It was the most visible reminder of the Emperor in all France, and an object of pride for all those who had fought for the Emperor.

Roussin went to his desk and opened the bottom drawer on his right. He drew out a black mahogany box and laid it on his desk. He opened the box to reveal his star of the *Légion d'honneur,* presented to him by the Emperor himself. He lifted the star out of the box and looked at it for a moment before rising and going to the window. He held it up so he could see the star and the arch at the same time, and he was overcome by a wave of nostalgia for the Empire. France had needed a strong hand to steer the nation and control the Paris mob; the Emperor had been the only man since Louis XIV to do so successfully. Roussin shook his head ruefully as he turned from the window. If only Napoleon had been able to control his ambition! He could have led France for decades, making France the most enlightened, advanced country in the world, then handed the throne to his sons, and France would have rejoiced.

He returned the star to its box and the bottom drawer again. He quietly bowed his head and wished Hornblower success.

The Russian port of Sevastopol was enjoying a cool evening breeze on this late summer evening. Captain Dimitri Eduardovich Baranov stood on the quarterdeck of his 44-gun frigate IRN *Brailov* and surveyed his surroundings. His own ship and the *Flora* were resupplied and ready for sea. But no orders had arrived. He was just beginning to allow himself to hope that nothing would come of that extraordinary meeting to which he had been summoned.

His chagrin was therefore understandable when he turned to see a court messenger boarding his ship with a packet in hand sealed with the tsar's personal seal.

He took the package to his cabin and opened it in private. Inside the envelope were three pages of neatly written text. Baranov skimmed them, then dropped the pages on the desk as though they were poison. He stared at them, wide-eyed and jaw hanging open. But the signature at the bottom of the last page was unmistakable.

Baranov reached out and picked up the orders again. He read them slowly, digesting them word by word before setting them down again and closing his eyes.

Baranov was ordered to take *Brailov* and *Flora* and patrol an area 100 to 200 miles north of the island of St. Helena. There he was to find and sink the French frigate *la Belle Poule,* and any escort ships accompanying the French frigate. Baranov was to use all resources at his disposal, including sacrificing his own ships, to prevent *la Belle Poule* from delivering the exhumed body of Napoleon Bonaparte to France. The closing paragraphs of his orders emphasized that there were to be no survivors from the French ship or its companion vessels. Any who survived the attack were to be cut down, without exception and without mercy. There were to be no witnesses.

Baranov tossed the orders on his desk and began to pace. He knew the tsar hated the French and detested their king, Louis-Philippe, as a weakling. Now this same king intended to welcome back to France the personification of the revolution that killed his uncle, the last true autocratic King of France.

Baranov frowned. The French king was France's problem. He did not like being ordered to murder people. Death in battle was one thing, but he was being ordered to gun down helpless survivors in the water or anywhere else they would be found. He was being ordered to turn his brilliant twenty-year naval career into that of a common pirate! The thought turned his stomach, to the point he thought he was going to be sick.

He went back to his desk and sat down. He picked up the orders and scanned them closely, looking desperately for a loophole he could exploit to save his career. A paragraph on page three said that intelligence reported that the British were sending Admiral Lord Horatio Hornblower to the exhumation as their official representative.

Baranov lowered the papers. Hornblower? Where had he heard that name? It sounded so familiar.... Of course! Riga. 1812. Baranov had been assigned to a sloop of war with the Baltic Fleet when Bonaparte invaded with a half-million soldiers. Many of the fleet's sailors were converted to infantry for the emergency. Hornblower had commanded a British squadron at the time, and his naval cannon fire was a great help in saving the city from the French and Prussian force that was approaching. Baranov sat up straight as he remembered Hornblower actually fighting on land. He had heard that the Englishman had been invalided home after contracting the plague during the fighting.

The Russian rubbed his chin. Hornblower's presence made his job much more difficult. A British admiral would almost certainly make the trip in a warship of some sort. A frigate at a minimum, and possibly a seventy-four. Whatever they sent, the British would not just stand by and allow him to attack and sink *la Belle Poule*. That meant he would have to fight and sink the British warship as well, killing its entire crew in order to fulfill his order of no witnesses.

The thought disgusted him. But what could he do? He had seen too many of his fellow officers simply disappear when they had disobeyed their orders. And now that he had seen these, he was certain he would not be allowed to live, should he decline the mission.

He turned and opened the drawer in the desk and withdrew a portrait of his wife and twin daughters, painted when the girls were very young. What would happen to them if he disappeared? Two tears fell onto the portrait, He carefully wiped them away before replacing it in the desk. He went to the door and passed the word for his first lieutenant, then returned to the desk to write out an invitation for Captain Filitov and his first lieutenant of the *Flora* to join him for supper.

The next night, as soon as it was dark, the two Russian frigates were warped out of Sebastopol harbor and disappeared over the horizon. They passed through the Dardanelles disguised as merchant ships. The British naval attaché in Constantinople paid them no attention, and the two ships disappeared into the Mediterranean Sea.

Alexandre Leclerc stood his watch as lookout in the fore tops of *la Belle Poule*, but his mind was not on his work. His mind was on the coded letter he'd received three days before they sailed. He was ordered to take every opportunity to prevent the remains of the Emperor from returning to France.

Leclerc looked out toward the horizon, lost in thought. For generations, his family had served the kings of France; one of his ancestors had been a musketeer during the reign of Louis XV. Of course, all that ended with the Revolution and the execution of Louis XVI and his queen. His grandfather and uncle lost their lives during the Terror. Alexander's young father was only spared by the fall of Robespierre, and he'd joined the navy as a way to avoid being drafted into the army. He'd acclimated well to naval life, although he never forgot to hate the Revolution and the Empire that followed it for what they did to his father and brother. He remained in the navy during the restoration, and his son followed in his footsteps. Alexander considered himself quietly but firmly in the camp of the Ultra-Royalists and worked for their cause whenever he could.

The letter had come as a surprise. Leclerc had not recognized the seal, but when he'd opened it and begun to read, the hairs on the back of his neck had stood on end. He's nearly fainted when he saw the signature of the duke of Angoulême at the bottom.

Leclerc leaned his back against the mast and looked out over the passing waves. At first glance, the chances of his carrying out the duke's wishes and living to tell about it were very slim. Even he knew the prince well enough to know that, no matter what his personal feelings, Joinville would carry out his orders to the best of his ability.

He closed his eyes, taking a slow, deep breath to calm his mind. It was a trick his father had taught him many years ago, and it usually worked. Soon his mind settled down, and he was able to enjoy the cool sea breeze on his face.

He opened his eyes. Unfortunatley, the first thought that crossed his calmed mind was that this assignment was, in all likelihood, a suicide mission. How could he possibly get close enough to the remains so as to destroy them completely without either the French or British killing him instantly in retaliation? A chill went down his spine, and in the back of his mind he heard his father's voice quietly chastising him for his cowardice. He felt the blush rise in his cheeks.

No, he thought, *I will not play the coward. If my life guarantees that a* true *son of the house of Bourbon sits on his ancestral throne, then it will be well spent. Thank you, Father.* He set his jaw and nodded to himself; problem one solved. Problem two was gaining access to the remains. That should be easy to fix—a word to his lieutenant should get him transferred to that detail. That only left problem three, which was the question of means. Many avenues were open to him here. He could plant a bomb in the chapel and set it off after the remains were aboard. He could also toss a bomb into the coffin as soon as it was opened. On the whole, he thought that his chances were better on board ship; that way he did not have to worry about transporting explosives to the grave site undetected.

Immediately, red flags went up in his mind. He remembered watching the ebony sarcophagus being loaded on the ship in Toulon. It was very solid and sturdy, and he had his doubts that a bomb exploding outside the sarcophagus would guarantee the destruction of the remains within. He gnawed on his bottom lip as he turned the problem over in his mind and came to the conclusion that he would need direct access to the remains themselves to guarantee their destruction. He also thought he remembered seeing a lock on the sarcophagus when it was being loaded; if that were so, it severely limited his options.

Leclerc sighed and closed his eyes again. Slowly, he withdrew the damnable letter from inside he shirt where he had secreted it. There was a tremor in his hand as he crushed the letter in his fist.

Leclerc sat at the table and ate his meal in sullen silence, ignoring his messmates as best he could. He stared blankly ahead, eating mechanically, his mind on other things.

He was not at all pleased. His attempts to be reassigned to the detail tasked with receiving the coffin had failed. That detail was limited to two men, due to the shortage of crew on this voyage. The new officer, Lieutenant Girot, was in charge, and his only help was a hand named Louis, an old man who had been in the navy all his life and was not much good for anything else. Leclerc dabbed the last of his bread in the leftover sauce and chewed it, wondering what to do. His mission became much more difficult if he could not get on that detail.

Leclerc drained the last of his grog. He wiped his mouth on his sleeve and frowned. There was no alternative; he had to get on that detail. For him to get on, something had to happen to Louis. But tough old birds like Louis didn't just roll over and die. Leclerc scowled and looked down at his empty tray. He hated the idea forming in his mind. He again heard the voice of his father in the back of his mind warning him against cowardice and urging him to do what he must to accomplish his mission.

His musings were shattered when his messmate, seated next to him, shoved him into the bulkhead, and he became aware of uproarious laughter going on all around him. Leclerc rebounded off the bulkhead and knocked the man to the deck with a single backhanded blow. He stood over the man, his eyes blinking back his rage and his mind only now realizing what he had done. He looked around at his messmates, half of them standing, all of them staring at him and wondering what had gotten into him. "Just leave me alone," he said, and he left the mess.

Hornblower came on deck to watch the gunnery practice; afterwards he complimented the crews on their speed of reload and accuracy of fire. As the exercise broke up and the crews were securing the guns, he turned to Brewer.

"We shall be passing near the Canary Islands, will we not?" he asked.

"Aye, my lord," Brewer replied.

"I would like to stop over at Tenerife, if you please."

"Of course, my lord," Brewer said. He paused to see if any

explanation was forthcoming, and hurried on when none came. "I shall give the orders immediately. Please excuse me." He touched his hat and went to the wheel to give instructions for the course change to the quartermaster. He returned to the admiral minutes later.

"We shall arrive at Tenerife the day after tomorrow if this wind holds, my lord," he said.

"Thank you, Captain. I wish to do a little shopping before we head farther south. I am also hoping to meet up with someone."

Brewer wanted badly to know who that someone was, but he stood silent, hands behind his back, biting his tongue.

It was six bells of the afternoon watch when HMS *Iris* slid into the harbor at Tenerife. Ships crowded the harbor, and Brewer turned to Hornblower, who was standing next to him. "If it pleases your lordship," he said formally, "I can send Alfred and Mac ashore with your shopping list."

Hornblower glanced at his captain, catching the tone beneath his statement and ignoring it. "That will do nicely, Captain," he said. "I gave Alfred the list and my purse yesterday."

Brewer blinked at that. "Aye, sir. I shall see to it at once." After he turned away, Hornblower smiled.

"Captain," he said, "please pass the word to your lookouts. I want to know about any warships in the harbor."

"Aye, my lord. Anyone in particular?"

"French."

Brewer turned at that. He nodded, understanding now. He quickly passed the word to the lookouts, and a message came back of two French ships across the harbor. Brewer and Hornblower went to the rail and raised telescopes to their eyes for a closer look.

"The small one off to the left looks like a sloop," Brewer said.

"Yes, Hornblower agreed, "but I believe the French call them *corvettes*."

"Look to the right, my lord," Brewer said.

To the right was the largest frigate Brewer had ever seen. He had heard of the French building sixty-gun frigates armed with 80-pounder Paixhans guns; this must be one of them.

"She's huge, my lord!" he said. "More than 300 feet longer than *Iris* at a guess, and two or three times our displacement."

Hornblower lowered his glass and thought for a moment. "Captain, send the third lieutenant in a boat to that frigate. I shall write out a note for him to deliver. Excuse me."

He handed his glass to a midshipman and went below. Brewer passed the word for Mr. Cooksley and ordered the launch to be readied. Fifteen minutes later, Hornblower reappeared and handed a sealed note to Cooksley.

"My orders are for you to hand this directly to the captain of the French frigate," he said.

Cooksley saluted. "Aye, sir!"

He went forward and over the side. Brewer and Hornblower watched the boat pull away.

"My lord," Brewer asked, "who is on that frigate?"

"The Prince de Joinville," Hornblower replied. "Third son of King Louis-Philippe of France, and captain of that frigate we are admiring. That is the man and the ship sent to transport the Emperor's remains back to France."

Brewer turned to watch the launch navigate its way through the crowded harbor. "I see."

"Captain," Hornblower said, "join me for a drink while we await Mr. Cooksley's return."

The two men retreated below to the day cabin. Brewer was pleased to find a decanter of dark liquid and two glasses waiting for them.

Hornblower indicated the decanter. "Captain, if you would care to do the honors?"

Brewer filled the glasses and took one to Hornblower. He sat down and lifted his glass to his friend. Hornblower returned the gesture, and both men drank.

"Excellent, my lord," Brewer said as he held out the glass for inspection.

"A gift from my brother-in-law, the duke," Hornblower replied. "I have been saving it for a special occasion. William, I asked you to divert here for the specific reason that I hoped to find Joinville. I very much would like to talk to him before we arrive at St. Helena."

"Hence the note?" asked Brewer.

Hornblower nodded. "A request for an interview with his highness in my capacity as the official representative of the British government."

Brewer nodded thoughtfully and took another swallow.

One hour and twenty minutes later, Mr. Cooksley was admitted to the cabin by the sentry. He handed Hornblower a note, which the admiral a promptly opened and read.

"Well, well!" he said. "They are sending a boat to take me to the prince."

Admiral Lord Horatio Hornblower sat in the stern sheets of *la Belle Poule's* launch and wondered what he would discover when he stepped aboard the prince's ship. In what aspect would de Joinville receive him? The Captain or the prince? Hornblower strongly suspected the latter. Not that the idea bothered him; he'd been face to face with the Queen of England, the Tsar of all the Russias, and the Emperor of the French, so the prospect of meeting with a French prince did not overly concern him. The prince's age, however, was another matter.

The launch slowed as it approached the frigate, and Hornblower took advantage of the opportunity to study the ship. She was painted black throughout, a very unusual paint scheme for a warship and due, no doubt, to the nature of her current commission. He looked the hull over and decided that Brewer's estimate of her size was pretty accurate, but a closer inspection revealed that she had been extensively modified prior to leaving port. He could not be sure, but it looked as though the modifications had cost the ship most of her armament. Hornblower frowned; if the modifications had indeed cost the ship her guns, she would be vulnerable to attack on the voyage home.

He made his way confidently up the entry way and stepped out on the deck. The reception was one fitting a lord. An officer stepped up, and saluted.

"Admiral Lord Hornblower?" he said. "I am Colonel Hernoux, aide-de-camp to His Royal Highness. Welcome aboard *la Belle Poule*. Would you be so kind as to come with me? The prince awaits us in his quarters."

"Of course." Hornblower bowed and followed the Colonel to the prince's day cabin where a sentry admitted them. Hornblower was astonished by the size of the room—nearly as big as those on first-rates in the Royal Navy In the center of the room stood a young man who could only be his host, the Prince de Joinville. The prince was taller than he by an inch, standing fully six feet three inches when he did not slouch, and possessing a thin build. His hair was neatly combed, his face clean-shaven but for a trim moustache. He had dark eyes set wide apart, and Hornblower could see intelligence in them that gave credence to reports that the prince had not attained rank solely through nepotism. He knew his job.

"Admiral Lord Horatio Hornblower," Hernoux said, "may I introduce to you His Royal Highness, François d'Orléans, Prince de Joinville."

Hornblower bowed. "An honor, Your Highness."

Hernoux turned to his prince. "Your Highness, may I introduce Admiral Lord Horatio Hornblower, Official Representative of Queen Victoria and the government of Great Britain."

The prince bowed. "Lord Hornblower."

There was a gathering of men standing in the corner of the room; obviously they were waiting for a signal before coming forward. The Colonel gestured towards them. "If you will allow me, my lord, I shall present some of the dignitaries who accompany us to St. Helena. First, here is Captain Guyet, in command of the corvette, *la Favorite*. This is Philippe de Rohan-Chabot, commissioned by Minister Thiers to superintend the exhumation operations. You may remember Generals Bertrand and Gourgaud, who were with the Emperor on St. Helena. And this," he said, motioning to the final person, "is Emmanuel de las Cases, who, along with his father, also attended the Emperor."

Hornblower greeted each man in turn, until he got to Las Cases. This was the boy whose illness forced his father to take him back to France. How many times had Bonaparte rued that cruel twist of fate! He nodded to the lad and turned back to the prince.

"Your Highness," he said formally, "I thank you for taking time to speak to me."

"The King my father is grateful," Joinville answered just as formally, "that you have consented to attend the ceremony, Lord Hornblower. I have heard of your adventures, both during the wars and afterward, and am honored to make your acquaintance." He turned to the onlookers. "Excuse us, if you please. Lord Hornblower and I have much to discuss. Never fear, I shall ask him to make time to speak to each of you once we arrive at our destination."

The group bowed to the prince and made their way out. Once the sentry closed the door behind them, the prince visibly relaxed. Only Hornblower, Hernoux, Guyet, and the prince remained.

"Hernoux," he said. "some wine for our guest. Admiral, you must forgive the entourage, but when they heard you were coming aboard to speak with me, they begged the favor of meeting you. But for Chabot, each has a personal connection to Bonaparte. I hope you can make some time for them once we reach St. Helena."

"Of course, Your Highness. Thank you," he said, as Hernoux handed him a glass of wine. "Your Highness, I cannot tell you how pleased I was when I heard of this magnanimous gesture by your king."

Joinville smiled, but it was a smile with no joy behind it; a political trick or a habit picked up at court. "Yes," the young prince said. "My father says the time was right to bring Bonaparte home."

"I quite agree. And I presume you are ready, in case either the Ultra-Royalists or the Bonapartists attempt to disrupt your mission?"

Joinville's expression grew sardonic. "Yes, we are ready."

Hornblower would have like to press for specifics, but forbore. He was here as an ambassador, not a military advisor. "This wine is excellent, Your Highness. May I invite you and your companions to HMS *Iris* to dine with Captain Brewer and myself? Say tomorrow, at noon? We can then coordinate what will happen on St. Helena."

De Joinville glanced at his companions before replying, "I accept, Admiral." He rose, and the others followed suit. "And now forgive me, but there are matters that require my attention. Colonel Hernoux will see you to the boat."

Hornblower bowed. "Thank you again for receiving me, Your Highness."

After Hernoux led the Englishman from the cabin, the prince looked to his companion. "Well, Guyet? What do you think?

The Frenchman shrugged. "We must remember that this man was governor of St. Helena and was said to be on good terms with Bonaparte. It has been reported by several who were in a position to know at the time that Hornblower did not cower before Bonaparte. He stood nose-to-nose with the Corsican and did not back down."

The prince nodded slowly as he drained his drink and considered. Perhaps he would be wise not to dismiss the Englishman out of hand. He, too, had heard of Lord Hornblower's reputation, but he had not taken it seriously before tonight. Now, after meeting him, the prince had no doubts that the reputation was earned. There are something about the man, a sense that he was one of the men who genuinely earn the respect the are accorded. De Joinville smiled to himself; suddenly, he was very glad he had accepted his lordship's invitation.

The forenoon watch the next morning saw a flurry of activity aboard HMS *Iris*. Captain Brewer and his first lieutenant made sure all was in readiness to receive the Prince de Joinville. Lord Hornblower was present to receive the prince and Colonel Hernoux when they stepped up on the deck.

"How good it is to see you again, Your Highness," he said

cheerfully. "May I present to you William Brewer, Captain of HMS *Iris*, and his first officer, Lieutenant Dean."

The prince returned the officers' salutes. "In the name of my father, King Louis-Philippe of France, I thank you for this invitation to your fine ship, and also for your participation in this great adventure."

"We are honored by your royal father's invitation," Hornblower replied, "as we are by your presence aboard our ship, Your Highness. If you will follow me, we shall retreat below."

Hornblower led his visitors below deck and aft to finally settle in the day cabin. Alfred appeared, carrying a silver platter with four glasses filled with the Admiral's best Madeira. Hornblower raised his glass.

"Gentlemen, a toast. To Queen Victoria and King Louis-Philippe! May they reign long and do great things for our respective countries!"

"Here! Here!" rang around the room. Hornblower and the prince sat on the settee, while Brewer and Hernoux took the chairs placed opposite.

The prince turned to his host. "My lord, I thank you for this invitation. It seems a much more... *private* setting than we had aboard *la Belle Poule*."

Hornblower smiled. "I thought the matters we had to discuss would be better done in private, Your Highness."

"And you are correct." De Joinville drank from his glass and set it down.

"I believe you are aware of the circumstances of my appointment?" Hornblower asked.

"I am."

"Then you must be aware that someone in your government or mine—or both—has grave concerns that you will be able to fulfill your mission."

"Sir!" Hernoux exclaimed. "Are you saying that His Royal Highness is incompetent?" His hand actually reached for the sword that was not, perhaps fortunately, at his side.

Hornblower raised a quelling hand. "Gentlemen, allow me to make one point perfectly clear," he said in low, authoritative tone. "With all due respect to His Highness, we do not have time to waste on distractions or pleasantries. Shall we dispense with the posturing as well? Nothing that will be said today is meant to impugn anyone's honor or service. Hard questions will need to be asked and answered—most likely by both sides—before we reach St. Helena, if we are all to survive this adventure, and today is most likely the only chance we shall have to discuss them."

"I agree," said the prince. He rose and went to the side table where Alfred had left the decanter of Madeira and refilled his glass. He brought the decanter back with him and refilled the other glasses before returning it and resuming his seat. "Ask your questions, and then I shall ask mine."

"How much of your armament did you lose due to the modifications made to your ship?"

De Joinville looked to Hernoux and nodded once. When the Colonel remained silent, the prince shot him a look that needed no interpretation.

"We lost forty-four of our sixty guns," he said in a low voice. "We have only fourteen 30-pounder carronades distributed on our forecastle and quarterdeck."

"I see," Hornblower said. He took a drink and looked to the prince. "And who do you and your government see as the greater threat to our success, the Ultra-Royalists or the Bonapartists?"

De Joinville smiled. "For whom shall I answer? For my government or myself? I fear the answers may be very different."

"I should like to hear your thoughts."

"Very well. The Ultra-Royalists would no doubt like to see my ship and Bonaparte's remains at the bottom of the Atlantic Ocean, but they fear the Paris mob almost as much as my father does. The events of 1789 are burned into the memories of all who survived them. The Bonapartists, on the other hand, will most likely try to take advantage of the Emperor's return. They are less likely to disrupt the return, although they may attempt to exploit it.

"But there is also this: it is not outside the realm of possibility for The Pretender to order his uncle's remains destroyed, in order to create an excuse to go to war, as it were, with the Ultra-Royalists."

Hornblower nodded slowly. "I fully expect one or the other of our adversaries, perhaps *both*, to make an attempt at disrupting your mission. To my mind, they are most likely to act either at the opening of the grave itself, or during our return voyage to France. I consider the latter scenario more plausible, if only due to the presence of the British garrison of St. Helena at the exhumation ceremonies."

"But where would either the Ultra-Royalists or the Bonapartists get a ship to sink us during our voyage home?" Hernoux asked.

"Ships," de Joinville said. "One ship could not guarantee success."

"I agree," Hornblower said. He picked his glass and drained it in a single draught. "I know of nowhere that the Bonapartists could obtain the ships necessary. The Ultra-Royalists, however, do have an ally to whom they could turn."

"The Tsar." It was the prince who whispered the words.

"Yes," Hornblower replied. "Nicholas is the one man in Europe with both the ships available and the autocratic nature to order the deaths of everyone aboard."

"So what can we do?" Brewer asked. "We cannot sink approaching Russian ships on sight."

"No," Hornblower said. "We are not at war with the Tsar, and I am sure that the Queen would wish me to keep it that way. No, we shall have to try to avoid the Russians during our voyage back to France. Perhaps we might make a detour by way of the Caribbean?"

The prince shrugged. "Perhaps."

Hornblower set his empty glass down and turned to his guest. "Forgive me, Your Highness, but you do not seem overly concerned."

De Joinville turned and looked at his host, and the look in his eyes told Hornblower that his guest was not bored but overwhelmed by the feeling that he was being forced to do something very much against his personal wishes.

"What would you have me say?" he asked. "My father bends to the demands of the mob and orders the return to France of my uncle's murderer. On top of that, he orders my ship, the finest frigate in the French navy, stripped of her arms in order to be turned into a giant funeral barge, complete with staterooms for the mourners."

"Bonaparte did not murder your uncle," Hornblower said.

"Perhaps not with his own hand," de Joinville said quietly. "But the Revolution murdered Louis XVI, and the Revolution made Bonaparte."

Hornblower looked hard at his guest. "With all due respect," he said, slowly and deliberately, "I need to know, will you carry out your mission to the best of your abilities, regardless of your personal feelings in this matter?"

De Joinville's face became a mask, hardened by his royal upbringing and devotion to his duty.

"Yes," he said. "I will do my duty."

"I was hoping you would say that," Hornblower said, with a hint of a smile at the corner of his mouth.

Joinville smiled as well. He was about to say something when he was interrupted by the appearance of Alfred in the doorway to announce that dinner was ready. The four men rose, and Hornblower led them to the table. Mac and the stewards brought out soup for the first course, followed by platters of roast duck and mutton chops, bowls of carrots and peas, freshly baked bread and a pudding. The prince eyed the service.

"I confess," he said, as he helped himself to the carrots, "I am disappointed in the fare. I had hoped to be served the same feast you served Alexander."

Hornblower looked up and laughed. "Oh, you have heard that story, have you? I must admit, the Tsar was a good sport about it; he ate ship's fare without any complaint." He paused to select a slice of bread. "I don't imagine he changed the menu at the palace to include ship's biscuit."

Hernoux asked Hornblower about his experiences in Russia, and the admiral told them of the fighting during the siege of Riga. The food disappeared as the conversation went on; the chops seemed to draw particular attention, Hornblower and the prince going so far as to use the last of the bread to sop up the gravy that remained on the platter. Alfred and his stewards cleared the table, and Mac returned to refill their glasses. The prince took a sip and looked at Hornblower over his glass.

"A question," he said, "if I may. It is my understanding that you were sent to St. Helena as governor to control Bonaparte. You were expected to bring him to heel?"

Hornblower's eyes met those of his guest. "My instructions were to find a way to deal with him in the hopes that he would behave."

"And were you successful?" Hernoux asked.

"Yes," Hornblower said, "I believe we were. Wouldn't you agree, Captain?"

The Frenchmen turned to Brewer, who raised his glass in agreement. "I would indeed, my lord."

"Ah, yes." Joinville turned to Brewer. "I had forgotten that you were there as well, Captain. Tell me, what was your opinion of your prisoner?"

Brewer hesitated and looked to Hornblower. The admiral smiled and shrugged. Brewer answered with his eyes and turned back to the prince.

"Your Highness," he said, "I think Bonaparte is the greatest tragedy in European history."

"Really? How so?"

"Well," Brewer sat forward and rested his forearm on the table, "look at all the good things he did for France."

Hernoux spoke up. "France suffered nearly six million dead from his wars."

"And that is part of the tragedy. For all his inarguable brilliance, both military and administrative, he never knew when to quit. He did not want to join the ranks of European rulers, he wanted to conquer them, to dominate them and break them to his will. In doing so, he doomed the entire continent to wars of extermination that would only end when he was gone or they were."

Joinville nodded thoughtfully. "And if he had stopped?"

Brewer looked him in the eye. "He or his descendants would still be ruling France, and France would be far more prosperous than it is today."

Hornblower watched the exchange with interest, hiding his smile behind his glass. Hernoux sat back, astonished that anyone would speak thus to a Prince of France. For his part, de Joinville listened without comment, his face polite and attentive throughout. When Brewer finished, the prince pursed his lips as he considered what he'd heard. "Possible," he said quietly. "What you say sounds quite possible."

He looked to Hornblower. "I once met Clausewitz during a state visit to Berlin. I was representing my father at some function or other at the Prussian court. I had a chance to sit with him for well over an hour one afternoon, and that is where I learned of your tenure as governor. He also told me of your aid during the siege of Riga, which is where I learned that you had entertained the tsar aboard your ship. Clausewitz told me of your treatment of Bonaparte, how you stood before him without cowering or wavering, and how you did what you could to improve his living conditions. On behalf of France, or at least the millions of peasants who still love him to this day, I thank you for that." He turned to Brewer. "There are times, Captain, when I, too, wish the Emperor could have turned against his own nature and made decisions based on the welfare of France rather than his own ambition. During those times, I, too, wonder what France could have been, had Bonaparte left war and turned his mind and his energies to the development of his adopted country."

"My Prince!" Hernoux exclaimed.

De Joinville laughed. "Do I shock you, dear Hernoux? Do you think I speak treason? No, I merely indulge in some harmless dreaming, as his lordship and the good Captain surely know."

"And what will you do when you are king, Your Highness?" Hornblower asked.

The prince laughed and leaned back in his chair. "I am afraid we shall never know the answer to that question. To begin with, I am my father's third son, and by way of conclusion..." his face darkened and all traces of mirth left his face, "I do not expect my father to last long enough to hand down the crown."

Hornblower looked to Hernoux, who was silent and looking at the deck below him. Obviously, this was a topic they had discussed before.

"You expect your father to be overthrown?" Brewer whispered, shocked.

"Sadly, yes," de Joinville said quietly. "My father bends to the will of the mob like the willow to the wind. Now he brings back to France the one personage whose standard as a ruler —and I am not even speaking of warfare, Captain—he could never hope to equal. No, I fear the next time the mob exerts its will, it will be to depose my father and proclaim a republic. I can only hope we will be allowed to leave the country and live as émigrés in England, rather than be guillotined in the streets."

Hornblower tapped the table with his fingertip. "If you expect your father to be overthrown, what do you think would happen if the Ultra-Royalists regained the throne?"

De Joinville smiled, a sad, terrible smile. "If the duke of Angoulême ever ascended to the throne, my prediction would be that within two years he would suffer Louis XVI's fate." The prince looked at each of them in turn, leaving no doubt as to what he thought of Angoulême.

"You have asked your hard questions," he said. "Now I wish to ask you a hard question."

"By all means, Your Highness."

"Will the British fight to protect *la Belle Poule* and Bonaparte's remains if the Russians do appear?"

Hornblower looked briefly to Brewer before meeting the prince's eyes again. "Yes, Your Highness. If the Russians attack, HMS *Iris* will fight."

"I thank you."

Hornblower saw the prince visibly relax at his promise. "So," he said, "when do you sail?"

"We shall be here another two days. There is a little celebration tomorrow night, a ball to be held in my honor. Would you care to attend?"

Hornblower smiled. "A gracious invitation, Your Highness, but we sail on the morning tide. My entire purpose in diverting here was to have the opportunity to speak privately with you before we arrived at St. Helena."

"I would not be in too great a hurry, were I you. From here, we go to Bahia for fifteen days of balls and festivities before finally heading for St. Helena."

"I see," Hornblower said, then he smiled. "Oh, to be young again!"

The prince rose, and everyone else followed. "Lord Hornblower, Captain Brewer, I know I speak for Colonel Hernoux when I thank you for your hospitality and the enlightening conversation. I look forward to seeing you again when we reach St. Helena. I bid you good day."

Hornblower bowed. "Thank you for coming, Your Highness. Captain Brewer will show you to your boat. Colonel, a pleasure to see you again."

Brewer led their guests out and returned a few minutes later to find his mentor seated on the settee with his arms crossed over his chest and his brows drawn in thought. "My lord?" he said. "Shall I leave you?"

"What?" Hornblower said, shaken from his musings. "No, Captain, not at all. In fact, I'd be obliged to you if you could coax two cups of coffee from that coxswain of yours. We have much to discuss. Tell me, what did you think of the prince?"

Brewer ordered the coffee and returned to sit beside the Admiral. "I don't know exactly, my lord. He is hard for me to read."

"I know what you mean," Hornblower agreed. "I get the impression that his independence extends beyond his opinion of his father's future. According to the Admiralty, de Joinville is considered a competent naval officer."

Brewer stirred. "Pardon me, my lord, but it seems as though the prince knows he himself will most likely never be king, so he does not care about it one whit."

Hornblower considered for a moment before answering, to allow Alfred to deliver his coffee. He picked up his cup and raised it in salute. "William, I believe you are exactly right."

CHAPTER 10

Later, when he was alone at his desk, Hornblower paused while trying to write his report to send to London before they sailed. He set the pen down and frowned. Why was this report giving him so much trouble? Was the Prince de Joinville that hard to put into words? Hornblower shook his head. *The real question,* he realized, *is who will read this report?* He had to be careful what he put down on paper; if Palmerston got hold of it—and Hornblower thought this entirely possible, especially with this Egyptian business going on—he might feel compelled to show it to the queen. Hornblower rested his elbow on the arm of his chair and stroked his chin as he thought. No, it would be best to send a bare-bones report, stating that the prince was aware of the potential dangers on the return trip and that they would most likely return to France in company, by way of the Caribbean.

He picked up his pen and completed his report in short order. When he was done, he folded the report neatly and sealed it with wax. He stretched for a moment before pulling out his watch—the gold pocket watch that had been a gift from Barbara on the occasion of their twentieth wedding anniversary, reputed to be the most accurate timepiece then in existence. He set it on the desk and pulled out a fresh sheet of paper. He was determined not to miss a chance to write Barbara a letter.

Louis stood at the fantail of *la Belle Poule*, enjoying the solitude and the cool sea breeze. Three bells sounded in the middle watch, and Tenerife was far below the horizon. It was the middle of the night, and the deck was practically deserted. Louis liked it that way.

He cherished this time when he could be alone with his thoughts. Normally, the solitude and soothing rhythm of the waves of the ship's wake had a calming effect on him, but tonight nothing helped. His mind was full of thoughts of the Emperor's return and the part he would personally get to play in it. It also brought back many memories. Louis leaned against the rail and folded his arms across his chest. His chin dropped to his chest, his eyes closed.

Louis was a very old man for a sailor, and he had been in the French navy for nearly fifty years. In all those years, the voyage he remembered most had been in the fall of 1799 when he was a ten-year-old ship's boy on the frigate *Muiron*, assigned to the Mediterranean Fleet protecting General Bonaparte's Egyptian expeditionary force. His ship had escaped damage in the Battle of the Nile, in which Nelson had effectively destroyed the French fleet. Louis still remembered the explosion of the French flagship *L' Orient*. He tilted his head back and looked at the stars, and the memories came

It had been the latter part of August when *Muiron*, along with three other ships, received orders to moor by the shore as night fell. The crew worked furiously through the night to prepare the ship for sea. Supplies were brought aboard and stowed—Louis only realized much later that they were probably looted from the surviving ships of the squadron. He remembered the captain and first lieutenant huddled together on the quarterdeck in quiet conversation; he could still see the worried face of the captain. Just before dawn, Louis discovered the cause of the captain's distress. General Bonaparte himself had come on board, and the ship set sail for France. The biggest surprise of all happened when the captain summoned Louis to his quarters. He was ushered into the day cabin to find the captain and first lieutenant having wine with General Bonaparte and his aide. The captain introduced him to the general and informed him that he was assigned as the general's servant for the duration of the voyage.

The general had leaned forward and called to him. He had approached nervously until he stood before the great general, and Bonaparte had reached out and tweaked his ear as a gesture of good will. He'd smiled.

Then Bonaparte had said, "The lieutenant tells me you are from Corsica."

"Oui, mon Général."

"And what is the name of your village?"

"Ajaccio, mon Général."

Bonaparte smiled. "That is my village as well, little one. We shall talk more of home, eh?"

Louis bowed. *"Oui, mon Général."*

Louis spent nearly the entire voyage in Bonaparte's presence. In his cabin, which he insisted be in the gun room so as not to inconvenience the captain, Louis quickly learned to lay out the requested uniforms and to serve the general's needs efficiently. On deck, Louis was required to remain always within earshot, in case the general required anything. On the whole, Louis thought it was good duty, and he enjoyed his time in the general's service.

The voyage had lasted 41 days, during which the ship was forced by contrary winds to seek shelter in Ajaccio itself for several days. Bonaparte took advantage of the delay to take Louis ashore. They spent three days trooping through the hills around the city, visiting relatives and renewing old acquaintances. The lad noticed that everyone they met bowed to the general—with the sole exception of his mother. He asked the general about it later.

"Ah," Napoleon had said, touching the side of his nose with his forefinger as though he were sharing a secret, "no mother will bow to her child being a mere general, nor should she. But one day, perhaps... Yes, one day."

Louis smiled at the memory of the general's words, because he also remembered what had happened the first time the Emperor's mother was presented to him after his coronation. He held out his hand for her to kiss, as he had with everyone else in the reception line, only to have her swat him across the knuckles publicly with her fan. Louis chuckled and pushed off the rail. He turned and stared wistfully at the ship's wake.

Leclerc watched the old man from his place on the deck between two of the quarterdeck carronades. He had laid his plans carefully. He'd learned the old man's habits and had watched several nights, waiting for the ideal opportunity. This was it; the quarterdeck was deserted and Louis's back was turned. At his side, Leclerc had a shoulder bag weighed down with coal. He hefted it from the deck and crept aft. He moved swiftly and silently in his bare feet. He came up behind the old man, stunning him with a savage blow to the back of the neck. He put Louis's shoulder and neck through the strap of the coal bag and silently heaved the nearly-unconscious man over the side. He sprinted back to the quarterdeck carronade, so he could emerge from there again after the splash sounded. In mock concern he ran to the fantail and looked over the side. He was quickly joined by the officer of the watch, who happened to be Louis's lieutenant, Mr. Girot.

"What has happened?" Girot demanded.

"Not sure, sir," Leclerc lied. "I thought I heard a splash, but I don't see anything in the water."

Leclerc watched as the lieutenant looked over the side himself, before turning to scan the deck.

"Have you seen Louis?" he asked.

"Who, sir?"

"Louis! The old man who works with me. He usually comes up on deck in the middle of the night."

"No, sir," Leclerc deadpanned, "I haven't seen him tonight, but I was asleep over by the carronades. The splash woke me."

Girot became concerned. He looked over the side again before coming to a decision.

"Man overboard!" he cried. "Quartermaster, heave to! Inform the captain! Bosun, launch crew!"

The prince and Lieutenant Charner came up on deck.

"Report!" de Joinville said.

Girot saluted. "My Prince, we heard a loud splash. My assistant, Louis, is missing. He often stands alone at the fantail at this time of night. I believe it is possible he has fallen overboard. In accordance with standard protocol, I ordered the quartermaster to heave to and the bosun to put the launch over the side."

De Joinville nodded and looked over the fantail. "I don't see anything."

"Nor did I," Girot said. "But I thought it best to be sure."

"You did right, Mr. Girot," Charner said. "I will take the deck. Please go below and write your report."

Girot came to attention and saluted. "Aye, sir." He bowed

to the prince and went below.

Leclerc watched everything from his position between the carronades. All was proceeding better than he had hoped.

He stole below. He looked in to the gun room and found Lieutenant Girot at the table, hard at work on his report. He knocked and Girot looked up.

"Come in," he said. "You were on the deck. Excuse me, but I don't know your name."

"Leclerc, sir. Alexandre Leclerc."

"Come in, Leclerc. I am just working on my report for the prince. A search of the ship has turned up no trace of poor Louis. It must have been he who went overboard." Girot looked at the table miserably. "I did not see him in the water. I fear he is gone."

Leclerc felt unhappy over the pain and suffering he had caused, but his mission from the duke had to take precedence over his duty to the navy. Not that the realization helped.

"I'm sorry, sir." It was all he could say.

Three days later, Leclerc was summoned to the chapel. He forced himself not to run; he didn't want to seem eager, but he hoped he was about to take the next step in his plan. He entered the chapel and reported to Lt. Girot.

"Ah, yes, Mr. Leclerc. Thank you for coming. As you know, the prince has declared poor Louis lost at sea, so I need a new assistant to help me prepare to receive the Emperor's remains and care for them during their return to France. I am offering you the position."

Leclerc bowed his head to hide his smile. "I accept, sir."

IRN *Brailov* sailed through the darkness of the Mediterranean, still maintaining her disguise as a merchant vessel. Her current position was 150 miles south of Malta.

First Lieutenant Yuri Sominov had just given the order to change their course to NNW. Their ultimate destination, which Sominov alone among the crew knew, was the Straits of Gibraltar and the Atlantic Ocean. Not that it was hard to guess from their course, but silence was the order of the day.

With the new course set, Sominov went below to report. He knocked on the cabin door and entered. He found Captain Baranov sitting at the table with an empty cup before him. The bottle of vodka was half empty.

"Our course is now NNW, Captain," the first lieutenant reported.

For a long moment, Baranov did not move. Then, "Come, Yuri," he said. "Drink with me." He got up, found another cup, and returned to the table. "Sit!"

Baranov poured vodka, filling both cups, and then both men drank. Baranov rose and went to his desk; he brought back their orders and laid them before his first lieutenant.

"The time has come for you to know our orders, Yuri," he said as he sat down hard in his chair. He poured himself another drink as Sominov began to read. In Baranov's current state of inebriation, it was difficult not to laugh at the expressions that crossed the first lieutenant's face. The last look was one of utter disbelief.

"I, I do not understand, Captain," he stammered.

"Then read them again until you do. They are, after all, fairly straightforward. And definite."

Sominov shook his head. "That is not what I meant, Captain." He struggled to find the words to express his thoughts. He finally looked around the cabin before leaning in close to his captain and whispering, "Has the Tsar lost his mind?"

Baranov grunted. "You may well think so. Still, those are our orders."

"Did you show them to Captain Rossokovich when he came aboard during our passage through the Dardanelles?" Sominov asked, remembering the raised voices heard outside the cabin during the visit.

"Of course."

"What did he say?"

Baranov threw his hands in the air in exasperation. "What do you think he said? He likes it no more than I do. I believe his exact words were, *'So, now we are ordered to be open murderers?'*."

Sominov sat back, dumbfounded and confused. "What will we do?"

His captain laughed. It was not a cheerful sound. "What will we do, you ask? Our duty, Yuri! Never doubt that; we will do our duty." He shook his head. "But I find myself hoping they go home some different way, so we cannot find them."

HMS *Iris* sailed smartly under all plain sail on a southerly course, on which they skirted the African coast. Brewer had chosen this route because he hoped to encounter either pirates or slave ships bound for America. His crew was hoping for either prize money or head money during this voyage, something Brewer himself would not mind in the least. In fact, he had issued a standing challenge that whoever sighted a pirate or slaver that was taken and sold, the lucky tar would get £10 from the captain's own share. Nearly every daylight hour found the rails and shrouds crowded with off-duty seamen scanning the horizon.

Hornblower came up on deck to find a clear, late morning. He had finished his morning walk hours ago and returned to his cabin, where he wrote a letter to Barbara. Now he found the captain in conversation with Mr. Dean and the quartermaster.

"Good morning, my lord," Brewer said as he touched his hat at Hornblower's approach.

"Good morning, Captain. Gentlemen." Hornblower motioned toward the men in the shrouds. "I see your incentive is working, Captain."

Brewer shrugged. "It worked before, so I trust it will again. Besides, I seem to recall Captain Bush saying that you yourself employed a similar tactic on more than one occasion. Rather successfully, too, if I recall the stories correctly."

His lordship smiled. "True enough, although I never went as high as £10! Every whale you come across will be a slaver if you're not careful!"

The men laughed, and Brewer scanned the ship. True, the shrouds and rails were crowded, but it kept the men occupied. The captain knew that the number of slavers traveling to the Americas was nowhere near what it had been when he last patrolled these waters fifteen years ago, but there was still a chance of catching one and cashing in on the prize money. Plus, there were pirates rumored to prowl in these waters, and the chance of taking a pirate ship already full of treasure was not something anyone on board would let slip by. Brewer nodded to himself; yes, it was well worth £10.

He started to speak to Hornblower but was interrupted by a cry from the foremast shrouds, portside.

"I see something! I see something!"

Brewer went to the rail and saw that it was young Mr. Paddington, pointing wildly off the port bow. He was so excited that he would have dropped his glass to the deck below had it not been for the strap around his neck. The captain was about to head forward and remind his young midshipman about how to make a report when he saw that his first lieutenant was already on the way. He turned to Mr. Priestley and ordered an intercept course.

"Mister Paddington!" Dean yelled when he arrived on the scene. "What's the meaning of this? Do you have a report for me?"

Paddington nearly fell when he heard the first lieutenant's voice, but he managed to retain his grip on the shrouds. "Aye, sir!"

Dean stood below him, fists on his hips and a scowl on his face. "Well, make it then!"

"A ship, sir!"

"Where, Mr. Paddington?"

"Over there, sir!"

Dean sighed beneath his scowl. "Get down here, Mr. Paddington!"

The midshipman bounded to the deck and stood before the premier.

"What's this?" Dean said. "Stand to attention when you report to me, sir!"

The midshipman's eyes grew to saucers, and he came to attention.

"Now, then," Dean said in a calmer tone, "is that how you make a report, Mr. Paddington?"

The boy's eyes darted from side to side as he desperately tried to recall his training. "No, sir."

"Let's have a proper report, Mr. Paddington."

"Sir, I have sighted a sail off the port bow."

"Much better. Where away?"

"Over there, sir." The boy turned and pointed.

Dean decided that was the best he was going to get and thanked the midshipman. He went to the rail and put his glass to his eye. He quickly found the patch of white on the horizon. He lowered the telescope, turned to head aft, and nearly tripped over Mr. Paddington, still standing at attention.

"Well done, Mr. Paddington," Dean said. "You may return to your other duties."

"Thank you, sir!"

Dean headed to the quarterdeck and made his report to the captain. When he was done, he passed the word for Mr. Ford, the senior midshipman.

The young gentleman arrived and touched his hat. "You sent for me, sir?"

"Yes, Mr. Ford," Dean said quietly. He led the senior midshipman to a secluded spot by the aft rail to speak privately to him. "Did you happen to hear Mr. Paddington's outburst when he sighted that sail? One of your responsibilities is to educate the men under you in proper behavior aboard ship. From this moment on, Mr. Paddington and Mr. Youngblood are to get extra instruction. Get Mr. Cabot to help you; he'll be a senior midshipman soon enough, so you may as well teach him how to act as an instructor now. I don't *ever* want to hear anything like that from an officer on this ship again, Mr. Ford. Do you understand?"

"Aye, sir," Ford said. "I'm sorry, sir."

Dean stepped back. "Dismissed, Mr. Ford."

Ford came to attention and saluted. "Aye, sir." He spun on his heels and headed forward.

The premier watched him go forward and mentally kicked himself. He should have looked after Ford more closely. After all, this was his first ship as senior midshipman. *I should have kept a better eye on him,* Dean thought. *I'll have to watch for a good chance to compliment him in the next day or so. Hopefully, that will restore his spirits.*

Dean rejoined the captain near the wheel.

"Steady as you go, Mr. Priestley," Brewer said.

"Aye, sir."

Just then young Billy, the youngest and smallest of the ship's boys, came bounding up and skidded to a halt in front of the captain. He saluted before bending over to catch his breath.

"What is it, Billy?" Brewer asked.

The boy stood up, his chest still heaving. "Mr. Cooksley's respects, sir. 'E says to tell you the foremast lookout says that ship has seen us and is crowding on sail."

Brewer looked up from the boy to see Mr. Dean already at the rail with his glass to his eye. After a moment of study, he lowered the glass and nodded once in confirmation to his captain. Brewer looked down to the boy and smiled.

"My compliments to Mr. Cooksley and the lookout," he said. "Please tell them I said, 'Well done.'" The boy saluted and turned to go when Brewer stopped him. "And Billy," he said loudly for all to hear. "Good job."

The boy smiled from ear to ear. "Thank you, sir!"

"Mr. Priestley," Brewer said, "Alter course two points to starboard. Call the hands to make all sail."

"Aye, sir." The sailing master repeated the change of course to the quartermaster's mates at the wheel as he picked up a speaking-trumpet. In moments the hands were leaping skyward up the shrouds to loose every stitch of canvas HMS *Iris* carried.

Hornblower stood near the lee rail on the aft portion of the quarterdeck and watched everything. Memories flooded his mind of times he and Bush had played out a similar scene. His eyes followed the hands skyward, and he made a mental note to congratulate Captain Brewer later on the training of his men. He considered what he had seen so far a noteworthy achievement for a captain on his first cruise with a new frigate. He looked back at the deck in time to see the captain heading his direction.

"My apologies, my lord," Brewer said. "I did not mean to leave you unattended."

"Posh, Captain," Hornblower replied. "I am hardly some bureaucrat whom you need to entertain. This actually feels like coming home after a very long absence."

"Thank you, my lord," Brewer said. He nodded forward. "So? What do you think, my lord? Slaver, pirate, or something else?"

Hornblower shrugged. "Hard to say. She seems to be running like a slaver, but in these waters it could be anything. What are your plans?"

"I shall try to overtake her. Slavers are usually built for speed, but part of the reason HMS *Iris* and her class were only armed with 26 guns was to get more speed out of her. Excuse me, my lord."

He stepped over to the first lieutenant.

"Mr. Dean," he said, "you have the deck. I shall be in my cabin."

"Aye, sir."

Brewer stepped back to his mentor. "My lord, it shall be a while before we can hope to overtake, and then a hot meal may be hard to come by. Shall we see if Alfred has something good for our dinner?"

"A capital idea, Captain. Lead the way."

The two men retreated below deck to the cabin. The captain was about to call for Alfred when he turned and spotted the faithful servant in the pantry door.

"Ah, Alfred. There you are," he said. "We will be two for lunch. What do you have for us?"

"I have a pair of small albatrosses that I can stew for you, sir, along with some cauliflower and carrots and a pudding for dessert, if that is to your liking."

Brewer nodded enthusiastically; stewed albatross (at least the way Alfred made it) was one of his favorites. He turned to Hornblower.

"What say you, my lord?" he asked.

"That will suit very well."

"Good. That will be perfect, Alfred. May we have some wine, please? Thank you." Alfred brought two glasses, one of which he handed to Hornblower. "Shall we sit in the day cabin, my lord?"

The two men sat on the settee beneath the frigate's stern window and allowed the sunlight to warm their necks as they drank. Hornblower noticed that his companion was staring out into space.

"William?" he asked. "Something on your mind?"

His words startled Brewer out of his trance. The captain shrugged and took a drink to cover his embarrassment. When he saw that his friend was still looking at him attentively, he lowered his glass.

"My apologies, my lord," he said, "but there are times when, for no reason I can fathom, I will think about people. Friends, subordinates, fellow officers or crew who are gone now. Their faces appear in my mind, and I think about them for a moment."

"Are these men lost in the line of duty?"

"Some, but not all. Mostly they're just gone, as in not with me anymore. Just now I was thinking about Captain Bush and how I wish he were here to share this adventure with us. After all, he was there the first time, and I thought it would be fitting, were he with us this time as well."

Hornblower looked down at his glass. "I know what you

mean, William. I think every officer who serves any length of time has moments like that. I thought of Bush many times when I was in the Caribbean without him, and many more when we thought he was dead." He took a drink. "Who else do you think of?"

A reminiscent expression flitted across Brewer's face. "Mr. Sweeney seems to pop up fairly often. He was my sailing master on *Revenge* and *Phoebe*, my lord. He taught me a fair bit when I was new to the captaincy, and he did it without ever seeming to forget his place—that may not sound quite right, but I'm not sure how else to say it."

Hornblower nodded. "I know just what you mean, William. Go on."

Brewer sighed. "He had a manner about him, a way that he dealt with me, my lord, that is hard for me to describe even now. He could make suggestions or point out options and leave me to make my own decision." He looked to his mentor. "In fact, it was rather like the methods you and Captain Bush used on me."

Hornblower smiled and raised his glass in a there-you-go gesture.

Brewer's countenance saddened. "In fact, it was in these very waters, while we were with the West African Squadron, that he died. He caught a fever and died of it two weeks later. I felt like my left arm had been cut off."

Hornblower nodded and took a drink.

"Then there was Dr. Spinelli," Brewer said. "You may remember him from the Caribbean, my lord. In fact, he was the surgeon who saved Gerard's life at Gibraltar."

"Yes, I remember him. Quite a character, that one. What became of him?"

"He said he had enough and wanted to retire. He used some of his prize money to buy a practice in a little village not far outside of London, and he's quite happy. In fact, he stays with us when he travels to or from London. Elizabeth says he is still as gallant as he was when we married, although I have a hard time believing it."

"Don't," Hornblower laughed. "Unless he's changed dramatically, he has something up his sleeve."

"I still remember," Brewer said suddenly, "losing Benjamin. That was off Morocco in a battle with a pirate ship."

Hornblower lowered his glass. "Benjamin?"

"I'm sorry, my lord," Brewer said, "I was lost in thought. Benjamin Greene was my first lieutenant on *Revenge* and *Phoebe*. I never knew how much you valued Bush until Benjamin and I... well, he was my strong right arm. To lose him early in that voyage, and then Sweeney later on to the fever, I felt so... *alone*, I guess would have to be the word, although I know it may not seem to fit."

"No, no, William," Hornblower said, "it's the very word. I have heard every captain use it who has experienced what you went through."

"I must say, it affected me. If it hadn't been for Dr. Spinelli being on board, I don't know what I would have done."

Hornblower smiled. "Yes, we are fortunate to have men like that around when we need them most."

"Someone was there for you, then?" Brewer asked. "Bush?"

Hornblower looked at the empty glass in his hands. "I sailed for the Pacific in HMS *Lydia* not long after the deaths of my children, Horatio and Maria. Maria was inconsolable, and stayed with her mother. I threw myself into the mission and captaining the ship, but I felt lost. I did not realize until years later how Bush saw me through, whether bearing my angry outbursts or taking tasks off my hands or just standing there like the Rock of Gibraltar, but he brought me through. I only wish now that I had realized it then and thanked him. I tried to thank him, years later at Smallbridge, and do you know, *he pretended not to remember?* William, I tell you, I thank Providence for the day I met William Bush."

Brewer smiled and looked at his glass. Empty, just like he felt when he thought of Greene. He wondered again, as he had so many times over the past fifteen years, whether he'd ever find another like him.

Both men were relieved when Alfred stepped in and said that dinner was ready.

After the meal was over, both men went back on deck. They found Lieutenant Dean in conversation with Mr. Priestley. Both men saluted as the captain and the admiral approached.

"Report, Mr. Dean," the captain said.

"We're closing the gap, sir," Dean replied, "but not by much, and not very quickly. Mr. Priestley here thinks she may be one of the American clipper ships."

"Long and narrow," Brewer said, "and built for speed."

"Aye, sir," the first lieutenant said. "Too bad we can't get our hands on the *Black Joke*."

"Black Joke?" Hornblower asked.

It was Brewer who answered him. "HMS *Black Joke* is a legend to anyone who's served on the West African station, my lord. She was an American clipper ship that was sold to Brazil and turned into a slaver. She was captured by Commodore Collins in HMS *Sybille* in 1827 and taken into the navy. She was so fast that she could catch slavers who outran everything else the navy had. In 1828, she set a record when she captured the *Vengador* with 645 slaves aboard.

She was burned at Freetown in 1832 after it was determined she was rotting away."

Hornblower vaguely remembered reading of the ship's adventures in the newspapers back in Smallbridge. If that ship they were chasing was anything like *Black Joke*, they could be in for a long chase.

Brewer turned to Lieutenant Dean. "Mr. Dean, let's go forward."

Hornblower watched as the captain and first lieutenant headed forward. He considered for just a moment before following. He found them next to the long nines, glasses to their eyes.

"Ha-hm" Hornblower cleared his throat.

Brewer turned and offered him his glass. "We were just estimating our chances of catching up to our friend out there."

Hornblower accepted the glass and raised it to his eye. The image that came into focus was not quite hull-up on the horizon, but it looked like a mountain of sail over a narrow hull, meaning a ship built for speed. When he handed the glass back to the captain, the look on his face was grim. "Unless I miss my guess," he said, "you won't catch her. Not unless something happens on board that ship or her captain does something incredibly foolish."

Brewer raised the glass, seeking to confirm the admiral's opinion for himself.

"My lord," Dean asked, "is there no other way?"

Hornblower shook his head. "None. He is currently outside the range of the long nines, and we are not closing the gap fast enough to have him before nightfall. All he has to do is sail in a straight line until darkness, and then he can disappear."

Brewer frowned.

"Agreed," he said. He turned and touched his hat to Hornblower. "My lord," he said, and walked aft without another word.

The two officers watched him go, then Dean spoke.

"My lord," he said quietly, "I am almost ashamed to say it, but I still have not figured him out."

"Really?" Hornblower looked almost bemused. "I should think him fairly straightforward. This is your first voyage as a first lieutenant, is it not?"

"Yes, my lord," Dean said, still watching the captain. "But I feel I should know him better by now. At least be able to anticipate him to a degree."

"It takes time to get to know someone, Mr. Dean," Hornblower said, "and you simply haven't had the time. Familiarity of the sort you are describing can take years to develop, and several battles in order to become close. Step over here, if you please." He led the first lieutenant to the rail for a little privacy.

"Let me tell you some things about your captain; perhaps these will help you get the measure of the man. He hates to lose, and he hates to give up. When he first arrived in the Caribbean in 1820, his ship was ambushed by the pirate El Diabolito. He hunted down that pirate and killed him. He cares greatly for the lives of his crew. If they do their duty, he will go up against the devil himself to defend them. That being said, he expects every man jack of you to toe the line; he has no patience for drunkards or slackers."

"Had a good teacher, did he, my lord?" Dean asked.

Hornblower smiled. "He was my secretary on St. Helena, yes, but the man who first saw his potential and mentored him was his captain, William Bush. Yes, the same Bush who sailed with me during the wars. 'Twas he who saw something in your captain and recommended him to me for the post of secretary, and he who mentored and molded him during battles against the Barbary pirates in 1818."

Dean looked aft again. "Thank you for telling me, my lord."

"Mr. Dean," Hornblower said, "remember, your job is not to anticipate your captain. Your job is to be his first lieutenant. Do that well, and he will be pleased with you. After that, let what doors open that may."

Dean turned to Hornblower and touched his hat. "Thank you, my lord," he said, and headed aft.

The pursuit carried on throughout the afternoon with HMS *Iris* barely closing the gap. Hornblower stood off to the side on the quarterdeck and watched the captain as he alternated pacing and checking the gap. Hornblower smiled to himself, remembering many times that he acted out this same scene. He looked forward, to judge for himself, and shook his head ruefully. The dark would fall far too soon. He glanced at Brewer and could see by the look on his face that he had come to the same comclusion. He saw Brewer frown and look at the deck, as though his gaze alone would bore holes in the planking, and he remembered doing the same thing himself.

Hornblower debated about stepping over to his one-time protégé but decided against it, knowing how he himself would feel. Finally, after all these years, he realized what Bush must have gone through all those times, and he marveled at his first lieutenant's restraint. He resolved to speak to Bush about it when he returned, and he smiled as he tried to imagine his friend's face at the prospect.

He looked up to see the captain stepping in his direction, the frown still on his face. He stopped about a step or so away and slapped his thigh in frustration.

"Two hours till nightfall," Brewer said. "We're not going

to catch them."

"I wouldn't abandon the chase just yet," Hornblower tried to encourage him. "You never know what may happen."

Brewer looked up at him with eyes that could kill. Hornblower watched as the captain opened his mouth to scream at him, then he blinked and caught himself. He closed his mouth and looked down at the deck, his frustration and anger swallowed up by his embarrassment.

"I am sorry, my lord," he said quietly. "Forgive me."

Hornblower stood there for a moment, unsure of how to respond. In the end, he stepped forward and put his arm on the younger man's shoulder. He leaned in and spoke softly. "There is nothing to forgive, William," he said. "You've done nothing wrong. You behaved correctly, and I am proud of you."

Brewer looked up at him, the embarrassment still evident in those eyes that searched the face of his mentor. Slowly, a smile crawled over his face, and he nodded once in acknowledgement.

He looked at the deck again and gathered himself. He stood up straight and took a deep breath, exhaling slowly and allowing the air to drain his frustrations and carry them away. He looked at Hornblower. "Well, as you say, my lord, something may happen. And if it doesn't, we shall just have to help it out."

Hornblower passed the two hours till dark walking up and down the deck and speaking to the hands. To a man, he found them to be proud to serve, and even those on their first voyage fairly knowledgeable of their work, considering their time at sea. He met the gunner, one Mordecai Sweet by name, an older, grizzled hand who loved his guns as though each was a fine Swiss watch. Hornblower found him servicing one of the long nines at the bow, and he asked the gunner if he wouldn't rather have an 18-pounder or even a 24-pounder here in place of the venerable long nines.

"It would give you longer range and more hitting power," his lordship said.

But the gunner merely shook his head and affectionately rubbed the barrel of one of the bow chasers. "I'm sorry, my lord," he said, "but I have to disagree. It would be... well, the only likeness I can think of is that of replacing a sharpshooter's rifle with a blunderbuss."

Hornblower had never heard that comparison. "Do you really think so?"

"Aye, my lord, that I do." He thought for a moment, then said, "'Twould be like taking the scalpel away from the surgeon and giving him an axe instead."

The admiral actually blinked at that. "Well, Mr. Sweet," he said, "I should like some time to consider what you've said, and then perhaps we can speak again."

Sweet knuckled his forehead. "At yer service, yer lordship."

Hornblower made his way aft, arriving on the quarterdeck just as darkness was falling. He stopped a few feet from where the captain was speaking to his officers.

"Clear for action, Mr. Dean, and be ready to beat to quarters if our friend tries to turn and we have the chance to cut her off."

"Aye, sir." Dean went off to give the orders, and HMS *Iris* underwent the transformation to get her ready for combat.

"Steady as you go, Mr. Priestley," Brewer said.

"Aye, sir," came the reply.

Brewer turned and saw Hornblower standing there.

Hornblower nodded forward toward the chase. "May I ask what your plans are?"

"To be honest, my lord, I am still waiting to see if something is going to happen."

"And if it doesn't?"

The Captain smiled. "In that case, my lord, I have one or two things up my sleeve I want to try. Who knows? We may just get lucky."

Hornblower smiled, encouraged by his captain's confidence. The two men stood quietly as the darkness closed in and swallowed their ship. Word came down from the lookouts that the visual contact with the chase was lost. The other ship had gone dark, and Brewer ordered visible lanterns extinguished all over the ship. They continued on their course for about a half-hour, then Brewer turned to his sailing master.

"New course, Mr. Priestley," he said. "Due west."

"West, sir?" The Sailing Master was clearly puzzled. "Oh, aye, sir."

Brewer stood by the wheel until the compass showed their course as due west.

"Hold this course until further orders," he said. He turned to Hornblower. "My lord, I believe I missed supper. Would you like to join me, to see what the good Alfred has available?"

The admiral bowed. "I would indeed, Captain. Lead on."

Brewer turned to Mr. Dean. "Who is the officer of the watch?"

"That would be Mr. Jason, sir."

"He has the deck, then. I shall be in my cabin."

"Aye, sir."

Brewer led his mentor to the cabin below. The sentry closed the door behind them, and Brewer tossed his hat on his desk. He found Hornblower in the day cabin.

"Something to drink to start, my lord? Alfred!"

The diminutive servant appeared. "You called, sir?"

"Yes," Brewer said. "Wine, if you please. And Alfred, we seem to have missed supper. What can you do for us?"

"I can have ham, peas, and kidney pudding in a half-hour, sir. Less, if you want something cold."

Brewer looked to his lordship, who merely shrugged. "That will be fine, Alfred. Thank you."

"Yes, sir." Alfred bowed and withdrew, returning with two glasses of wine on his silver platter. The Captain thanked him again, and he withdrew to prepare their meal.

Hornblower turned and went to sit on the settee in the day cabin. HMS *Iris*, being a brand new ship, was furnished in a grander style than in Hornblower's day, and the settee was particularly comfortable. He sipped his wine and watched his friend. Brewer had been a one-time protégé, but that was more than twenty years ago. This was the first chance Hornblower had really had to study what he had become.

William Brewer's career was one that any officer would be proud to call his own. He had served on and successfully captained ships in the Mediterranean, the Caribbean, the South Atlantic, in the Caribbean again, and off the coast of West Africa. With the single notable exception of an incident off the American coastline in the 1820s, his record was unblemished. A rare occurrence, especially in the peacetime navy where many officers feel the need to try to 'supplement' their incomes by various means, most of which were not legal. Brewer seemed uncommonly successful at not only staying on the right side of the law, but also in earning either prize money from pirate ships or head money from capturing slavers bound for Caribbean or American waters. The Navy had become his family after his father had disowned him for joining up, and to Hornblower's knowledge, Brewer had not been home since. He had regularly written to his mother and sisters until their deaths, but his only letter to his father had gone unanswered. His mother had advised him not to write again, and Brewer hadn't.

Now the admiral watched as Brewer drank wine and stared into space.

"Something on your mind, William?" he asked.

Brewer grimaced. "Excuse me, my lord. No, I'm fine; just frustrated that we were unable to close the gap with that slaver."

"Do you think that's what it was?"

Brewer shrugged. "As you said, it ran like one. I'm positive that she'll try to lose us during the night; I wouldn't be surprised if she's already altered her course. My hope is to anticipate their moves and have us close enough to take her when the sun comes up."

"Ah, hence the change in direction. Where do you think she was heading?"

"America, based on her course when we first sighted her. Ships bound for Brazil usually head south before venturing into the Atlantic." He took a drink and frowned. "At least, they used to."

"Sounds reasonable," Hornblower admitted. "What are your plans?"

Brewer drained his glass. "After we eat, I will go on deck and reduce sail. My belief is that they will head southwest for several hours in order to lose us, before turning northeast or north-northeast in order to head for America. They may have to stop in the Caribbean for supplies if they travel too far out of the way."

After their meal, Brewer led the way back on deck and gave the order to reduce sail. Hornblower felt HMS *Iris* slow as the ship plowed through the darkness alone. As before, he stood off to the side on the quarterdeck, not wishing to intrude or appear to impose himself on the captain. He well remembered how he felt at times like this and how the last thing he wanted was company. He turned to look at the captain, standing not far behind the wheel in the center of the quarterdeck, eyes looking forward into the darkness. Hornblower could well imagine the captain's thoughts, how he hoped that the sun would rise to reveal their adversary close at hand. Hornblower knew, as he was sure Brewer did, that the odds were astronomically against such being the case, but it was either that or abandon the chase altogether.

Hornblower knew it is wasn't just the prize money for himself and the crew Brewer was after; the captain wanted his crew to benefit from working their hardest together. Furthermore, Hornblower suspected, he wanted to interrupt at least one more slave run. England had outlawed the slave trade as inhumane on March 25, 1807, prohibiting it throughout the British Empire. Britain could not shut down the African slave markets, which had been in existence for a thousand years or more. Nor could Britain dictate policy to the Americans. British captains could, however, interrupt the transportation of slaves in open waters.

Eight bells signaled the changing of the watch, and still the captain did not stir. Hornblower saw McCleary, the captain's coxswain, come up on deck. He spoke briefly to a crewman, his eyes on his captain the whole time, and then disappeared below deck. A few minutes later, he reappeared carrying a small table and two chairs, followed by Alfred carrying a tray with a pot of tea and two cups. The coxswain set up the table and chairs by the fantail and went to speak to his captain while Alfred deposited the tray on the table and went below. Brewer turned to see the table and nodded to McCleary. Brewer headed for the table while the coxswain stepped over to Hornblower.

"Begging yer pardon, my lord," he said as he knuckled his

forehead, "but the captain sends his respects and asks that you join him for a cup of tea."

Hornblower looked past the coxswain toward the captain standing at the fantail, gazing out over the ship's wake, and wondered whether he should accept.

"Thank you, Mr. McCleary," he said.

"Aye, sir." The coxswain could see the conflict on the admiral's face, but he simply saluted and went below.

Hornblower stepped over beside the captain and was not surprised when it took a moment for Brewer to notice him.

"Ah, there you are, my lord," the captain said. "Thank you for joining me." The two men sat, and Brewer poured the tea. "My lord, I apologize...."

"William," Hornblower said quietly, "you need not apologize. I've been there, as you well know, and I expect you to put the ship first."

Brewer looked down at his cup for a moment. "I don't know why, but it's different for me, having you aboard. I feel almost like we were back aboard *Defiant* again. I'm unsure of myself."

Hornblower smiled at the memory as he sipped his tea. Brewer had assumed command of one of the largest and most powerful frigates in His Majesty's navy after her captain had been washed overboard during a hurricane, then had captained the ship during operations against pirates operating out of the north coast of Cuba, including the capturing of the pirate Jean Lafitte and his ship. Brewer's performance had been good enough to justify Hornblower's purchase of the pirate ship for the navy, recommissioning it as HM Sloop *Revenge* and granting Brewer a promotion to the rank of Master and Commander.

"Is there something on your mind, William?" Hornblower asked. "Anything besides the chase, I mean?"

Brewer's cup stopped halfway to his lips, and he stared at his mentor for a moment before chuckling and setting the cup down.

"It's that obvious?" he asked. He shrugged. "Going back to St. Helena is certainly stirring memories, but I've also been aware of a voice in the back of mind that's been there for a while now."

"And what is that voice telling you?"

"That maybe it's time to retire." Brewer looked at his cup.

Hornblower observed his captain through the steam from his own cup and wondered what to say. He judged Brewer to be between forty-five and fifty years of age, still young enough to maintain a command at sea, especially with his record. The problem would come if he retired, then ever wanted to go to sea again; another ship might be hard to come by, especially he you did not have a patron at the Admiralty.

"We do not need the money," Brewer said. "Elizabeth has turned out to be a wizard at investing my prize money. We have more than enough now to last us the rest of our lives and then leave a decent inheritance to the children."

"What would you do?" Hornblower asked.

Brewer looked up. "Do?"

"Yes. What will you do to occupy your time?"

The captain was thoughtful, thens said, "Spend time with Elizabeth. Travel. I'd like to take her to Paris, to see Bonaparte's grave, after he is buried there."

"You know you and Elizabeth are always welcome at Smallbridge."

"My lord, you know how much Elizabeth loves Lady Barbara, but her heart is in London. I may well have to kidnap her for the trip to Paris."

Hornblower drained his tea and rose. "Well, I'm sure

you'll figure it out, William. Let me tell you this: you have done your duty for king and country. Should you decide to leave the service, you need feel no shame."

Brewer rose and bowed. "Thank you, my lord."

"I am going below to get some sleep. Good night, Captain."

Brewer touched his hat in salute. "Good night, my lord."

Hornblower went below, automatically turning aft and ducking his head against the low ceiling. He entered the cabin and removed his hat and coat. Alfred appeared in the pantry door.

"Do you desire anything, my lord?" he asked.

"Yes, Alfred," he said absently. "Wine, if you please."

"Yes, my lord." The diminutive servant withdrew, returning with a goblet filled with the admiral's favorite Madeira. Hornblower thanked him and went to sit on the settee. He missed Barbara, and desperately wished she were here with him. He trusted her insight and advice as he did no other these days, and now he found himself walking into unknown dangers without it. He sat back and rested his head on the settee for a moment.

This trip to St. Helena had him again remembering Bonaparte. Hornblower was thankful to have met the Corsican when he did. Had they met at any other time, the friendship they'd developed would never have been. The combination of Bonaparte's acceptance of exile, and the chance to dote on Hornblower's young son, had changed him, and he'd allowed Hornblower entry to a place in his heart where no man had been before. Had Bonaparte treated him like he had his predecessor, Hornblower felt certain he would have broken under the strain of Richard's illness and the departure that also took Barbara from him.

He took a drink and wondered what Bonaparte would say

about the consequences of his return to France. Hornblower could only smile as he pictured the expression of disgust on his friend's face when he found there was not a single Bonaparte capable of taking the throne. He wondered what Napoleon would think of his nephew. Hornblower was sure Bonaparte would distain the Pretender, but he had been known to put family over ability when he was Emperor, and it was just possible he would have done so again.

Hornblower rose and got ready for bed. He climbed into his cot—feeling a twinge of pride that he could still do so unassisted—and settled in for the night. He briefly toyed with the idea of skipping the exhumation itself, preferring to remember his friend as he was the last time he saw him. Hornblower had no idea what Bonaparte had looked like by the time of his death, more than three years after Hornblower left the island. And if his death really had been due to a cancer of the stomach as reported (the veracity of which Hornblower held in doubt), it was probable that he had been badly ravaged by the disease. Yet, as soon as he thought it, he felt a wave of guilt and embarrassment. Of course he would attend the exhumation; and he would fulfill his debt of honor by seeing his friend's remains safely returned to France.

He rolled over and considered what Bonaparte considered the two worst mistakes of his later reign (strangely enough, the Emperor never admitted the invasion of Russia to be a mistake): not installing his stepson, Eugene, as King of Sweden; and the failure to withdraw from Spain in 1813. Bonaparte had said h'd toyed with the idea of putting Eugene forth as a candidate for the Swedish throne when the Swedes asked his permission to speak to Bernadotte, but he had not followed through with the idea, allowing Sweden to join the coalition against him in 1814. With Eugene on the throne, Sweden would have been neutral at worst and an ally at best, either of which could have allowed him to escape Germany with his armies intact. He could have retreated across the Rhine, leaving Eugene's Swedes and 80,000 Frenchmen to guard the border, while he took the remaining forces to Spain, defeated Wellington's British army, and then withdrew from the country entirely, fortifying the Pyrenees to guard France's southern border. Bonaparte said he would have accepted the Allies' proposal of the "natural frontiers" and lived in peace, turning his remaining energies inward toward improving his country's industrial base and enriching its citizens.

Hornblower rolled onto his back and the cot swayed. He wondered, as good as those plans sounded, whether they would have been feasible. He had no doubt that the Bonaparte he knew, the Bonaparte of 1818, tempered by defeat and exile, could have succeeded, but what about the Bonaparte of 1813? Sadly, in 1813, Bonaparte still had faith in his star, that it would rescue him from his perils if he would only fight on. Even with Eugene and his Swedes on his side, he would still have attacked the Allies in Germany and left Spain to its own devices. Hornblower shook his head. What a waste.

He wondered whether Bonaparte had ever finished his memoirs. And if they had been finished, how truthful were they? He made a mental note to ask Gourgaud or Bertrand when he saw them on St. Helena.

As he closed his eyes in sleep, the last thing on his mind was the slaver they were chasing...

Alexandre Leclerc was hard at work cleaning the chapel. He paused and looked around, shaking his head in disbelief. *Never thought I'd be glad me ol' Dad was dead and gone,* he thought. *He'd have a fit if he knew I was preparing to take care of Bonaparte's bones.* He eyed the ebony sarcophagus.

Nah, Dad would be proud of me, he thought, *surely. Our family's name will go down in history as the avengers of Louis XVI and Marie Antoinette.*

He took a deep breath, reaffirming his commitment to the cause. He focused on the sarcophagus, looked around once more to make sure he was alone.

During the voyage south, he'd remembered hearing about a kind of delayed detonation device perfected by the Swedish chemist Immanuel Nobel. During his shore leave in Bahia, he'd been able to procure such a device from a local chemist's shop. It consisted of a glass vial containing sulfuric acid. When this was broken, the acid fell onto potassium chlorate, which would then ignite and cause the gunpowder surrounding it to explode.

He stepped behind the sarcophagus and knelt down. One of the first things he'd done after getting this job was to convince Lieutenant Girot to enclose the sarcophagus's base in a red velvet curtain. He parted it now and checked his handiwork. Working in strict secrecy over the past several days, Leclerc had modified the base of the sarcophagus to contain the device. His grandfather's hobby of woodworking, passed on over many summers of working the old man's farm, had come in handy. He'd carved a small niche in the base and secured the vial of acid next to it. When the sarcophagus was lifted from the stand, the niche would expand just enough to allow the vial to roll into it. When the sarcophagus was returned to the stand, the additional weight would break the vial open and set the acid free. Ten seconds later, according to Leclerc's calculations, the quantity of powder he would secure within the base just before their arrival at St. Helena would explode.

Leclerc sat back on his heels and admired the stark simplicity of the device. It was quite literally foolproof, always presuming it was not disturbed once it was set. He pulled the curtain closed and rose, looking around the room. All he had to do now was make sure the device was not discovered before the sarcophagus was lowered on to the pedestal, and this entire portion of the ship would be engulfed in a fireball that would incinerate the Emperor's remains.

Leclerc had spent most of the voyage to Bahia ingratiating himself with some of the hands working in the magazines. He'd found a royalist sympathizer in the starboard watch and went to work on the man's sensibilities. Several bottles of wine over the weeks of the voyage had won the man over, and Leclerc had been able to secure bags of gunpowder for his purpose. He'd transported them to the chapel, one or two at a time, usually late at night. During their stay at Bahia, he'd been able to reposition them while most of the crew were out on shore leave.

He stepped out from behind the sarcophagus and looked around again, this time to make sure the area was spotlessly clean. An idea struck him, and he looked toward his device and frowned. It would be activated when the sarcophagus was raised from the base. The vial would slide into its niche, and be broken when the sarcophagus was lowered on to its base again. The only danger was if the sarcophagus was lowered onto the base prematurely. He shrugged and left the chapel.

Hornblower opened his eyes and realized the sun was up. He got up and dressed hurriedly. He came out into the cabin to find Alfred waiting for him.

"I heard you moving about, my lord," he said. "Will you have breakfast?"

"Not just now, I think. Has Captain Brewer already gone up on deck?"

"Sir, I do not believe the captain came down last night."

"Really?" Hornblower grabbed his hat and headed for the door. "Alfred, please bring coffee for two up on deck."

"Aye, sir."

Hornblower stepped up on deck and stood at the top of the stairway. Mac was stationed on the lee rail, watching his captain, who was standing by the fantail. Hornblower could tell by the captain's face that Alfred had been correct. He walked over.

"Good morning, Captain," he said.

Brewer touched his hat automatically. "Good morning, my lord."

Hornblower nearly asked Brewer if he had been here all night but decided it would be insulting. Instead he stepped over to the table where they'd had tea the night before.

"Won't you join me for coffee, Captain? I asked Alfred to bring some up."

He could tell from the tensed reaction of his shoulders that Brewer was exhausted and short tempered. Obviously his plans had not borne the fruit he had hoped for. Hornblower pulled out a chair and sat, knowing that Brewer would be compelled by good manners to do so as well. Alfred's appearance on deck cinched the matter. Brewer took the other seat and accepted the cup Hornblower poured for him, looking up just long enough to say his thanks. The two men sipped their coffees.

"Anything from the lookouts?" Hornblower asked.

"No, my lord."

Hornblower poured himself a second cup and studied his companion. Brewer was dead on his feet. Hornblower had been there himself, many times, and he knew now that everyone knew it then but himself.

"William."

Brewer looked up.

"It was a good plan, certainly worth the attempt, but it's over now. You're exhausted and in need of rest."

Brewer smiled, which Hornblower was glad to see.

"Are you trying to take command of my ship, my lord?" Brewer asked.

"Not at all, Captain, but if you don't go to bed, I shall be forced to drastic measures."

Brewer's brow rose. "Such as?"

His lordship snapped his fingers, and Mac appeared at his shoulder.

Brewer grunted. "Not you again. One would think you made your living at mutiny. First in the Caribbean, now this."

McCleary just smiled, and Brewer winked at him.

He turned back to the admiral. "Well, my lord, it seems you have the advantage of me. I think I shall go to bed." He rose, then looked back to Hornblower. "I'm just sorry I shan't be giving Mr. Paddington his £10." He stepped away from the table and saw his third lieutenant.

"Mr. Cooksley," he said, "you have the deck. Make your course south until the noon sighting. Once Mr. Priestley has figured our position, make your course for St. Helena. I shall be in my cabin."

"Aye, sir!"

He turned back to Hornblower, still seated with his coffee.

"Thank you, my lord."

"Pleasant dreams, William. Go with him, Mac."

"Aye, aye, my lord," the big Cornishman said. "Captain? If you please?"

Brewer eyed his coxswain for a moment before setting off. As he passed by, Hornblower heard him mutter, "One of these days, McCleary."

Mac smiled. "Let's hope so, sir."

When Brewer opened his eyes again, it took him a moment to realize where he was. He sat up as best he could in his cot and saw sunlight peering under the cloth used to close off his sleeping cabin. He rolled out of the hammock and quickly dressed. He stepped out into the dining cabin to find Hornblower sitting down to eat.

"Ah! There you are, Captain! And just in time to join me," Hornblower said. "Alfred! The captain's awake!"

Alfred's head appeared in the doorway. "Coffee coming right up, Captain!"

Brewer sat down opposite the admiral. "I'm starving, my lord. What's for supper?"

Hornblower smiled. "Breakfast."

Brewer looked up in surprise. "Excuse me, my lord?"

"Breakfast, William. You've slept almost twenty-four hours."

"No wonder I feel so stiff," Brewer said. Alfred arrived with a steaming cup of coffee.

"Eggs, ham and toast, sir?" he asked.

"Yes, Alfred, that will do nicely." Brewer turned to Hornblower. "What did I miss, my lord?"

"Absolutely nothing, Captain. Mr. Priestley got the sighting done and made the course change per your orders. He makes it just under three thousand miles to St. Helena. Three weeks, more or less." Hornblower paused while Alfred brought them their breakfast, which both men attacked with gusto.

"You know, my lord," Brewer said around a mouthful of eggs, "this reminds me of a visit I made to America. Must have been nearly fifteen years ago now. I was staying as a guest of an American shipping magnate in New York. It was the first time I ever had the chance to experience the big breakfast common to Americans. I tell you, my lord, I was astounded at the amount of food! Eggs, a slab of ham, and roasted potatoes were followed by huge biscuits covered with gravy. The meal was finished with the finest coffee I have ever tasted in my life. I will confess to you, it was the only time in my life I was tempted to desert and live in America."

Hornblower laughed and pushed his empty plate away from him. He wiped his mouth with his napkin. Both men adjourned to the day cabin, where Alfred brought them more coffee.

"Captain," Hornblower said, "I want you to use the next three weeks to exercise your gun crews and topmen to wartime standards. I want them ready to go into battle."

"Yes, my lord. But I thought we were going back to France via the Caribbean? Surely the Russians won't be looking for us there?"

"True, but I've got a nagging feeling that things aren't going to work out the way we think they will. I'm not willing to trust that de Joinville will not change his mind at the last minute and wish to take the more direct route." He set his cup down and frowned. "I wish I could give you something more definite, but that feeling is all I've got. I will tell you, William, that the worst mistakes of my life have come when I've ignored that feeling."

"I know precisely what you mean, my lord," Brewer said. "I shall set Mr. Dean and Mr. Jason to drawing up a suitable training routine, and we shall implement it as soon as possible."

CHAPTER 11

The next eighteen days saw the officers and crew of HMS *Iris* put through a training regimen unlike anything seen in the Royal Navy since Waterloo. Gun crews were put through the motions morning and afternoon. Live firing with powder and shot was severely limited, or else they'd have nothing left to fight with, but under the eyes of the captain or first lieutenant they practiced until the routines were as natural to them as breathing and just as necessary to their survival. The same went for training aloft. Nearly every daylight hour saw men ascending the shrouds to make sail or take it in, and maneuvers were practiced again and again until the men could initiate a sequence at practically the first word. Brewer would later say that he never had a crew that behaved so well or trained so hard as this one did.

He was not alone in that assessment. Admiral Lord Hornblower thought so as well, and he told the crew so one evening when they were within a day's sail of their destination. He came on deck just as the sun was beginning to set and asked the captain to assemble the crew aft. When Brewer had gathered his crew, Hornblower stepped forward.

"Men! I asked the captain to assemble you so I could have

a word," he said loudly and with feeling. "I have been in the king's service—and now the Queen's—for forty-five years, man and boy, and I have to say that I have never seen a crew work as hard as you have! If we had another few weeks, you would be ready to face the best the enemy threw at us during the Napoleonic wars; even with the short time you have had, I would put you up against any warship from any navy in the world, with no doubt as to the outcome!"

Cheers went up all around him, and Hornblower raised his hat to salute the men. Then he raised his arms for quiet.

"Men! You are as ready as we can make you, and you can make yourselves! I do not know if we shall have to fight before we see England again, but I am confident that, should an enemy decide to test our mettle, it will be the last and greatest mistake of their lives!"

The men roared approval. Hornblower walked over to where Brewer and his officers were assembled.

"I want you to know," he said to them, "you should be proud of this crew. I have never seen a peacetime crew in the Royal Navy train as hard and as seriously as these men, and the credit is yours. Each of you has led by example and shown yourselves ready to stand shoulder-to-shoulder with your crews, and believe me, they have seen it and are ready to follow you to the very gates of hell. Do not lose that faith they have in you. Guard it well; it is a rare thing to find in a wartime crew, let alone one in peacetime. Captain Brewer, please accept my most heartfelt congratulations on your ship and crew. Well done, gentlemen!"

The captain touched his hat. "Thank you, my lord."

Alexandre Leclerc made his way to the chapel as quickly and unobtrusively as he could. It was the middle of the night, so he moved quietly. They would reach St. Helena the day after tomorrow, and he wanted to check his device one last time.

He entered the chapel and lit a small candle he took from his pocket. He made his way to the back of the sarcophagus and knelt, settling the candle on the deck before him so he could part the curtain. He carefully picked up the candle and held it inside the curtain, but he could not see the vial or the powder he had secreted there. He pulled the candle out and reached in gently with his free hand to see if he could feel the vial, but his fingers found nothing but wood. Leclerc frowned and decided to risk a look inside. He carefully moved the candle inside and put his head inside just far enough to see. The vial was gone; in its place was a block of wood. He turned his head and saw the powder was also gone, along with the mechanism for lighting it.

Confusion gave way to terror as a cold chill gripped his heart. He pulled out of the curtain and sat back on his heels. Then a voice stopped him cold.

"Looking for something?"

Leclerc froze. His mind raced, searching for a way of escape, and excuse, anything; but he realized it was hopeless and he stood. Lieutenant Girot stood in the doorway, a lantern in one hand and a pistol in the other, pointed in the general direction of Leclerc's chest.

"Lieutenant Girot," he said, and swallowed hard. "Is there anything I can do for you, sir?"

"What were you doing here, Leclerc?" Girot asked. The pistol did not waver.

Leclerc had no idea what to say. Never had it ever entered his mind that he might get caught. He set his candle on the sarcophagus.

"Nothing, sir," he said nervously. "I just came in to check the arrngement one last time."

Girot raised the pistol to aim at the other's head. "One more chance," he said coldly. "What are you looking for?"

"Lieutenant!" Leclerc pleaded. "I don't know what you're talking about!"

"Have it your way." He cocked the pistol, and Leclerc feared he was about to be executed. Girot hesitated, then sighed as he uncocked the pistol and lowered it. He stood to the side, and Lieutenant Charner entered, followed by three marines and the Sergeant-at-arms. The marines had swords drawn, and the First Lieutenant's pistol was pointed squarely at the cornered tailor's chest.

"Alexandre Leclerc," Charner said formally, "you are under arrest for treason. Sergeant-at-arms, take him away."

"Wait!" Leclerc cried. He took a step back as the sergeant-at-arms approached. He looked to Girot and said, "What is the meaning of all this?"

"A magazine inspection discovered the missing powder," Girot said. "Your confederate confessed under questioning. Your explosive device was discovered, rendered harmless, and removed. A search of your locker yielded the letter from the duke of Angoulême."

"Sir," Leclerc pleaded desperately, "this can all be explained! If I could just see the prince?"

"You shall see him," the First Lieutenant said. "If he decides to court-martial you himself, that is! Take him away!"

Leclerc was dragged away by the two marines, bound for the cable tier. The sergeant-at-arms came to attention and followed them out. Charner watched them leave and turned to say something to his companion. His voice caught in his throat when he saw the look of betrayal on the lieutenant's face. "Girot?" he said, putting his hand on the other's shoulder. "Speak!"

The lieutenant jumped and spun, startled out of his misery. He looked at the deck and shook his head, before looking up to the Charner.

"He killed Louis?"

The premier sighed. "Probably. He had to get access to the chapel and the sarcophagus."

Girot drew a ragged breath. "Poor man. He was a good hand. He did not deserve this fate."

Charner patted him on the shoulder. "Come. The prince awaits."

They found de Joinville sitting in his day cabin, reading. He rose as the two officers entered and came to attention. The prince nodded his acknowledgment and turned to his senior lieutenant.

"Well?"

"Lieutenant Girot confronted him in the chapel, my Prince," Charner reported. "He admitted to the device found beneath the sarcophagus. When questioned, I expect he will admit to the murder of the sailor Louis as well."

De Joinville took a deep breath and exhaled loudly. "Lieutenant Girot," he said formally, "you have done outstanding work during this investigation. I shall note this fact with both the naval ministry and my father in my reports." He saw the miserable look on the lieutenant's face and said, "Girot, you are not to blame for this. Leclerc was a soldier with a cause. The Angoulême letter proves this. You could not have known what was in his heart. I want you to know, I am pleased with your conduct. You have served me and this ship with great honor."

Girot came to attention, bolstered by the prince's words. "Thank you, my Prince."

De Joinville smiled. "Return to your cabin and get some sleep. In the morning, write a report. Give it to the first lieutenant by the turn of the forenoon watch. You are dismissed."

Girot stood at attention for a moment before turning and leaving the cabin.

"It is very sad, Louis's death," Charner said. "

"Agreed," the prince replied. He walked to his desk and removed the Angoulême letter from a drawer.

"It seems my cousin can still command forces to carry out his schemes. Complete madness, of course. Had Leclerc succeeded, he may well have plunged France into a civil war. Had the Bonapartists prevailed, the Tsar, along with his Austrian and Prussian cronies, may have used it as an excuse to invade France—to prevent a second revolution."

Charner was aghast. "Your father would never permit such a thing!"

"My father would be dead," Joinville replied coldly as he resumed his seat, "followed by my brothers and then myself. The duke would see to that. He would not allow anyone to stand between him and the throne."

De Joinville paused for a moment before calling for the sentry to pass the word for Colonel Hernoux. He put the letter down on the settee beside him and sighed. "You have done well, Charner. I shall remember you to my father. Go now, my friend. Get some sleep."

The first lieutenant came to attention and departed. Joinville watched him go, only his eyes betraying gratitude.

He picked up the letter and read through it again. He was staring at the pages when the sentry admitted Hernoux.

You sent for me, my Prince?"

"Yes, my friend," Joinville said without looking up. "It is done. Sit, but first have them bring us something to drink, won't you?"

Hernoux stepped out and gave the orders before

returning and taking his usual seat, opposite the prince and off to the side. He waited while the steward brought two glasses of wine, handing one to Hernoux and setting the prince's on the table.

The colonel took a drink of his wine and waited. Soon the prince sighed and reached for his glass.

"So," he said, "this is what my life has come to, eh? Saving Bonaparte. What would my ancestors say, Hernoux? What could I tell them?"

The colonel shrugged. "You could always say you were under orders."

Joinville grunted. "I doubt they would accept such an explanation." He looked at the letter again and handed it to his aide. "It seems my dear cousin can still command forces to do his bidding. Read this."

Hernoux accepted the letter and scanned the first few lines. He looked up in surprise.

"The Angoulême letter?" he asked. Joinville nodded, and Hernoux read it hurriedly. He grunted when he was finished and handed it back. "I'd have thought he would have destroyed it."

"No, not someone like Leclerc," the prince said softly as he refolded the letter and returned it to the desk. "People like that do not burn a letter from their god."

De Joinville called for their glasses to be refilled as he resumed his seat. After the steward departed, he stared thoughtfully at his drink.

Hernoux recognized the look. "My Prince, your thoughts?"

Joinville set his drink down and sighed. "The same old ones, my friend. What if my cousin is right? Did Louis XVI make a mistake in not fighting for his throne? Did God entrust France to my family to rule and care for in His name?

If this is so, should I not throw my lot in with him?"

Hernoux was grim. They had had this conversation at least three times in the past. "You know that would mean your death—or his. Not to mention your sanctioning the murder of your father and brothers, to clear the duke's way to the throne."

Joinville picked up his glass and drained it. "I know." He looked at his aide and smiled. "Never fear. I know who my friends are, and where my duty lies."

Hernoux raised his glass in salute. "You always have."

Two days later, shortly after dawn, HMS *Iris* entered the harbor at Jamestown, St. Helena. Hornblower stood beside Brewer on the quarterdeck. From the deck of the ship, it didn't look as though much had changed in the more than twenty years since they had left.

What did you expect? Hornblower chided himself. *It looks almost as it did the last time he and I walked along the waterfront. My God, has it really been twenty-three years?*

Hornblower wandered to the rail, still looking at the town on the shore. He felt something at his arm and turned to find Mr. Midshipman Youngblood standing there silently, offering him a glass.

"Thank you, Mr. Youngblood."

The lad touched his hat and bowed. "My lord." He withdrew across the quarterdeck.

Hornblower brought the glass to his eye, and with it the memories came flooding back. He did not fight them, but neither did he want to experience them here on deck. He snapped the glass shut and turned to Brewer.

"Captain," he said, "please send an officer with a note to the governor, stating that I shall call on him at ten o'clock tomorrow morning, if that time is acceptable to him."

"As you wish, my lord," Brewer saluted and turned to his first lieutenant. "Write out a note for the governor and detail Mr. Jason to deliver it to him at once."

"Aye, sir."

Dean went off to do his duty, and Brewer stepped over to where Hornblower was once again scanning the shore with Mr. Youngblood's glass.

"Something feels different this time, my lord," he said simply.

Hornblower lowered the glass but did not look at his captain. Brewer tried to read his face, but he could not. After a moment, the admiral looked down at the rail and sighed.

"Captain, I believe that may be the understatement of the year," he said. "Let us go below."

Brewer turned to the wheel and said, "Mr. Cooksley has the deck until Mr. Dean returns. I shall be in my cabin."

The two officers retreated below deck to the safety of the day cabin. No sooner had they sat than Alfred appeared with coffee.

"Alfred," Hornblower said playfully, "I believe you are part witch. Thank you."

The servant bowed and retreated to his pantry.

"For a long time," Hornblower said, "years after we returned to England, I was bedeviled by the thought that I could have done more for him, especially there at the end, that all I did was to leave him to his fate. I do not know if Lowe was responsible for his death or not—personally, I believe he may well have been—but whatever the truth be, I felt that I had deserted him, after all he had done for me, especially after Barbara was forced to leave with Richard. I'm sure you noticed at the time, William, that I was a wreck. I was certain that when I said goodbye to them, I was seeing my son alive for the last time. How easy it would have been for him to pounce at that moment! I was completely defenseless, and the Allied Commissioners would have had the best gossip possible to send back to their European courts." He looked at Brewer. "He didn't do that, as you yourself know full well. In fact, William, I don't think anyone knows more about that time than you; not even Barbara knows the full story."

Brewer didn't know what to say, so he did the best thing and said nothing.

"I still cannot believe," Hornblower continued, "how Bonaparte held me up during those trying days. He was discretion personified, speaking only when we were alone in the office or out on a walk by ourselves. I owe my sanity to Napoleon Bonaparte, William, if not my very life."

He took another drink and watched the designs of the clouds, beyond the windows. "I took years to come to terms with his death, ashamed that I'd abandoned him to the wolves who gathered for the final kill. I felt guilty that I never went back to thank him." He grunted. "Not that I would have been allowed to set foot on the island while he was alive! That would have been all the proof that the liberals—not to mention the Tsar—would have needed to 'prove' that I had succumbed to Bonaparte's famous charms! I couldn't even say thank you!" His voice caught in his throat.

Brewer suddenly felt uncomfortable in his lordship's presence. He set his cup down and made to rise.

"If you'll excuse me, my lord?"

Hornblower looked up suddenly. "No, William, stay. Please." He straightened made an effort to regain control. "I apologize for burdening, but it was good to get it out after so long. That had been building up since Minister Roussin asked me to attend the exhumation. I told you what he said, didn't I? They wanted someone there to look out for the Emperor!" He looked at the deck beams above. "Well, at least

I get to do something to repay my debt."

Brewer resumed his seat. "Knowing him as I did, my lord, I'd say he would consider any debt owed him by you to be paid in full."

Hornblower turned to him, a quizzical look on his face. "Do you think so?" He shook his head in doubt.

Brewer smiled. "Aye, my lord. I'm sure."

"Well," Hornblower said with a hint of hope in his voice, "let's hope so."

The sentry knocked at the door and announced the first lieutenant. Dean stepped into the room and stood inside the door, feet apart and his hands clasped behind his back.

"Well, Jeremiah?" Brewer asked.

"Mr. Jason has returned, sir," he said. He turned to Hornblower. "The governor says ten is fine, my lord."

"Good," Hornblower said.

It was ten o'clock the next morning precisely when Hornblower stepped into the outer office for his appointment with the governor. A young man in uniform was sitting behind Mr. Brewer's old desk. He rose when the admiral entered. "May I help you, sir?" he asked.

"Yes. I am Admiral Horatio Lord Hornblower, and I have an appointment with the governor."

"Of course, my lord." The young man came around the desk. "If you'll give me a moment, I'll inform the general you're here."

"Thank you."

The secretary went to the door, knocked once with his ear to the door, then entered. A moment later, he emerged. "The general will see you now, my lord." He stepped back into the roomto allow Hornblower entrance.

Hornblower found the Governor standing in front of his

desk.

The secretary spoke. "Sir, may I introduce Admiral Lord Horatio Hornblower, Special Representative of the Crown for the exhumation of Napoleon Bonaparte."

The governor bowed.

"My lord," the secretary said, "may I present Major General George Middlemore, Governor of the island of St. Helena."

"Governor, thank you for seeing me," Hornblower said.

"A pleasure, my lord."

The general stepped forward and shook Hornblower's hand, a limp handshake that told Hornblower much. Middlemore was a good six or eight inches shorter than he, with gray, curly hair that was bald on top, and a bushy moustache, and the look on his face told Hornblower that his visit was anything but a pleasure. The governor led the way to the same two overstuffed chairs before the window that had been there when Hornblower was governor. They settled themselves and a servant brought wine.

"Thank you, John," Middlemore said. "That will be all."

He handed Hornblower a glass and raised his in toast.

"To Her Majesty's good health."

Hornblower raised his glass as well, and both men drank.

Hornblower set his glass down. "Are you aware of why I am here, Governor?"

"Yes, my lord," he answered. "Lord Palmerston sent a fast packet to me as soon as you accepted the French request. In fact, the Queen herself sent a note, stating that I was to extend every courtesy to the French when they arrived."

"Good, that simplifies matters," Hornblower said.

"Can't say I like it, though," the general said. "I didn't fight against him in the Peninsula just to show the upstart courtesy now."

"You fought in the Peninsula?"

"Of course! I say, aren't you kin to the Duke of Wellington?"

"He is my brother-in-law."

"Best fighting general I ever knew! He beat every marshal Boney sent against him in Spain, and then he gave it to the man himself, at Waterloo. Yes, indeed! The best England has ever produced."

Hornblower grinned. "My wife would agree with you." He drained his glass and looked around. "I see the office hasn't changed much. When did you become governor?"

Middlemore shifted in his seat. "I was appointed in 1836, when the crown took over administration of the island from John Company."

"Do you have many visitors to see Bonaparte's gravesite?"

"Some. Nothing like they see in London, I'm sure. A moment, if you please, my lord."

The Governor rang a bell on the table, and a servant entered and silently refilled their glasses. He bowed before retreating from the room.

Hornblower raised his glass. "Thank you. I had quite forgotten the heat." Both men drank. "Governor, a moment ago, you said something to the effect that you were opposed to the return of Bonaparte's remains. Is that your position?"

Middlemore set his glass on the table and sat back in his chair. "Yes, my lord."

"May I ask your reasons?"

The general shrugged. "I fought with the duke on the Peninsula, my lord. The French were the enemy, and as far as I'm concerned, they still are. Bonaparte was determined to have war. He was showed mercy once, when he was given Elba rather than being put to death, but he threw that aside and returned to France, causing the wars to start again.

Fortunately, the duke put an end to that quickly enough, and Bonaparte was imprisoned here for the rest of his life. I don't think we should allow him to influence French or European events now that he is gone. I say leave him where he is, mostly forgotten and powerless."

Hornblower drained his glass and thought for a moment. "I see. Tell me, Governor, will you be able to do your duty when the French arrive?"

Now it was Middlemore's turn to think. He rubbed his chin with his thumb and forefinger as he stared out the window. Hornblower was content to wait for his host's decision. He took advantage of the lull to look around the room again, and he was flooded with memories of the many conversations he'd shared with Bonaparte in this very room. He looked over to the fireplace and remembered how Lord Cochrane had visited Bonaparte at the behest of Chilean dictator Bernard O'Higgins and offered the Corsican the future throne of a United South America. Bonaparte had pronounced Cochrane "mad", but said it would be interesting to talk to him again in five or ten years. Sadly, that never came to pass, as Bonaparte was dead in slightly more than three.

Middlemore shifted in his seat, pulling Hornblower back to the present. The governor drew a deep breath and let it out slowly.

"My lord," he said simply, "I will not participate."

Hornblower's face became an unreadable mask. The governor's answer was not unexpected, but that didn't mean that he was pleased to hear it. "Sir, I must ask you to reconsider. The Queen will not look kindly on your decision."

Middlemore shrugged. "I can designate Colonel Hamelin Trelawney to act in my behalf. He is the garrison commander." He reached out and rang the bell again. The servant appeared in the doorway. "Have a message sent to

Colonel Trelawney stating that he will be acting as my official representative and dealing with all matters concerning the exhumation when the French arrive."

"Yes, Governor." The servant bowed and departed.

Middlemore looked at his guest. "Will there be anything else, my lord?"

Hornblower rose. "That is all, Governor. As the Queen's ambassador, I shall make sure that she learns of your decision. More than that, I can assure you that the duke will hear of it as well."

That got the Governor's attention. His eyes narrowed.

Hornblower rang the bell on the table. The servant appeared in the doorway and was surprised when it was Hornblower who addressed him. "Send a second note to Colonel Trelawney to ask him to meet me at once at Bonaparte's grave. That will be all." The servant bowed and retreated from the room. Hornblower turned to Middlemore again.

"If you claim to know my brother-in-law, then you may remember his opinion of officers who refused to obey orders. I would not look forward to seeing him again, if I were you; I think I can say that meeting will not turn out well for you. My advice to you, *Governor*, is that if you have decided that you can no longer fulfill the duties and obligations of your office, *give it up!*" Hornblower went to the door and turned back again. "Do not interfere with any of the proceedings regarding the exhumation and removal of the remains, sir. If you do, I shall have you arrested for violation of my orders, given on authority of the Queen's letter to me. Do you wish to see it?"

"No, my lord," Middlemore said in a low voice.

"Farewell, sir." Hornblower left without looking back.

Outside on the street, Hornblower turned in the direction

of Longwood and the gravesite and started walking. He paused at the last sidewalk café on the edge of town and sat down under a shaded canopy. He ordered a cool drink and thought about the governor and his decision. The waiter returned with his drink. He took a reviving sip of the beverage before a voice interrupted him.

"My lord? Is it really you?"

Hornblower looked up to see a man of roughly his own age, but shorter and with broad shoulders and powerful arms. He had a felt hat over curls that had gone gray, and a gray beard hid the smile under questioning eyes. The skin on his face and arms was toughened to leather by St. Helena's sun and wind.

"I am Lord Hornblower. Do I know you?"

"Begging yer pardon, yer lordship," he said as he jerked his hat off, "My name's Harry Dickens, my lord. I worked the wharves when you was governor. I remember seeing you and old Boney walking the shoreline and streets all the time."

"Good to see you again, Mr. Dickens," Hornblower said. "Please, sit down. Waiter, another drink!"

"Oh, no, my lord, I couldn't let you do that!"

"Too late, I'm afraid," Hornblower said. "It's already ordered."

Dickens laughed and tossed his hat on the table. "Are you here for this French business?"

Hornblower nodded as the waiter returned with Dickens' drink. "Yes. The Queen has appointed me the official representative of Her Majesty's government." He glanced around. "My ship just arrived yesterday, and I only came ashore this morning for a meeting with the governor. I must say, it doesn't look like much has changed in twenty years."

Dickens shook his head. "Not much, my lord, not much, let me tell you." He leaned forward. "My lord, pardon me for being so forward, but how is your family?"

"They are fine, Mr. Dickens," Hornblower answered warily. "Thank you for asking."

"And your boy? The one who left due to the sickness?"

Hornblower smiled with relief. "He has completely recovered. He is a doctor now, with a practice outside of Edinburgh."

"What?" Dickens said. "Not a navy man?"

Hornblower put on his best mock-frown. "We don't talk about that, Mr. Dickens."

Dickens roared with laughter at that, and after a moment Hornblower joined him. This was just what he needed, a talk with a friendly stranger who remembered the past.

"Did you know Bonaparte?" Hornblower asked.

Dickens shrugged. "More or less, my lord. He would come down to the waterfront from time to time, especially when he was expecting something from France or America. Sometimes he brought one of his men to interpret for him, but sometimes he would come on his own and practice his English on us. Those were the fun times; I can tell you! My lord, whenever he could not come up with the right word in English, he would... *explode* into this string of French! It was bloody hilarious, believe you me! He was probably cursing everything from the fish in the sea to the English language itself! But he was good about it; every time, when he was done cursing, he sat back down and learned whatever the right word was. I remember how hard we laughed with him when he offered to teach us all how to 'swear like a sergeant' in French!"

Dickens laughed again, and Hornblower smiled and shook his head. He could see Bonaparte doing just that.

Hornblower set his glass on the table. "Mr. Dickens, what happened after I left?" Hornblower watched his guest's face fall and knew the news would confirm his worst fears.

"I couldn't rightly say, my lord. You see, after you left the island, we saw less and less of Boney. Lowe—he was the governor after you, remember?—he took away Boney's freedom to travel. He insisted that Boney was a prisoner and that he had to have guards with him everywhere he went. Anyone he talked to could be arrested by the garrison and questioned to see if he was a French spy! Once that became clear, Boney just stayed at Longwood. Lowe tried to make him present himself once a day, but Boney refused. When Lowe said he would come in and see for himself, Boney threatened to shoot him if he put one foot across his doorstep! After a while, Boney hardly ever left Longwood." Dickens shook his head. "It was sad to watch, my lord. Lowe treated Boney like a thief locked up in Newgate. I don't pretend to understand the politics of him being here, but I don't think Boney deserved that."

"Nor do I, Mr. Dickens," Hornblower said.

Dickens could see how sad his words made his host, and he wondered if the rumors that he was friends with Boney might be true after all. He leaned forward and touched the table with his fingertip to get his lordship's attention.

"There's one thing I *can* rightly say, my lord. I was working the wharf the day Boney arrived on the island, and I saw him many times before, during, and after you was here. What I can say is that while you were here were the happiest days he spent on the island. You can lock me up for treason if you like, and I ain't no Frenchie spy neither, but that's the God's truth. He smiled more, and he talked to the townsfolk. They loved him dearly, my lord. He was kind to them and joked with them. I was here for the whole thing. I saw it all, and that's what I can say."

Hornblower sighed. "Thank you, Mr. Dickens. What you say means the world to me. I'm no French spy either, and I think Boney was a good man. I'm talking about the Bonaparte we knew here on St. Helena, not the tyrant who tried to rule all Europe and destroy England. I think that was a different man than the one we knew, you and I."

Dickens bobbed his head. "I would say so."

Hornblower pulled out his watch and looked at the time. "You must forgive me, Mr. Dickens, but I have an appointment I must not miss. It was good to speak with you." He rose and held out his hand, and after a moment's hesitation Dickens rose and shook it heartily.

"God bless you, my lord," he said. "Please give my best to the missus and son."

"I shall," Hornblower said as he stepped out into the street. "Goodbye, Mr. Dickens."

Hornblower made his way from Jamestown to Bonaparte's grave. He was in no particular hurry, wandering about and re-familiarizing himself with the island as he went. He found the gravesite in a place called the Valley of the Tomb. Hornblower knew the place as Geranium Valley. The tomb was marked by a plain slab, level with the ground, surrounded by a wrought iron grille and shaded by a weeping willow tree. The whole thing was surrounded by a wood fence, and there was a spring nearby. Hornblower remembered drinking its fresh and clear waters on some of his walks with Bonaparte.

He stood outside the gate, looking at the plain slab that covered the tomb. Sadness and frustration welled up inside him. Was Lowe so petty that he condemned Bonaparte to a nameless grave?

He heard a throat being cleared behind him. "Yes," a voice said, "he's really there."

Hornblower turned to see a British Army colonel

standing about ten feet away. The newcomer saluted. Hornblower returned the gesture. "Colonel Trelawney, I presume," Hornblower said.

"Yes, my lord," he said. "I received your message directly after the governor's."

Wordlessly, Hornblower pulled out the Queen's letter and handed it to Trelawney. The colonel's eyebrows rose as he read, and he handed the letter back to Hornblower.

"Forgive me for being blunt, Colonel, but after my interview with your governor, I feel this needs to be said. I do not care what your personal feelings are regarding the return of Bonaparte's remains to France. The only thing I care about is that we accomplished the task given us by Her Majesty, which is to turn the remains over to the French with appropriate dignity and decorum. I would prefer to do so without causing an international incident. Have you been briefed at all?"

"No, my lord."

"We are awaiting the arrival of the frigate *la Belle Poule,* in company with the corvette *Favorite.* She is commanded by the Prince de Joinville, third son of the French king. When the prince arrives, we shall meet with him to hammer out the details of the proceedings. My main concern, Colonel, is security. I fear there may be an attempt to sabotage the ceremonies. To my mind, the obvious place for such an attack would be when the coffin itself is opened. That would be the opportune time for someone to toss a bomb inside and obliterate the remains entirely. The garrison will have to be out in force. I want to see your preliminary plan for security arrangements by sundown tomorrow."

"Yes, my lord," Trelawney said. "When are we expecting the French to arrive?"

Hornblower shrugged. "I'm afraid your guess is as good

as mine, Colonel. The prince has scheduled a number of festivities at various ports of call along his way here. Remember, sir, the French are not the enemy. Not anymore. Neither is Bonaparte. The Queen wants to improve our relations with France. Do your job well, and I shall see to it that your name figures prominently in my report to her."

Trelawney bowed. "Thank you, my lord. Is there anything else?"

"Not at the moment, Colonel. We shall meet again tomorrow. Why don't you come and dine on board? I shall have a boat at the wharf at sundown, and we can discuss your report afterwards."

"A pleasure, my lord. Thank you. Now, if you'll excuse me, I'd best get started." He turned to go, but Hornblower stopped him.

"Before you go, Colonel, tell me, when did you arrive on St. Helena?"

"I've been here for two years, my lord."

"I see. Thank you, Colonel."

Trelawney touched his hat in salute. "My lord."

Hornblower heard him retreat. He was alone with his thoughts again, or so he thought.

"You the one going to take him away?"

Hornblower turned to see a small old lady standing there. She had on a long dress that must once have been a beautiful gown but now showed definite signs of wear. She also wore a shawl across her shoulders despite the rising heat, and a bonnet on her head. Her eyes were narrowed and accusing, her lips pressed in a firm line.

"I beg your pardon?" he said.

"You heard me," she barked. She nodded toward the grave. "You takin' him away, aren't you?"

Hornblower looked to the grave and back to her. "No,

madam, I am not. The French are coming to do that."

She snorted in derision. "Same thing. He'll be gone."

He wondered what she was getting at. "May I ask your name, madam?"

"I am Lady Torbet," she answered, "and I own this land. I allowed the governor to use this plot to bury Bonaparte." She turned to the grave and sighed. "Now I don't know what I'll do."

"What do you mean?"

"I make my income here, selling drinks and cakes to those who come to visit the grave. After you take him, that's gone."

Hornblower studied her. She looked at the grave with a sad expression on her face.

"Did you know him?" he asked.

She nodded, and after a moment she wiped a tear from her eye. "He came by often when he was allowed the freedom of the island. He liked this spot, sitting under the shade of the willow and listening to the water as it flowed past. He always said it would be a nice place to rest. So, when he died, I allowed the governor to bury him here."

Hornblower smiled. "I remember him saying something similar. He brought me here a few times, and I saw how happy this place made him. He seemed more at peace here than anywhere else on the island."

Lady Torbet turned to him and stared, trying hard to place his face. Her eyes grew wide when she succeeded, and Hornblower laughed.

"Lord Hornblower? It *is* you!" Her hand went to her mouth in embarrassment. "Oh, my lord! I pray you'll forgive my harsh words!"

"Think nothing of it, Lady Torbet. It pleases me more than I can say to see him remembered and honored. It was a good thing you did for him. I know he would have been grateful to you."

He thought for a moment she would blush, but she just smiled, as at a memory. "Thank you, my lord."

Hornblower walked over to her and pulled out a £5 note. He handed it to her, but she tried to refuse. "Oh, my lord, I can't..."

"Nonsense," he said. He nodded toward the grave. "Think of it as a thank-you gift from him. And I hope something turns up for you."

He bade her goodbye and headed for the shore.

CHAPTER 12

A week went by with no sign of *la Belle Poule*. A packet ship arrived shortly before noon. As soon as its anchor hit the water, a boat from the packet was pulling toward HMS *Iris*. They tied up alongside the ship only long enough to take the ship's mail bag with them and to leave a bag of incoming mail and a package for the admiral. Mr. Dean signed for the package and carried it below.

He found the admiral in the day cabin talking with the captain.

"Begging your pardon, my lord," he said and held out the package, "but a packet from England just pulled into the harbor. Her boat brought this straight here for you."

"Thank you, Mr. Dean." Hornblower took the package to the table.

"Was there any mail?" Brewer asked.

"Aye, sir. Your clerk has the bag and is sorting the contents now."

"Here's hoping!" Brewer said, rubbing his hands together. "Thank you, Mr. Dean. That will be all. Please let us know if we have any mail."

"Aye, sir." Dean came to attention and left.

Brewer walked over to find Hornblower scowling as he read. "What is it, my lord?" he asked.

"Trouble I don't need right now," Hornblower answered. "It seems the French Prime Minister, Thiers, has brought France and England to the brink of war over his support for the Egyptian renegade Muhammad Pasha. Palmerston has sent a fleet to bombard Beirut if Pasha doesn't restrain his ambitions, but he is resisting, based on his expectations of Thiers and France coming to his aid. Thiers is threatening war now."

"What does that mean for us?"

"Nothing," Hornblower said thoughtfully. "Our mission remains unchanged. This may be the one action that makes either Thiers or Louis take a step back and tone down the rhetoric somewhat."

There was a knock at the cabin door, and the sentry allowed Mr. Paddington to enter.

"Begging your pardon, my lord," he said formally, before turning to Brewer. "Captain, a French brig has just entered the harbor."

"Is it *la Favorite*?" Hornblower asked.

"No, my lord," the midshipman answered. "If we are reading it correctly, it appears to be named *l'Oreste*."

Hornblower looked to Brewer. "Possibly bringing the same information to de Joinville." He went to his desk and wrote out a note, which he folded and sealed. "Who has the deck, Mr. Paddington?"

"Mr. Cabot, my lord."

"I see." The admiral considered. "Thank you, Mr. Paddington. Please pass the word for Mr. Cooksley."

"Aye, aye, my lord!" The midshipman came to attention and left the cabin.

"May I ask your intentions, my lord?" Brewer asked.

"Indeed, Captain. The note I wrote out is an invitation for the captain of the French brig to have a drink with me. I intend to ask the third lieutenant to deliver it."

A knock at the door announced the arrival of Lieutenant Cooksley.

"You sent for me, my lord?" he asked.

"Yes. A French brig, *l'Oreste*, has just arrived. I would like you to take a boat and deliver this note to her captain. If he accepts, you may bring him back with you if he is agreeable. If not, ask when he will come."

"Aye, my lord."

The lieutenant departed on his mission, and Brewer excused himself to work on a letter to Elizabeth.

My Darling,

We have arrived at St. Helena. I have not gone ashore as yet, but Jamestown appears the same, at least what I can see of the waterfront. I wish Captain Bush had been able to come along, but His Lordship says his health is not up to the journey. I may sound mad, but I almost expect to see ghosts of the past walking on the shore, Bonaparte especially. I wonder what the Emperor would say?

Sailing with Lord Hornblower is very strange—on my part, not his. For some reason I cannot explain, there are times when I feel like I am a lieutenant at his side again, feeling thankful for his patronage as I was in the Caribbean before I first met you. I don't know that he has done anything to elicit these feelings within me; just being in his presence seems to be the cause. Fortunately, he seems to be handling it better than I.

I must close now. I do not want to miss the

possibility of a mail boat while in an English port. Besides, duty calls. A boat is alongside, bringing a visiting French officer. I shall write again soon.

All my love,
William

He had heard the report made to Hornblower that Mr. Cooksley was returning with an officer accompanying him. Hastily he sealed the letter and gave it to Alfred to post for him. Then he presented himself to the admiral.

"My lord, shall I escort the French captain?" he asked.

"If you please, Captain."

Brewer came to attention, picked up his hat and left. Hornblower stared at the door, so he did not notice Alfred appear beside him. "My lord," the servant said, "what shall I serve?"

Hornblower looked at him. "I'm sorry, Alfred, I did not hear you approach. Madeira will be fine, I think."

"As you say, my lord," came the reply. "Will there be anything else?"

"Not right now, Alfred."

Brewer waited at the entry port. Mr. Cooksley climbed up, followed by a French officer. He was shorter than Brewer, but possessed of a much thicker frame, well-muscled, with shoulders like an ox. Cooksley stepped forward.

"Captain, may I present *Capitaine de Corvette Doret* of the French brig *l'Oreste*?"

Brewer bowed. "*M. le Capitaine,* welcome aboard HMS *Iris.*"

Cooksley turned to their guest. "*Capitaine,* may I present

your host, Captain William Brewer of Her Majesty's frigate *Iris*?"

Doret came to attention and snapped off a sharp salute, which Brewer returned.

"Captain," Doret said, in very clear English, "it is a pleasure to make your acquaintance."

"The pleasure is mine, *Capitaine*. Now, if you will follow me, Admiral Lord Hornblower awaits."

The two officers made their way below. Hornblower received them in the day cabin, and Brewer made the appropriate introductions. The men settled themselves cofortably.

"A pleasure to meet you, *Capitaine*," Hornblower said. "Although in truth, I was hoping your ship was the *Favorite* heralding the arrival of *la Belle Poule*."

"Thank you," Doret said, when Alfred set a drink before him. "I am sorry to disappoint, my lord. I await the prince's arrival myself. I am glad to have arrived early, however; it will give me a chance to go ashore and pay my last respects to the Emperor."

"Did you know the Emperor, *Capitaine*?" Brewer asked.

Doret smiled. "I had the honor to meet him on several occasions," he recounted proudly, "and I dined with him twice. The last time I saw him was in Rochefort, almost three weeks after his defeat at Waterloo. I was just an ensign then. Two of my fellow officers and I came up with a plan to spirit the Emperor away from Rochefort, hidden in a luggar. We would sail under cover of night to Ile de Aix, where we would put the Emperor into a fast sloop, which would take him to America. Unfortunately, the Emperor declined our offer. He thought the plan undignified, saying it was too close to running away for his liking. We begged him, pleaded with him not to throw himself on the mercy of the Allies, but he said the English would listen and perhaps come to some sort of reasonable arrangement with him. The rest, as they say, is history."

"A fascinating tale, *Capitaine*," Hornblower said. "I wonder what would have happened had the Emperor said yes."

"It may interest you to know, *Capitaine*," Brewer said, "that Lord Hornblower was governor of St. Helena and knew the Emperor well. In fact, not many know that the Emperor inducted him into the *Légion d'honneur*."

The French captain looked at Hornblower in surprise.

The admiral shot a look at his one-time protégé. "Since we are telling secrets, *Capitaine*, I know you will be interested to learn that the last person the Emperor ever inducted into the *Légion d'honneur* was our Captain Brewer here, only days before we left the island. He did not have a star to present him, so the Emperor removed the one from his own uniform."

Doret stared at Brewer as though he was a god. "Is this true, Captain? May I see it?"

"Yes, what his lordship said is true. Unfortunately, I left it at home with my wife."

Doret shook his head in sad regret. "That is too bad."

Hornblower brought the meeting to order. "*Capitaine*, I presume you have some vital information to convey to the prince upon his arrival."

Doret's eyes narrowed. "That may be true, my lord," he replied cautiously.

"I have reason to believe I have received similar news from my government." He pulled a note sealed with wax from his pocket. "After you have seen the prince, please give this to him from me."

Doret looked from the note to the admiral and back

again. Finally, he took the note and put it in his pocket.

"It will be as you say, my lord," he said.

"Thank you. I wish you well on your journey to the Emperor's tomb."

The Frenchman rose and bowed to Hornblower before Brewer led him back to the boat. When he was alone, Hornblower picked up the updates he'd received from the packet and read them again, wondering if England was, at that very moment, already at war with France.

Three days later, *la Belle Poule* and *Favorite* sailed into the harbor. Not long after they dropped anchor, a boat was observed pulling from *l'Oreste* toward *la Belle Poule*. Hornblower stood on the quarterdeck and wondered what de Joinville would make of the news—and whether his information sources were more recent.

"What do you think the prince will do if Doret reports that France and England are at war?" Brewer asked.

Hornblower took a deep breath. "I would expect him to weigh anchor and leave immediately. He would not want to be caught in an English port and interred for the duration. The next two hours should tell."

It was two and a half hours later that a knock came at the cabin door. The sentry admitted the first lieutenant.

"I beg your pardon, my lord, Captain," he said, "but I wanted to tell you myself. There's a boat pulling this way from the French frigate."

The two men followed him back up on deck and went to the rail.

"The officer in the stern sheets," Brewer said, "is it...?"

"Yes," Hornblower said. "That's de Joinville. Captain, make ready to receive him. I shall be in the cabin."

"Aye, my lord."

The Prince de Joinville stepped onto the deck, followed by Colonel Hernoux and a third man Brewer did not know, and was received with all the pomp that was his due. Captain Brewer met him and bowed. He was surprised when the prince offered his hand; he hesitated only a moment before shaking it warmly.

"I realize this is strange, Captain," the prince said quietly while holding Brewer's hand firmly, "but we have much to discuss, and I want you to know my commitment to this process is unshaken."

"Thank you, Your Highness," Brewer said. "If you will follow me?"

Joinville hesitated, then indicated the newcomer. "Captain, may I present Philippe de Rohan-Chabot? He is commissioned by my father and Minister Thiers to superintend the exhumation proceedings."

Brewer bowed. "Monsieur, I greet you in the name of His Lordship. Colonel, it is good to see you again. Now, gentlemen, if you'll follow me?" He led the way to the cabin.

"Thank you for coming, Your Highness," Hornblower said upon their arrival. "I am pleased you got my message."

The prince nodded but said nothing.

Hornblower also recalled M. Chabot and greeted him warmly. Then he addressed the prince. "Allow me to be direct. Did the information given to you by *Capitaine* Doret state that our two nations are at war?"

"No, my lord," came the reply. "It did not. However, the Egyptian Ali's actions have come close to forcing Minister Thiers to break with England in order to support the renegade, which o would almost certainly lead to an armed conflict, if not outright war. But, I would not concern myself, if I were you, my lord."

"And why not?"

"Because my father would never allow it," Joinville said with conviction. "My father is not a warrior. I cannot see him going to war over something that directly concerned France's interests, let alone something as secondary as the Egyptian's cause. My father will call Thiers into his office and tell him that there *must* be peace."

Hornblower considered what the prince had said, and he could find no fault with his reasoning. "Then we proceed with our mission."

"I do have one concern," the prince said, "and that is that some English ship will try to stop us."

"HMS *Iris* will sail in company with you back to France."

"That is well," Joinville said. "In light of these developments, it would be best for us to forgo our planned course home through the Caribbean in favor of the most direct route."

Hornblower studied his guest through narrowed eyes. "You realize, Your Highness, that if Angoulême has succeeded in convincing Nicholas to give him ships—and I think this likely—then we may be delivering ourselves to them by doing what you suggest."

"*Oui*," the prince said simply, "but I consider it worth the risk. It is imperative to return expeditiously and distract the people of France, and the politicians, with a splendid gesture. My question now becomes, are you still with me?"

Hornblower sat back with a sigh to consider his options. He shot a questioning gaze to Captain Brewer and saw nothing but trust in the captain's eyes. He looked back to the prince.

"HMS *Iris* will sail in company with *la Belle Poule* to France."

Hornblower saw the tension drain from Hernoux and

Chabot at his pronouncement.

"Thank you, Admiral," the prince said. "Now let us get down to our business. We should like to exhume the body of the Emperor—"

"One moment," Hornblower interrupted. "Forgive me, but the British will disinter the body and turn it over to you."

This caused a stir among the Frenchmen, particularly Chabot, but Hornblower held firm.

"I believe this is in all our best interests," he said, "from a security standpoint, if from no other. We have spoken of this already, Your Highness, and my opinion is unchanged. The exhumation is a golden chance for sabotage, and I intend to prevent it. The garrison will be out in force, and the British will exhume the remains. The French may be there to observe, but from a distance. I will allow certain individuals to be in close proximity—M. Chabot, of course, and yourself—along with some of the personages you brought with you."

"I cannot accept," de Joinville said. "I cannot be present at work I do not direct."

"I am sorry, Your Highness," Hornblower said, "but those are my conditions. Can we not come to some sort of agreement?"

"Admiral," Chabot said, "you cannot keep His Highness from the exhumation!"

"M. Chabot," Hornblower replied calmly, "I am doing no such thing. I have simply stated that British soldiers will perform the exhumation and not French sailors. It is the prince who has said that he will not attend."

De Joinville sat silently, watching Hornblower with hooded eyes, the slightest hint of a smile at the corner of his mouth. Hornblower waited a moment, and when the prince did not speak, he continued.

"Regardless of the prince's presence, the exhumation will

take place. Today is October 9. I propose the exhumation take place on Thursday next, October 15. That is twenty-five years to the day since Napoleon Bonaparte arrived on St. Helena. It seems fitting that it also be the day he leaves. What do you think?"

Hernoux said, "That date is fine, my lord, but what of the prince?"

Hornblower looked at de Joinville as he said, "My dear Colonel, I have already said that the prince is free to attend. You must take up the matter with him."

Joinville folded his hands in his lap. "I see your reputation is well earned, my lord. What I propose is this: the British shall take care of the exhumation under the watchful eye of M. Chabot and those who wish to attend. M. Chabot can direct the transfer of the body from his tomb to the sarcophagus we have brought to carry him back to France. The British garrison can provide escort to the end of the jetty, where I shall be waiting to receive it. There the body shall be transferred to French custody. What say you?"

Hornblower looked to Brewer, who shrugged. He looked back to the prince and nodded. "Your Highness, I accept your offer."

The prince stood, and the others followed suit. "Thank you, Lord Hornblower. My party and I shall make a pilgrimage to the tomb tomorrow morning. I shall be pleased to have you attend as well."

Hornblower bowed. "I shall be honored, Your Highness."

"Good. Shall we say ten o'clock? *Bon.* We shall see you then, my lord. Good day."

Brewer moved to the door to escort the Frenchmen back to their boat. Hornblower sat down and wrote out a note, which he handed to Brewer when he returned. "Please have this sent ashore to Colonel Trelawney, Captain," he said. "I need to inform him of arrangements."

Brewer went to the door and passed the word for Mr. Ford. The senior midshipman arrived and stood to attention.

"Stand easy, Mr. Ford," the captain said. "I want you to take a boat and deliver this note to Colonel Trelawney of the island garrison. It goes from your hand to his. Do you understand?"

"Aye, aye, sir!"

"Dismissed."

"Sir!" Ford turned and departed on his task.

It was in the dead of night that IRN *Brailov* and IRN *Flora* sailed past the Pillars of Hercules, leaving the Mediterranean Sea behind and entering the Atlantic. Captain Baranov stood on the quarterdeck of his ship and savored the moment. He was still dressed as a merchant master, but starting tomorrow the deception would be cast aside. Despite what his orders said, he could not bring himself to fight as anything other than a Russian naval officer. He would carry out his orders, but not as a pirate.

He lsurveyed the deck. The disguise had been effective; there had been no indication that they were anything other than two Russian merchantmen bound for the Caribbean. *At dawn tomorrow,* he thought, *Yuri will give orders to take the costumes off, and the ship will again become the best frigate in the Tsar's service. Then we turn south and look for the Frenchman.* A thought struck him—what if a British ship was accompanying the French frigate? Baranov shrugged the way only a Russian could. *If the British are there when we find the French, then they must die, too.*

At ten o'clock the next morning, Hornblower stood on the wharf, waiting for the arrival of the prince and his party. He could see their boats approaching and did his best to be patient.

The prince climbed up on to the wharf and greeted Hornblower.

"Good morning, Admiral. Please forgive our tardiness; some last-minute additions to the party."

"Of course, Your Highness."

The prince strode ahead. Hornblower was about to follow him when he found his way blocked by a man he had never seen before. Head and shoulders shorter than Hornblower, the newcomer had thick, dark hair just beginning to gray at the temples. He had dark eyes and a long Roman nose in the center of a thin face.

"You are Lord Hornblower?" he asked. "You were the governor?"

"You have the advantage of me, sir," Hornblower said, trying to be polite.

He was rescued by the arrival of Hernoux. "Allow me to make the introductions, Lord Hornblower. May I present to you Louis Marchand, valet of the late Emperor during his time on St. Helena?" He turned to Marchand. "M. Marchand, this is Admiral Horatio Lord Hornblower, official representative of Queen Victoria at these proceedings and former governor of St. Helena."

The two men bowed to each other.

"I have long hoped to meet you, Lord Hornblower," Marchand said. "The Emperor spoke of you often. He once told me he was glad he had fought your brother-in-law on land rather than you on water. He feared the result for him would have been far worse."

"The pleasure is mine," Hornblower said. "Did we meet while I was governor? Forgive me, but I don't remember."

"We did not, sir. I rarely left Longwood. But the Emperor

would talk at great length in the evening or during his bath. You earned his respect," the valet said. "Not an easy thing to do, I assure you."

The party mounted horses and departed. They made their way to the tomb first. Hornblower was not surprised to see that Lady Torbet had set up a stand to sell refreshments to those attending the proceedings. At the gate of the enclosure, de Joinville dismounted and stepped up to the iron grille. His party followed suit, Hornblower included. The prince stared in silence at the grave. After a while he raised his head and stared at the tomb, his face in no way divulging his thoughts. After about a half-hour, he replaced his hat and remounted his horse. The rest of his party did likewise, and they continued their pilgrimage to Longwood, or rather what was left of it.

Hornblower was shocked by the sorry state into which Bonaparte's house had fallen. Marchand acted as guide and gave the prince a tour, explaining to him what each room had been used for and what it had contained during the Emperor's stay. Hornblower trailed along at the rear of the group. He had never been here during his term as governor, but he had authorized many improvements and hated what he saw now.

He suddenly realized he was not alone, and turned to find General Bertrand walking beside him. "Allow me to show you something, my lord," he said quietly. He took Hornblower by the elbow and steered him to a patch of wall. He pointed to a crown drawn on the wall where the wallpaper had been torn away.

"The day they buried the Emperor," he said, "I tore that piece of wallpaper off and drew that crown. I still have the fragment of wallpaper in my bedroom." He sighed. "It is my reminder of my Emperor."

They caught up with the group at the front door, just in

time to hear Marchand relating to the prince how the Emperor withstood the English governor Lowe's attempts to force him to present himself twice a day. Hornblower burned with shame at the behavior ascribed to an Englishman, but he had to admit, it fit with his own brief impressions of Lowe.

On the way back to Jamestown, Hornblower noticed that Bertrand seemed downcast and asked him what was wrong. "Forgive me, my lord," he said, "but hearing Marchand describing things to the prince has brought back sad memories for me. I remember the Emperor saying that Lowe reminded him of a Sicilian policeman." He chuckled, but then his face grew serious. "Later he told me, *'They've sent me more than a jailer. Lowe is a hangman.'* I firmly believe his job was to kill the Emperor. He succeeded."

Hornblower could say nothing in reply, being of somewhat the same opinion himself. The two rode back to town in silence.

Back at the wharf, Hornblower bade farewell to the prince and made his way to see Colonel Trelawney. He found him at the inn having lunch.

"Good day, my lord!" the Colonel said. "Join me, won't you? This inn has a wonderful ragout of pork, or perhaps you'd prefer the roast rabbit?"

Hornblower chose the ragout o. It was every bit as good as the Colonel advertised, especially when washed down with a pint of ale. The two men sat back, satisfied, as the innkeeper cleared the table and brought them each a cup of tea.

"Thank you, George," Trelawney said to the innkeeper. He turned to Hornblower. "I eat here often. George and his wife run the best inn on the island. What can I do for you, my lord?"

"I have spoken with the Prince de Joinville and his principle advisors, and we have hashed out a basic schedule for the proceedings." Hornblower went on to explain the process for the exhumation, to be observed by Chabot, and the processional to the jetty where the remains of the Emperor would be handed over to the prince.

"There's just one thing, my lord," Trelawney said. He hesitated before continuing. "I have found in the papers given me by the governor a letter from Lord Palmerston stating that he is to be known as 'General Bonaparte'."

"I don't think we need worry about little things like that," Hornblower replied, patting his pocket that contained the Queen's letter. "I suggest we go along with whatever title the French wish to give him. I'm sure Her Majesty would approve."

Trelawney sighed with relief. "As you say, my lord."

The Colonel excused himself and left Hornblower alone with his thoughts. He was not entirely happy with the schedule of events, but he believed them to be the best compromise available. He was so lost in thought that he did not notice his visitor until he heard a familiar voice.

"Lord Hornblower?"

Hornblower looked up to find Marchand, the Emperor's valet, standing a few feet away.

"M. Marchand," he said, "how may I help you?"

"You must pardon me for intruding on your meal," the valet said, "but I was hoping to speak to you privately."

"Sit, Monsieur, please." Hornblower indicated the chair opposite him. "Waiter, an ale for my guest. Now, Monsieur, what would you like to talk about?"

"I have long desired to meet you, but I was not sure if it was appropriate. Now fate has put us together. It is probable you do not know what change there was in the Emperor after your arrival on the island as governor. Before you came, boredom was his constant enemy, and I feared that it would corrupt him beyond reason. He was quickly becoming petty and cruel, especially in the way he treated those he considered inferiors. Unfortunately, this included the governor prior to yourself, as well as all the Allied Commissioners except Clausewitz. I will tell you privately, sir, there came a time when I began to fear for his sanity."

The valet took a drink of his ale. Hornblower could read on his face the conflicting emotions that memories were causing him.

Marchand took a deep breath and continued. "When we heard that the governor was to be replaced, I remember the Emperor rubbing his hands together with a fiendish smile and saying, *'Ah, Marchand, fresh meat!'* When you arrived and were in your office, he hurried off to confront you, to take your measure, so to speak. Let me tell you, my lord, when he returned, he was a different man."

Hornblower smiled. "You should have seen the look on his face when I introduced myself. It took him perhaps ten seconds to recall who I was and that I had escaped from captivity in 1810. He even recalled the name of the officer in charge of my detail and informed me that he had died at Wagram."

The valet nodded earnestly. "His memory was prodigious, and it stayed with him right to the end."

Hornblower realized that here before him was the one man in the world who could answer the question he had lived with for nearly a quarter of a century. It was a golden opportunity. "I am curious, monsieur, did your master say anything when he returned from that first meeting between us?"

Marchand sat back in his seat, searching his own memory. Hornblower took advantage of the interval and ordered coffee for them both.

Finally, the valet's eyes lit up. "Ah, yes. Pardon me, my lord, but I was trying to recall his exact words, and I believe I have them now. As I said, he was a changed man when he returned. Even the look in his eye was different. It was a focused look, as though he had a new challenge to tackle, one he took seriously. I have seen this look twice before, my lord, on the eve of Leipzig and during the campaign of 1814 around Paris. It meant that he considered you worthy of his attention, if you will pardon my saying so."

Marchand paused while the innkeeper placed their coffee on the table. He took a sip before going on.

"I asked him what had happened, but he did not answer me. His mind was that busy considering all the implications of your arrival. It was not until his bath after supper that he said, 'The new governor's name is Lord Horatio Hornblower. He was a British sea captain during the war and earned his peerage through his victories against me. Finally, the British have sent a governor worthy of me. Perhaps I can deal with this one.'"

Hornblower laughed softly at that.

Marchand said, "I asked him once what was so special about you, monsieur, and do you know what he said? 'I signed his death warrant twice, Marchand, and he is still alive. Do you know of anyone else who can say that? That is what makes him special.'"

Hornblower lowered his head at the valet's words. They had hit a sensitive spot, and he didn't want to be seen with tears in his eyes. He blinked them away as best he could, drew a silent deep breath, and raised his head. He found the valet looking at him with a smile in his eyes.

"I want you to know, monsieur," he said quietly, "just what—and by that, I mean *how much*—your presence meant to the Emperor. As I said, the Emperor told me that you had earned his respect. In the history of the Empire, do you know the number who can claim that feat? To my knowledge, there are five, not including yourself." Marchand counted them off on his fingers. "Desaix, Davout, Masséna, Ney, and Eugene, his stepson. That is all. And you were unlike the others; you were someone with whom he could talk and share things he was unable to share with his followers. His conversations with you, along with the improvements you sponsored at Longwood and the freedom you granted him to ride, helped him not to hate this place, for a while at least. You helped to dispel the melancholy that was overwhelming his heart. Sadly, it returned, but for a while he was able to live free of its effects."

"Thank you, monsieur," Hornblower said. "Let me say privately to you that he was as important to me as you say I was to him. Did he tell you about my son getting sick?"

"Yes, monsieur. I remember him returning to Longwood and immediately calling for the doctor. When he described the boy's symptoms, the doctor agreed that the only hope was to get him off the island. The Emperor looked downcast at the news, and I heard him say, *'It is Las Cases all over again. The poor governor!'*"

Hornblower shifted in his chair. "He was a tower of strength to me in those dark days. Always discreet, always guarded so as not to cause me trouble with the Allied Commissioners. I owe him a great deal for that. That is why I am here, monsieur, to repay that debt."

"I believe the Emperor would be honored by your presence, monsieur. I know he regretted that you were forced to leave the island. He missed you a great deal."

Hornblower was about to reply when they were approached by General Bertrand and a young man with him.

"My lord, M. Marchand," the general greeted them. "I

hope you do not mind the interruption, my lord, but I wanted to introduce you to my son." He indicated the young man next to him. "This is my son, Arthur. He was born just prior to your arrival, my lord." He laughed. "When we presented him to the Emperor, we told him Arthur was the first Frenchman to come to Longwood without a permit!" Both he and Marchand laughed heartily at the memory.

Marchand rose. "If you will excuse me, my lord, there is much to do before we receive the Emperor. Thank you for a very pleasant afternoon." He bowed, and the three Frenchmen left together.

In accordance with the French request, Hornblower was standing on the shore at the end of the wharf. The sun had long since set, and the sea breeze was cool on his neck. The French delegation, led by Count Rohan-Chabot, had just landed and was approaching.

"My lord," Chabot greeted him. Hornblower saw Bertrand and Gourgaud standing behind him.

"The prince did not change his mind?" he asked.

Chabot shook his head. "We could not prevail upon him to attend. He sent his first lieutenant as his representative. The prince has assured me that he will meet us on this very spot to accept the transfer of the Emperor's remains."

"Very well, then," Hornblower said. "Shall we go? Colonel Trelawney and his men will meet us at the grave."

The procession marched through the town and toward the gravesite in silence. As they approached the burial ground, Hornblower was pleased to see that Trelawney had the entire area lit bright as day by torches. He nodded politely to Lady Torbet, who despite the lateness of the hour, had her booth set up one last time to sell refreshments to the visitors and soldiers working through the night.

The iron grille surrounding the grave had already been removed. Hormblower spotted the Colonel talking with two soldiers beside the grave and saw Chabot join them. On the other side of the willow tree stood a large blue and white striped tent that had been erected the previous day.

The meeting at the grave broke up, and Trelawney was coming over to report. He saluted and pointed to the grave.

"We are ready, my lord," he said. He pulled out his pocket watch. "Seven minutes to midnight, my lord. We shall begin on time."

"Very good, Colonel," Hornblower said. "Carry on."

Trelawney saluted again and went off to get the work started. Hornblower quietly took out his own watch and waited. The first spade went into the ground at one minute past midnight.

General Bertrand stepped up beside him. "It is hard for me to conceive that it was twenty-five years ago that we were brought to this island. The Emperor was only forty-six when we arrived. He would have turned seventy-one this year." The general shook his head. "He was taken from us too soon."

"Yes," Hornblower agreed.

"My lord," Bertrand said, indicating the soldiers who were digging around the stone slab of the grave, "they are going to be busy for many hours. Might I suggest we purchase some refreshments?"

They bought two iced drinks and two tarts from Lady Torbet and made their way to the tent. They sat in two camp chairs placed off to the side. There were two large biers under the tent, one of which held the large polished ebony coffin brought by the French to take Bonaparte home. The sarcophagus was huge, measuring more than two meters in length, a meter wide and nearly a meter deep. Each of the four sides was decorated with a gilded bronze N, and the lid bore the following inscription:

Napoleon
Emperor
died at St. Helena
5 May 1821

Hornblower turned to his companion. "Do you really think it will take them that long to get the coffin out of the grave?"

Bertrand stared at him. "Ah!" he said. "I forget that you were not here for the burial. Following the autopsy, the Emperor's body was placed in a tin coffin, which was soldered shut. The coffin also contained his heart and stomach, which had been removed during the autopsy but were placed in two silver urns for the burial. The tin coffin was placed in a wooden one, which was screwed shut. These were in turn placed in a lead coffin, which was soldered shut as well. These three were placed inside a fourth coffin, this one of mahogany. The tomb itself was lined with stone slabs, themselves being three meters deep in a brick-lined pit. The coffins were lowered in, and the top was sealed with a giant stone slab, which was fixed in place by a layer of cement. The next day, another layer of cement was laid. This was covered by two meters of stone and clay and finally topped by three stone slabs."

When the general was finished, Hornblower could only stare at him. Bertrand shrugged. "Apparently, the governor at the time did not want anyone to steal the body."

Bertrand's words regarding the time needed proved prophetic. The work of removing the slabs and breaking through the masonry surrounding the coffin went on all night and into the morning. The last slab was not lifted clear until 9:30 a.m., finally exposing the coffin to view. Abbe Coquereau, the *almonte* of the French squadron, got some water from the nearby spring, blessed it, and sprinkled the coffin.

Laboriously, the mahogany coffin was raised, carried to the tent, and placed on the bier. The ends of the outer casket were sawed off in order to extract the lead coffin. This coffin was placed inside the ebony one brought by the French. The lid was then removed. The wood coffin inside looked remarkably well preserved. Its lid was unscrewed with difficulty and removed, allowing the lid of the tin coffin to be unsoldered and removed as well.

The body inside was covered by a white cloth—the white satin lining of the coffin lid had fallen over time to cover the body like a shroud. A French doctor named Guillard stepped forward and rolled the lining back, beginning at the feet, to reveal the body. The uniform was remarkably well preserved, although the buttons and decorations were a bit tarnished. The face was instantly recognizable, although Bertrand would later say the face was that of the thinner First Consul rather than the middle-aged Emperor. The doctor noted that the hands were perfectly preserved; there were long white fingernails. Hornblower noticed that the boots had cracked, exposing all but the big toe of each foot.

Gourgaud and Bertrand dropped to one knee, and the rest of those assembled followed suit. Many of the French wept. Bertrand and others hung their heads, overcome by emotion. The company rose in silence. Dr. Guillard proposed that he continue his examination of the body and went to open the silver urns. Gourgaud became angry and ordered the coffin to be closed at once. Trelawney looked to Hornblower, who nodded his assent. The doctor replaced the makeshift shroud, and the lids to the first two coffins were replaced, although they were not secured. The lid to the lead coffin was re-soldered in place, and the lid to the ebony coffin was closed and secured with a combination lock.

The ebony coffin was placed in a giant coffin made of oak, designed to protect its contents during the voyage home. This coffin was lifted by forty-three soldiers onto a solid hearse and draped in black. The hearse was pulled with great difficulty by four horses, also draped in black.

The procession moved slowly toward the bay. When the column was visible from the harbor, the fort and the French ships began firing salutes. From the edge of town, they marched through the streets lined with garrison soldiers at attention, their arms reversed as a show of respect.

The procession reached the end of the jetty at 5:30 in the evening. Joinville was standing there, arms at his side. Hornblower and Trelawney marched up to him.

"Your Highness," Hornblower said, "on behalf of Queen Victoria, I now return to you the mortal remains of Napoleon Bonaparte."

"Thank you, my lord," Joinville replied. "On behalf of my father, King Louis Philippe of France, I accept the remains and thank you and your queen."

The three men stood aside and watched as the oak coffin was placed with great care in the launch for the passage to *la Belle Poule*. Joinville, joined by Hornblower and Trelawney, stepped into the stern of the launch, and the launch left the jetty.

As soon as the boat left, the French ships, which up to now had been showing signs of mourning, hosted their colors and fired their guns in salute. The atmosphere changed from mourning to one of celebration, of welcoming a long-lost hero home.

The coffin was hoisted on to the deck, and its oaken outer protective layer was removed. Hornblower turned to the prince.

"What will be done with the oak?"

"It will be divided up and given to the hands," Joinville replied. "This way, the men will have something to cherish from this voyage."

The ebony coffin was carried to a candlelit chapel at the stern of the ship. The next day Hornblower attended a mass there, after which the coffin was lowered below deck to be placed in the chapel that had been constructed in the steerage.

Once the coffin was settled in for the trip, Joinville visibly relaxed. "My lord," he asked, "would you care to join me for a drink?"

"I would be honored, Your Highness," Hornblower said. "I would also like to discuss our plans for the voyage to France."

François Courbet strode down the hallway toward his master's study in answer to his summons—a rather frantic summons, judging from the rapid and prolonged ringing of the bell in his office. He paused just long enough for his customary two knocks at the door before entering. He found his master, Louis-Napoleon Bonaparte, writing frantically at his desk.

"You sent for me, my Prince?" he asked.

"Yes, François," Louis answered without looking up. "Pardon me while I finish this thought... it must be exactly right.... There!" He put the pen down and sat back in his chair. The broad smile on his face made François wonder what was going on.

"François," Louis said, "I have long thought that something was missing in this enterprise—I mean, my uncle's return to France—and now I have figured out what that something was. *I* was not involved. *I* almost let the greatest opportunity of my life pass by unnoticed!"

"My Prince," François interrupted, "what are you talking about? What opportunity?"

Louis sprang from his chair and came around the desk to grab his secretary by both shoulders. "France, François! My uncle is returning to France! *And I must be there to greet him!*"

Louis squeezed his childhood companion on both shoulders before returning to his chair. François, frozen in shock, stared wide-eyed. *Return to France!?!?*

"My Prince," he said, trying desperately to keep a calm voice, "Are you sure? Will it be safe for you to try to reenter France? Remember, the Minister of Justice said they would execute you if they caught you on French soil again."

Louis dropped his pen and sat back in his chair. His eyes had an unnatural gleam that François recognized and always feared. The last time he had seen it was at Strasbourg.

"My friend," Louis said, "I tell you, *now is the time for us to strike!* The French people are with us, and that fool who calls himself king has all but delivered the nation into our hands!"

"Forgive my bluntness," François said firmly, "but remember Strasbourg! We thought the people were with us then, too."

Louis waved the objection aside. "I was betrayed by the garrison! This time, all will go well."

"But where will you go?" François asked.

"Boulogne," Louis said. "It is *perfect,* I tell you. Where better to start our revolution, where better to enter France than at the port where the Emperor departed the country? We shall engage a ship for the journey, and I shall outfit a small cadre of men to accompany us. My 'Old Guard', shall we say?" His face beamed and he winked. "I shall march to Paris and sit on my uncle's throne!"

François was aghast. It was Strasbourg all over again, only *worse!* At least in Strasbourg, they had a regiment of the garrison they knew they could count on. But this time? *Boulogne!?!?* Even during the end of the Empire, that entire area was overwhelmingly Royalist in its sentiments. *No,* he thought desperately, *I cannot allow... I promised his mother...*

"My Prince," he gasped out, but his words caught in his throat when Bonaparte turned to him. The maniacal gleam was gone. Now the eyes were cold; his face and the set of his shoulders were ones of disappointment. François feared he had finally gone too far.

Louis rose and came around his desk to face his childhood companion. "You have been with me nearly my whole life, through the best of times and those not so good. Even at my lowest points, you never deserted me. Therefore, I cannot find it in my heart to blame you now if your nerve fails you. No, no, it is as I say, my friend. Do not worry; your place is in my heart as it ever was. For this mission, you shall remain here, in England, and keep this house as our base of operations. Never fear; as soon as I am installed in my uncle's palace in Paris, I shall send for you. I could not go on without you by my side. Leave me now; I must complete my plans. Make arrangements for a ship to convey us to France, if you please. I want to leave within the month."

With that, Bonaparte turned away and he was dismissed. As he left the room, closing the door behind him, François' eyes filled with tears. He feared disaster, and there was nothing he could do to prevent it. He made his way down the hall, and anyone passing close by would have heard him saying the same thing over and over under his breath. *I'm sorry, Mama Hortense. I have failed you.*

CHAPTER 13

The little convoy left the harbor with the morning tide. *Favorite* went first, followed by *la Belle Poule,* with HMS *Iris* bringing up the rear. They cleared the harbor and set their course to the northwest, to get around the western hump of the African continent. As they passed Ascension Island, lookouts were doubled. They reached their next scheduled course change without incident, and the convoy moved north.

By prior agreement, they sailed through the night without lights or bells, each ship striving to keep to the prearranged course and speed, to avoid discovery and still avoid collisions, and to have the dawn find them together.

It was on the morning of their third day heading north that something happened.

“Deck there!” the lookout's cry shattered the calm. “Signal from *la Belle Poule.* The corvette's sighted a strange sail to the nor'west. She's ordering her to investigate.”

On the quarterdeck, Hornblower and Brewer brought telescopes to their eyes and watched as *Favorite* turned away from her frigate toward the unknown sail, which was still below the horizon to the British.

So, Hornblower said to himself, *it begins.*

"Captain," he said, "you may clear for action."

Brewer tucked his telescope under his left arm and touched his hat. "Aye, my lord. Mr. Rivkins, clear for action."

Rivkins saluted. He picked up a speaking trumpet and began barking orders. HMS *Iris* began the transformation that would prepare her for the coming battle.

Hornblower stood in the midst of the activity, waiting as patiently as he could for *Favorite* to return. Out of the corner of his eye, he could see the captain standing not two feet from him, eyes forward and hands clasped behind his back, awaiting his next orders. How many times had he seen Bush strike that exact same pose? The thought gave him confidence.

Lieutenant Rivkins reported to his captain that HMS *Iris* was cleared for action.

"Ship cleared for action, my lord," he repeated.

"Thank you, Captain. Now we wait to see what news *Favorite* brings us."

They didn't have to wait long. An hour had not passed when the lookout made himself heard again.

"Deck there! The French corvette's coming back! She's signaling to her frigate, but I can't make out the flags, sir!"

Hornblower felt his breath catch in his throat in anticipation. He moved to the rail for a clear view of the corvette, but he had no better luck reading the message.

"Deck there!" the lookout called. "Signal from the French frigate! *'Two unknown ships on intercept course!'* She's making all sail, sir!"

"You may beat to quarters, Captain," Hornblower said as he watched *la Belle Poule* crowd on sail. The arrangement was for the Frenchman to run for Cadiz while *Iris* and *Favorite* did what they could to ensure she got away.

Joinville had argued fiercely at their planning session against this plan, saying honor demanded his ship stay and fight rather than run away. In the end, he changed his mind when Col. Hernoux reminded him, rather forcefully, that his mission was not to fight but to safeguard the Emperor's remains and ensure their arrival in Paris.

Brewer issued the appropriate orders, and HMS *Iris* exploded into action. He stepped to the waist.

"Mr. Dean!" he called, and the first lieutenant appeared. "Load your guns, but do not run out until ordered."

"Aye, sir!"

The Captain turned to the midshipman of the watch. "Pass the word. I want the fo'c'sle carronades loaded with chain, the quarterdeck with grape. Do not run out until ordered."

"Aye, sir!" the lad saluted and disappeared.

Brewer returned to his lordship's side. They were as ready as they could be.

Aboard the IRN *Brailov*, Baranov could not believe his luck. *The gods have smiled on us,* he thought. *The only way this could have been better would be if we had sprung upon them out of a fog bank or a storm. No matter; I have them now.*

He strode to the lee rail and raised his glass to his eye. "Lookout! What do you see?"

"Large ship with a black hull off the port bow, Captain!" came the reply. "It looks like she's crowding on sail. The small ship is heading for her! There's another ship coming up from the south; she's making sail as well."

Baranov studied the scene before him. The large black-hulled ship must be the Frenchman carrying the Corsican's remains. That meant the ship approaching from the south would be the British escort.

"We shall beat to quarters!" he roared. The Imperial Marines drummer began to beat out his rhythm that would send his crew to their battle stations. He turned to the midshipman of the watch. "Signal *Flora* to engage the British ship approaching from the south," he said. To the sailing master: "Make all sail! I want every stitch she'll carry! We shall overtake and engage the black ship to the northeast!"

The crew responded well, and he felt the ship jump forward as they settled in on a course to pursue their quarry. He turned in time to see *Flora* turn SSW to intercept the approaching frigate.

Hornblower stood by the larboard rail amidships studying the growing patch of white on the horizon.

"What do you see, lookout?" he called.

"They're hull-up now. Looks like two frigates chasing *Favorite*. No flag on them!" came the reply.

Hornblower couldn't see the hulls yet from his position. He crossed the deck to see *la Belle Poule* turn ENE to escape the newcomers.

The lookout reported again. "Deck there! Ships are definitely frigates! Still no flags or pennants flying on them! Frigates are splitting up! The lead ship is going after the Frenchman, but the second one is turning for us!"

Hornblower and Brewer focused their attention on the approaching frigate. The captain noticed his superior tense.

"My lord?" he asked. "You recognize him?"

"Russian," Hornblower replied. "I recognize the construction." *So,* he thought, *the Tsar has decided to play his hand, has he? Very well.* "Now, Mr. Russian, which kind are you?"

"What kind, my lord?" Brewer asked.

"I learned in Russia that there are two principle builders of frigates for the Tsar's navy," Hornblower explained, "and they build their ships very differently. I don't recall their names, but the first builds their ships very light and swift. These ships can almost fly across the water and possess a tight turning radius with very little loss of speed. The downside is that they are easily disabled or sunk. The other builder is almost exactly the opposite. Their ships are built very solidly. They are not as fast as their counterparts, nor do they turn as quickly, but they do well in a pounding match with another frigate."

The Russian's course was just east of south, aiming to come between *Iris* and *la Belle Poule*. Hornblower suddenly realized that he had stationed *Iris* too far to the south. Now he would have to fight his way to his charge's side. Brewer stirred beside him.

"Shall we take her down the starboard side, my lord? Permission to run out the starboard battery?"

Hornblower nodded, and Brewer went to issue the orders. Before he could utter a word, the Russian cut swiftly to starboard across their bow, exposing the starboard battery that the British had not seen them run out. Brewer's eyes grew wide.

"Down!" he shouted to the deck at large. "All hands down!"

He hit the deck just as the Russian broadside erupted. He hugged the deck and covered his head with his arms, listening as ball and grape tore through *Iris's* upper works and those of his crew who had not moved fast enough. He heard the whisper of shot passing over his head and closed his eyes tight to hold down his fear.

When it was over, Brewer lifted his head and saw the Russian pulling away to port. He pushed himself off the deck and turned in time to see Mac getting off the admiral and helping him to his feet. Mr. Priestley and the quartermaster rose from behind the wheel and immediately went to check on two of the mates, who were not rising. Brewer went to check on the admiral.

"Are you all right, my lord?" he asked.

"Yes, Captain," Hornblower replied, "thanks to Mr. McCleary here."

Mac resumed his position behind his lordship.

"Well, my lord," Brewer said, "at least now we know which kind the Russian is."

Hornblower humphed. "We do indeed, Captain. Run your guns out, if you please. Mr. Priestley, hard to larboard. Pursuit course."

HMS *Iris* came around smartly, but the Russian continued to pull away. Brewer looked forward to ensure that the wounded were being taken below before walking to the rail. A moment later, he returned.

"This is no good, my lord. Shall I run in the guns? That may get us another knot or so."

Hornblower shook his head. He glanced over his shoulder at the shrinking form of *la Belle Poule*, with *Favorite* following close behind her and the second Russian in hot pursuit. "The Russian is leading us away from the prince," he said. "Captain, bring us about. Make for *la Belle Poule*."

Brewer spoke to his sailing master, and the ship swung about, on a heading of roughly ENE. "May I enquire as to your plan, my lord?" he asked.

Hornblower waited until the ship steadied up on her new course, then he looked back at the enemy frigate. The Russian had seen his move and was coming about herself. He sighed.

"We need to close with *la Belle Poule*," he said. "Our friend out there is probably armed with 12-pounders;

wouldn't you agree?"

Brewer looked again at the damage caused by the Russian's broadside and considered. "Aye, my lord."

"It would be difficult for a ship so light and swift to carry anything larger," Hornblower continued. "I am hoping to kill two birds with one stone, William. That ship has orders to engage us, at the very least to occupy our attention so we cannot help the prince. Do you think HMS *Iris* can turn just fast enough to get off a broadside to keep our friend out there at bay and then resume course without losing too much time about it?"

Brewer smiled. "You camayn count on it, my lord."

"Good. Mr. Priestley, a moment if you please." The sailing master joined them, and Hornblower outlined his plan. "The Russian will do his best to make us turn and engage him, but he doesn't dare go where we might hit him with a broadside. Therefore, his aim is to try to rake us across the stern. Depending on where he is, I will simply say 'starboard' or 'larboard'. Mr. Priestley, you will put the wheel hard over in that direction, and Captain, you will inform Mr. Dean to fire that battery as soon as we turn. He will have to fire all at once, because, as soon as the broadside is away, Mr. Priestley will put us back on our present heading. Do you both understand? Do not wait for any additional orders."

"Aye, sir," Brewer said, answering for them both.

Priestley went to inform the quartermaster, and Brewer informed Mr. Dean and posted Mr. Paddington at the waist to relay the order below. He looked around the deck again and returned and took his place beside his mentor.

"We are ready, my lord."

Hornblower turned about to watch the approach of the Russian frigate and tried to guess the range at which *Iris's* 24-pounders could reach her long before her return shot had a chance of striking home. Finally, he thought the moment had come.

"Starboard," he said.

The order was repeated, and the ship swung sharply. As soon as she steadied up, the thirteen 24-pounders on the deck below sang out in near unison. The ship recoiled, but Mr. Priestley almost immediately returned to their ENE course. Brewer and Priestley joined the admiral in observing the fall of the broadside. The Russian captain had reacted as soon as he saw the British ship turn, swinging to port to avoid the broadside. And agile as the ship was, it succeeded in dodging the broadside. Even so, Mr. Priestley's prompt return to their course gained them a slight breathing space by opening the gap somewhat. Hornblower and Brewer raised their telescopes.

"No hits," Hornblower said.

"But you had the range, my lord," Brewer commented. "The splashes looked just beyond her."

A half-hour later, Hornblower called for the maneuver again.

"Larboard."

The order was repeated, the ship swung to larboard and the cannon below roared. Again, the Russian turned the opposite way and avoided the broadside. Hornblower lowered his telescope and stared at his quarry through narrowed eyes.

Everyone on the deck of *la Belle Poule* could hear the gunfire from the battle to their south. Joinville stood at the fantail, watching the flashes of the broadsides and wishing he was closer, so as to observe the damage and be able to present a report to his superiors on the state of gunnery in the Royal Navy.

In accordance with his agreement with Hornblower, *la Belle Poule* was on a course away from the battle area, his destination Cadiz. He did not like it, however; it went against all his training and also his nature to run from a fight. This was the main reason he would never be any good at politics, and the major reason he was often at odds with his father.

His ship now flew every stitch of canvas she could carry, and still the enemy frigate was gaining. Joinville knew his best hope was to hold his lead until sundown and then try to lose his pursuer in the darkness. In the distance, he could see *Favorite* closing, as per the plan, but Joinville wondered what good she would do. Hornblower's idea was that she would play the gnat to the enemy's bull with distracting hit-and-run stings. The corvette's 8-pounders could possibly do some damage to the frigate's stern—if there were no stern chasers.

The prince shifted his gaze farther south and was disappointed to discover that their advancing speed had pushed the battle below the horizon. For the moment, at least, he was on his own.

He turned and surveyed the deck of his ship. The carronades—his ship's sole remaining armament—were manned and ready, awaiting the command as to which ordnance to load. His passengers were nowhere in sight. He had ordered Hernoux to get their guests below for their own safety. The result had been total confusion. Joinville had never before in his life seen a living example of sheerest anarchy, but that was the only way to describe what he had witnessed. The passengers had reacted to the order to go below by scattering all over the deck. Some ran forward, perhaps thinking they could outrun the danger, while others headed aft, to see what the trouble was. Several tried to take refuge behind masts. The most humorous part of the entire episode to Joinville was watching Bertrand and Gourgaud.

The two combat veterans stood near the waist and watched the entire escapade with a look that was a cross between amusement and exasperation. He even saw Hernoux pause to apologize to them as he raced around the deck, trying to corral his charges.

Finally, Gourgaud had had enough and grabbed a speaking trumpet. He raised it to his lips and yelled "SILENCE!" at the top of his lungs. That got the attention of the entire deck. The general continued, "His Highness has ordered Colonel Hernoux to take us below deck for our safety. Now everyone get below! Anyone who disobeys this order, I will kill him myself!"

Joinville's eyes had widened at that, but he did not question the general as to his intentions. Neither, apparently, did anyone else. One by one, they made their way below deck. The two generals were the last to descend, bowing to the prince before going down the stairs.

The prince picked up a glass and turned his attention to the approaching frigate. He saw that her captain, in his hurry to overtake the French ship, had crowded on so much sail that her gun ports on her starboard side were very nearly under water. He turned his attention slightly to the left and saw *Favorite* overtaking the enemy ship. Fortunately, Captain Guyet also noticed the enemy's condition. Joinville watched with admiration and envy as hands on *Favorite* raced up the shrouds and took in sail, slowing the ship to pace the enemy. Guyet fired two broadsides of grape that swept the exposed deck of the enemy. After the second broadside, Guyet peeled off to starboard and got away.

Joinville turned to his first lieutenant, Francois Charner. "I want every other carronade in the larboard battery loaded with grape, and the ones in between with ball. Do you understand? Every other one. I want to be ready to hit that frigate if she gets close enough."

Charner saluted and rushed off to explain the prince's orders to the individual gun captains as well as their divisional lieutenants. Joinville turned his attention back to the Russian frigate. Her captain had recovered from *Favorite's* attack. He reduced sail and altered course a couple of points, which allowed the ship to level off and, more importantly, raised his starboard battery out of the waves and made it useful again. Joinville pursed his lips in thought. The Russian was now on a course roughly parallel with his own, keeping pace but staying just outside of gun range.

Joinville left the fantail and began to pace the quarterdeck. His steward appeared with a glass of wine and a plate of cold meat. He told the prince he had missed his noon meal. Joinville nearly ripped into the man, but his stomach reminded him the steward was right. He accepted the gift and thanked the steward for his thoughtfulness.

The prince sipped his wine and munched on the meat. A battle raged inside him: one part urging him to turn on the Russians and attack, and the other arguing that he had to stick to the plan agreed upon with Hornblower. His temperament and pride overcame the urgings of prudence.

"We shall attack," the prince said finally. "Charner, bring the ship about and make for the Russian frigate."

The first lieutenant hesitated and looked to Hernoux.

"You cannot do this, my Prince," the Colonel said quietly, stepping between the prince and his lieutenant. "You have your orders."

"I do not take orders from minor English nobility," Joinville said stiffly.

"I was referring to your father," Hernoux answered.

Joinville narrowed his eyes and did not reply.

"Your orders are to bring Bonaparte's remains back to

France," the Colonel continued, "not get entangled in a fight with the Russians or anyone else because your pride does not like doing what you have been told."

Joinville stood firm, saying nothing but his body language speaking volumes.

Charner stepped around Hernoux. "I beg you to reconsider, my Prince. In our present condition, we cannot fight that frigate and win. All we have are carronades! All they have to do is stay out of range and pound us into kindling! And what would you say to the nation when a stray ball destroys the sarcophagus of the Emperor?"

The prince shrugged.

Hernoux exploded. "You *dare* to be so cavalier? *YOU DARE!?!?* I tell you truly, Your Highness, you do *that* when the Paris mob asks the question of you, and they will bring the guillotine out of hiding for your neck!"

It was Bertrand who stepped between them and pulled the unfortunate Hernoux away. "You have said enough," the general told him. "Truth, every word, but enough. It is his decision now."

They turned to see the prince staring at the deck, as though his mind were racing. Bertrand stepped over and lightly touched his arm. "My Prince?"

It was enough. Joinville blinked. He straightened and brushed the front of his jacket. "Of course," he said. "You are perfectly correct. My apologies, gentlemen; I don't know what got into me. Hernoux, Charner, my thanks. We shall say no more of this."

Standing on the quarterdeck of the IRN *Brailov*, Captain Baranov was not at all happy with how the battle was going. He had pulled off a miracle and found the French ships, only to discover they were accompanied by a British frigate. He dispatched Captain Rossokovich in IRN *Flora* to deal with the British while he pursued the Frenchman, but apparently Rossokovich had allowed the British to get the better of him. Baranov had seen the British frigate cut across *Flora's* stern and put a broadside into her before both ships fell too far away for him to tell what was happening. He had to assume that *Flora* was now disabled—or worse. Then, to add insult to injury, he had allowed himself to be caught out of position and raked with grape by the French corvette when he was unable to reply.

Now his best speed was barely equal to that of the French frigate, and he was having trouble closing the gap. He had to slow her down somehow, but how? Baranov folded his arms across his chest and stared at the horizon as he thought. He realized now that his mission was going to fail. For him to sink the two French ships, killing everyone on board, as well as the British frigate that disabled or sank *Flora,* bordered on the impossible. He sucked his teeth (a habit held over from childhood) before deciding to concentrate on what was most important.

"Yuri," he said to his first lieutenant, "if and when I discover how to slow that ship down, I want you to have at least two boarding parties ready. If we cannot sink her, that may be our only chance. One group is to find Bonaparte's remains and destroy them with grenades. The second is to fight their way to the frigate's magazines and blow them up."

Sominov stared at his captain, not believing what he heard. The look in his captain's eye convinced him. He swallowed hard and nodded. He saluted his captain and went forward on his errand. Baranov watched him go and grunted. Yuri had the easy job; his was slowing the French frigate.

"Captain!" a midshipman called. He pointed aft. "Ship approaching off the starboard quarter!"

Hornblower was fast tiring of the game. Four times now, HMS *Iris* had turned and thrown a broadside at the pursuing Russian frigate, and four times the Russian had turned in the opposite direction and avoided the hail of shot. To make matters worse, the last two times the Russian had turned back fast enough that they managed to close the gap slightly.

"This is getting us nowhere," he growled in a low voice to Brewer. "We must deal with this Russian before we drag him into the fight for *la Belle Poule*. Here is what I want to do. We shall go about as we have before. If the Russian turns opposite again, we shall put the wheel hard over and come about, continuing the turn until we can hit them with a broadside. Then we shall cross their bow and feed them another broadside."

"Yes, my lord!" Brewer saluted. "With your permission, I shall go and make arrangements."

Hornblower nodded, and Brewer departed on his mission. The admiral watched him confer, first with his sailing master and then with Mr. Paddington and the first lieutenant at the guns. Hornblower envied the captain his easy rapport with his crew. It was something that had never come easily to Hornblower; it had taken him years to achieve it just with Bush.

Brewer returned and took his place beside his mentor. "We are ready, my lord."

"Thank you, Captain." Hornblower turned about and raised his glass to his eye. Brewer waited for the word.

"Starboard," Hornblower said, the glass not moving.

"Starboard, Sailing Master," Brewer repeated. HMS Iris began her turn. Now it was up to the Russian.

"Now, Captain," Hornblower said.

"Now, Mr. Priestley!" Brewer cried. "Larboard battery, Mr. Paddington!" The ship heeled terribly on the reversal of course. Brewer looked aft for the Russian. The enemy was caught by surprise by Hornblower's move.

"Steady, Quartermaster," Hornblower called. "Steady... that's it... straighten her out, Mr. Priestley! That's it! Fire, Captain!"

"Fire!" Brewer repeated, and Mr. Paddington echoed the command below.

HMS *Iris's* larboard battery belched smoke and flame as all thirteen guns went off. Hornblower did not wait to see the results.

"Hard to larboard, Captain," he said. "I want to cross her bows."

"Aye, my lord," Brewer said. "Hard to larboard, Mr. Priestley; take us across the Russian's bows. Mr. Paddington, doubleshot the larboard battery with grape over ball."

The ship came around and took them out of the smoke. This time the Russian frigate looked damaged.

"Lookout!" Brewer called above. "Did you see any hits?"

"Aye, sir!" came the joyous reply. "At least four hits for sure! We hurt her good, Captain!"

The Russian was very nearly in irons, trying to double back on her turn. This allowed HMS *Iris* to get the advantage.

"Stand by, Mr. Paddington!" the captain called.

"Stand by!" the midshipman repeated.

"Fire as your guns bear, Captain," Hornblower ordered.

"Aye, my lord!" Brewer replied. He nodded to Paddington.

"Fire as your guns bear, Mr. Dean!" the midshipman repeated. Brewer heard Dean acknowledge the order.

"The carronades, my lord?" Brewer asked. Hornblower nodded.

"Mr. Paddington!" the captain called the midshipman

away from the waist. "Go forward and repeat the order to Mr. Jason! Tell him that after he fires, reload the carronades with chain!"

"Aye, sir!"

He turned to Lieutenant Cooksley, commanding the quarterdeck carronades. "You heard the order?"

"Aye, sir! Fire as we bear, then reload with chain."

They stood on the quarterdeck and watched events take their deadly course. Within minutes, they would be crossing the Russian's bow, when he would be at his most vulnerable. HMS *Iris's* turn had carried them closer than he thought it would; the range was down to barely more than pistol-shot. Hornblower could see that his enemy was beginning to regain control. In a few moments he would be under way again, but by then it would be too late. Brewer stepped over to the fantail, obviously hoping to see the fall of the first shots before smoke obscured their view. Hornblower joined him.

Just then the first carronade fired, followed a moment later by the first of the 24-pounders. The two officers raised their telescopes to their eyes. Geysers rose on either side of the Russian frigate before they saw woodwork errupt into clouds of splinters. Then the broadside was over, and their quarry was hidden behind a wall of smoke.

"Reload immediately, Captain," Hornblower emphasized. "I want to circle around and rake their stern for good measure."

"Aye, my lord," Brewer replied. He called to Mr. Paddington to repeat the order to Lieutenants Dean and Jason, before turning to see Mr. Cooksley signal his acknowledgement as well.

HMS *Iris* ran out from behind the smoke. Hornblower studied his quarry. The Russian had suffered badly from multiple hits, and his foremast was hanging over the larboard rail, held there by the ship's rigging. He could see hands working feverishly with axes to cut away the debris.

Hornblower smiled grimly. The Russians never were good sailors, but they knew how to die with bravery and honor. He turned to the sailing master and ordered a turn to larboard.

He turned back to the rail, only to have his complacency shattered. The Russian was running out his cannons! McCleary sprang into action, tackling the admiral to the deck just as the Russian broadside boomed. Hornblower lay on the deck, his arms covering his head and the big coxswain on top of him, and heard the sounds of iron balls smashing into *Iris*. There were screams from wounded and dying men, taken out by direct hits or impaled by splinters. Hornblower cursed himself for forgetting that the Russian still had teeth.

The broadside passed, and McCleary rose and helped Hornblower to his feet. He turned to see Brewer on one knee with his head down.

"Mac!" he said. "Quickly!"

"Aye, my lord!"

The big Cornishman rushed to his captain's side and helped him to his feet. Brewer put his hand out to the coxswain's arm to steady himself. Hornblower came over and put his hand on the captain's arm.

"I'm all right, my lord," Brewer said. "I heard a tremendous *whoosh* rush past my ear. I can only imagine that one on their balls missed me by inches!"

Hornblower straightened. "Are you fit, Captain?"

Brewer looked up at the tone of his mentor's voice. He stepped away from Mac.

"I am, my lord."

"Then get me a damage report."

"Aye, my lord."

Hornblower turned away and surveyed the deck. Armed only with 12-pounders, the Russian shot had still done damage to *Iris's* sides. Hornblower was thankful that the Russian navy followed the French model of gunnery, aiming, for the most part, at the rigging and sails more than the hull. Even so, a quick scan forward told him that a moderate number of the crew had been injured. He watched as the wounded were helped below.

Brewer appeared on the gun deck, having already walked the upper deck and received the reports on the carronades and upper works. He'd set the bosun and his mates to making emergency repairs to the lines before he came below. Now, as he surveyed the damage, years of training took over.

"Mr. Dean!" he called. The first lieutenant looked up and, seeing his captain, came to report. "Report, Mr. Dean."

"Sir, we have two guns out of action," Dean said. "One dead, six wounded taken below to the doctor."

"Can you put the two guns back into action?"

"Not in time, I'm afraid, sir."

Brewer's eyes closed, more due to the pounding ache in his head than Dean's remarks. He forced them open again and gave his first lieutenant a curt nod, which caused the headache to spike horribly. "Do your best."

"Aye, sir," Dean said to his captain's retreating back.

Brewer came up on deck and reported to his lordship. Hornblower acknowledged the report without a word and turned away. Brewer noticed that the delay had caused them to sail past the Russian frigate, which was turning to pursue them. Hornblower stood at the fantail, watching the enemy ship come around and take up the chase. Brewer walked up and stood beside the admiral, remaining silent and studying the Russian through his glass.

Hornblower was busy berating himself for a mistake that was inexcusable in a new lieutenant, let alone an admiral with his experience. *Bloody fool!* he raged. *Thirty years ago, I would never have been so complacent, so high-and-mighty, and now look at the cost! Blast!*

Out of the corner of his eye he saw the captain, studying the approaching Russian and awaiting his orders. Hornblower closed his eyes and inhaled deeply and slowly, forcing his mind to focus on the task at hand. He exhaled silently and felt the rage dragged from him with his breath. His jaw set; he was not looking forward to writing this part of his report to Palmerston and the Admiralty.

He raised his glass and studied the Russian. Her upper works were damaged, but she was still able to make a good clip across the calm seas. She was gaining on them, slowly but surely.

"Captain," he said, "Given *Iris's* present state of damage, I want you to tell me if the following is possible. Shortly I will give the command to back our foresails, bringing the ship almost to a stop, just long enough to let our friends catch up. Then I want to heel over to larboard and cross the Russian's bow with a broadside from the larboard carronades, followed by an immediate turn to port to give them a full broadside of 24-pounders from the larboard battery. We will then round her stern and hit them again with the carronades and any 24s that have reloaded in time." He lowered his glass and looked at him. "Can we do it?"

Brewer put his telescope under his arm and came to attention. "We will make it so, my lord. Excuse me."

Brewer went to the wheel and explained the admiral's plan to the sailing master and quartermaster, ignoring the worried look on Priestley's face. He also sent Mr. Ford and Mr. Paddington to relay the orders to the battery officers and ordering them to reload with grape over ball. Lastly, he went to find the bosun.

"Sir?" the bosun said as he saluted.

"At his lordship's command, we are going to back the foresails. Be ready to turn them right around again, because he is going to order the wheel hard to larboard to strike the Russians across their bows with the larboard carronades. Then another larboard again so the guns can hit her broadside, and a third turn to larboard to rake her stern with whatever's reloaded." Brewer looked the man in the eye. "I just want you to know what's coming."

"We'll make it so, Cap'n," the man nodded confidently. He saluted and headed for his mates.

Brewer returned to the quarterdeck to find the admiral again at the fantail, studying the approaching Russian frigate. Brewer joined him and raised his glass to his eye. He had to admit he was beginning to develop a grudging admiration for the Russians; they had been hit hard and were still coming back for more. He hoped his lordship was correct about this fellow being lightly built for the sake of speed. If he was, the admiral's plan might be enough to put the Russian out of this fight.

He caught a movement out of the corner of his eye and lowered his glass. The admiral was stirring; it wouldn't be long now. Ninety seconds later, Hornblower lowered his glass and nodded.

Brewer turned. "Now, Mr. Priestley!" he shouted.

Orders rang out to the hands at the braces, and the ship shuddered at the sudden loss of speed when the foresails were backed. The gap with the Russians closed very quickly. Hornblower watched the ship intently, timing the order to set things right and make the turn to larboard. Too early, and the Russian would have time to prepare and possibly prepare his own larboard battery for a counter-broadside; too late, and the ships would collide. He lowered his glass and turned his head to the captain.

"Now, William."

Brewer left his side, shouting orders to the sailing master and the bosun. Within moments, Hornblower felt the ship surge forward and heel over as the turn was made. He put the glass under his left arm and walked calmly to the larboard rail to watch the carronade broadside.

The guns went off singly or in twos, firing as they bore. Even without the glass, the Russian was close enough for him to see men struck down by the grape, and privately he was thankful that the roar of his own guns would drown their screams. His vision was soon obscured by the smoke of the quarterdeck carronades, and he stepped back to where Brewer was awaiting him. The clock in his head was timing the next turn. He paused for a moment after joining the captain, before turning to him with a rueful smile.

"You may make your next turn, Captain," he said.

"Aye, my lord." Brewer barked the orders to the sailing master before telling Mr. Paddington to have Mr. Dean fire as his guns did bear.

Hornblower was haunted by the need to dispatch his foe swiftly so he could rejoin *la Belle Poule*. Normally, he would not be concerned about the prince's ability to handle a single Russian frigate, but the French ship was without its most powerful armaments. Time was of the essence.

HMS *Iris* came out of her turn and made her way down the larboard side of the enemy frigate. Hornblower took advantage of the break in the smoke to make a quick survey of the damage the carronades had done. He was pleased to see several Russian fo'c'sle carronades upended and a few more without crews, and he made a mental note to have Brewer pass his congratulations to the carronades' gun crews.

Iris's powerful cannon opened up, one or two at a time, their captains taking careful aim. Hornblower had a tin ear—and he would be the first to admit it—but it was music to his ears to hear a broadside fired by British guns. He felt the ship shudder, and then again. The Russians had a couple of gun captains who were alert enough to get their rounds off. He hoped *Iris* was sturdy enough to take the 12-pound shot the enemy was tossing at them.

He joined Brewer at the rail as the smoke cleared. The 24-pounder broadside had proved devastating to the lightly built Russian frigate. Hornblower judged a minimum of six of their cannon were now out of action. The wheel was gone, and their mizzen mast had fallen over the side and taken the main topmast with it. The ship was staggered; now was the time to deliver the knockout blow.

"Captain," he said, "make your turn as you see best. Guns to fire as they bear. Let's end this."

"Aye, my lord."

Iris came around and crossed the Russian's undefended stern. The broadside was decisive, as nearly every 24-pounder was able to join the carronades. When they came out of the smoke, Hornblower nearly turned away. It was the worst carnage he had ever seen on a naval vessel. The British broadside left the Russian a derelict, devastated and sinking by the stern.

"Captain," Hornblower said, "make your course for *la Belle Poule*. Call the hands to make all sail. We need every knot *Iris* can give us. Also, have Mr. Dean get those 24-pounders back into action. I have a feeling we're going to need them."

"Aye, my lord."

Baranov went to the rail and raised a glass to his eye. The small shape of the British frigate came slowly into focus, coming his way under all sail. *Well,* he thought, *that tells me all I need to know.* The British were still a good way off. He might yet be able to destroy the French frigate before she could arrive on the scene.

"Captain!" It was the midshipman again. "The French corvette returns!"

Baranov turned to see the corvette trying to make a dash to join his frigate. Suddenly, Baranov got an idea that might just solve his problems. He looked swiftly from the corvette to the French frigate and back again. *Yes,* he realized, *it just might work!*

He turned to the midshipman of the watch. "Load the carronades with grape, main armament with ball. Run out the guns when they are loaded."

Lieutenant Sominov returned. "I have the boarding parties ready. What are your orders, Captain?"

"Yuri, we are about to turn hard to starboard and pounce on the French corvette. If all goes well, their frigate will see what is happening, and their captain will turn back to help."

For the first time in days, Sominov smiled.

Captain Baranov turned to the quartermaster and ordered the wheel put over hard to starboard.

On board *la Belle Poule*, the Prince de Joinville was about to head below deck to rest when the cry came from the fantail.

"Your Highness! The Russian is turning to starboard! He's going after *Favorite*!"

Joinville hurried to the fantail and saw at once that what the midshipman said was right. The Russian was indeed heading to pass in front of *Favorite* and pummel her with a free broadside. The prince grunted. *He'll probably do a wide turn and come back to rake Guyet's stern,* he thought. *Favorite* was in trouble, and there was nothing he could do to help. *Or was there?*

The prince spun. "Hernoux! Charner!" he called. "We must turn about and go to *Favorite's* rescue."

Charner's eyes went wide, but it was Hernoux who stepped forward.

"My Prince, you must not!" the Colonel remonstrated. "We have been through this already. You have the most important responsibility, not only to the king your father but also in the eyes of the nation. You *must* fulfill your mission."

"If we do that," the prince bit out, "*Favorite* will be destroyed, and Guyet and all his crew will perish. Don't you see? The Russian only attacks the corvette to entice me to turn about and engage."

"Exactly my point," Hernoux jumped. "You must not give in to the enticement."

"If I don't," Joinville said, "Captain Guyet and his brave crew will perish."

Hernoux's eyes brimmed with tears, and he looked at the deck. "So be it," he whispered.

Joinville looked about in exasperation, trying desperately to find an argument that would move his officers. His eyes fell upon General Bertrand.

"Tell me, General," he pleaded, "what would the Emperor do in a situation such as this?"

Bertrand looked at his Prince, then he looked at the other two men in turn, before turning back to Joinville. "The

Emperor," he said, "would risk all to go to the rescue of his men."

Joinville looked at the other two. "Gentlemen," he said, "I believe the question has been answered. Have either of you anything to say?"

Neither man answered.

"Thank you for your counsel," the prince said. He turned to the quartermaster. "Bring the ship about. Hard to larboard. Ready the larboard battery."

"Aye, my Prince," came the reply.

Captain Guyet looked about him with tears in his eyes. His proud ship was destroyed. The Russian frigate—he was sure it was Russian—had put two broadsides into her, one across her bow and the other cross her stern. Most of his guns were disabled, and nearly all his guns' crews were dead. Guyet himself was wounded in three places. Still, he was proud to have served his Prince and his nation one last time. His death and that of his crew would ensure the success of the mission given them by their king.

His eyes fell on the dead and wounded that littered the deck. "I'm sorry," he said quietly. "I know you deserved better."

He turned to find his antagonist. The Russian had swung a wide arc to his larboard side and was now coming around to deliver the death blow. *Go ahead!* Guyet thought, *for all the good it will do you! You will never catch the prince, nor will you prevent Emperor Bonaparte's triumphant return to Paris! Vive le France!*

He heard a cheer go up forward, and he turned to see what it was about. He was shocked, dismayed to see *la Belle Poule* coming about and heading in his direction. He could not believe his eyes. His head snapped back despite the pain to see if the Russians had noticed the prince's maneuver. They had, and they altered course to engaege the main quarry.

Guyet turned in agony to look back at *la Belle Poule*, knowing that the prince had reversed course only to try to save him. "Oh, my Prince," he whispered through the pain, tears streaming down his face, "No, please.... No!"

He collapsed on the deck.

Admiral Lord Hornblower paced the quarterdeck of HMS *Iris*, listening to the lookouts keeping him updated on what was going on up ahead.

"Deck there!" called the lookout. "The French frigate has come about!"

That news stopped Hornblower in his tracks.

"What?" he cried. "Lookout, say again?"

"The French frigate has come about!" the lookout repeated. "She's making for the corvette!"

Hornblower turned forward and cursed beneath his breath. He *knew* Joinville would not be able to keep his word. He went to the rail and tried to see what was happening, but they were still too far away. "Captain!" he called. "I need more speed!"

The one man who was happy with the current turn of events was Captain Baranov. He ordered IRN *Brailov* to turn away from the wreck of the corvette and instead prepare to put a broadside into the French frigate.

"We will take her down the larboard side, Yuri," he called. "Stand by!"

Baranov now had his first chance to study his adversary up close. She was twice the size of *Brailov*, and her carronades on the upper deck were run out,. It was not until he was almost ready to fire that it occurred to him that something was not right. Suddenly, the French ship turned sharply and closed the range to half-pistol shot.

"Fire!" he yelled.

His broadside went off in decent order, the carronades sweeping the Frenchman's deck while his main battery pounded her hull. A moment after he gave the order, the French replied with their own volley from their carronades. He heard the screams of his crew as they were cut down by grape or lost an arm or leg to solid shot.

"Bring her about!" he bellowed to the quartermaster, who put the wheel hard over to starboard. He called to a midshipman for a glass, which he used to study the enemy frigate. Now he knew what seemed strange. For whatever reason, the French were not using their main battery! They were limited to carronades! Now he knew how to beat them.

"Alter course to larboard," he ordered.

"Captain?" It was the first lieutenant. "What are you doing?"

"They only have carronades, Yuri!" he said. "We can pound them to kindling from long range!"

The Premier looked to the enemy frigate in disbelief. Baranov shrugged. His guess was confirmed when the French altered course to try to shorten the range.

The two ships engaged in a deadly dance of sorts, each trying to turn so as to gain an advantage over the other, and each firing a broadside whenever their guns were brought to bear. The general direction of the dance was southwest, with *Brailov* trying to lengthen the range and *la Belle Poule* giving chase in an attempt to close and bring her carronades to bear. Baranov grew desperate. He crowded on sail to try and pull away, hoping a lucky shot would dismast his enemy.

Baranov was so focused on his work that he did not notice that the course of the running fight was carrying both ships directly toward HMS *Iris*, which was sailing north under all sail.

"Captain!"

Baranov turned to the source of the cry, a midshipman on the larboard rail. "Yes?"

The boy pointed to the south. "The English frigate approaches!"

Baranov went to the rail to see for himself. Sure enough, the British ship was nearly in gun range.

The first lieutenant appeared at his side. "Captain, what shall we do?"

Baranov thought desperately. "We must play to win *now*, Yuri, and risk all on one throw of the dice. We shall turn suddenly on the British frigate and take her across the bows, then continue our turn and rake the Frenchman across the stern. Then we shall board her and turn your boarding parties loose."

Sominov looked aghast. "It is suicide."

Baranov shrugged. "It is destiny."

The younger man looked at the deck, and the captain put his hand on his lieutenant's shoulder.

"I am proud to serve with you at this moment," he said.

"As am I, my Captain."

Baranov patted his friend's shoulder. He turned to the quartermaster. "Hard to larboard. Ready the starboard battery."

Hornblower stood beside Captain Brewer on the quarterdeck of HMS *Iris*, monitoring their progress as they closed on the battle.

"Nice of them to bring the battle to us," Brewer remarked.

"Yes," Hornblower answered.

"Enemy frigate closing, sir!"

"Stand by, Captain!" the admiral said. "Run out the guns!"

"Run out the guns!" Brewer repeated.

Hornblower studied the enemy and soon realized what he was trying to do.

"He means to cut across our bow and rake us! Hard to larboard! Captain, stand by the starboard battery!"

Brewer stood at the waist and called down, "Starboard battery stand by!"

HMS Iris came around.

"As they bear, Captain."

Brewer watched the turn and marveled at his lordship's timing; they were going to get their licks in first. They came around so their broadside pointed right into the enemy's starboard bow.

"Fire!"

Death and destruction spewed forth from the British guns. But then it was the Russian's turn.

Brewer murmured, "For what we are about to receive, may we be truly grateful."

Both ships were continuing their turns, so the broadside hit *Iris* just forward of her starboard quarter. HMS *Iris* was built rather lightly, being designed to carry a relatively small number of very big guns with speed, so when the 18-pound shot of the enemy broadside crashed into her side, the damage was considerable.

Hornblower dove to the deck by pure instinct. He felt the waves of wind and splinters pass above him, and he heard the screams of those whose instincts had not served them as well.

Leaping to his feet he turned his glass on the enemy frigate. He felt a surge of satisfaction that HMS *Iris* had given better than she got. The enemy appeared to have several guns out of action, and many casualties from grape and splinters. He turned to ask for a damage report.

"My lord!"

Hornblower spun to see Brewer on the deck, his left shoulder bloody and a long splinter impaled in his left thigh. McCleary, the captain's coxswain, was kneeling over him.

Hornblower rushed over and knelt.

"How bad?" he asked.

"Hard to say," the coxswain answered. "I need to get him below."

"Keep me informed, Mac." Hornblower rose.

"Aye, my lord." Mac called for a couple hands to help carry the captain below to the doctor.

Just then *La Belle Poule* cut across the enemy frigate's stern and poured a broadside into her. Obviously Joinville was not about to quit now that he had joined the fight. The enemy reversed course round to starboard and made straight for the French frigate.

"My lord," Lieutenant Dean said, "does he intend to board her?"

"So it seems," Hornblower said. He turned to the quartermaster. "Bring us around to half-pistol shot. Mr. Dean, you are to take command of the starboard battery. When we pass by, I want every ball put into the enemy frigate!"

"Aye, my lord!"

Hornblower turned to the midshipman of the watch. "Pass the word for the second lieutenant." He said to the quartermaster, "After we fire, bring us around to board the French frigate from the other side."

Lieutenant Jason arrived and saluted. "You sent for me, my lord?"

"Yes. We are going to board the French ship. I want you to organize three boarding parties. I will take one and secure Bonaparte's remains. You will lead a second and secure the French passengers; they are probably below deck. Mr. Dean is currently working with the starboard battery. He will command the third party and secure the Frenchman's main deck."

Jason saluted again. "Aye, my lord."

"Mr. Paddington, my compliments to Mr. Dean. Please tell him to report to me on deck after he has fired his broadside."

"Aye, my lord!"

Hornblower stood back. For the moment, he could only watch.

CHAPTER 14

Baranov picked himself up from the deck and checked to make sure he was not injured. *Damn the British!* he thought savagely. They'd got in their broadside first, and now his precious frigate was in trouble.

"Fire!" he yelled.

His guns replied with all their fury, but Baranov didn't bother to check the damage done to the British. He turned instead to the quartermaster, who was standing amongst the remains of two of his mates as he manned the wheel alone.

"Continue your turn, Vasily," he said. "When the starboard battery bears on the French ship, we shall put a broadside into her, then turn into her and board."

"Aye, Captain."

He turned to find Sominov standing there, blood on his tunic and his hair disheveled.

"Are you hurt, Yuri?"

The first lieutenant shook his head. "One of the hands nearby took a direct hit. The blood and mess are his."

Baranov pointed at the French ship. "Prepare to board, Yuri. After the broadside we will turn into her. You know what to do."

Sominov looked at his Captain with the traditional Russian look of stoic acceptance of one's destiny. Baranov was proud of him. "Aye, Captain." Sominov saluted and went forward.

Baranov went to the waist. "Run out the starboard battery! Prepare to fire as your guns bear!"

As *Brailov* came around, he saw the French run out their battery of carronades. The two ships fired almost simultaneously, and Baranov felt his ship shudder at the impact. His men screamed and his mizzen mast fell over the larboard rail. He turned to the wheel and saw the quartermaster still standing there.

"Now, Vasily! Hard to starboard!"

The Quartermaster put the wheel over as hard as he could, but he was alone in his efforts, so the turn was not as sharp as it could have been. Rather than ramming the French, the Russians only managed a hard nudge. Fortunately, Sominov was prepared and quickly lashed the two ships together.

"Now, Yuri! Board! I am right behind you!"

A cry worthy of a Cossack charge across the steppes arose from the Russian bow as Sominov led his teams over the rails and on to the French frigate. Almost immediately, Baranov heard the clang of metal striking metal and shrill cries. He went to the waist and called the gun crews up on deck, taking them with him as he moved forward, gathering every man along the way who could still stand and hold a sword or a pike. When he reached the bow, Baranov turned to address the fifty or more men.

"We will board the French ship," he shouted, "and fight our way aft. Our primary objective is the enemy quarterdeck! Take no prisoners! Are you ready?"

His men let loose a battle cry that rivaled that of their shipmates earlier, and Baranov raised his sword and leapt over the rails. He landed and launched himself at once into the battle. He did not care about the numbers against him; he knew his men were right behind him.

The Prince de Joinville was caught off guard when the Russian frigate turned into his ship. He was shaken from his shock when *la Belle Poule* shuddered from the impact.

"They mean to board!" he cried. "Hernoux! Take twenty men and go to defend the Emperor! Charner, take twenty more and go to defend the passengers! The rest remain with me to defend the deck!"

The French scrambled madly to repel the boarders, but they were not in time. A yell erupted from the bows while Joinville was still organizing his defenses, and armed men began pouring over the rail. The prince now regretted not protesting more fervently before leaving France when he'd been informed that most of his gun crews would be left behind in Toulon in order to make room for his passengers. *Besides,* he had been told, *their guns will not be there, so they will have nothing much to do.* The prince thought they might have plenty to do at this moment.

Charner reached the passenger cabins to find Bertrand and Gourgaud. The first lieutenant explained what was happening and stated that he was there to protect them. The two generals stared at him.

"Young man," Gourgaud said, "I was fighting the enemies of France at the Emperor's side when you were nothing more than a gleam in your father's eye. I assure you, my sword arm is still quite strong."

Bertrand rested his hand on the hilt of his sword. "Mine also," he said. "The general speaks for me as well."

"And me."

The men turned to see Bertrand's son Arthur with two pistols in his belt.

Charner drew his sword. "Then we are ready."

Back on the deck, the Russians—Joinville was sure of their nationality, after hearing their cries—were pouring over the rails onto *la Belle Poule*. The prince drew his sword.

"We shall make our stand at the quarterdeck," he cried, "then move forward as we can."

"My Prince!" It was the midshipman of the watch who approached and pointed to the south. "The British frigate approaches!"

Joinville raised his sword. "Help is on the way, my men! Let us see if we can kill these Russians before the English get here!"

Hornblower watched in helpless frustration as the enemy boarded *la Belle Poule*. *Well,* he said to himself, *we won't be helpless very much longer*. He paced the quarterdeck as HMS *Iris* made her way into firing position. Hornblower walked to the waist.

"Fire as your guns bear, Mr. Dean! Remember your target!"

"Aye aye, my lord!"

The admiral walked back to the quarterdeck. He watched the gap closing between the ships and judged he had about ten minutes before anything would happen. He turned to the quartermaster.

"I shall be in the sickbay. You have the deck."

"Aye, my lord."

Hornblower made his way below and forward to the sickbay. He paused as he crossed the threshold and allowed his eyes to adjust to the dimmer light. He could just make out the doctor and his mates hard at work on one of the injured. He stepped further inside, speaking to those of the wounded who were conscious, reassuring them that the battle was going well. He found one of the attendants. "Excuse me," he said, "how is the captain doing?"

"My lord!" he said. "The captain's over here, my lord. Doctor Sisk said a ball went clean through his upper arm, just below the shoulder, but missed the bone. He also pulled three splinters out of the captain's thigh. He's going to be sore for a while, but he should recover."

"Thank you. The Captain's dear wife would never forgive me if I brought him home in less than one piece." He looked around. "I see the doctor is busy, so I won't bother him. Tell him I shall return after the battle."

"Aye, my lord," the mate said as he knuckled his forehead. "Good luck."

Hornblower smiled, thanked the man, and left.

He arrived on deck just as Mr. Dean was preparing to fire. Hornblower walked to the waist. "Mr. Dean?"

Dean appeared below. "Ready, my lord!"

"As they bear, then."

Hornblower walked to the wheel. "Steady as you go, Mr. Freemantle."

"Aye aye, my lord."

The broadside went off in twos and threes, Mr. Dean obviously moving from gun to gun to check its aim before firing. Hornblower was pleased to see Mr. Jason doing the same with the carronades.

HMS *Iris* moved past the smoke, and Hornblower got a good look at the damage caused by the attack. The Russian frigate would never make port again. Dean had aimed some of his 24-pounders at the waterline, and Hornblower was sure that he would soon see her begin to settle in the water. Better still, the ship's rudder was gone. He turned his attention to the battle raging on *la Belle Poule's* deck. His surmise was confirmed: the enemy was Russian; he recognized the distinctive uniforms and hats from his time in the Baltic. He turned to Freemantle.

"I want to board on the other side."

"Aye, my lord. Around her bows it is, and we'll meet her starboard quarter."

Mr. Dean appeared. "Reporting as ordered, my lord."

"Well done on the broadside, sir," Hornblower congratulated him. "We are going to board the French frigate to help them repel the Russian boarders. You will command a team and secure the main deck. I shall secure the remains, and Mr. Jason the passengers. Mr. Cooksley! We are about to board the Frenchman! You shall remain here in command of the ship."

Mr. Cooksley was clearly not pleased to be left out of the fighting, but he saluted Hornblower and acknowledged his orders. Lieutenant Dean went forward to prepare. Freemantle guided the ship around the bows and nestled her in with barely a nudge against their starboard quarter. Dean led the first group over the rail. He raised his sword and led his group into battle. The momentum of their rush pushed the fighting forward, making room for the boarders behind them.

Hornblower led his men below and aft, toward the chapel and the remains. They encountered a group of Russians trying to fight their way aft and fell on them from behind. One Russian stopped to throw lit explosives at the casket, but

Mac stepped in front of him, bringing his sword down hard on the man's arm before running him through. The Russian dropped the explosives, then his body fell on top of them and took the full force of the explosion. A second Russian threw more explosives, but they bounced off the casket, and a French sailor dove on top of them, sacrificing himself to save his shipmates and the Emperor's remains.

The arrival of the British forced some Russians to turn around, making them fight back-to-back between the French and British. Mac made sure to stay close to the admiral, and he had to admit to himself that the Old Man could still fight. Mac blocked a thrust by one of the Russians and pulled his dagger from his belt. He embedded it in the Russian's rib cage and pierced his heart.

Hornblower parried a slashing attack from his right, then quickly brought his sword down hard into the man's thigh. The Russian screamed and went down on his good knee. Hornblower brought the hilt of his sword down on the back of the man's head. He fell forward onto the deck and did not move. Hornblower placed himself beside Hernoux, in front of the casket, but he needn't have bothered; the enemy forces were nearly dead to the man. But the price paid was high. Hornblower counted seven Frenchmen and 5 British among the dead. He turned to the Colonel.

"If you will remain here on guard, I shall take my men and begin to search the ship, to make sure we account for every Russian boarder."

"As you say, my lord," Hernoux replied. "Don't tell the prince, but I believe the Emperor would be proud of us today."

Hornblower leaned against the coffin for a moment to rest and catch his breath.

Mr. Jason led his men forward from the staircase in search of the passengers. He was confronted and challenged by a French officer.

"I am Lieutenant Paul Jason," he explained, "second officer on HMS *Iris*."

Bertrand vouched for him. "It is true, M. Charner. I have seen him with Lord Hornblower." He said to Jason, "Lieutenant, may I present Lieutenant François Charner, the prince's first lieutenant."

The two officers saluted one another. Jason looked around.

"Have the Russians come this way?" he asked.

"Very few," Charner said.

A voice piped up from somewhere in the rear. "Monsieur, I just saw some strangers proceed below deck."

"What?" Charner cried. "When? Why did you not speak up before now?"

An old man stepped forward. He was trembling.

Bertrand said, "This is M. Coursot, one-time servant to the Emperor on St. Helena."

"M. Coursot," Charner said, "tell us where they went!"

"Below," the old man said. "I saw them go below."

"Below? For what purpose?"

"What's...?" Jason searched for the answer, and suddenly his eyes widened with fear as it came to him. "The magazine."

"Of course!" Charner said. "They will try to blow up the ship! Lieutenant, you and your men accompany me. The rest of you, stay and guard the passengers. I want one man to report this to the prince."

"I'll go!" one of the French sailors cried. He ran for the staircase.

"Follow me!" Charner headed for the forward staircase. Jason and his men followed.

Bertrand looked at Gourgaud. "I am going with them." He trotted forward. His son went with him.

Gourgaud looked around and spotted a midshipman whose name he could not remember. "You!" he called, pointing at the lad. "I leave you in charge here. I am going to safeguard the Emperor."

Charner ran forward and dove down the stairwell, with Jason and his men hot on his heels. At the orlop deck, he paused only for a second to listen, then turned aft and soon caught up with the invaders. The Lieutenant launched an immediate attack, but was cut down by a savage blow to the neck from the nearest Russian. Before Jason could act, Bertrand ran past him and dispatched the Russian with a strike to the man's chest, his blade sliding expertly between two ribs and piercing the heart. The general knelt to check on his fallen comrade as his party swarmed past him and into the fray. He stood and shook his head.

"I have seen many young warriors fall," he murmured, "but none lately. I find it still hurts as much as it used to." He looked to Jason and realized the lieutenant was very young. He guessed this was his first combat. Instinct took over, and he assumed command of the group. "Come, Lieutenant, we must save the ship!"

Bertrand charged forward into the wedge of Russians, blocking and parrying between thrusts and slashes that bit into his enemy's flesh. Jason and his remaining men followed close behind, fighting for their lives. Jason looked past the throng and saw several Russians enter the forward magazine. He immediately informed Bertrand.

"Lieutenant," the general said, "choose four men to accompany you. Leave all your weapons here except your swords–no dirks, no pistols. We shall fight our way to the magazine, then you and your men go in to deal with the Russians inside. The rest of us shall deal with the threat out here."

Jason immediately saw the logic in the general's plan; they would take nothing into the magazine that could cause a spark and initiate the very destruction they were trying to prevent. He quickly chose his men and gave them their instructions.

"We are ready," he said to Bertrand.

"Then let us charge the enemy! *Bonne chance, mon ami!*"

Jason raised his sword and followed the French general into the melee. He saw a Frenchman to his left go down after a Russian saber dug deep into his chest. The Russian pulled his blade free and turned on Jason, who barely had time to raise his blade and parry the blow. The Russian's momentum carried him into his opponent, and by sheer reflex, Jason grabbed his attacker by the lapel so they both went down to the deck. The Russian landed on top, but before he could strike again, Jason saw his face contort in pain and felt the Russian collapse upon him. The lieutenant pushed him off to find a hand waiting to help him up. It was Yulee, a topman from *Iris*.

"Up you go, sir," Yulee said as he pulled the young lieutenant to his feet. "No time to lay down on the job!"

The two men dove into the brawl again, heading for the magazine. Jason heard Yulee gasp and turned to find a sword point sticking out of the topman's chest. Jason remembered Alfred's training. He spun around his shipmate and dove his sword point into the blackguard Russian's ribs. He sword was wedged in good, so he dropped it and picked up Yulee's. He headed for the door.

The fighting was as bad as any Bertrand had ever experienced, including when his unit repelled a Russian charge at Borodino. He was thankful that he had faithfully practiced his fencing; it was his preferred method of exercise, and it certainly came in handy now, as two Russians blocked his path. He feinted toward one, causing him to go on the defensive, then turned in mid-thrust and brought his sword down on the neck of the second. Meanwhile, the first had recovered and struck quickly, slicing open Bertrand's arm above the elbow. He kicked out with his foot, catching his antagonist on the inside of his knee and dropped him to the deck. The genera drove his sword deep into the unfortunate man's back.

They reached the door of the magazine, and Jason and his team threw down their swords and ran inside.

They found four Russians inside, two tipping powder kegs over with the third preparing to light them off. The fourth was across the magazine, breaking open a box of grenades. Jason made straight for this last man. He struck out with all his might, his fist smashing into the Russian's face and sending him tumbling back over some barrels and into the bulkhead beyond. Two others of his team went for those preparing the powder and the last two took out the one who would spark the explosion.

Jason and his men secured their prisoners—the one Jason attacked had broken his neck when he hit the bulkhead and was dead—and marched them out of the magazine. All was quiet outside, and Jason found seven Russians dead on the orlop. Sadly, nine of his team and the gallant Charner were also dead. He looked to Bertrand.

The general shrugged. "I remember from 1812. Russians don't surrender."

"Let's go," Jason said. "We can hold these prisoners in the fo'c'sle."

On the deck, the fighting raged on, as more and more Russians were leaving their own wrecked vessel to board *la Belle Poule*. The French and British were doing all they could to prevent the Russians from advancing on to the quarterdeck. Dean and Alfred fought side by side at the starboard gangway, holding their own, but just barely. The Lieutenant was amazed at the way the Russians charged, regardless of the risk to their own lives. The French marines in the tops made the difference on one or two of the charges.

Captain Baranov had paused just long enough to see Sominov lead his team below in search of the ship's magazine, before returning his attention to the fight. He charged forward with his sword in one hand and a pistol in the other. He shot a Frenchman who was waiting in the mainmast shrouds to leap on one of the invaders; the man spun off the shrouds and disappeared into the sea. He roared in rage as he saw a huge Frenchman strike down one of his men, and attacked. The Frenchman was surprisingly quick for his size, and Baranov quickly found himself on the defensive. His enemy's blows were powerful, but Baranov was an old hand at this sort of fighting. He had sharpened his skills over many battles with the Turks, and his instincts were still good. He feinted to his left, and when his opponent reacted, he ducked and stabbed upward with his dagger, piercing his enemy's chest below the sternum and killing him instantly.

At one point, Dean and Alfred ran to help the prince and his forces on the other side of the deck, after the Russians had succeeded in pushing them back. The intervention was enough, and the Russians were pushed forward.

"Alfred," Dean said, "I want you to stay with the prince. Watch his back."

"Aye, sir," Alfred said, and he took his place at the prince's side.

Joinville scowled. "I do not need a nursemaid, Lieutenant, especially one so small."

Dean was about to reply when a Russian swung over the quarterdeck using a line he had cut. He landed with a cry behind them and immediately went for the prince. Alfred stepped in between them and parried the man's thrust just short of Joinville's chest. Alfred pulled his dagger from his belt and stabbed the man in the thigh, then he jumped back and brought his sword down savagely on the man's neck. He fell to the deck, dead, and Alfred looked at the prince. Joinville stared in amazement.

Dean just smiled and went back to his men. He got there just in time to save Turner, a gun captain in the starboard battery. Two Russians had him cornered against the rail. Turner was holding his own until one of the Russians sliced open his thigh. The cut must have gone deep, because Turner dropped his sword and grabbed his leg as he fell to the deck. Dean cried out and leapt on the back of the nearest Russian, driving his dagger into the base of the man's neck. The two men went down to the deck together. Dean thought he was done for, but his rash attack had distracted the second Russian long enough for Turner to pull his pistol from his belt and shoot the man in the face. Dean got to his knees, staying low so as not to attract any attention, while he examined Turner's wound. The cut was bleeding badly. Dean looked around for a bandage of some sort, finally cutting the dead Russian's shirt from his body and tying it around Turner's leg. Then he removed the dead man's belt and secured it above the wound to reduce the flow of blood.

"Now you sit tight," Dean said, as he handed Turner back his sword and a loaded pistol. "I'll be back for you as soon as I can."

"Aye, sir," was all Turner could say before Dean was gone.

Near the bow, Baranov rested for a moment as he nursed a wound in his upper arm before rejoining the battle. It was not going according to his plan, let alone his wishes. The French had proved difficult, and the arrival of the British had all but sealed his fate. To add insult to injury, he had been wounded before he could fight his way to the French captain.

He sighed and looked back at his beloved ship. *Brailov* was beginning to settle in the water. The damage below the waterline from the last British attack was far too much for his pumps to overcome. He knew what he had to do now. No matter what, he could not allow The Tsar to be brought into this. He, his ship, and his men were dead now; the only thing left to do was to take as many French and British with them as they could, and hopefully, Bonaparte's remains as well.

"You two, come over here," he called to two hands.

"Captain, you're hurt!" cried one of them.

"It is nothing," Baranov said. "I have a job for you. Return to the ship. Get the wounded into the water; lash them to anything that will float. Set as many fires as you can, then go to the magazine, and empty one barrel of powder onto the floor. That will help the fires detonate the magazine."

"But Captain!" the second said. "The ship will explode!"

"Yes, and take this one with it," Baranov confirmed. "We will not be able to finish our mission and return home. The nature of the mission is such that we must make sure The Tsar cannot be blamed for this. Do you understand?"

The second man—the younger of the two—made to protest, but the first man prevented him.

"I understand, my Captain," he said. "It shall be as you say."

"Good," Baranov said. "Now, off with you both."

Hornblower and Colonel Hernoux looked around to make sure there were no Russians left below. The entire force lay dead around them. French and British casualties had been heavy, but their numbers had carried the day. The casket containing the remains was safe, and the threat neutralized—for the moment.

They looked up as they heard renewed fighting on the deck above.

"I shall take what men I have left and go forward," Hornblower said. "We shall ascend to the deck and attack the Russians from the rear. I suggest you remain here with about ten men to guard the Emperor, in case some Russians break away from the fight on the deck and make their way here."

"Agreed, my lord," Hernoux said. "Good luck."

Hornblower raised his sword and led his men forward.

Baranov was just about to make his way aft to lead his men below when he turned at a noise behind him. A dozen British sailors were emerging from the companionway, led by an officer. He bellowed for help and led eight of his men against this new threat. He realized that both of the teams he had sent below decks must have been wiped out, or it would have been his own men ascending to the deck. Now he had to keep the British busy long enough for *Brailov* to blow up.

He approached the officer and attacked. The man blocked his blow and quickly tried to strike at his head, but Baranov dodged the blow. The officer made a thrust that he parried, but it forced him off balance, just enough that he could not dodge his opponent's thrust at his thigh. He cried out as the blade bit deep, and he fell to the deck. The officer stepped back, as though looking for another opponent, giving Baranov the chance to quietly pull a pistol from his belt and raise it. He cried out again as a sword blade flashed past his head and sank into his chest. He just had the strength to look at the man standing by his head before he died.

Hornblower turned when he heard the cry behind him to see McCleary with his sword buried into the chest of the Russian he had just wounded. He saw the pistol next to the dead man's hand. He looked to Mac and saluted him with his sword.

"Thank you, sir," Hornblower said. "Now I know how your captain has survived all these years." He looked aft and saw maybe ten or twenty Russians still fighting, presumably trying to make their way below deck. He was about to order his men to attack when Mac cried out.

"My lord!"

Hornblower turned to see wisps of smoke ascending from the sinking Russian frigate. Either the ship had caught fire, or the Russians were blowing up their own ship in an attempt to sink the French ship and its precious cargo. The two men ran to where the ships were lashed together and began hacking at the ropes with their swords.

"Excuse us, my lord!"

Two hulking tars came up with axes in their hands. Hornblower and Mac moved aside and let them take over.

"Mac," he said, "find some pikes, or something we can use to push that ship away. Have someone signal Cooksley to move *Iris* away."

"Aye, my lord." The big Cornishman returned with three pikes and handed two of them to the hands after they cut the last lashing. The three of them managed to get a yard or two of separation between the ships. Not as much as Hornblower would have liked, but enough for *la Belle Poule's* canvas to nudge the ship to safety. The British watched as the flames began to lick upwards through the hatches and gun ports of *Brailov*. The ship exploded about a hundred yards off the larboard quarter. The blast sent pieces of masts and chunks of canon skyward, and burning sails billowed as they fell.

The explosion stopped the fighting for a moment as men on both sides gazed, aghast, at the destruction. The remaining Russians realized that they had a new enemy force at their rear. That, and having no ship to return to, was enough to take the remaining fight out of them, and they threw down their swords.

CHAPTER 15

All that was left was to secure the prisoners. Twenty-three Russians had been taken, most of them wounded. French and British casualties combined added up to forty-two dead and sixty wounded. Joinville was saddened to hear of Charner's death; Bertrand told the prince that his friend died bravely in battle and that his actions contributed greatly to saving the ship.

Hornblower took HMS *Iris* to look for survivors of *Favorite*. They rescued a total of seventeen, one of whom was the faithful Marchand, to Hornblower's great joy.

Hornblower stepped below to the sickbay while the ship made her way back to *la Belle Poule*. He found Captain Brewer awake and talking with Doctor Sisk.

"My lord," the captain greeted him, "I hear you did it again."

"Nonsense," came the reply. "You have an excellent crew, Captain, and the French fought well." He shrugged. "Things went our way. I just wish we could have prevented the Russians from boarding the prince's ship."

"How badly was she damaged?"

Hornblower shook his head. "Not too badly. Cables to splice, sails to mend, some general repairs to be made. She was fortunate that she took the Russian broadsides forward for the most part. I think only one ball made it near the chapel, and the casket was untouched through it all." The admiral smiled. "Bonaparte would probably credit that to his star. His destiny required him to be buried on the Seine, he would say."

Brewer laughed at that. "I can hear him saying those very words, my lord."

It took three days to make repairs on *la Belle Poule* and *Iris* and get under sail again for France. All those rescued from *Favorite* were transferred to the French frigate, save for M. Marchand, who asked to sail on HMS *Iris* as far as Cherbourg. Hornblower was delighted to grant his request.

Captain Brewer was back on his feet before the week was out, and Hornblower made sure his injured leg got exercise by inviting the captain to walk with him on the quarterdeck. His recovery was slow and painful going at the first, but by the time they made Cherbourg he was walking almost normally.

Marchand's presence on board was a delight to Hornblower. The two men talked often, either in the cabin or walking on the deck. Hornblower asked him many questions about his time with the Emperor, and Marchand told him many stories.

On the last night before their arrival in Cherbourg, Hornblower invited the former valet to the cabin. Captain Brewer was also invited. The three men shared a vintage bottle of Cognac.

"Monsieur," Hornblower said, "I have one last question to ask, and I should be very glad to hear your opinion. I have long thought that all that transpired on St. Helena during my tenure as governor was only possible because the Bonaparte I knew was not the Bonaparte of 1805. He had changed since then, becoming more moderate in his tastes and attitudes. I do not know if his final defeat or his exile or a combination thereof was responsible for the change, but I want to know what you think."

Marchand looked at his host with a strange gleam in his eyes. He sipped his Cognac and then stared at the liquid inside the glass. Brewer was about to comment on his silence, but a glance at Hornblower told him to wait him out. Finally, the valet shifted in his seat and spoke. "My lord," he said, seemingly searching for the right words, "you are the only one besides myself who has raised this question. I first noticed the change begin on Elba. That was when, I think, he first realized that he was no longer who he once was. You may be interested to know that the Emperor very nearly did not leave the island. He developed the habit, as he got older, of talking out both sides of a proposition himself when he was alone, and he often did so when I was in the room, attending to my duties.

"I happened to be present when he debated with himself the possibility of escaping Elba. He went back and forth for nearly two hours. At one point, he seemed to have convinced himself to stay, the thought being that if he went and was beaten again, his fate would be much worse. This line of thinking overjoyed me; I was quite content to serve him there for the rest of my life. The Emperor could still rule there, he was able to receive visitors with relative ease, and the populace adored him."

The valet paused to draw a ragged breath and shook his head. "But fate would not allow this. I saw the last vestiges of the old Napoleon rear his ugly head, the invincible conqueror, you see, who could solve all his problems with one more great battle! He did not know, he had not realized that those days had ended with Wagram." He paused again to gather himself, showing a small smile of embarrassment. He continued, "So, we went. We reached Paris on a wave of popular support. France was glad to have him back, but the rest of Europe objected mightily. I remained in Paris during the Waterloo campaign, and when he came back, he was devastated. He briefly considered trying to escape to the United States, but decided he would look like a criminal and surrendered to the British instead."

Marchand wiped his eyes with his handkerchief. "I apologize for my emotional response, my lord. To answer your question, yes, I agree with your comment. The Emperor of 1805 was a completely different man."

Hornblower raised his glass in a toast. "Then I am glad to have met the man I did. To the Emperor, may he rest in peace."

Marchand raised his glass as well, and the two men drank in silence.

"What will you do now?" Hornblower asked when they were done.

The valet shrugged. "I have a little money put aside."

"May I suggest that you write about your experiences with the Emperor, monsieur? You have insights into the second half of the Empire, as well as his two exiles, that no one else knows except the Emperor himself."

Marchand looked concerned. "What about the Emperor's expectation of confidentiality from me?"

"I think the Emperor would not mind," Hornblower said. "After all, he never asked you for your silence, did he?"

The valet shook his head.

Hornblower shrugged. "Then I see no problem, as long as what you write is the truth and not sensationalized or slanted to make the Emperor look good. I believe, monsieur, that he would rather have you, who was there, tell his story rather than others who were not. It is my opinion, based on my conversations with him, that he would approve."

The valet thought it over. "I shall consider your proposal, my lord. Thank you."

Hornblower stood next to the wheel the next morning, as HMS *Iris* followed *la Belle Poule* into Cherbourg harbor. Captain Brewer stood proudly beside him, with Mac standing just behind, in case the captain's injured leg gave him trouble. They dropped anchor a short distance from the French frigate so as to have a first-rate view of the ceremonies to be held when Bonaparte's remains were transferred from the ship.

Early the next morning, Hornblower, Brewer, and the entire crew of HMS *Iris* were turned out to witness the momentous event. The paddle steamer *Normandie* approached *la Belle Poule* and backed up to the big frigate. A large gangway was laid from the frigate's deck to the steamer's, allowing the passengers to transfer safely. M. Marchand bade them farewell and was rowed over to the steamer.

A large derrick was constructed aft on the frigate which lifted the black, flag-draped casket from the hold, swung out over the rail, and lowered the coffin on to the steamer's deck. Several hands moved immediately to secure the casket, and once that was done, the ship pulled slowly away from the frigate and made her way upstream toward Paris.

Hornblower watched as the steamer rounded a corner and disappeared from his sight, and he wondered if his debt to the Emperor was truly paid in full.

Later that afternoon, Hornblower and Captain Brewer were reminiscing in the day cabin, retelling stories of their time on St. Helena. There came a knock at the door, and the sentry opened the door. Mac entered with a note in his hand.

"What's that, Mac?" Brewer asked.

"Don't rightly know, sir. Quartermaster said this was delivered by boat. It's addressed to his lordship." He handed the note to Hornblower.

The admiral broke the seal and unfolded the page flat on his knee. He read the note slowly, and the more he read, the higher his eyebrows rose.

"My lord?" Brewer asked.

"It is from Louis-Antoine d'Artois," Hornblower said slowly. "He is the duke of Angoulême and the Legitimist Pretender to the French throne." He looked up and saw the name meant nothing to the others. "He is the leader of the Ultra-Royalists," he explained.

"What does he want, my lord?"

Hornblower looked at them in disbelief. "He asks that I come to his chateau outside Cherbourg to meet with him. The note says there will be a carriage for me at the wharf at seven o'clock this evening."

"Why does he want to see you, my lord?" Mac asked.

"The note does not say."

"Is it a trap, my lord?" Brewer asked.

Hornblower tapped the note. "I wouldn't think so. What profit would he gain by kidnapping or killing me now, when Bonaparte is already on French soil? Besides, if anything were to happen to me, I'm sure Alfred would hunt down those responsible and avenge my death. Isn't that so, Alfred?"

Brewer and McCleary turned to see the servant standing in the pantry door.

"Yes, my lord," he said.

Brewer looked from one man to the other but was unable to tell if either of them was kidding.

"Will you go, my lord?" he asked.

Hornblower read the note again. He had to admit he was intrigued by the idea.

"Yes, I believe I will," he said. He pulled out his pocket watch. "I have just over an hour to meet the carriage. Excuse me, gentlemen, while I change."

He stepped out of the boat and onto the wharf with ten minutes to spare. Mac volunteered to conn the gig and wait for him to return, and Hornblower gratefully accepted the offer. He walked to the end of the wharf to find the carriage waiting, his door held open by a footman in expensive livery.

"Lord Hornblower?" he asked.

"Yes."

"His Grace awaits you. If you please?"

Hornblower entered the carriage and the door was shut behind him. He glanced out the window at the festivities that accompanied the arrival of the Emperor's remains, and he wondered what the duke thought of the celebrations.

The journey was a short one. Soon the carriage turned up a tree-lined way that ended at a gilded two-story chateau complete with a fountain in front. His door was opened, and he stepped out to find the duke himself waiting at the top of the stairs. Even if he had not seen a recent portrait of him, the way this man carried himself would have identified him.

"Welcome, my lord," he said. "I am Louis-Antoine d' Artois, Duke of Angoulême."

Hornblower bowed. "Your Grace, thank you for the invitation."

"Not at all, my lord," he answered. "Come. We have certain matters to discuss."

Hornblower wondered just what these matters could be as he climbed the stairs. He bowed again when he reached the top of the stairs, and the duke reciprocated. Without a word, the duke led the way into the house. Hornblower followed him into a magnificent library with a fire blazing in the huge fireplace against the chilly November air. The duke closed the door behind them, then surprised Hornblower by going to the table himself and pouring them each a glass of wine. He handed one to his guest and led him to some comfortable chairs in front of the fire.

Hornblower tasted his wine and looked to his host. "What can I do for you, Your Grace?"

"I merely wished to congratulate you on a job well done, my lord," the duke said, "and to let you know your success will not change anything in France."

"Thank you, Your Grace, for your hospitality; but I did not do what I did for France but for my Queen, and I care not one whit for your country's internal political affairs."

"Of course you don't, my lord," the duke said with a smug smile on his face. "That fool of a cousin of mine who calls himself king cannot possibly survive much longer, and with the Bonapartist pretender in prison, I am the obvious choice to assume the throne and restore France to the glories she possessed under my ancestors."

Hornblower started. "Bonaparte is in prison?"

"Indeed he is, my lord, indeed he is!" Angoulême crowed. "The *imbecile* tried to stage a coup in Boulogne, which, naturally, fell apart; he was arrested."

"Has he been tried yet?" Hornblower asked.

"Not yet," the duke replied. "Were I on the throne, there would be no trial; Bonaparte would be executed at once for sedition and treason. However, with my cowardly cousin on the throne, I doubt he will even come to trial. The king would not wish to offend the Bonapartists and risk a civil war." Angoulême took a drink and shook his head. "No, my cousin will let him languish in prison for a time and then quietly send him back into exile." He looked at his guest. "I am sorry you went to all this trouble for nothing."

Hornblower drained his glass. "Have you had any communication with the tsar lately, Your Grace?"

Angoulême glared at him; his guard was up now. "No, my lord, why do you ask?"

Hornblower shrugged. "I thought he might want to know where his two frigates are."

The duke's face grew cold. "And what frigates are those?"

"The ones he loaned you to sink *la Belle Poule* and stop Bonaparte's remains from reaching France."

The duke waved the inference away. "I know nothing of this."

"Come now, Your Grace," Hornblower said. "Where else could you have obtained the ships? And who, besides yourself, could have planted the idea in the tsar's head? Your plan failed. We sank both ships."

"Take care, my lord," the duke said menacingly. "It is not wise to make unsubstantiated accusations."

Hornblower's face grew hard. "Hardly unsubstantiated, Your Grace. We took prisoners from the Russian boarding parties. I do not know what Joinville did with his, but we have ten aboard my ship, including the first lieutenant of one of the frigates."

Angoulême stared at his guest over his glass for some time, his hooded eyes revealing nothing of what he was thinking. Hornblower set his glass on the table, and sat back to wait. The duke finally set his glass down as well and folded his hands in submission in his lap.

"What do you want, my lord?"

Hornblower leaned forward to dictate his terms. "Neither you nor your followers will interfere in any way with the internment of Bonaparte's remains in his new tomb, nor will you disturb the tomb in the future. The moment I hear that mischief has been done, I will place my evidence before the Queen herself—as well as the press." He smiled a terrible smile, full of menace. "The Paris mob would put *you* on the guillotine."

The duke glared at his guest with undisguised rage and hate. Hornblower rose.

"I'm glad we understand each other, Your Grace," he said.

He left the room without looking back.

The next morning, Hornblower invited the captain and first lieutenant to breakfast with him. The three men sat down to one of Alfred's special breakfasts—eggs, slabs of ham, fresh baked bread, butter, jam, and fresh fruit.

"When do we leave for Paris, my lord?" Greene asked between mouthfuls.

"The British trade representative at the port office has booked us three passages on a river packet for Paris. We must be aboard before nightfall. I have been guaranteed that we will arrive before the festivities begin."

Brewer swallowed a mouthful of ham and smiled mischievously. "Say, my lord, I wonder what our friend would say about your finally making it to Paris?"

Hornblower chuckled. "I believe he would arrange a tour of the Bastille for us, just so I can see what I missed." He wiped his mouth and rose. "I believe we shall take our coffee in the day room."

His companions rose and followed Hornblower aft. They sat and Alfred brought their coffee. A knock at the cabin door came suddenly, and the sentry admitted Mr. Ford.

"My lord," he said, "there's a boat pulling this way, and I believe the prince is on board!"

The two officers looked at each other. Brewer rose. As he did, Mac appeared in the doorway.

"I shall go receive him, my lord," the captain said. "Let's go, Mac."

Hornblower called for Alfred to prepare a cup for their guest, and he wondered, as he heard the scurrying of feet over his head, what was the meaning of the prince's visit. Soon he heard the door open and the Prince de Joinville was shown into the day cabin. Hornblower bowed.

"An unexpected honor, Your Highness," Hornblower said. "To what do I owe the pleasure of your visit? May I offer you coffee?"

"Yes, please."

"Please, sit, Your Highness. How may I be of service?"

Alfred entered the cabin with the prince's coffee on his silver tray. The prince took the cup and raised it to the servant. "Before we get to that, my lord, allow me to toast one of the best swordsmen I have ever met and to say that to fight at his side was a great honor for me. M. Alfred, to you, sir!"

The two officers raised their cups as well, and Alfred bowed deeply, humbled by the tribute. He backed out of the room without a word.

"That was kind of you," Hornblower said by way of thanks.

The prince waved his hand dismissively. "I shall be the first to confess to you that when your Mr. Dean posted the little man as my protector, I scoffed at the thought. That was before I witnessed him in action. I should be invincible with him at my side!"

"I know what you mean," Brewer agreed. "He has saved my life on countless occasions."

The prince turned to Hornblower. "I came to thank you again for your swift actions during our voyage home. Your presence saved my ship and my life."

"I fulfilled the mission given me by my Queen," Hornblower said. "If I was able to assist you in the process, I consider that my honor and my privilege."

The prince's face grew serious. "I have also come upon a second matter, my lord. I was having a late dinner with Minister Soult last night when a messenger arrived."

Hornblower shot his guest a questioning look. "Soult?"

Joinville lowered his cup. "Jean-de-Dieu Soult, the new Prime Minister of France. My father appointed him to replace Thiers on 29 October. He was also," he paused to sip his coffee, "a Marshal of the Empire under the Emperor."

Hornblower nodded, and the prince continued.

"My lord," he asked, "pardon my intrusion, but were you ashore last evening?"

Brewer reacted to the question, his eyes narrowing as they darted from the prince to Hornblower and back. Hornblower himself remained outwardly calm. He set his cup down in front of him.

"Yes, your Highness," he replied. "I received an invitation to visit someone in the town."

Joinville looked down at his hands, folded in his lap, before looking Hornblower in the eye.

"And was that someone the duke of Angoulême?"

Hornblower's brow furrowed slightly as he wondered where this was going. "Yes, your Highness, it was."

The prince looked at his hands again and sighed. It was a

sad sound, the kind made by a friend about to deliver bad news.

"I feared as much; that is what the messenger reported to Minister Soult last night." He looked up and took a deep breath, obviously steeling himself for what he must now do. "You must understand, my lord, that Minister Soult has only recently been thrown into a very precarious position when my father asked him to take over as prime minister. Thiers very nearly drove my nation to war with yours over his support for the Egyptian, Muhammad Pasha. Soult must smooth relations with Britain while at the same time overseeing the internment of the Emperor on the banks of the Seine. As a result, he has become overcautious when it comes to security." Joinville paused, misery on his face. "My lord, the fact that you had conversations with the leader of the Ultra-Royalists has disturbed Minister Soult greatly. It is my sad duty to inform you that he has forbidden you entrance to France. You will not be permitted to attend the ceremonies in Paris. I am sorry."

Dean leapt to his feet, poised to fight, outrage bursting from every pore of his being. He was only restrained by his captain's hand planted firmly in the middle of his chest. Brewer, for his part, tried to maintain his self-control. His right arm restrained his aggrieved first lieutenant, while his left hand quietly closed into a fist. His countenance was one of death to the Frenchman. All he needed was a signal.

But Hornblower sat impassively, his eyes never leaving the miserable Joinville. After a time, the Frenchman drew a ragged breath and raised his head. "I wish it were not so, my lord," he said quietly. "Minister Soult thought to inform you through a note delivered by an officer from the port navy yard, but I thought it better to come from me. I told the minister that we had fought together, and he said he understood."

"As do I," Hornblower said. He called for Alfred, who came and refilled their cups. When they were alone again, he looked to the prince. "Your Highness, I thank you for bringing me this news yourself. You are right; it is easier to swallow, coming from one who has fought at your side." Hornblower set his cup down and rose. The others followed. "Captain, make preparations to sail for England on the morning tide. Please give me a moment with the prince."

"Aye, sir," Brewer replied. He and Dean came to attention and left the room. Hornblower turned to his guest and held out his hand. The prince took it.

"I want you to know," Hornblower said quietly, "that I harbor no ill will toward you. We may be on different sides where the return is concerned, but you set your feelings aside and did your duty. I know from experience that is not something easily done. You have done well, especially for one as young as yourself. Personally, I think it a shame that you will never sit on the throne of France."

"Thank you, my lord," the prince said.

"If you are ever near Smallbridge, please come to visit us. My wife would be delighted."

"I will."

Hornblower escorted the prince to the entry port, where he was joined by Captain Brewer. Salutes were exchanged, and Joinville departed.

EPILOGUE

The debriefing in London took several days, especially after Palmerston learned of the battle with the Russian frigates. Hornblower handed over his written report and answered every question put to him. In the end, he was strongly admonished by Palmerston not to breathe a word about the Russians to anyone, something he had no intention of doing anyway.

Hornblower found his wife in the library when he finally arrived back in Smallbridge. She rose and greeted him with a kiss.

"All went well?" she asked.

"More or less," came the answer. "I left after he was put on the river steamship for the journey to Paris."

She was surprised. "I'd have thought you would see him all the way to the tomb."

"No, I got him back to France. He will be safe now. My debt is paid."

She looked at him as if questioning his statement, but her husband went silent, and she knew better than to press him. He walked over to the platter decorated with a painting of the *Grande Armée's* camp at Boulogne in 1804, a gift from Bonaparte. She joined him, taking his arm and leaning on his side.

"Remembering?" she asked.

"Yes," he whispered. "I wish I could have done more for him when he was alive."

Barbara patted him on the arm. "You did all you could. I think he understood that, and he loved you for it."

He regarded the platter and hoped that was true.

THE END

About The Author

James Keffer

James Keffer was born September 9, 1963, in Youngstown, Ohio, the son of a city policeman and a nurse. He grew up loving basketball, baseball, tennis, and books. He graduated high school in 1981 and began attending Youngstown State University to study mechanical engineering.

He left college in 1984 to enter the U.S. Air Force. After basic training, he was posted to the 2143rd Communications Squadron at Zweibruecken Air Base, West Germany. While he was stationed there, he met and married his wife, Christine, whose father was also assigned to the base. When the base was closed in 1991, James and Christine were transferred up the road to Sembach Air Base, where he worked in communications for the 2134th Communications Squadron before becoming the LAN manager for HQ 17th Air Force.

James received an honorable discharge in 1995, and he and his wife moved to Jacksonville, Florida, to attend Trinity

Baptist College. He graduated with honors in 1998, earning a Bachelor of Arts degree. James and Christine have three children.

Hornblower and the Island was the first novel James wrote, He has self-published three other novels. He currently lives and works in Jacksonville, Florida, with his wife and three children.

If You Enjoyed This Book
Please write a review.
This is important to the author and helps to get the word out to others
Visit

PENMORE PRESS
www.penmorepress.com

All Penmore Press books are available directly through our website, amazon.com, Barnes and Noble and Nook, Apple iTunes, Kobo books and via leading bookshops across the United States, Canada, the UK, Australia and Europe.

BREWER'S LUCK

BY

JAMES KEFFER

After gaining valuable experience as an aide to Governor Lord Horatio Hornblower, William Brewer is rewarded with a posting as first lieutenant on the frigate HMS *Defiant*, bound for American waters. Early in their travels, it seems as though Brewer's greatest challenge will be evading the wrath of a tyrannical captain who has taken an active dislike to him. But when a hurricane sweeps away the captain, the young lieutenant is forced to assume command of the damaged ship, and a crew suffering from low morale.

Brewer reports their condition to Admiral Hornblower, who orders them into the Caribbean to destroy a nest of pirates hidden among the numerous islands. Luring the pirates out of their coastal lairs will be difficult enough; fighting them at sea could bring disaster to the entire operation. For the *Defiant* to succeed, Brewer must rely on his wits, his training, and his ability to shape a once-ragged crew into a coherent fighting force.

BREWER'S REVENGE

BY

JAMES KEFFER

Admiral Horatio Hornblower has given Commander William Brewer captaincy of the captured pirate sloop *El Dorado*. Now under sail as the HMS *Revenge,* its new name suits Brewer's frame of mind perfectly. He lost many of his best men in the engagement that seized the ship, and his new orders are to hunt down the pirates who have been ravaging the trade routes of the Caribbean sea.

But Brewer will face more than one challenge before he can confront the pirate known as El Diabolito. His best friend and ship's surgeon, Dr. Spinelli, is taking dangerous solace in alcohol as he wrestles with demons of his own. The new purser, Mr. Allen, may need a lesson in honest accounting. Worst of all, Hornblower has requested that Brewer take on a young ne'er-do-well, Noah Simmons, to remove him from a recent scandal at home. At twenty-three, Simmons is old to be a junior midshipman, and as a wealthy man's son he is unaccustomed to working, taking orders, or suffering privations.

William Brewer will need to muster all his resources to ready his crew for their confrontation with the Caribbean's most notorious pirate. In the process, he'll discover the true price of command.

BREWER AND THE BARBARY PIRATES

BY
JAMES KEFFER

It is said that a man is grown by his past, and so it was with William Brewer. Before he took command of HMS Defiant in a hurricane and before he hunted pirates in HMS Revenge, Brewer endured a crucible of fire that molded him into the legend he became. Fresh from the tutelage of Napoleon Bonaparte on St. Helena, Brewer signs on for a cruise under Captain Bush in HMS Lydia to the Mediterranean to battle the Barbary Pirates. Here Brewer learns to fight, but he also learns what it means to command men in battle and what it takes to order men to their deaths. Their enemy is a Scottish renegade who is responsible for the deaths of dozens of his fellow sailors over the years and the selling of hundreds of Europeans into African slavery. Along the way, Brewer is introduced to new heroes and new devils. He also receives sage advice from no less than the Duke of Wellington himself. In the end, Brewer has to use all he's learned – not to mention going beyond all that – to save HMS Lydia from total destruction at the hands of pirates.

MIDSHIPMAN GRAHAM AND THE BATTLE OF ABUKIR

BY

JAMES BOSCHERT

It is midsummer of 1799 and the British Navy in the Mediterranean Theater of operations. Napoleon has brought the best soldiers and scientists from France to claim Egypt and replace the Turkish empire with one of his own making, but the debacle at Acre has caused the brilliant general to retreat to Cairo.

Commodore Sir Sidney Smith and the Turkish army land at the strategically critical fortress of Abukir, on the northern coast of Egypt. Here Smith plans to further the reversal of Napoleon's fortunes. Unfortunately, the Turks badly underestimate the speed, strength, and resolve of the French Army, and the ensuing battle becomes one of the worst defeats in Arab history.

Young Midshipman Duncan Graham is anxious to get ahead in the British Navy, but has many hurdles to overcome. Without any familial privileges to smooth his way, he can only advance through merit. The fires of war prove his mettle, but during an expedition to obtain desperately needed fresh water – and an illegal duel – a French patrol drives off the boats, and Graham is left stranded on shore. It now becomes a question of evasion and survival with the help of a British spy. Graham has to become very adaptable in order to avoid detection by the French police, and he must help the spy facilitate a daring escape by sea in order to get back to the British squadron.

"*Midshipman Graham and The Battle of Abukir* is both a rousing Napoleonic naval yarn and a convincing coming of age story. The battle scenes are riveting and powerful, the exotic Egyptian locales colorfully rendered." – John Danielski, author of *Capital's Punishment*

THE DISTANT OCEAN

BY

PHILIP K ALLAN

Newly returned from the Battle of the Nile, Alexander Clay and the crew of the Titan are soon in action again, just when he has the strongest reason to wish to abide in England. But a powerful French naval squadron is at large in the Indian Ocean, attacking Britain's vital East India trade. Together with his friend John Sutton, he is sent as part of the Royal Navy's response. On route the Titan runs to ground a privateer preying on slave ships on the coast of West Africa, stirring up memories of the past for Able Sedgwick, Clay's coxswain. They arrive in the Indian Ocean to find that danger lurks in the blue waters and on the palm-fringed islands. Old enemies with scores to settle mean that betrayal from amongst his own side may prove the hardest challenge Clay will face, and a dead man's hand may yet undo all he has fought to win. Will the curse of the captain's nephew never cease to bedevil Clay and his friends?

Raider of the Scottish Coast
BY

Marc Liebman

Which serves a Navy better? Tradition and hierarchy, or innovation and merit?

Two teenagers – Jaco Jacinto from Charleston, SC and Darren Smythe from Gosport, England – become midshipmen in their respective navies. Jacinto wants to help his countrymen win their freedom. Smythe has wanted to be a naval officer since he was a boy. From blockaded harbours and the cold northern waters off Nova Scotia and Scotland, to the islands of the Bahamas and Nassau, they serve with great leaders and bad ones through battles, politics and the school of naval hard knocks. Jacinto and Smythe are mortal enemies, but when they meet they become friends, even though they know they will be called again to battle one another.

"This is Marc Liebman's first foray into the age of sail, and what a densely packed, rattling yarn he has produced... The twists and turns of the breathless plot see the two main protagonists cross again and again in a story that never lets up its pace." ~ Philip Allan, author of the award-winning Alexander Clay series about the Royal Navy during the Age of Sail.

PENMORE PRESS
www.penmorepress.com

CPSIA information can be obtained
at www.ICGtesting.com
Printed in the USA
LVHW022353130821
695160LV00001B/108

9 781950 586837